CHILDREN OF 1

First published in 2009 by

WOODFIELD PUBLISHING LTD
Bognor Regis ~ West Sussex ~ England ~ PO21 5EL
www.woodfieldpublishing.co.uk

ISBN 1-84683-090-7

Children of the Wave

JOHN GODWIN

Woodfield

Woodfield Publishing Ltd

Woodfield House ~ Babsham Lane ~ Bognor Regis ~ West Sussex ~ PO21 5EL
telephone 01243 821234 ~ **e-mail** enquiries@woodfieldpublishing.co.uk

Interesting and informative books on a variety of subjects

For full details of all our published titles, visit our website at
www.woodfieldpublishing.co.uk

To my wife Elizabeth
for her constant support
and to my children Veronica and Ben
for suspending their incredulity for so long.

'All that is necessary for the triumph of evil
is that good men do nothing.'
Edmund Burke, *MP for Bristol 1774-80*

About the Author

John Godwin was born in Essex, was educated at King Edward VI Grammar School, Chelmsford and Leeds University and has had a lifelong interest in history. He has lived in the West Country for many years and has been a solicitor in practice in Bristol, a university law lecturer and is currently a South Gloucestershire councillor. He has stood as a candidate for Parliament in two General Elections. He lives with his wife in South Gloucestershire; they have two children.

John Godwin

Author's Preface

This novel has been a long time in gestation. I have wanted for some time to bring together my love of history with my career as a lawyer and local politician. *Children of the Wave* is a work of fiction but I have tried to be faithful to the period and any anachronisms are mine.

However, I made a conscious decision to bring forward by perhaps a decade the beginnings of the anti-slave trade movement in Bristol to coincide with the early stages of the struggle by the American colonists for independence. I apologise to purists for this but I wanted to deal with both issues and their effect on Bristol's politics and business.

I was pleased to find a title for the novel in the writing of Thomas Chatterton, the Bristol boy poet and I am indebted to the Victorian writer G.E. Weare for his book *Edmund Burke's Connections with Bristol 1774-80*, which provided much of the background for the by-election with which this novel culminates.

All the characters are fictitious and political colleagues will look in vain for modern comparisons, although I believe the nature of politics does not change.

I am grateful to my good friend Nigel Rushworth for reading the text and making many helpful comments. Any errors are mine alone.

I would also like to express my thanks to Woodfield Publishing for their support and advice.

Prologue – November 1770

The body was eventually dragged ashore at Redcliffe Wharf. For several minutes four urchins had been pelting it with stones and clods of earth, trying to divert its course down-river to bring it closer to the bank. Now their eager hands dragged it clear of the water and onto the quayside.

They had come out at first light, as they always did the morning after the market, and made their way to the new stone bridge to relieve themselves over the side and to look out for anything that may have drifted down-river. They knew that the stall-holders of Old Market tossed unwanted scraps into the water near King's Orchard and often something useful would wedge against the bridge or in the rushes nearby.

It was a damp November morning with no wind and a mist hanging in the air, trapping the stench from the open sewers that ran down from the town into the river. Coming from the hovels of Lewin's Mead, a slum area in the centre of the prosperous city of Bristol, the boys were undeterred by either the cold or the smell, and as darkness gave way fitfully to daylight they had peered down through the gloom to the dark waters below.

Today the sight of a body wedged against one of the stone pillars had rewarded their early morning rendezvous. This in itself was not unusual. They had seen bodies in the river before, usually vagabonds drunk on gin who had fallen in from Castle Street, or sometimes a wretched whore, her throat cut by a client whose ship would be half way across the Atlantic before the victim was found. But today they were lucky. The sodden corpse looked well dressed, which meant rich pickings.

Dislodging it from the pillar with long staves left from the market, they had waited for the current to bring it under and out the other side of the bridge. It was close to the Redcliffe side of the river and a few well-directed stones thrown into the water on its offside pushed it even closer. The boys ran from the bridge and chased after their quarry as it drifted with the current. At Redcliffe Wharf the river swung round sharply to the right in the direction of the Avon Gorge. Here their poles were long enough to hook the body into the side before the outgoing tide could take it round the bend and away down-river towards the sea.

Despite the muffling effect of the mist, an orchestra of sound drifted across the river from the quayside at Welsh Back. Ships creaking at their moorings, the splash of a rat, or slops being thrown into the water, and the dull, resentful voices of sailors completing the provisioning of their already loaded ships ready to sail on the early morning tide.

By land, river and sea Bristol's port acted as an emporium for the world's trade, and as such served several functions. It was the main market for grain, crops and dairy produce from the Midlands and South Wales, the Welsh trade using and giving its name to the recently extended quay known as Welsh Back. The city also imported industrial raw materials, timber from the Forest of Dean for shipbuilding, wool from Milford and Cardiff for the Cotswold woollen industry. Although some of these imports were transported by road inland, others were used by local manufacturers who in turn exported glass, soap, refined sugar, and bricks.

As well as the local trade Bristol had strong trading links with the West Indies, particularly Jamaica, and with Virginia and the Carolinas, importing tobacco, sugar and rum, and exporting manufactured goods and, via West Africa, slaves. Bristol was without rival in domestic trade and local navigation with only London and Liverpool competing in international commerce. The city boasted many wealthy merchants and shipbuilders, many of them owning plantations in the Colonies.

The boys knew they would have to hurry for soon the river would be alive with rowing boats and other small craft as the day's activities began. Working in silence, they went through the dead man's pockets, looking for anything that might be worth a few pence. His wig was missing but the ribbon tying back his hair was soon removed, to be sold later to one of the ladies of the city's drinking dens. Then, using a sharp stone, one of the boys prized open his mouth to look for gold fillings. They were unmoved by death and took no notice of the state of the body. Their cold fingers moved quickly, for rigor mortis was setting in and the limbs had started to swell, making their task more difficult.

It was clear that the wretched man was wealthy. They could not pull the rings off the swollen fingers, but a fob watch, a pouch of soaked tobacco, and a few silver coins were like an Aladdin's hoard to these scavengers, for whom a penny or two, earned begging or stolen, was the most they usually possessed.

They turned their attention to his clothes. The shoes were already gone. Two of the boys started to roll the silk stockings down over the swollen feet while the other two fumbled with the buttons on the full-length silk waistcoat.

Suddenly a sound caused them to freeze, like animals sensing danger. Sharp-eyed, they looked round but could see nothing through the swirling mist, yet they detected a muffled crunch of footsteps on the stony track leading to the quay. As the sound grew louder they saw the dim glow of an oil lamp moving towards them and, as one, they left the body, running for cover behind the nearest shed from where they could watch. Seconds later they saw the familiar figure of Constable Skinner holding the lamp and leading a dog on a length of rope, followed by a second man who they did not recognise.

By the cut of his dress, the second man was as wealthy as the corpse lying motionless on the quayside. There was no reason why the boys should recognise him, for Bristol had burst out of its medieval walls nearly a century earlier and no longer did the wealthy and poor live alongside one another. In the time of Queen Anne the merchant class had started to build houses away from the central area, south to what became Queen Square and west in the direction of Clifton. This left the poor in the centre of the city from where the boys had never strayed, the confines of their world being the old city boundaries of the Frome and Avon rivers to the west and south and Old Market to the east.

The frustrated urchins watched the two men make their way across the quay. It was now inevitable that the newcomers would discover the body, so the boys abandoned their prey and scrambled up the bank behind the warehouse to work their way along Redcliffe Street and back to Lewin's Mead.

A final glance back from the top of the bank saw the officer and his companion kneeling over the forlorn corpse.

~ CHAPTER 1 ~

Richard Stourton, pupil to Lawrence Willoughby, Attorney at Law, stood in the centre of his principal's office waiting for him to speak. In the three years of his pupillage since leaving Oxford he had learned that an early morning summons meant that Lawrence Willoughby had something of importance to say and that he was expected to wait in silence until the older man was ready to share his thoughts. On such occasions Richard felt by turns amused and frustrated by the lawyer's idiosyncrasy, but his gratitude for the opportunity to follow a professional career enabled him to suppress any uncharitable feelings.

Lawrence Willoughby was sitting in his leather armchair, fingertips together, staring out of the window and across the street to the Exchange opposite. He was a heavily built man, almost to the point of obesity, with thick dark eyebrows, a bulbous nose and jowls as loose as those of his bloodhound, Xerxes, lying asleep at his feet. His waistcoat was unbuttoned and his wig lay on the desk behind him.

It was a morning ritual to turn his chair to the window to watch the comings and goings at the Exchange. Willoughby had told Richard that he could judge the buoyancy of business in the city and who was trading with whom and, for a lawyer who strove to maintain his position as one of Bristol's leading practitioners, such information was important. The shifting undercurrent of business alliances and transactions almost always gave itself away at the entrance to the dealings hall and from his vantage point high up in his chambers opposite, Lawrence Willoughby could see all. Today there was more than the usual number of traders standing together in groups, talking animatedly, some occasionally pointing in the direction of Wine Street.

'Come and have a look at this, my boy.'

Richard walked round the desk and joining the lawyer, stared out of the window at the assembly of people on the cobbled road opposite. It was a damp morning with a fine drizzle and no sunshine, not a morning that would normally bring people out onto the streets.

'Do you know what they are talking about, Richard?'

'No I don't. Has anything untoward happened? '

'Indeed it has. Councillor Jackson is dead. Murdered. His body was dragged out of the river at Redcliffe Wharf this morning, his skull fractured. Constable Skinner and I found him. '

Willoughby turned his head and looked at Richard.

'Skinner frightened off some body robbers. But they were only urchins. They wouldn't have been responsible for his death. Attacked up river I would guess, the body thrown in afterwards. '

'He was robbed then?'

'His pockets were empty. But whether he was robbed by his attackers or by those who found him, we may never know. He must have been walking in the Castle Street area late last night. Goodness knows what he was doing there. He could afford a better class of dolly-mop than Old Market provides.'

The Castle Street area had been notorious for thieving and prostitution since before the castle had been destroyed over a hundred years before. Then, criminals and vagabonds had lived in the castle ruins, but now they mostly lived in the slums of Lewin's Mead. They came up to the newer shops in Castle Street and Old Market to catch unsuspecting tradesmen or merchant seamen who came into the city for business, then entertainment in the drinking dens in the city centre and ten minutes with a whore on the river bank, or in some squalid room.

Willoughby turned back and stared out of the window once more, no doubt contemplating mortality, Richard thought. During the time of his clerkship with him, he had learned that beneath the brusque manner and unemotional approach to his work there was a deep humanity. Richard was sure that his principal was feeling sorry for the dead man but that he would never show it.

He knew better than to disturb the older man's thoughts and waited patiently for what he knew was coming next. Willoughby would not want to go through the councillor's possessions now that he was dead; that would be a job for a younger man for whom death was but a future possibility. He looked round the floor at the various boxes, chests and piles of manuscripts but could see nothing connected with the late Ben Jackson. Steggles, the managing clerk, will have removed his papers already, he thought.

After some minutes, Willoughby turned his chair away from the window and rested his arms on the mahogany desk in front of him, as if to signal that his moments of personal grief were over.

'You had met Ben Jackson, hadn't you?'

'Yes, I had.'

The dead man had been a client of the firm for many years and Richard had met him on several occasions. He shuddered at the thought of that genial man now lying dead with his skull broken. He knew that most people in the city knew of him by reputation. The news would be a blow to civic life. One of its wealthiest citizens, he had been a generous benefactor and the city had much for which to thank him.

Willoughby continued. 'I would like you to go through the deceased's box, if you would be so kind. Steggles will give it to you. The dead man's brother, his next of kin, will be in to see me later today to instruct me to look after the estate. He and I are executors. I know most of his affairs of course but a wise man does not tell his lawyer everything, and Councillor Jackson was a very wise man.'

Richard saw his eyes twinkle at this self-deprecating remark and he smiled back, admiring the older man's fortitude as much as his humour.

He returned to his own room to find the black tin box already on his desk, key in lock. As he opened the lid and saw the accumulated jumble of certificates, papers and deeds, his mind went back to the last time he had seen a man's life telescoped into one tin box. That was on the death of his own father. His mother had died when he was just a boy, but his father's death had been only six years ago, when Richard was nineteen. He remembered the terrible last few days as if it were yesterday; the agony his father had suffered as he struggled for life. But his illness was terminal and Richard had been powerless to do anything but watch him grow steadily weaker.

He had not always seen eye to eye with his father, but had loved and respected him nonetheless and felt more than a filial sorrow at his going. The manner of his death had left a bitter legacy. A successful timber importer, Thomas Stourton had been persuaded to invest heavily in merchant shipping, and along with a number of other investors had lost everything.

At the time, the crash had been a major shock to the city. Bristol was growing fast as a mercantile port, some four hundred ships entering and leaving every year. Its trade had grown so rapidly that it seemed that every venture would bring vast profits. Importers and distributors saw it as a logical step to invest in the shipping that was handling their trade. A young councillor and merchant, Joseph Terrill, had a growing merchant fleet and invited investment. Thomas Stourton's life savings, and those of several others, disappeared within months. No one had been able to prove fraud but it angered Richard that Terrill himself appeared to have emerged unscathed with no check to his growing wealth. Thomas Stourton lost his business and his home, became ill with grief, and died. He had left just enough to pay for Richard to study law at Oxford University and pay a small premium to Lawrence Willoughby for his articles of clerkship but thereafter he would have to make his own way. Richard had vowed that some day he would find out the truth about the failed venture. Besides, he owed it to his sister, his only close relative, to make something of himself and restore the family name and fortune. Julia was just eighteen and he had been fortunate to find her a position as a companion to the young daughter of a wealthy Gloucestershire family.

As he looked round his room he couldn't help wondering whether he really wanted to spend his working life there. It was dark and musty with very little natural light and the oil lamp on his desk threw shadows on the wooden racks set around the walls. These racks were filled with files and boxes containing people's hopes but more frequently evidence of unfulfilled expectations. And there was the smell. Not too repellent, for he was used to it, but of damp, disintegrating documents, here and there mixed with the odour of a decaying mouse dead on a surfeit of chewed parchment.

He walked over to the window and wiping away a patch of condensation with his sleeve, stared out. Not for him the view of Corn Street and the Exchange, for his room was at the back of the building. All he could see was the derelict gardens of his building and the Bush Hotel next door, the gardens overgrown with dead couch grass, patches of nettles, and in one corner the broken brickwork of a former outhouse long since disused. In the opposite corner a gnarled and dying fruit tree, moss turning its bark a dirty grey. What would his career as an attorney bring but an eventual transfer from this room to Willoughby's room at the front, a meagre reward for a life's work?

He shivered, as if to pull himself together, knowing that it was the association of ideas following Ben Jackson's death that had sparked a moment's depression. He felt grateful for his education and to Lawrence Willoughby for the opportunity to become an attorney. Yet that didn't prevent him feeling frustrated too. His years at Oxford had brought him into contact with young men who were far wealthier. They could travel to Europe, or the Colonies. He could not. They were destined for political and public life. He was not. In his darker moments he felt it would have been better not to have been educated; his expectations would have been less. But those low moments soon passed. His education had opened some doors already. Who knows what other opportunities might come along?

It took Richard most of the morning to sort, then schedule, the many bonds and stock certificates and to read and digest the various trust deeds and contracts the dead man had left behind. Next he started on the correspondence, most of which comprised of letters of a personal nature. But one caught his eye. It was a packet from London marked private and confidential. It had obviously been opened and then re-sealed. Gently breaking the seal, he read the contents with a growing sense of amazement. It was dated three months earlier.

27 New Broadwick Square
London
17th August 1770

Dear Friend,
We now have reliable evidence that on 16th May 1764 the Demera sunk off the Guinea Coast in a gale. Four hundred and twenty Negroes drowned together with fifteen of the crew. The captain and twenty-five of the crew survived. In a confidential settlement the insurers paid for the loss of cargo, that is to say, the Negroes. The captain, Jasper Cox, still sails from Bristol and is frequently to be found when ashore, in the Flying Angel in Marsh Street where we believe a number of his crew were recruited. I believe we are beginning to gather the evidence about this pernicious trade in human lives that will enable us to make our case public. It would greatly assist our cause if contact could be made with Captain Cox or any of his crew from that voyage.
Yours truly,
Henry Scrope,
Secretary to the London Committee
for the Abolition of the Trade in Slaves.

Richard felt his hands tremble as he read the letter. He fully realised the importance of what it contained. Councillor Jackson had been involved in the highly unpopular anti-slave trade movement. He slumped back in his chair to consider the full implications of what he had read. He knew that slave trading was a major commercial interest of the Bristol merchants and that some years ago Bristol had overtaken London as the leading slaving port. Those who were not involved in the trade nevertheless supported it. The city had benefited greatly from the triple profits generated by the triangular trade – manufactured goods such as brassware, muskets, copper pans and hats exported to Spain or West Africa, slaves taken across the middle passage to the West Indies or American Colonies, and tobacco and sugar back to Bristol.

Few voices in England had been raised against the trade and even fewer in Bristol. Richard knew that recently a small but growing number of people in London had begun to voice doubts about the morality of trading in human life, and one or two had even condemned the ownership of slaves. But no such doubts had troubled the sleep of the Bristol merchants who owned many of the plantations and the slaves who worked them. Yet here in his hands was evidence that one of the city's most prominent citizens, a former mayor, was in league with those who sought to stop the very trade that had given the city much of its wealth. And was it just possible that the letter was connected with his death?

There was something else about the letter that nagged in the back of his mind. One of the reasons his father was ruined was because ships were lost at sea apparently with inadequate or no insurance and the letter referred to an insurance settlement. Had his father invested in slave ships? Could the *Demera* have been one of them? No, the coincidence would be too great, he thought, but he could not put the possibility out of his mind.

'Richard, allow me to introduce Mr Frank Jackson'.

Lawrence Willoughby extended his hand in the direction of a middle-aged man sitting in a leather armchair at the side of the lawyer's desk. Richard bowed slightly to the client but quickly turned his attention to the other guest sitting on a high-backed wooden chair on the opposite side of the room.

'And this is Mr Jackson's daughter Sarah. Frank, my pupil Richard Stourton has been helping me sort through Ben's papers.'

Richard expressed his condolences and was content to let the two older men talk leaving him to study father and daughter, but rather more the daughter. He judged her to be about twenty. She had a round face, brown eyes and hair in ringlets worn close to her head. She wore a plain dress and cloak, with no trace of the extended hooping that had become more fashionable and extravagant of late. Her demeanour suggested to him that her modest appearance and dress were natural to her, not worn out of respect for her dead uncle. Yet Richard thought he noticed a trace of impatience in her eyes as she sat silently, hands at rest on her lap, waiting for her father to conclude his business with the lawyer.

After some minutes Richard was invited to read through the inventory that he had prepared. The two visitors listened in silence as he recited the details of the deceased's estate and the various bequests made and charitable trusts established.

'The contents of the will have, of course, been known to me since it was drawn up,' said Willoughby when Richard had finished. 'After these bequests have been made, the remainder of the estate passes to you for life, Frank, and thereafter for Sarah absolutely. In other words, you have the use of the income, and on your death, Sarah receives the capital. Everything is as I expected to find it. There was nothing more, was there Richard?'

Richard felt his body tense. It was the question he had hoped would not be asked, but knew it would. Since finding the letter from Henry Scrope he had wondered whether he should reveal it. He knew he should hand it over to Frank Jackson but had wanted more time to think through the consequences of what he had read. And did Lawrence Willoughby already know about it?

Richard looked at his principal but could read nothing in his eyes. 'Nothing more, except a few letters which appear to be personal.' He handed a small bundle to Frank Jackson. The Scrope letter was not among them.

'A few letters telling of his occasional indiscretions, no doubt,' said Willoughby with a wry smile.

It struck Richard how Willoughby, in common with all lawyers he had so far encountered, seemed to wish to give the impression of knowing something about everyone, usually to their disadvantage.

'Richard, take Miss Jackson through to your room for a few minutes, if you would be so kind. Mr Jackson and I have some further business to discuss concerning the executorship and I am sure she would prefer your company to listening to us.'

Richard needed no second bidding and ushered Sarah out of the room. The corridor to his room was narrow and dark, the candles along the walls throwing light upwards towards the ceiling.

'Please be careful of the uneven floor,' he said. He lightly touched her arm to guide her and the contact made him tremble slightly.

In his room they sat opposite each other in silence for a minute or two. Richard had had little experience of society, save that which he had gained at the male preserve of Oxford, and none of society women, particularly one so young. Yet her bright eyes and open countenance seemed to welcome him and he thought he detected a kindred spirit behind her polite silence.

His mind had been in turmoil since reading Henry Scrope's letter that morning. Was it for him to make its contents known, perhaps sullying the dead man's reputation in the eyes of his peers? Yet had he any right to suppress it? His own instincts were against the slave trade too. At Oxford he had been taught Roman legal principles, that slaves were personal possessions, but he could not accept this as a modern thesis. It may have been the way of life in Ancient Rome, and was still regarded so now, but he could not hold to that view no matter what others might think. The few minutes he would have alone with the dead man's niece provided him with an opportunity to discuss the letter. Should he take a chance and speak to her about it? He felt his palms sweating as he tried to start a conversation that would lead him in the direction of the letter. He would have to hurry. The ticking of the ornamental clock on the mantelshelf warned him that his chance would soon be lost.

He watched her as she took in the dark surroundings of a lawyer's office.

'I am sorry we have met under such dreadful circumstances, Miss Jackson.'

She nodded by way of reply. He could see she was struggling to hold back the tears.

'Would you care for a cup of tea?'

'That would be kind.'

Richard walked to the door and called down the corridor. 'Mr Steggles.' As if anticipating a summons, a thin wiry middle-aged man with a shock of black hair sticking up in all directions came down the corridor towards him.

'Miss Jackson would take tea. Can you manage that for her?'

'Certainly Mr Richard, sir. I have taken the liberty of boiling a kettle in readiness. I will be with you directly.' He shuffled off back down the corridor and was as good as his word, returning within two or three minutes with a pot and two cups.

This distraction and a few sips of tea seemed to settle Sarah's composure and Richard felt able to resume the conversation.

'Were you close to your uncle, Miss Jackson?'

'Yes. He was a kind man. I was very fond of him.' Her voice broke a little as she spoke and Richard recognised her obvious distress.

He waited for her to regain her composure before speaking again.

'He was very popular in the city, I believe?'

'He was generous. That leads to popularity of a kind.'

'You sound a little cynical, Miss Jackson. Did you disapprove of his business activities?'

A flash of puzzled anger crossed her face. 'Certainly not. You misunderstand me, Mr Stourton. My uncle was above reproach. But a man who is wealthy and generous often attracts those whose spirit is less noble and their motives less honest.'

Richard was encouraged by this unguarded confidence. 'Was he involved in any clandestine business activities that you are aware of?'

As soon as the words were out, he realised the tactlessness of his question. Sarah stood up and started to walk towards the door. 'Your question is intolerable Mr Stourton. My uncle was a completely honest man. To suggest otherwise, and at such a time...'

'Please, Miss Jackson, you quite misunderstand me. Allow me to explain.'

Sarah stopped. 'I think you had better do so Mr Stourton. I didn't expect to come here and be insulted '

'I am sorry. I did not intend to suggest he was not an honourable man. But was he involved in any activities that may have upset anyone less scrupulous than himself?'

Sarah returned to her seat. 'Not that I know of. What are you trying to tell me?'

Richard knew the moment had come. He would either have to share his secret with Sarah or forget about the letter altogether. He crossed the room and sat on the edge of the chair next to hers.

'Miss Jackson, I need to take you into my confidence about something relating to your uncle. Do you know if he was in any way connected with the slave trade? Or rather, was he strongly opposed to it?'

Sarah looked startled. 'My uncle may have been a merchant but did not have any investment in slaves because he was opposed to the trade. As I am myself.'

'Did he tell you so?'

'Yes, we discussed it frequently. You may be aware, Mr Stourton, that Bristol's share of the slave trade has been declining over the last few years. Some of the city merchants have been seeking ways of recovering this lost business. They recently prepared a petition to Parliament for help defending the trade. But he refused to sign it'

Her face was defiant in grief. Richard recognised her as someone whose confidence he could share, and was prepared to take the risk.

'That is what I suspected. I have come across some evidence that your uncle was involved with the London Anti-Slave Trade Committee. I should like to know how deep his involvement was.'

He watched as Sarah fiddled with the drawstring on her reticule, the only sign of her nervousness.

'Are you suggesting, Mr Stourton, that his death was more sinister than a mere robbery?'

Richard shrugged his shoulders. 'There are a lot of people heavily involved in the trade who would lose a considerable income if it were stopped. Whether that would lead to murder I do not know.'

He walked over to his desk and, taking the letter from a drawer, handed it to her. After she had read it, they sat in silence awhile, both thinking through the implications of what he had said. If Ben Jackson was killed to deter the Anti-Slave Trade Committee, then the perpetrator could be as well known in the city as the dead man.

Sarah turned to Richard, her features now pale. 'I will give you what help I can. But I do not think we should mention this to my father. He is not in the trade, but he is not antagonistic towards it.'

'I agree.' Richard was equally firm. 'And I have said nothing to Mr Willoughby. He does not believe in lawyers expressing political opinions. And he certainly would not wish to upset some of his wealthier clients. You might be able to help me by discretely talking to some of your father's friends. There may be other opponents of the trade in slaves among them.'

'I have friends of my own, Mr Stourton. I may only be a woman, but I have political contacts in the city quite apart from my father's circle. Uncle Ben was not alone in disliking the trade in slaves and I will speak to those who shared his views. But what do you intend to do?'

Richard now felt able to relax. Their misunderstanding seemed to have been overcome. Here was a girl with spirit who was apparently willing to flout the social conventions of the day.

'Well, I have only one lead, the Captain Cox referred to in the letter. I am going to try to find him to see what he knows of your uncle's activities.'

~ CHAPTER 2 ~

Richard knew that Marsh Street at night was not a place for the faint-hearted. As he turned into this notorious thoroughfare from the more familiar, and safer, King Street, he gripped his cane a little tighter, and kept a distance between himself and the unlighted doorways. For several generations Marsh Street had contained a series of lodging houses and pubs, almost all owned by Irish families, each dwelling opening its ground floor to the pleasures of the night. Drinking dens, gambling rooms and whorehouses stood alongside one another, sometimes all three in one building.

In nearly every doorway he saw young girls, who from their appearance he judged to be as young as twelve or thirteen, beckoning him to pleasure. Occasionally they shared the doorway with a lifeless body, drunk with gin or beer, slumped against the doorjamb and to the casual passer-by apparently dead, but in reality merely insensible until the grey morning cold prompted it to stir.

Richard tried to shut his mind to these scenes around him, but without success. The cold night air quickly dispelled the smell of stale beer and urine that assailed him every time he passed an open door, but the noise of singing and shouting in one establishment had not subsided before the next reached his ears. He had to make his way carefully, avoiding groups of men and women staggering along the pavement. He knew that where there was entertainment and money changed hands there was also crime. A seemingly innocent collision in the street could be a prelude to losing his wallet.

On reaching the Flying Angel he stopped momentarily before entering. As he did so, he felt a tug at his coat.

'Want some pleasure sir?'

He looked round to see the emaciated figure of a girl, dressed in a torn, dirty frock, and barefoot, despite the cold. He took a penny from his pocket. 'I am looking for a Captain Cox. If you can take me to him you shall have this.'

The girl looked up at him with some surprise, and nodding to him to follow she disappeared through the half open doorway. As he entered, he recoiled at the stench of stale beer, cheap wine and the sweat of many bodies in close confinement. All round the room were groups of drinkers sitting before tables laden with beer and food. Most of the revellers were men but at each table there were two, and sometimes three, gaily dressed and heavily powdered and rouged women to make sure the patrons parted with their money in sufficient quantity. Small boys worked their way from table to table collecting empty tankards and replacing them with full.

Richard wiped his eyes with his pocket-handkerchief, so much did they smart from the rancid smoke of the foul smelling pipes most of the men were smoking. Momentarily he thought of leaving, but realised he had to go through with it if he were to find Cox. He pushed through the throng to try to keep up with his guide. The flickering candles in the sconces around the walls gave little assistance to him in seeing his way.

Being taller than most, he could see the bar in the centre of the room behind which a stout middle-aged man was directing operations. Despite the noise made by the drinkers, some shouting, others attempting the popular ballads, the barman seemed to be able to pick up shouted orders from all round the room, and single-handedly was directing the boys to collect, and then serve, mugs of beer and porter.

Although strong enough to shoulder his way through the heaving mass of people, Richard was unable to keep up with his guide who stopped twice to let him catch up. When he eventually reached the bar, he found the girl already in conversation with the barman. He strained unsuccessfully to hear what they were saying and waited patiently until the barman turned towards him and started a shouted conversation.

'The captain's in the back room. Who shall be wanting him?'

'My name is Stourton, Richard Stourton, but he won't know me.'

'Are you a magistrate, or a special?

'No. An acquaintance of Councillor Jackson.'

The barman nodded to him. 'Will you be waiting here then?'

He said something to the girl who darted off across the room and through a door at the back. Moments later she reappeared and waved Richard over. 'You can go in now. But no trouble, mind, else he'll belt me. And where's me penny?'

Richard held the coin tantalisingly before the girl. 'What's your name?'

'Nancy'

'Nancy who?'

'I ain't got no other name.'

'How old are you, Nancy?'

'Fifteen. But don't ask no more questions.' From the way she fidgeted with a stray strand of hair hanging over her eyes Richard could see she was uncomfortable being the centre of attention. He guessed she had not had anyone take any interest in her before. He gave her the coin. Without another word she stuffed it into her bodice and made off into the crowd.

Richard jostled his way into the back room, closing the door behind him, at the same time shutting out most of the noise. He looked round and saw that he was in a small parlour, a quiet sanctuary after the noise of the public bar. But there was no respite from the tobacco smoke, which filled the room, there being no open window providing an escape. To the left was a blazing log fire and through the gloom of the smoke and dim candlelight he could see in the centre of the room a table around which sat four men, all smoking long clay pipes. Mugs of beer to hand, the men were engrossed in a game of cards. Coins lay in uneven piles on the table in front of the men, representing the ebb and flow of fortune.

Richard glanced nervously from one to another for a sign of recognition. None of the men took any notice of him. 'Captain Cox?' he asked, of no one in particular.

One of the four took his pipe from his mouth and laid it on the table in front of him, signifying that he was the one who would reply, but only in his own time. He was a thickset man, with greying temples and side-whiskers and wearing a stained blue jacket over a dirty woollen shirt and black breeches. He spoke with a drawl, not taking his eyes off the cards he was holding.

'Sit down, Mr Stourton, and state thy business.'

Richard's confidence was fast disappearing. He perched on the only available seat, a stool by the fender.

'Thank you Captain. I work for an attorney and am investigating the affairs of Councillor Ben Jackson, who died a few days ago. I believe you may have met him.'

The seaman took a long pull at his pipe, then spat on the floor. 'I might've. Me memory's a bit shaky. A jug o'beer might help it along.' He lifted his tankard and downed the last few drops. Richard nodded in acquiescence, and opening the door called to a serving boy and paid the bribe. Cox visibly relaxed.

'I remember your man. Came here one night just as you 'ave. 'Bout three weeks ago I'd say.'

Richard leaned forward, warming to his task. 'What did he talk to you about?'

Cox was in no hurry and took another draw at his pipe before replying. 'Well he were interested in my commands. Particularly the *Demera*.'

'What did you tell him?'

'He wanted to know 'bout the loss o' the ship. I told 'im how we foundered. And how me an' me mate 'ere survived along wi' a few others. It were just off the Guinea Coast. We'd only that day made sail. The storm came up an' 'it us afore we knew it. A few of us made it back to the shore in a dinghy. The rest 'o the crew went down.'

He took another mouthful. The three other men laid their cards down and smoked contentedly. Richard began to feel that Captain Cox was leading him on, perhaps to find out what he knew, or why he wanted to know. Yet he had no choice.

'And what about the slaves?'

'All the cargo was lost. You will understand, Mr Stourton, that for the proper running o' the ship it were necessary to chain the Negroes. Otherwise they'd fight. An' some'd jump overboard. When the ship foundered there weren't no time to set 'em free.'

'You -' Richard hesitated. 'You let them drown?'

Richard saw four pairs of cold, hostile eyes fix on him. It was one of the other men who broke the silence. 'Mr Stourton, there were four hundred and thirty tightly packed and chained Negroes in the hold. The ship was sinking. D'you know what would 'a happened if we'd gone down there to set 'em free? The first dozen we'd freed would 'ave killed us, left the others to die an' tried to swim ashore. Besides, the cargo was insured. We weren't.'

'These gentlemen here are mighty thirsty Mr Stourton,' prompted the captain. Richard dutifully obliged and felt emboldened to press the men further. 'Who owned the ship?'

'Your dead friend asked me that,' said Cox, 'but truth is we don't know. That's oft the way. I get signed up by the agent. He pays me an' I find the crew an' pay 'em. "Taint none o' my business more'n that.'

'Then can you tell me who the agent is? Perhaps I can talk to him.'

The captain leaned back and laughed.

'To be sure I can tell 'ee. His name's Amos Kettle. But you won't find 'im. He's out in the Colonies now. A plantation manager in Virginia. 'ee won't be back no more.'

Turning away from Richard the captain picked up his cards, signifying that the interview was over. Richard stood up to leave. 'Thank you for your help. But do you know why anyone would wish to murder Councillor Jackson?'

Two of Cox's companions stood up, fists clenched, and Richard could see the menace in their eyes. One of them took a step towards Richard but Cox restrained him. 'Goodnight Mr Stourton.'

Richard nodded and with considerable relief left the room.

Richard fingered his cravat nervously as he stood on Frank Jackson's doorstep in Clifton Hill the next morning. He had spent a sleepless night thinking over the events of the previous forty-eight hours. An idea had planted itself in his mind but there was no one with whom he could discuss it except perhaps Sarah. The tension within him had carried him to her home from his lodgings as if he were in a trance, but the compelling jangle of the doorbell brought him back to reality and doubts began to push their way into his mind. There was no certainty whether he would even see Sarah, much less have an opportunity to talk with her alone.

The maid who let him in invited him to wait in what he guessed was Frank Jackson's study, an exquisitely appointed room dominated by a large mahogany bureau and two matching bookcases. Restlessly he opened one and took down a book and his fingers idly turned the pages. But he was not reading nor even knew the title. He was thinking of Sarah. He had felt an instant attraction to her, but did he have the right to speak intimately with a woman he hardly knew and had met but once? He had already overstepped convention on that previous occasion and had done so clumsily. Another such mistake and the informality of their relationship would be at an end. Yet he could not forget the warm smile and friendly brown eyes. Could he hope to impress her with the audacity of his plan?

By the time the maid returned he had resolved not to draw back and with his heart thumping he followed her up the stone staircase to the back of the house on the first floor and into the drawing room where several people were standing talking.

'Richard, good morning.' Frank Jackson greeted him warmly. 'I am pleased to meet you again. Allow me to introduce everyone. My daughter you already know.'

Richard turned and bowed to Sarah, seated by the fireplace. His first wish had been granted. She rose and walked over to him, her smile lighting up her face with pleasure, her eyes sparkling. 'Richard, how kind of you to call. We are so pleased to see you.'

Frank Jackson touched Richard's arm. 'Have you met our Mayor, James Walter? And Councillor Joseph Terrill?'

So here he was. The man to whom Richard's father had lost his fortune. Richard could barely bring himself to greet the man politely but managed to acknowledge both men civilly. The Mayor was an elderly man, probably in his early seventies, Richard thought. He was dressed in the manner of his generation: waisted coat, wide in the skirts and short in arm, revealing a full white shirt beneath and of a length falling to the tops of his stockings rolled to above the knee.

But Richard's attention was more naturally drawn to Joseph Terrill, the man he believed had ruined his father and perhaps contributed to his early death. Richard could not accept that his father's fortune had been lost through ill luck and Terrill, a man he had not met until today, was the object of his hatred. He recognised Terrill for what he was; a beau. He wore a coat of bright green velvet, elaborately laced, red shoes and a powdered and curled wig. His face was sharp, with a pointed protruding chin, his small eyes made smaller by his curled, sneering lips. Richard was surprised how young he was, not more than his early thirties, he thought.

'Mr Stourton is in chambers with Lawrence Willoughby,' said Frank Jackson. 'You have called on official business, Richard?'

'I have sir. I have brought some papers for you to look through at your leisure.'

'I am much obliged to you. I will deal with them directly. These gentlemen have called to discuss with me a suitable memorial for my dear brother. Perhaps you would like to hear what they are proposing?'

Richard was pleased to stay but not for the suggested reason. The longer he was there the better the chance there was of speaking privately to Sarah. And though he felt he hated the man, he was fascinated by the presence of Joseph Terrill and felt that knowing him would somehow help bring him nearer to solving the question of his father's unhappy end.

'I was just explaining,' said James Walter, 'that in addition to a memorial service we should seek a more permanent form in which to remember our late colleague. Such as a public subscription for a memorial tablet....'

'And I think that such a gesture would be wholly inadequate for such a generous benefactor,' said Terrill, showing no concern at interrupting the Mayor. 'All our major city institutions have benefited from his work. Something more fitting is required. I suggest a statue be commissioned. What do you think, Stourton?'

Whatever Richard felt he was not going to endorse this opinion and stood silent for a moment, conscious that all eyes were upon him. Sarah's smile encouraged him to reply.

'Well Mr Terrill I am not at all sure that your former colleague would have wanted a large sum spent on him in that way. Although he was a generous man, I understand he was frugal in his personal habits. Perhaps he would have preferred any remembrance to have a more practical application such as an endowment to the Grammar School.'

'Nonsense,' Terrill sneered. 'Endowments are two a penny. You obviously do not understand how the city fathers think. A statue for him would guarantee a memorial plaque for most of the other leading councillors when their turn comes. Less than that for him would mean that when they die they would barely be remembered at all. That's how it works, is it not, Miss Jackson?'

Sarah bowed her head slightly, then looked Terrill straight in the face. 'If you say so, Mr Terrill. I bow to your greater wisdom in these matters.'

Richard looked at Terrill's mocking face and his instant dislike of the man was confirmed. His knuckles whitened as he clenched his fists behind his back and tried to control his anger. His annoyance at being put down by Terrill was compounded by Sarah siding with him. He glared at her but said nothing. She was taking no notice of him but had turned to listen to the Mayor who was apparently unmoved by Terrill's interjection.

'The question is, will the councillors of Bristol take the view that Ben's contribution to the life of the city was exceptional? They will not want to create an unfortunate precedent. What is your opinion, Mr Jackson?'

Frank Jackson seemed to Richard to be as reluctant to express an opinion as he had himself been. 'I agree with our young friend here that my brother was not ostentatious about his good works and not given to unnecessary personal spending. In fact he was most abstemious in his habits. But I will defer to the collective wisdom of the council. Mr Terrill may be expressing the view of the majority and I would not wish to go against the general feeling.'

This seemed to bring the discussion to an end. Richard prepared to leave but Sarah invited him to stay. 'Perhaps I can offer you some refreshment before you go, Richard?'

She led him back to her father's study. No refreshment appeared leading Richard to assume that Sarah had contrived the opportunity for private conversation. Pacing up and down the room, he soon gave vent to his feelings. 'I did not care for that Mr Terrill, Miss Jackson. How could you bring yourself to agree with him?'

'Calm yourself Richard, and come and sit down. I was just being polite. My father rather likes him and he is a frequent guest here. It is not my place to give offence.'

'But he is so opinionated.'

Richard could see that he was driving Sarah into unnecessary support for Terrill but could not prevent himself from speaking out. Sarah replied, a little too sharply for Richard's liking. 'He has made quite a fortune in business and is anxious to take a place in society. I am told that he is much sought after by society hostesses seeking a successful marriage for their daughters.'

This last remark did nothing to improve Richard's humour and he felt a queasiness in his stomach. 'If I may say so, I don't think Mr Terrill is a good influence on you.'

Sarah laughed. ' You are being very presumptuous, Richard.' She spoke with a gleam in her eye and a smile that showed she enjoyed teasing him. 'Who is being opinionated now? But enough of Mr Terrill. Tell me about your investigation.'

Richard began to feel calmer. 'I went to Marsh Street last evening. The Flying Angel is an unwholesome place as you may imagine. But Cox was there.'

'Were you able to speak with him?'

'I did indeed, though in the presence of three of his friends. He said little more than I already knew. He confirmed that the slaves had drowned and some of the crew too.'

'Did you find out who owned the ship?'

'No. According to Cox, they never knew. The agent who hired them is now in the American Colonies. This morning I asked Mr Willoughby about the *Demera*. He told me that the matter was never really made public and that there was a private insurance settlement.'

'Why should it be private? Surely slaves are dying all the time on these voyages?'

'Yes. But mainly from illness or disease. Letting a whole cargo drown without attempting to release them is a different matter. Public opinion might have found that unacceptable. The insurers were a little nervous.'

'But what do you intend to do now? You seem to have reached the end of that enquiry.'

Richard smiled.' I intend to carry on your uncle's work and help the anti-slave trade movement.'

'But how?'

'By obtaining extended leave of absence from Lawrence Willoughby and signing on a slave ship. I can probably get a berth as a tally clerk'

Sarah stared at him, clearly speechless.

'You seem surprised.'

'I don't know what to say, Richard. Would Mr Willoughby allow it?'

'There is no reason why he should know all the details. I will tell him I wish to travel, which he knows to be true. He will approve of that. There will be no need to worry him with the exact details. I will certainly tell him I intend to visit the American Colonies. But not how.'

Sarah, recovering from her shock, looked thoughtfully at him. She put her hand on his arm. 'I applaud your enthusiasm. But is it not a little foolhardy? You will be running terrible risks. Such a voyage is full of danger.'

'I realise that. But I feel committed to it.' And if it wins your esteem, he thought to himself, so much the better.

'There is another reason,' he continued, 'perhaps a selfish one. I wish to travel but do not have the means to do so. To see a little of the world, and at the same time do some useful work is too good an opportunity to miss.'

Richard felt the passion in his own voice and perhaps for the first time realised what motivated him. Sarah would never understand, he thought. She has as much money as she needs. If she believes in a cause she no doubt contributes money to it. He could only give himself. His head was in a whirl at the prospect before him, with its various motives and reasons. And opposite him sat this sweet girl, entirely oblivious to the tensions churning inside him.

He was minded to tell her of his father, and of his own suspicions about Terrill, but he did not. Something held him back. He was not yet ready to share his private grief, not even with this young woman in whom he recognised openness despite their different social positions. Deep down inside him, deeper even than his liking for Sarah, his dislike of Terrill, his desire for travel, deeper even than his desire to follow the trail of Ben Jackson's murder and support the anti-slavery cause there lurked the as yet unarticulated desire to restore the family name and position.

'I was not just thinking of the physical danger,' Sarah continued, 'but what of your career in Bristol afterwards? When you make your disclosures public you will upset a great number of influential people. Even my father might turn against you.'

This thought distressed Richard. 'But I thought your father had nothing to do with the trade.'

'That is true. Nor do a great many Bristolians. But that is not the same thing as actively campaigning against it. Even people wholly disconnected with the trade would feel offended at what they would see as your interference.'

Upset that she appeared to be discouraging him, Richard stood up and again started pacing the room.

'I understand what you are saying but I will not be put off. I have thought through all the implications and made up my mind. I want only your approval.'

He looked at her and could tell from her eyes that she had given in and even approved of his intention. Her smile told him that she not only supported the cause but that she was pleased he had sought her commendation.

'I admire your spirit Richard. Perhaps if I were a man I would be tempted to join you. I will give you my support if you agree to fulfil one condition. I would wish you to talk to the London Committee first. You should not take this on alone. Only if they approve and believe your journey to be necessary will I venture to give my blessing.'

Richard was jubilant. 'I readily agree to that. I would welcome the backing of the Committee. And your support means a great deal to me too.'

The following Saturday Richard breakfasted early and walked the four miles to Henbury to call on his sister Julia. It was a clear, dry morning sufficiently frosty to keep his road firm and passable on foot. He enjoyed the walk after a week of the smells of Bristol and the stuffiness of his office. Although wealthy merchants were extending the city with their confident stone houses, there was still plenty of open country between the city and Henbury for him to enjoy. Most of the trees had shed their leaves giving him a clear view for some distance in all directions, and clear visibility gave him some protection against possible surprise from footpads. Julia did not like him making the journey alone and on foot but he felt he had little to fear, most highway robbers being down and outs who rarely troubled the young and strong. But it was as well to be alert and the lack of tree cover for ne'er do wells gave him an advantage.

He had been a frequent visitor to the home of Sir John and Lady Elizabeth Manners and he had met them, their daughter Jane and son Nicholas, on several occasions. As he walked up the gravel driveway and studied the square stone façade in front of him he could not help comparing the solid certain life of the occupants with what lay ahead for him. He guessed that his sister was looking out for him for as soon as he reached the front door it opened and Julia stood there in welcome.

She showed him into the empty morning room. A fire had been lit but as yet had done little to warm the room so they sat either side of it to enjoy such heat as there was.

'Are you still happy here Julia?' It was always his first question. He felt personally responsible for his sister's situation though both knew that was not the case.

'I am content. Lady Manners and Jane are both kind and considerate towards me, Jane in particular. I think she regards me as an older sister rather than a companion. It pleases me, though I am insufficiently experienced to be her counsellor.'

'And Nicholas?'

'He is very kind. Perhaps a little too gentle for his father's liking. I am not sure he feels comfortable as part of his father's business, but has little choice really. He is not so hard a businessman.'

Richard studied her. What a fine young woman she is growing into, he thought. Tall, fair haired, neat in dress and modest in manners, he felt sorry she was unable to enjoy the social life usually available to young ladies in a thriving city like Bristol.

'I am sorry your life is so restricted.'

'It's not your fault Richard. I consider myself fortunate in the circumstances. But how are you?'

'Well enough. Mr Willoughby keeps me busy.'

Both stared into the fire as if willing it to keep burning and for some minutes neither spoke. At last Richard broke the silence.

'Julia there is something I want to tell you. I am planning to go abroad for a while. Not yet, and not for too long. But I wanted you to know what I have in mind.'

Years of close companionship as brother and sister, latterly with no other relatives, had bred the habit of total confidentiality, so once started on the narrative of events, Richard was able to tell her the whole story.

'Can you afford to go that distance, Richard?'

'I will earn my passage.' He told her of his intention to work on a slave ship.

'That sounds very dangerous,' she said quietly. Richard could see concern in her features.

'The risks are not great. Many thousands of people cross the Atlantic each year quite safely, including those on slave ships.'

'It is not only that. Sir John owns a plantation in Virginia and he owns slaves to work it. He relies on regular replacements to farm the tobacco crop. He will not be pleased to hear you are planning to act against the family's interests.'

'I see no reason to tell him Julia.'

Their conversation was interrupted by the arrival of Sir John and Lady Manners, and two exuberant cocker spaniels. The dogs bounded up to Richard and started to jump up at him, clearly pleased to find someone new from whom to seek attention.

'Richard, good morning,' said Lady Manners. 'I am sorry about the dogs. Rufus, Blackie, get down will you?'

Although a tiny, soft voiced woman, the dogs knew who was in charge and left Richard, to seek a friendly pat from Julia before settling down on a rug in front of the fire.

'Good day Ma'am.'

'We saw you arrive. I have rung for coffee. Won't you join us for a cup after your long walk?'

'Thank you Ma'am, yes.'

'And how is life in the city, Richard?' said Sir John, a bluff red-faced man with a portly figure to go with it. 'Is Willoughby keeping you busy?'

'He is indeed, Sir John.'

'Bad business about Ben Jackson. Does anyone know what happened?'

'I don't think so. The general opinion is that it was just thieves and Mr Jackson tried to resist, with fatal consequences. No other explanation has come forward.'

'Do you know his family? Lovely people. Such a tragedy for them'

'Yes, his brother Frank is a client of the firm. I have met him and his daughter. They are very upset as you may imagine.'

'He wasn't married, was he?'

No, so there are no children. I think he gave his life and energy to the city. And may I ask how business is with you, Sir John?'

'Damned hard to tell, if you want the truth. Well enough right now, of course, but some of the American colonists are getting ideas above their station. Causing no end of trouble for our Government. It makes life very difficult for those of us with property and businesses over there.'

'You mean they resist paying the tea levy?'

'I do indeed, sir. We pay for their defence from privateers, from the French, and from the natives but they don't want to share the cost.'

'Is your plantation much affected?'

'Not directly. The main problems are in the north. There are a lot of inflammatory leaflets coming from Massachusetts and spreading to other northern Colonies. The King may have to insist on a firm hand.'

Out of respect for his sister's position, Richard did not give the reply that had formed in his mind and said nothing more. Julia quickly changed the subject. 'Richard is hoping to go over to the Colonies himself soon.'

'Is that so?' said Sir John. 'Well, if you do, let me know. I might have some letters for you to take for me.'

'Of course, Sir John. I would be happy to do so.'

As he made the return journey to Bristol later that morning, Richard realised he had now committed himself to the journey and wanted only the backing of the London Committee to bring it about.

~ CHAPTER 3 ~

The first flakes of winter snow were falling as Richard walked up Corn Street towards the White Hart Hotel in Broad Street where he was to board the coach for London. Ahead of him the sky showed a light purple over All Saints Church and he was thankful that it was a still morning. It would be cold enough on top of the coach without the biting wind that frequently blew across the Wiltshire Downs.

Although barely dawn, the street was busy. Chestnut roasters were setting up outside the Exchange opposite the Bush Hotel, and two road sweepers were working along the street shovelling away dung and other refuse, much of it being pushed into the open sewer channel running down the centre of the road towards the River Frome at the bottom of the street. It was a little after high tide and two ships at the quayside two hundred yards away were beginning to unload. Richard had stopped briefly to watch the dockers at their task as he had passed from his lodgings in Frogmore Street. Although brought up in a seaport he had never been much interested in the docks, but now that he was planning a voyage the ships that creaked and rocked gently at their moorings seem to have become part of his life.

Before he reached the top of Corn Street he could see the Exchange was already open. The tides determined the hours of business and an early tide meant an early start, for there was much trading to be done. Imports from Spain, North Africa, and the American Colonies were being unloaded, some to be auctioned on the quayside, the rest to be haggled over in the Exchange. At the same time new insurance contracts were being negotiated for outgoing freight to be shipped aboard when the holds were empty.

At the top of the street, all was bustle and noise. Above, seagulls that had followed the tide wheeled and screamed at one another. Their calls were answered by the whinnying and snorting, and the stamping of hooves, of the horses waiting impatiently between the shafts of the coach. On the Exchange side of the road, the hustle of business; across the road in Broad Street, the chaos and disorder of travellers sorting out luggage and arguing over seats.

Richard did not hurry. He had purchased his fare in the six-seat coach and was well prepared for the journey, wrapped in overcoat and scarf and carrying blankets. He glanced up at the window of his chambers, which were next to the hotel, and wondered if Willoughby had yet started his morning ritual. The old man would not have been surprised to see Richard, for he knew of his intended trip to London, though not its purpose. He had assumed his pupil was off on a youthful frolic, and thought none the worse of him for that.

Ten days had passed since his discussion with Sarah, the time needed for his letter to be delivered by post boys to the London Committee and a favourable reply to be received. They had not known of Ben Jackson's death and were shocked to hear of it. Richard's interest in continuing his work was appreciated and, as he had requested, he was invited to meet some of the members to discuss what assistance he could give.

Now, he was off on the first stage of what he believed would be a momentous change in his life. As the horses clattered down High Street and over Bristol Bridge towards the Bath road, Richard looked out at the cold water of the Avon below as the snowflakes touched the surface and disappeared. He shuddered at the thought of Ben Jackson ending his days there. His thoughts centred on the riddle of the man's death, and his own growing commitment to the dead man's cause. As the coach left the city he barely noticed the jarring potholes, the rutted road with its frozen verges, or the fields beyond, covered in a light powdering of snow. His mind was now in Africa, and no one disturbed his thoughts, for it was too cold to talk and the other passengers remained muffled. Richard was grateful for their silence.

Lawrence Willoughby had not been stationed by his window when the coach left the White Hart Hotel. Had Richard left his lodgings some thirty minutes later he would have met the familiar figure of his principal walking slowly down Corn Street towards Broad Quay, the faithful Xerxes at his heels.

Coat collar turned up, and with the aid of a stick, he walked slowly along the quayside inspecting each moored ship as he passed. At last he stopped and watched a cutter being loaded. A gang of six men was unloading crates and boxes from a wooden sledge, the most frequent way of moving goods in the city where carts were not allowed. Willoughby walked over to one of the loaders who stopped work on seeing him.

'Morning Mr Willoughby.'

' Good morning Abel. I've been looking for you.'

Abel Jacobs was a thin, wiry man in his early thirties, of medium height, wearing black breeches and waistcoat and with long greasy black hair hanging down the back of his neck. Rubbing his hands together to keep warm he waited to hear what was wanted of him.

'Are you off on the morning tide?'

'That I am sir, to Bordeaux. I've regular work now. No more slave ships for me.'

'I'm pleased to hear it Abel. I understand the Bordeaux run gives an opportunity for a little personal enterprise. Is that right?'

'Aye that it does sir. What do you have in mind?'

'I have a few clients who would appreciate the opportunity to buy wine at a...a fair price.'

Both knew he meant free of excise duty, but neither said so.

'How much would you be looking for sir?'

'Just one crate each trip would suffice. I think you owe me that.'

Jacobs nodded. Like many in the city he owed his liberty to his lawyer. In his younger days he had lived by thieving until eventually caught. Willoughby had persuaded the magistrates to release him on a promise he would go to sea. Finding a berth had not been easy for an inexperienced sailor with a criminal record, and the slave ships were all that would take him on. After ten years aboard slavers, he had now found himself a more congenial berth.

He was more than willing to repay his lawyer by a little smuggling. Although it was itself a crime, only the government and the excise service regarded it as so. Almost the entire population of the coast and port areas saw smuggling as a legitimate business occupation and no one, not even a number of magistrates, would turn down the opportunity for occasional excise free goods.

'I can do that, Mr Willoughby.'

'Good. My man Steggles will see to the details. When you return, report to him at my office. He will give you further instructions and arrange payment.'

He nodded to the seaman, turned, and walked slowly away. Xerxes, who had been inspecting the quayside for his own purposes, followed on his heels, looking forward to the warmth and comfort of chambers.

It was another cold morning as Richard rang the bell in New Broadwick Square for his appointment with two members of the committee, Henry Scrope and John Combe. He was glad to be ushered into a large drawing room with a blazing log fire. There were three men in the room rather than just the two he had expected and he waited with some interest to learn who the third man was. Two of the men were middle-aged, dressed soberly in dark coat and tails with plain white cravats. The third man was younger and dressed in a bright green coat with white shirt-sleeves and collar. One of the older men came over to Richard and introduced himself.

'Mr Stourton, it is good of you to come. I am Henry Scrope. This is John Combe.' He indicated the older man, who bowed. 'And may I introduce Sir Edwin Bulwer, who is a Member of Parliament. You are most welcome.'

'Thank you, sir, for your warm welcome. I am grateful to you for sparing the time to see me.'

Henry Scrope bade Richard join them in armchairs around the fire and poured him a glass of sherry before speaking.

'Ben Jackson's death was a great shock to us as you may imagine. But I understand from your letter that you wish to help us?'

Richard nodded. 'Yes. I have in my possession the letter you wrote to Councillor Jackson concerning Captain Cox. I have made contact with Cox myself. He has confirmed the details of the sinking of the *Demera* but claims to know nothing about the financing of the voyage or who owned the ship. Apparently it was all arranged by an agent, one Amos Kettle, who is now a plantation manager in Virginia.'

'Excellent, Mr Stourton. At least we have found Cox.'

'We may have, Mr Scrope, but I doubt he will be prepared to testify about the loss of the slaves. It was his decision to abandon ship and cargo and he will be none too keen to testify to that in court. The insurance claim was settled in private. Cox himself still captains slave ships and has no interest in re-opening the matter.'

'There is our difficulty, Mr Stourton,' said John Combe. 'Our problem as a committee is that we are all London based. We have little active support in either Bristol or Liverpool. As you may be aware, the bulk of this vile trade is through ships now operating out of those two ports. Yet every time we find a sympathiser or gather some information we find we cannot use it.'

'Is there no support in Bristol?'

'Very little, I fear. You must have seen yourself how Bristol's economy is tied to the trade. Not just regular slavers. There are many traders for whom buying and selling slaves is just one part of their business. Then there are the plantation owners who rely on a regular supply. And the craftsmen employed in the ship-yards. The suppliers of textiles and other products that are shipped out to Africa. And the sail makers, coopers, ships' chan-dlers, right down to the small retailers providing provisions for the crew and horse beans for the slaves. And dare I mention the builders who build the fine buildings and the lawyers who draw up the contracts?'

Richard began to feel uncomfortable and looked across at Edwin Bulwer.

'Is Parliament not able to put a stop to it?'

Bulwer stared at Richard a moment, then roused himself in his armchair.

'It could. But it won't. There is too much vested interest, dear boy. Those who know about it won't act. Some are in the trade themselves. Others won't upset influential constituents, and turn a blind eye. Parts of the country have grown rich on slaving. They won't vote for their own impoverishment. Even if some of them abhor the trade, they think that making it illegal for British traders would simply enrich our rivals abroad.'

He slumped back in his chair as if to signify that he had said all he intended to say on the subject for the time being. There was silence in the room as all present sank into contemplation. Richard began to feel frustrated at the lack of optimism. But he was not prepared to leave matters there. Here was an opportu-nity to help a cause dear to his heart, and an opportunity to travel too. And who knows what he might find, even a connection with the ruin and death of his father, though he could see no obvious link as yet. But Bristol was a small commercial world, who knows what might come to light?

'Mr Scrope, what evidence do you think might move Parlia-ment to act?'

Scrope continued his contemplation of the burning logs before replying.

'There is a certain amount of sympathy for the crews of these ships. More so than for the slaves. A slave ship is the worst berth a merchant seaman can get. The crew are often treated as badly as the slaves. If we could rouse public opinion on their plight, Parliament might just be persuaded to act.'

Richard saw his opportunity.

' I have a mind to sign up on a slave ship, probably as a tally clerk. I would then witness everything at first hand. We could have no better evidence. And if I could find a ship going to Virginia I might be able to make contact with Amos Kettle.'

The three men stirred uneasily in their chairs each waiting for one of the others to react.

'You realise the dangers involved, do you, Mr Stourton?' enquired Henry Scrope hesitatingly. 'The death rate on these ships is abnormally high. Illness and disease is almost as rife among the crew as the slaves. You would be risking serious illness, or even death.'

'Oh come now, Henry,' cut in John Combe. 'It is out of the question that Mr Stourton should do this. We cannot expect a young man to put himself at such risk. It is not good enough just to warn him of the danger. We must refuse. It would do the reputation of our committee no good at all if we were to be seen to be encouraging such a foolhardy enterprise.'

'On the contrary, I am not encouraging him,' said Scrope. 'Rather the opposite. But if I am satisfied he is aware of the dangers, and is still determined to go, then I will give him my support. But encouragement? No.'

Richard began to feel the argument drifting away from him.

'I appreciate your concern gentlemen, and I am grateful for it. But I do understand the dangers involved, and the unpopularity I will attract in Bristol if I am successful. I have to say that the more I have thought about it the more determined I am to do it. With or without the support of your committee.'

He watched the faces of the three men as he threw out this final challenge. He knew it was a bluff and that without their support he would not go. After what seemed to Richard an interminable silence, Edwin Bulwer stirred in his chair once more.

'We must let him go, and with our blessing, John. After all, what have we achieved so far? Absolutely nothing. This campaign will be won at sea, not here in London. Mr Stourton has made up his mind. Are we going to turn away any evidence he brings back? Of course not. Then we must support him before he goes.'

'We could make some funds available for you Mr Stourton. But once you are aboard ship, you will be on your own,' warned Scrope. 'No one will be able to help you. But we can give you a letter of introduction to a Quaker family near Bristol who will provide you with support before you sail. Charles and Hannah Penney believe that there is that of God in all men and that the peace of God does not include one man enslaving another.'

The four men fell silent. Richard felt satisfied as he watched the colours of the flames in the grate and thought of the months ahead. The others sat watching him.

'Can you tell me what else is being done?' Richard asked at last.

'Indeed we can,' replied Edwin Bulwer. 'Now that it is clear that you are among our sympathisers, I can tell you more of our plans. There is a political problem in Bristol that needs to be dealt with. We are forming a movement in the city to unseat one of the two Members of Parliament there. One of the younger Bristol Councillors, Robert Harford by name, is organising this group. As you may know, for some years there has been an understanding between Whigs and Tories that each would nominate one Member of Parliament unopposed. This is largely justified by the expense of a contested election. Unfortunately both sitting members protect the slave trade and one has invested in it himself. Our intention is to force a contest when the opportunity arises by fielding a candidate who will support our movement.'

'Would such a candidate stand any chance of being elected?'

'A good question,' said Bulwer. 'On that issue alone, no. But combine it with the problem over the American Colonies and the picture changes. As I am sure you know, there is deep anxiety in the Colonies over the King's insistence on taxing the colonists. Many of Bristol's merchants own or have investments in plantations and do not wish to see a ruinous war. A candidate advocating peace with our Colonies and fair conditions for our merchant seamen would have a strong appeal. But even then we cannot be sure of support over the slavery issue.'

'Surely people can't ignore the inhuman treatment of the slaves?' enquired Richard indignantly.

'One of our difficulties, Mr Stourton,' said John Combe, 'is that to a great many Englishmen the Negro is regarded as sub-human.

And in law a slave is a chattel, to be disposed of as its owner wishes. Slaves are treated as being no different to crops, or animals. Until quite recently even the Established Church regarded slaves as God's gift to Europeans. Most of the ordinary seamen on these ships are enlisted by force or bribery and are treated appallingly. We must use this to our advantage. If we have to concentrate on the treatment of the crew, we will do so.'

'Surely crew members will testify as to the treatment they and the slaves receive?'

John Combe shook his head.

'I am afraid not, Mr Stourton. The fact is they are too frightened. Their physical safety is at risk as well as their livelihood. Slave ship owners also run other trade routes. And they are none too scrupulous. We are dealing with dangerous men who will stop at nothing to protect their interests.'

Richard's face paled as he thought through the implications of that last remark.

'Even murder?'

'Even murder.'

'Is it possible that Ben Jackson was murdered just for asking questions?'

'We fear that might be the case,' said Henry Scrope. 'And you have been asking the same questions of the same people in Bristol. You may be regarded as too unimportant to worry about. But you may already be at risk.'

Three days later Richard was back in Bristol sitting at the back of the Council Chamber to listen to the deliberations of the Common Council. This was a privilege granted by the Council who usually met in private. But the Mayor, who presides over the meetings, had obtained the consent of the Council to admit their late colleague's relatives and legal adviser to listen to the discussion about the proposed memorial for Ben Jackson. He was there at the request of Lawrence Willoughby who wanted an eyewitness account of the debate. Sitting a few yards away from him in the seats reserved for distinguished guests were Sarah and her father. Joseph Terrill was with them prior to taking his seat in the chamber itself. Despite having no claim over her, nor ever likely to have, Richard felt irked that of the three occasions he had seen Sarah, Terrill was with her on two of them.

His thoughts were interrupted by a call to order by the Mayor, James Walter, whose duty it was to formally announce the death of one of their number. He outlined the political and business career of Ben Jackson and gave a brief description of how he met his end.

'I would remind members that the first item of business at out next meeting will be to elect a new member to fill the vacancy. But I know that some members here will wish to comment on this tragic occurrence and there will be opportunity to do so when formal business is concluded.'

As he sat listening to the proceedings Richard found it ironic that not even the brutal death of one of their senior colleagues could divert the council from its usual routine. Yet it was clear what councillors really had on their minds.

At first the regular business was dealt with perfunctorily. There was little of the usual squabbling or point scoring between one faction and another, as if behaving thus would sully the memory of their late colleague.

Surveying the scene before him, Richard wondered about these representatives of the city. The Common Council members included the city recorder, aldermen, former mayors, sheriffs, and a dozen others. A few whispered conversations were going on. Several members appeared to be asleep despite it being only nine in the morning. Occasionally he saw the flash of a brandy flask being opened under the benches at which the representatives of the citizenry sat. How many of these good gentlemen had investments in plantations in the Colonies, he wondered? And how many of those purchased slaves to work them? Did they care that the Jasper Coxes of the merchant fleet were snatching men, women, and children from their homes in Africa to provide the labour to make them rich?

How civilised and remote this building and these proceedings were from what was happening in their names in another part of the world! Richard looked round the chamber itself. Built early in the century it was both comfortable and comforting. He admired the classical style with its panelled walls covered by huge hanging portraits of the city's distinguished former mayors. How much of this, he wondered, was paid for by the pain and sweat of others?

Richard watched Terrill sitting motionless in his seat on the Tory benches. Is he as self-confident as he seems, thought Richard, or is it that I just don't like him? And why don't I? Is it because of my father, or the friendship that he apparently has with Sarah and her father?

Richard's attention was brought back to the proceedings by a call from the Mayor.

'Mr Robert Harford.'

Richard recognised the name as the person mentioned by Edwin Bulwer who was organising a group to attempt to oust one of the sitting MPs. He watched with interest as a man he judged to be about thirty rose to put a question arising from a previous minute. He was tall, very slim, with a closely fitting grey coat over dark knee length breeches. He wore his own hair, lightly powdered, but no wig. Modern, Richard noted, without being showy. Harford put his question.

'I have a petition from the business community of this city to ask the Sheriff to what extent the city constables are instructed to assist the excise officers operating in the Avon Gorge.'

Richard knew that the Bristol Channel was alive with smuggling, regarded by most as a form of tax avoidance. For many years smugglers had operated by sailing up the channel at night and dropping their contraband on the Somerset coast. But nowadays they sometimes stored it aboard legitimate traders, unloading the lawful cargo in Bristol by day and the rest by night. This practice was common knowledge so Richard was not surprised to hear the reply that smuggling was the concern of the Government and not the Council.

For three quarters of an hour councillors received reports, drafted petitions, and debated motions. Then formal business over, the Mayor once again returned to the death of Ben Jackson. Richard wondered why it was that only in death were politicians spoken well of outside their own party. Was that the only time members thought of their own mortality?

Richard could see Terrill sitting impatiently on the edge of his seat waiting his opportunity.

James Walter said: 'if I detect the mood right, there is perhaps a wish for Council to mark the passing of our colleague in some way. I open the floor to contributions.'

Terrill leapt to his feet before more senior and less agile members could do so.

'Mr Mayor. We were all shocked to hear of the savage attack on our respected colleague and I am sure I speak for all here when I say I hope the perpetrators of this foul action will soon be brought to justice.'

There were nods and mutterings of approval from all sides. Terrill continued: 'But that is for others. This Council has to consider the consequences of the death. I have two proposals to make. The first is that party leaders should agree that Mr Frank Jackson, the deceased's brother, should take the vacancy on the Council unopposed.'

Almost as one, the councillors sat up, alert and many angry. The sleepers became wide-awake, the brandy bottles disappeared. Three councillors stood up and gesticulated wildly at Terrill, then started shouting. But Terrill stood his ground, fiddling with his wig as a gesture of defiance towards the interrupters. To Richard's disappointment, Terrill appeared not in the least discomfited by the furore he had created and stood calmly waiting for the disorder to subside.

'I say so for this reason,' he continued. 'Violence should not be seen to succeed. To contest the vacant seat suggests that violence can influence the exercise of political power. By accepting my proposal we are saying that it is business as before.'

'Liar!'

'Hypocrite!'

Several members stood up, shaking their fists and waving order papers at him. But this time he was supported by others of his party who shouted back, trading insult for insult, until almost the entire body of men were on their feet shouting. Only Robert Harford and his surrounding group kept out of the fray, Harford scribbling furiously on the back of his order paper. The Mayor, also now standing, banged his gavel and shouted for order, in vain, then sat back powerless, to let the storm blow itself out.

Then, as quickly as it had begun, order reasserted itself and calm and quiet was resumed. Terrill stood up. Again the smile on his face disclosed how much he had enjoyed being the centre of attention. He looked round, preening himself before Council and public, before continuing his speech.

'My second proposal concerns a memorial for our late colleague. I am sure members will agree that it is difficult to recall anyone who has served this city with such distinction. We all know his generosity to the Grammar School, the Free Hospital, and to numerous other charities. I know I have considerable support in this chamber when I propose that a subscription be opened for a statue to be commissioned and erected in a suitably prominent place.'

Richard looked across at Sarah and her father with exasperation. They were both sitting listening to Terrill without betraying any emotion. Richard was sure that Terrill had set out to win the affection of Sarah and was using her uncle's death to further his cause. He was perplexed that they could not see this. To his eyes Joseph Terrill was an actor playing to the gallery.

After Terrill had finished, Robert Harford rose to speak.

'Mr Mayor, I oppose both proposals. What this Council and the country needs are more elections not fewer. It is a disgraceful suggestion that the Tories should seek to replace a member with one of their own choice, however suitable that choice may be. With respect to Mr Frank Jackson, against whom I impute no dishonour, Councillor Terrill and the Tories may wish to find placemen they can appoint to do their bidding but I will have none of it.'

Terrill stood up, fists clenched, and leaned across towards Robert Harford.

'I resent that remark. If Councillor Harford is challenging my honour, then he will have to do so in the time honoured way, outside this chamber.'

Immediately the uproar started again. A dozen councillors stood up and resumed their shouting. One jumped up and down, shrieking. It was a revelation to Richard how one remark could ignite political passions which for most of the morning had lain dormant. It was a warning to him that beneath the opulence and order of the city lay a dangerous turbulence and potential strife.

He looked across at Sarah and her father, the unwitting victims of the disorder. They continued to sit motionless and silent staring at the uproar before them. Richard, beside himself with fury at Terrill's remarks, could not understand their composure and felt excluded from their class and their world.

After some minutes of further banging of his gavel, the Mayor gradually brought proceedings under control, and order was completely restored when he threatened to prorogue the meeting.

Robert Harford was allowed to finish his speech in silence; how he thought there was too much election rigging already without making it official and that good works were rewarded in heaven not in expensive statues. Richard took a liking to him, and not just because he spoke against Joseph Terrill.

There were no more interruptions and one hour after it had started the debate came to an abrupt end when councillors realised what the guests had long since appreciated, that nothing new was being said. But the passion had not run its course for there then followed a procedural wrangle as to whether the two proposals should be voted upon singly or together. The councillor who had been jumping up and down shrieking now ran to the Mayor's dais and started haranguing him. But the Mayor stood his ground and ruled that the two propositions should be treated separately. After more name calling the proposal to offer the vacant seat to Frank Jackson was defeated. But Joseph Terrill was invited to open a subscription for a statue to be commissioned, with the Council undertaking to find a suitable site. Terrill sat back looking well pleased with himself, his self-satisfied smile directed towards Sarah.

When the meeting ended Richard waited in the lobby for Sarah and her father. Much to his chagrin they emerged from the Council Chamber in the company of Terrill, who, flushed with success, was obviously ready for another joust.

'Ah Mr Stourton, I trust you enjoyed the proceedings? You will have noted that the Council agreed with me about the statue.'

Richard rose to the bait. 'But your other proposal was not so successful, Mr Terrill.'

'No? We shall see. My party will nominate Mr Jackson as its candidate. We shall see if anyone opposes him. I doubt anyone will.'

He smiled ingratiatingly at Richard who clenched his fists behind his back in frustration. Sarah could see that the sparring would end unpleasantly and diverted the conversation to safer channels.

'How was your trip to London, Richard?'

'It was very successful, thank you, Miss Jackson. It achieved its objective handsomely. As a matter of fact I was wondering whether with your father's approval, I might call on you tonight to tell you about it.'

Sarah hesitated, then looked towards her father before replying.

'I'm afraid that won't be convenient, Richard. Mr Terrill and other guests are dining with father and I this evening. I believe Mr Terrill wishes to discuss the statue project.'

Terrill smiled again at Richard's discomfiture.

'That is so, Miss Jackson. We must act whilst the unfortunate death is still in the public mind. Now if you will excuse us, Mr

Stourton, I have a carriage waiting for Mr and Miss Jackson. I bid you good day.'

Richard wished them well then stood on the steps of the Council House watching the carriage make its way towards Broad Quay and Clifton beyond. Turning back to his offices, he pulled his cape round his shoulders and disconsolately retraced the few steps to report to Lawrence Willoughby.

~ CHAPTER 4 ~

As Richard walked home that afternoon in the direction of the river, and his lodgings beyond, he became aware of a figure watching him from the shadows of the doorway of a draper's shop on the junction of Clare Street and Corn Street. He quickened his pace but the figure flitted in and out of the doorways, keeping close but slightly behind. It was evident that someone was following him, but in the dark he could not make out who it was, even if it was someone he knew. From the corner of his eye he could tell that his pursuer was nimble, quite short, and darted in and out of the doorways like a child playing a game.

He crossed the river in the direction of St Augustine's Back and headed up narrow Denmark Street towards Frogmore Street. Here the overhanging buildings almost met, shutting out such natural light as remained. Richard was aware that he was still being followed, so turning into Frogmore Street he immediately concealed himself in the first doorway and waited. As the figure came round the corner he stretched out and grabbed at it.

''Ere, what d'yer think yer doin'?'

Richard found himself holding on to a struggling bundle of rags and saw it was a young girl.

'Now calm down, I'm not going to hurt you.'

Gradually the struggling subsided but Richard held the girl's wrists tightly. He pulled her close towards him and looked into her face.

'Aren't you Nancy from the Flying Angel?'

'What's it to you if I am?'

'I want to know why you are following me.'

The girl's head dropped. Richard was surprised that she could stand still without shivering, for she wore just a thin, torn frock with a shawl round her shoulders. She said nothing. He gradually relaxed his grip, sensing that the girl had calmed down and was unlikely to run away.

'Where do you live, Nancy?'

'I ain't got no 'ome.'

'Where do you sleep then?'

'All over. Me parents are dead. I sleep where I can find some place for me 'ead.'

Richard took hold of her arm. 'You'd better come to my lodgings for a few minutes. I would like to talk to you. It's too cold out here.'

' 'ow much will you pay?'

'No, it's not like that Nancy. You can have something to eat and a warm drink while we talk. You can go when you like, I shan't harm you.'

He could see suspicion and fear in her eyes but after releasing his grip she walked by his side until they reached his lodgings. She briefly shrank back as he took out his key and opened the door, but followed him in nevertheless.

Richard rented the two downstairs rooms and scullery of a small house at the far end of Frogmore Street from the owner, Mrs Browning, a widow who lived upstairs with her two young children. He had lived there since returning to Bristol from Oxford. It had been the best arrangement he could afford at the time but he had found it suited his needs well and he had no inclination to move. It was the quieter end of the street, away from the noise of the Hatchet Inn further along. He paid his rent regularly plus a little extra for his laundry and was left undisturbed.

It was early evening but already bitterly cold and his rooms were scarcely any warmer. He settled her down in an armchair close by the fireplace and gave her a blanket to keep her warm while he lit a candle and made up a fire. He could see her looking round his room, and he too looked round, trying to imagine how a new pair of eyes would see it. It was ill furnished with an assortment of furniture, cluttered by modern standards because he had kept as many of his father's possessions as he could. But the wonder in Nancy's eyes told him that to her, to whom indoors meant a slum building or a pub, his room was a palace.

He left her by the fire while he went to make some tea, but on his return found her handling some china on the dresser across the room.

'Is this all yours?' she said.

'Most of it, yes. '

'You 'ave a lot of nice things.'

'They belong to my sister and I. We were left them by our father.'

''Ee's dead?'

'Yes, and our mother.'

She looked puzzled. So you ain't got no parents neither?'

'You ask a lot of questions, Nancy. My sister is a ladies companion and lives at her house. She has nowhere to store her possessions.'

He put the tea and some bread and cold meat on the table.

'Here you are Nancy. You eat this. I expect you haven't eaten much today.'

'I get by.'

Whilst it was undoubtedly true that she did get by, she nevertheless ate everything on offer with a speed that suggested acute hunger, or a fear that it would be taken away again before she had finished. Richard sat some distance away from her and asked no questions until she had finished eating.

'Now. Tell me. Why were you following me?'

'To see where you live.'

'That won't do Nancy. Why would you want to know that?'

'I... I...' She stopped, clearly still frightened. 'I wanted to warn you. To keep away from Jasper Cox. It won't do you no good askin' questions. You'll end up in trouble.'

Richard spoke softly to coax her on.

'Why is that, Nancy?'

'The captain nor the mate like people askin' questions about them slavers. 'Specially the one you was on about.'

Richard recognised that the girl knew something about the affair. He crossed the room and sat down beside her, and putting his face close to hers, whispered to her.

'Now Nancy, you just tell me why and I won't ask you any more questions.'

'I can't. They'd do for me if they found out.'

'I promise they won't.'

He could see from the knitted brows that she was undecided and waited.

'Promise?' she said at last.

He smiled. 'I promise.'

'Well. That ship you was on about. It weren't like they said.'

'What did they not tell me?'

'They threw some of them Negroes overboard.'

'Threw them overboard? Why?'

'To get rid of the load. So as they could get through the storm. They was too low in the water in the rough seas. They threw 'bout seventy overboard. But it weren't no good. The ship still went down.'

Richard sat upright, thinking aloud. 'So they kept it quiet and told the insurers that the entire cargo went down in the ship when she finally foundered. Nancy thank you for that, it is very important for me to know about it.'

'Can I go now?'

'Yes, of course. I said you could go when you wanted. And here is another penny for you. Where can I find you when I want to talk to you again?'

'I ain't talkin' no more. 'Specially about that. But I often sleep at the Angel. Down in the cellar mostly.'

Nancy was up and over to the door before Richard could say any more. She turned back.

'An' you keep away from Cox like I said. You've been kind to me. I don't wish you no 'arm.'

With that she was gone. Richard sat in silence for a few minutes staring into the firelight and thinking of the cruel world into which he had stumbled.

'Julia, do listen to this.'

Julia put her book down on the table beside her as Jane Manners burst into the room and sat near her.

Jane continued. 'You remember the death of that poor Bristol boy, Thomas Chatterton, in London in August? Well this is a copy of two of his poems. It is said he saw some African slaves at the docks and they looked so sad he could not forget them and wrote these poems.'

'Do you think your father would approve of you having them Jane?'

'Oh, father is not interested in books, only his newspaper. As for poetry, he thinks it a waste of time and too frivolous to heed. Here is the first.

She started reading.

> *'The children of the wave, whose pallid race*
> *Views the faint sun display a languid face*
> *From the red fury of thy justice fled*
> *Swifter than torrents from their rocky bed*
> *Fear, with a sicken'd silver, tinged their hue;*
> *The guilty fear when vengeance is their due'*

'Isn't that beautiful Julia? And so sad for those poor slaves.'

'Jane are you sure you ought to read on? The poem is talking about slave owners. You know your father owns slaves in Virginia.'

'I am sure he does not mistreat them, Julia.'

'Do you think he should own them?'

'I know that slavery can be cruel in some ways, but so are lots of other things and we could not manage without slaves to work the tobacco crop. I believe father is a humane man and does only what other investors have to do in the Colonies to make a living. And it is better for them to work for Christian owners than be slaves to other godless people in Africa.'

But Julia's comments had dampened Jane's enthusiasm for the poem and soon the pamphlet was cast to one side.

'Do you think much of the future, Julia?'

'What a strange question, Jane. I suppose I do sometimes, but not often. I don't know what the future holds for me, so there is not much point in thinking about it. Do you?'

'Oh, yes. Well, not too far ahead. I look forward to the balls I can now go to. I so love dancing. And the theatre. But I don't think much beyond that though I think my future is already planned by father. And for Nicholas too.'

Julia sat back and laughed. 'And what does your father have in store for both of you?'

'Well Nicholas is to become overseer at the plantation for a while; to get to know the business so that he can take over when father retires. As for me, well I expect he wants me to marry into a well-connected family, he thinks it his duty to see our family improve generation by generation.'

'Has he said so?'

'Well, not directly. But mother has hinted at it and I have seen older friends follow the same path.'

'Do you welcome it?'

'I should like to marry and have children. And it is always better to have money than not. We are fortunate as a family. That is just how it is.'

'Do you think slaves have the same thoughts, Jane?'

'Don't be silly Julia. It is different for Africans. We live in Bristol. That is how it is for us. But let's talk about something else. Mother and father have been invited to the civic ball at the Assembly rooms in April and we are included in the invitation. Shall you come?'

'I don't know, Jane. I really have little experience of dancing of late and have not met most of the people who will be there.'

'I shall keep on at you until you agree. I won't enjoy it so much if you are not there.'

'We'll see,' said Julia.

Xerxes raised his head off his paws, satisfied himself that the person coming through the door was a familiar one, then lowered his head again to continue in his blissful state of semi-consciousness. Richard crossed the room in some trepidation and stood by Willoughby's desk watching him finish a letter.

'Sit down my boy.'

'Thank you, sir. Can you spare me a few minutes?'

Willoughby carefully replaced his quill into the inkstand and sat back, for the first time looking up at his pupil.

'Is anything troubling you?'

'Nothing sir.' Richard knew that his nervousness had communicated itself. 'I have a favour to ask of you.'

Willoughby bowed his head slightly. 'If I can be of service, I will.'

'Thank you. For a while now I have had it in mind to travel. To see a little of the world. I was hoping you would have no objection to me taking extended leave of absence.'

Willoughby eyed him cautiously. 'You want to do the European tour, do you? Well, there's nothing wrong with that. How long do you want? Three months?'

'No sir. What I had in mind was to visit the American Colonies. I can't afford to travel round Europe as many young men do. But my situation is a little different. My future lies here in Bristol in the legal profession. With you I hope. As many of our major clients have interests there, I would like to turn my travels to good account. To visit the Colonies, and the plantations. To learn more about the businesses of the people I hope to represent.'

Willoughby sat back and stared at his pupil. 'A noble thought Richard.' He paused, taking up his usual position, head back, fingertips together. 'You will need longer than three months. Probably seven or eight. That is a long time to be away from the business. But perhaps you would be able to execute a number of commissions for me while you are there. You do realise that the situation is a little tense out there at the moment?'

Richard did. He knew that during the seven years since the French War had ended relations between the British Government and the Colonies had been deteriorating. The imposition of excise duties on the colonists, when they had no voice in Parliament – taxation without representation they called it – had led to considerable ill feeling and a number of violent incidents had occurred. The coming to power of Lord North's Government earlier in the year had quietened the situation a little, but no one expected that to last. There was a very real danger that the colonists might try to break away from British control, and if King George III had his way, this would be forcibly opposed.

'I am aware of the situation. But I believe the hostility is confined to British officials. Trading is continuing uninterrupted. I see no personal danger.'

'Then I have no objection Richard. But how will you manage financially? I can advance you some of your capital, and pay you whilst on firm's business. But that will not be enough to cover all your expenses.'

'I can manage, thank you. I intend to seek a working passage. As tally clerk if possible. The voyage would pay for itself. I would like to be away for longer than seven or eight months. About ten months would be better, if you will agree. I am grateful to you for your support. I would like to leave early in the New Year if that is convenient to you.'

'Of course. Ten months it is then. Give me a month to arrange for the business to cope with your absence. And if you can let me know where you intend to travel when over there I can make ready the various transactions I would like you to conduct.'

On the very morning Richard was tackling Willoughby for extended leave of absence, Sarah and her maid left home early for a meeting the details of which she did not disclose to her father.

As her carriage took her the mile or so to her destination in Kings Down, she reflected on the relative freedom she was fortunate enough to enjoy. She felt grateful for the opportunities that she had, then thought of her dear dead mother. Perhaps had she lived, her own freedom would have been much curtailed. As it was she intended to make the most of her situation.

Her carriage turned into the drive of a mid-century mansion standing in its own grounds. The iron gates were open and Sarah was driven to the front door, leaving her but a short step into the hallway and the warmth of a blazing log fire. There to meet her were Councillor Robert Harford, the owner of the house, and his wife Mary.

She was ushered into the drawing room where three other people were sitting drinking coffee.

'Sarah, I believe you know Hugh Berry, his wife Frances, and John Powell.'

'Yes, we have met before, Robert.' She knew them to be some of the members of a group of young businessmen and politicians known in the city as having liberal views and of which Robert Harford was the acknowledged leader. Harford poured her coffee and continued.

'Sarah we were all shocked and saddened to hear of Ben's death. He was a fine man. As a matter of fact he was party to some of the matters I wish to talk about this morning and I need hardly tell you, he was very supportive.'

He continued. 'I'm grateful to you all for coming this cold morning and will come straight to the point. As you perhaps know, there is a great deal of concern here in Bristol about the poor relations between our Government and the American Colonies. A number of Bristol merchants have substantial investments there and view with alarm the growing disturbances. I'm sure you know the reasons. Briefly, the King and his Ministers feel the colonists should pay towards their own defence – and towards the cost of the recent French war that is still a drain on the nation's purse. The colonists say they shouldn't be taxed if they are unable to sit in our Parliament.'

He stopped and looked round at his audience. They sat silent, content to let him continue.

'I think all of us here feel the colonists have a powerful case and that unless something is done quickly, there is likely to be armed conflict which can only damage our interests. Unfortunately our two Members of Parliament, although one a Whig and the other a Tory, both support the King's Party, so our views find no expression in the House of Commons.'

'More's the pity,' growled Hugh Berry.

'Quite,' Harford resumed. 'And one of them, Henry Croder, owns a plantation in Virginia worked by slaves. A number of people in our city feel something should be done before it is too late. What has been suggested is that the rather too convenient arrangement between the two political groups to share the seats uncontested should be broken. To achieve this, I have decided to stand as a candidate at the next General Election, whenever it comes.'

'And a good thing too,' said John Powell. 'There are many who feel this is necessary. But it will be difficult to achieve. Blackman and Croder are well entrenched and have formidable friends. How do you propose to tackle it?'

'I have had a number of informal discussions,' continued Harford, 'and it is clear that there is more support for our views amongst Whigs than Tories. I intend to seek the Whig nomination either with or in place of Henry Croder. If that fails, I will stand as a radical candidate against both the others.'

Sarah intervened. 'How do you feel I can help? We women have no political power, not even a vote.'

Harford laughed. 'You may not have power, Sarah. But you certainly have influence. We need to know how many of the leading Whigs in the city would be likely to support us. This can be done more discretely through their wives. We mustn't declare our hand too soon. If suspicion is aroused we can say it is mere wives idle chatter – if you will forgive me, ladies.'

Sarah winced at this, but with no malice towards Harford, for she knew he was right. It irked her to find her world so dominated by men but recognised the role she could play.

'But how can we fund a contested campaign?' said Hugh Berry. 'I'm told the last contested election in Bristol cost each candidate £20,000. How can we raise that amount of money?'

'There are many in Bristol and in the Colonies who are at risk to lose a great deal more than that,' replied Harford. 'We ought to be able to raise a substantial subscription once our campaign is firmly established. Sarah, do you know how your father stands on these issues?'

Sarah looked thoughtful.

'My father is a little old-fashioned and doesn't discuss politics with me. He rarely expresses his opinions openly, preferring to build houses for Whig and Tory alike. He used to leave politics to my uncle. But I do know he is under some pressure to declare for the Tories.'

'Will he do so?' Harford was alarmed. 'That would make things very awkward for you.'

'I'm not sure that he will. The Tories are trying to persuade him to take my uncle's seat on the Common Council in the belief he would feel sufficiently indebted to them to give his support. But I doubt he will. My father may not hold strong opinions of his own, but he will not allow others to foist theirs on him.' She smiled. 'But even if he did, he would not mind me taking a different course, or feel that I was being disloyal. He is not old-fashioned in everything.'

'What about the colonists themselves?' enquired Berry.

'I'm sure we can raise finance from them,' replied Harford. 'But we need someone to go over there as soon as possible to organise it. And it should be someone who will not arouse too much suspicion.'

'I think I can help with that,' said Sarah. 'I know someone who is planning to make the journey shortly and I am sure would do this for us.'

The person Sarah had in mind was back in Marsh Street two evenings later, looking for Nancy in the Flying Angel. Richard found her in the kitchen preparing food. She was clearly agitated at his presence and started scrubbing a pot with exaggerated force.

'You shouldn't've come 'ere.'

'Why not?'

'Jasper Cox don't like me talkin' to you.'

'But I must talk to you. Is there somewhere quiet we can go?'

With some reluctance Nancy put the pot down, and drying her hands on a cloth, nodded to him to follow her. At the back of the kitchen were some stone steps down which Nancy led him into the cellar. Richard shivered. He could see the walls were damp with fungi growing in patches, plaster peeling off the walls in other parts. There was a smell of damp, and of rats. Clearly its main use was as a storeroom, but on the floor in one corner was a dirty mattress with straw sticking out of protruding holes. A few empty sacks lay on it.

'Is this where you live Nancy?'

'I don't live nowhere. I sleep 'ere most nights. Not always, mind, but if I 'elp in the kitchen 'ee lets me stay the night 'ere.'

'But it's no place for a girl to grow up.'

''Tain't no worse'n most of us 'ave. Better than a shop doorway. An' it ain't too cold.'

Richard said no more about it. He realised the girl knew no different and regarded herself as fortunate. It was all according to what you were used to.

'What d'yer want to talk to me about then?' Nancy jolted Richard's mind back to the reason for the visit.

'I want to find a ship that's doing the slave run. To sign up as crew.'

Nancy's mouth opened in astonishment. 'You're daft if you wanna do that. 'Tain't for the likes a' you.'

'I have my reasons Nancy. Every ship needs someone who can tally the stock. I can turn my hand to that – and look after myself.'

'You'll end up dead, that's what,' said Nancy discouragingly.

'It's my choice Nancy. Can you help me?'

She seemed reluctant to do so. ''Spose I can. You do what you want. It's your life. There's a Captain Joel Pinney looking for crew for 'is slaver that's leaving in January. He's usually to be found in the Queen's 'ead along the street. He's a nasty bit o' work mind. You'll get no favours from 'im.'

'Do you know where he's heading after leaving Africa?'

' 'ee ain't goin' to the India Islands but more'n that I don't know.'

'Thank you Nancy. You've been a great help.'

She looked solemn. 'I dare say this'll be the last time I shall see you. If you've a mind to go on a slaver I won't expect you back.'

Somewhat discouraged by Nancy's pessimism, Richard left the Flying Angel and walked the few yards to the door of the Queen's Head. He was no stranger to this way of life now, but was still shocked at the number of times he was accosted by young women loitering in unlit doorways between the two drinking dens.

The Queen's Head was a similar establishment to the Flying Angel but he soon found that it outclassed its neighbour in the volume of noise and the smell of stale beer. The sawdust on the floor looked unswept for many a day and the crush of people made progress into the half lit interior difficult. But he had no difficulty finding Captain Pinney in the corner of the public room sitting at the end of a long wooden table, playing cards with a number of young men whose noisy and restless behaviour immediately told Richard they were the worse for drink The captain himself seemed in good spirits and was joining in the revelry with the young men, but with a slight reserve which suggested some play acting on his part, an indication that he at least was sober.

Joel Pinney was a thick set man, about forty, Richard thought, with greying hair and wide grey sideburns meeting down under his chin. He wore a dark navy singlet, full of holes, and black breeches. At the opposite end of the table sat another seaman who Richard was soon to realise was a confidant of the captain and who was keeping the beer mugs filled.

His first impressions were not favourable. He felt something menacing and unreal about this display of good humour. As he reached the Captain's table he was conscious of several pairs of eyes watching him from adjacent tables.

'Captain Pinney?'

Everyone at the table put down their cards. The Captain looked up at him and gave him a withering smile. 'That's me. Have you come to join our game?'

'Thank you, but no. My name is Richard Stourton. I am told you might be looking for a tally clerk on your next trip.'

The Captain smiled again, but without any warmth. 'Aye, that I am. Have you someone in mind?'

'I'm looking for such a berth myself. I wish to travel to the American Colonies and am seeking to earn my passage.'

This brought roars of laughter from the young men around the table. 'Don't go wi' 'im,' one of them shouted. 'There's no telling where you might end up.'

This was greeted with another burst of laughter, the Captain and his companion joining in. But Captain Pinney had his answer ready.

'We're bound for Virginia, calling first in West Africa for a little business. I might be willing to take you on.'

'That would suit me, if you are prepared to take me. When do you plan to sail?'

The reply came from a swarthy man sitting at the opposite end of the table.

'I'm the mate, Samuel Baillie. We plan to leave 'bout the fifteenth of January.'

'I could be ready by then. Have you signed up the rest of the crew yet?'

'No, not all.' Baillie smiled and leaned across to Richard whispering 'some of 'em are here now, but they don't know it yet.'

Richard's unease grew but he told himself this was to be expected. He settled down on a wooden bench alongside the captain, ordered a tankard of ale and awaited developments. He was not sure whether the Captain had accepted him or not. As he watched the men playing, he saw the piles of coins that had been in front of the young men gradually disappear and reappear in front of the Captain and Baillie. After an hour all their money had gone and the young men were signing bills to cover their losses. As their drunkenness increased so did their debts.

Just before midnight the game came to an abrupt end. For close on an hour, Pinney and Samuel Baillie had kept up a conversation about the benefits of sailing with them and the game ended with two of the young men agreeing to sign up as crew. From their slurred speech it was clear they had little idea of what they were doing. Pinney immediately produced two written contracts, which the new recruits were induced to sign, although writing even their own names required the help of Samuel Baillie. Richard doubted whether they were literate even when sober.

The other two young men refused to sign up even though under heavy pressure to do so. One of them clumsily attempted to stand up, pushing his chair over noisily in the process. He needed to grip the table to keep upright and seemed to retain little idea of what was going on.

'You're not getting me to sign up on no slaver,' he shouted, his voice slurred. 'I ain't going with you.'

Richard noticed that the other patrons of the King's Head took little notice of the outburst. He assumed they had seen it all before.

The captain smiled at him. 'Well Mr Nathan, it's the debtors prison then for you and your friend. You'll not be able to pay up on these bills in twenty years never mind next week an' the debtors court will have you in Newgate soon enough.'

The young man spoke falteringly. 'I've been tricked into this,' he said bitterly, 'no court would allow this debt to stand.'

'And who's goin' to believe you?' enquired Pinney in a mocking voice. 'Everyone here saw you play cards and lose. Your only way out is to make this one voyage and your debt will be wiped out. You'll witness what I've said won't you, Mr Stourton?'

Richard's inclination was to have nothing to do with it, but he knew he would see far worse before the voyage was finished.

'Yes of course.'

Nathan knew he was beaten and fell back in his chair. Then, slowly, he leaned across to Pinney, took up the document and signed his mark where instructed.

'Mr Stourton,' said Pinney, 'I'll take you on as you wish. You'll be a welcome member of my crew. The usual terms. No payment whilst on board, food and drink only. Payment of £15 when we reach Virginia. The same amount again when we're back in Bristol. We'll be docked in Virginia for about five weeks. That's free time for you 'cept the first few days when we sell the stock and again the last few when we re-load for the return journey. We should be away just short of a year all told.'

'Who owns the ship, Captain Pinney?'

'Sebastian Sedgehill. You'll have heard of him no doubt. He's in a good way of business.'

'Yes I have. He lives in Queen Square. He transports convicts to Maryland I believe.'

'Aye, that he does. But not this trip.'

As Richard made his way back to his lodgings later that night he felt both depressed and satisfied. He had soiled his hands in slavery business; yet obtained his first piece of evidence.

CHAPTER 5

Christmas and the New Year passed quickly for Richard for there was much to do in preparation for the voyage. His work for Willoughby needed to be put into order and the various commissions organised that he would be undertaking in the Colonies. His leave of absence started during the second week in January, four days before he was due to sail. Most of this time was to be taken up by his new duties for Captain Pinney.

His first visit to the Amelia was on the morning after he had left Willoughby's chambers for the last time. The ship was moored at Bathurst Basin where final repairs had been carried out prior to loading. He arrived just after daybreak to find activity and confusion on the quayside and the ship. Ropes and canvas scattered across the quay; crates and boxes piled high around the gangplank; seagulls circling and crying; cats already walking the deck in search of rats. And always the shouting from the many sailors and vendors, opportunistic thieves and beggars, and a crowd of boys come to watch the fun. He was surprised how small the three-masted slave ship seemed for the voyage ahead, perhaps no more than one hundred and twenty tons, he thought.

As he walked up the gangplank he could see three men talking at the stern of the ship. They broke off as he approached. Captain Pinney and the mate Samuel Baillie he recognised but not the third man.

'Morning, Stourton,' said the captain. 'Glad to see 'ee on time. We've started loading. There'll be no rest for yee for the next couple o' days.'

Richard nodded, then looked at the stranger, who introduced himself.

'My name's William, William Daniel. I'm the ship's surgeon. You must be the tally clerk, Richard Stourton isn't it?'

'Aye, that he is,' said Captain Pinney. 'Our surgeon here will be the busiest man aboard once we set sail for Virginia, Mr Stourton. Mr Daniel, perhaps you would like to show Mr Stourton round while the mate and I organise the crew.'

They were interrupted by a scuffle and shouting near the gangplank and Richard could see one man, who appeared to be drunk, trying to resist being carried aboard by three others.

'This way Mr Stourton,' said William Daniel. 'Take no notice of the commotion. Some crewmen are a little reluctant to join ship, but they soon settle down.'

There were other crewmen standing around on deck looking sullen and resentful and Richard wondered how many of them had been tricked or forced into signing up.

He followed the surgeon down into the hold. It was dark, smelled of rats, and was extremely cramped, requiring him to stoop as he moved about. Around the sides, and at regular intervals across the floor, were iron chains. There seemed to be no more than a few inches between one chain and the next.

'Are all these chains to be used?' he asked.

'Yes. The Captain is what's known as a tight packer. He says that a certain number of slaves will die on the journey whatever we do for them, so the more we start with the more we shall have at the end.'

'As a medical man, do you believe that?'

Daniel laughed. 'I'm not really a medical man. I'm a sailor. I picked up a few ideas on how to keep crew and cargo alive and that's enough to warrant me being a surgeon on a slaver. My main task is to organise fresh air and exercise for the slaves and try and keep most of them alive.'

'What medical supplies do you have on board?'

'Not too much that you would recognise as medicines. Gum camphor, cinnamon water, mustard and bitters are the stock items. Fresh air, exercise, clean quarters and fresh food are the best medicine, but not always available.'

Richard noticed that Daniel had not given his opinion on the Captain's views about tight packing. He was learning fast. He said nothing more and followed the surgeon back up the stairs to the crew's living quarters and the deck. The officers and Richard each had their own cabin though in Richard's case it was really a small office for the keeping of the records with a bunk bed in one corner. The crew were to sleep on deck. Richard's cabin had barely enough room to move about in but he was grateful for a private refuge where he would be able to escape the brutal world around him, and compile a diary unnoticed.

'I see we are well armed. How many cannon are there?'

'Nine. One trained on the slave quarters for when they come up on deck for exercise. The others to fight off any pirates.'

'Are they common?'

'The pirates? Well not so many as when we are at war. But there will always be those who will let you do the hard work collecting the slaves, even taking them across the Atlantic, then try and take them from you. Off the African coast and close in to the American coast are the two most dangerous times.'

'How many slaves will we be transporting?' he asked.

'About four hundred and twenty,' replied Daniel. 'And it's my job to make sure that as near to four hundred as possible arrive in saleable condition. Every dead slave represents a loss of profit on the run, and the Captain takes none too kindly to that. Especially as I have to select the most suitable slaves when we are in Africa.'

'How much are the slaves worth?'

'About £30 each. For a strong young male perhaps £40.'

'And how many crew?'

'About twenty five.'

'That's not many. Is it a safe number?'

'Oh yes. And that allows for some loss. But don't be alarmed, tally clerks usually survive, they don't come into contact with the slaves or do any of the hard work.' He grinned at Richard who smiled weakly in return.

'What food are the slaves given?'

'Some of the food we take with us. The rest we buy in Africa. Each slave can expect a daily ration of yams and beans with biscuits, flour and salted beef occasionally. They have two meals a day.'

'Is that sufficient?'

'The flux and scurvy are the biggest dangers. They are given a mouthwash of vinegar or lime juice every morning which helps.'

To Richard it seemed a small number to manage the ship on such a long voyage with its large and potentially troublesome cargo. But he said nothing, and settled into his first task which was to record all the cargo being boarded and stored for the first stage of the voyage, from Bristol to West Africa.

Apart from food and water for the crew the ship was loaded to capacity with exports for sale or exchange. Brassware, pots and pans, gin, several hundred rolls of cotton, clothes, hats, guns and ammunition were all recorded and stowed aboard, all of which could be used to purchase slaves. Preparing the inventory took him two days leaving just the day before sailing to make his farewells. He noted that the goods for trading were worth about £1,000. The slaves purchased with these goods would be worth many times more.

'So, Richard, you will soon be gone.' Richard could see the sadness in his sister's eyes that she could not conceal.

'The sooner gone, the sooner I will return.' His voice was too full of emotion to sound convincing. 'Will you be comfortable whilst I am away?'

'Yes. Please don't worry on my account.'

'You know I don't regard our situation as a permanent one.'

'What do you mean?'

'I think it is possible father was defrauded out of his fortune. I am trying to find out the truth.'

'Do you think that is wise, Richard?'

'Why should I not?'

'It could lead to bitter disappointment, not to say danger. I wonder whether we might do better just putting the past behind us and accept our situation. After all, we are not badly placed. You have your career, I a comfortable situation. There are many less well circumstanced than us.'

Richard stirred in his seat as he listened to what his sister was saying.

'Julia you may be right. But not quite yet. I have already told you why I am going to the Colonies, and how. Yet there could be links to father's affairs. I have no direct evidence but there could just be a connection between the merchant ship owner, whoever he is, whose ship *Demera* foundered, and father's losses. It is not much more than a feeling at present but whilst I have the opportunity to investigate further, I will do so. I promise you that if it comes to naught, I will give up and try and be as contented as you. People have made a success of their lives starting with less than we have.'

'Richard I am relieved to hear you say so. Harbouring regret or a feeling of injustice could cast a shadow over your life. But there is something else I wish to talk to you about.'

'What is that? Not a serious problem I hope?'

'No, not really. It is Nicholas. He has been a little more attentive than his position requires. Not over familiar, his reserve prevents that, but he has shown signs of affection. I can tell he is worried his father will find out and send me away. When his parents are about he becomes more distant.'

'Have you encouraged him in any way?'

'No. But I am nearly always here so cannot escape.'

'Do you like him, Julia?'

'Oh yes. Very much. But I feel that if I show him the slightest encouragement I will be accused of enticing him. His father has other plans and would not tolerate such a relationship.'

'What does Sir John expect of his son?'

'I am not sure exactly. To spend some time on the plantation in Virginia, then come home and marry a wealthy young lady of his own class I expect.'

'Does Jane know?'

'No, nor Lady Manners. In truth, Nicholas has said little but is very thoughtful and kind. I can tell though, and I don't know whether to discourage him or just pretend I do not see what is happening.'

Richard grasped and gently squeezed her hand. 'Poor Julia.. The loss of fortune and status is so much harsher for a woman. I don't know what to advise, save only to continue as you are and see what develops. Be polite and friendly but not forward. If Mr Nicholas is serious in his intentions, he will speak to his father sooner or later and make it clear you have offered no encouragement. While I am away you must feel able to call on Miss Sarah Jackson. She is a discreet and wise young woman and has been a good friend to me. You can confide in her.'

Richard sympathised with his sister. Were his feelings for Sarah a parallel? Did he feel affection for Sarah? Or was it simply gratitude for the interest she had taken in his plans? As he made his way back to the city he had much to occupy his mind. Not the least how the loss of a modest fortune had impinged on the status in society of both Julia and himself.

Where there is trade, so there are traders' clubs. Such was the case in Bristol. Some were formal, some exclusively so, some just a loose gathering of like-minded people. Their members are always male, and centred at coffee houses in the mornings or hotels if they chose to meet of an evening. Except in the more rigidly constituted clubs, members were generally self-selecting, a symbiosis of opinion or interest usually being sufficient. It was rare for Whig and Tory to frequent the same gatherings unless a single issue brought them together.

Such a single-issue gathering met once a month in a private room at the back of a coffee house in Broad Street. All who owned businesses that relied on, or were involved in, the supply of African slaves to the West Indies or the American Colonies were at liberty to attend.

On the second Monday morning of the New Year Sir John Manners and his son Nicholas had ridden down to the city to attend the monthly meeting. They found fifteen or sixteen others already there including the Councillor Joseph Terrill, and Henry Croder, one of the city's MPs. Despite the eminence of some of those present, it was usually left for Sir John to direct proceedings.

'Gentlemen, I wish you all a prosperous New Year. May I say what a pleasure it is to have one of our Members of Parliament with us today. I have already told him of our concerns, which we have discussed here before and I know he is sympathetic to us. Is that right Mr Croder?'

'Indeed it is so, John. As I understand it you have two concerns. The first is the development of some public sympathy in this country against the trade in slaves, particularly in Quaker and Evangelical circles. And the second, the rising outspokenness of some of our cousins in the American Colonies against His Majesty and His Government.

'With regard to the first of these I think you need not feel too concerned. There is a very small group of Members of Parliament, led by Sir Edwin Bulwer, who profess to be against the trade but they have little influence. Most are London members and are driven in my view by the fact that London has lost out in the trade in slaves to Bristol and Liverpool. Nothing was heard from them when their city was making money.

'The Quakers, and a few in the Established Church, have also raised questions but there seems to be no popular support. The King's friends, who are the strongest force in the Commons, are steady for the trade as are the vast majority in the Lords.'

'And the Opposition in the Commons?' asked Joseph Terrill.

'The Opposition is by and large of a like mind,' continued Croder. 'The general view is that to retain our pre-eminence in trade both here and overseas we must retain our share of the transportation of labour. Trying to stop it would probably be fruitless for if successful it would simply hand it over to the

French, Spanish or Portuguese, and our plantations would then be at their mercy.'

There was a murmur of assent round the table. To a man, those present had substantial holdings in the plantations or the shipping companies who provided the transport.

'The second question is more difficult,' Croder said. 'The King's Party in both Commons and Lords takes the view that we must stand firm against the demands made of us. As a plantation owner myself, I agree, as does my fellow member Ralph Blackman. Whilst I confess there are a growing number of voices in the Colonies complaining about the taxation imposed, a firm hand should, and I hope will, quell any incipient discontent and even acts of disloyalty.'

'I agree,' said Sir John. 'We must take a firm line. We have to think of our livelihoods and families. What practical steps do you think we can take Henry?'

The MP thought for a moment. 'I suppose the answer is to organise, and persuade. That's what our opponents are doing. Don't let our case go by default. With regard to the Colonies, a petition of loyal support to His Majesty from the Common Council would be well received.'

'I will gladly do that,' said Joseph Terrill. 'But what about the slave issue?'

'Most of the criticism against the trade in slaves is in respect to the alleged conditions that our merchant seamen have to endure, not concern for the cargo,' continued Henry Croder. 'Well, there is an economic case to be made here. The work is difficult and dangerous and therefore expensive. There is no future for any of us if we lose out to foreign competition. I suggest you form a Bristol League of Support for the African Trade. As one of Bristol's three representatives on the committee of the Company of Merchants Trading in Africa, I would find such an organisation to be of great assistance.

'In the Colonies we must separate the two issues. However the matter with the colonists is resolved, using slave labour must continue, as will the demand for future supplies. All of you who have plantations over there must persuade your neighbours of the value of strong links with His Majesty's Government and that you will not allow a break with the English Parliament.'

'And what about agitation in Bristol?' said James Walter.

'There are only one or two I believe,' said Sir John, ' and we can deal with them.'

❖ ❖ ❖

Richard had seen little of Sarah during these last few weeks, but at the instigation of his daughter, Frank Jackson had invited him to dinner on his last night before sailing.

Early on that final afternoon and some hours before he was due to go to the Jackson's house, he was disturbed by a knock on the door. He found Nancy outside and in a distressed state. Blood was pouring down her cheek and around her left eye he could see severe bruising.

'Come in Nancy. For goodness sake, what's happened?'

' 'ee 'it me. Like I said 'e would.'

'Who hit you?'

'Captain Cox.'

He asked no more for the present, but sat her down and fetching water and towels did his best to staunch the flow of blood and tidy her up. This calmed her and she was able to give an explanation.

' 'ee kept askin' questions about you, an' what you was after.'

'Did you tell him?'

'Not to start with. But 'ee kept on threatening me. So I told 'im as how you was looking for a berth. But I didn't say as you'd got one. Just where you could find one. Then 'ee 'it me. 'ee said it would be worse next time if I was to talk to you again.'

'Is there no one who can protect you? Constable Skinner?'

'Where I come from we don't 'ave nothin' to do with the law. We sort ourselves out. It'd be the worse for me if I was to bring a constable in.'

'But what are we going to do with you? I sail tomorrow.'

'I can take care of meself.'

'It doesn't look like it. You shouldn't go back to the Flying Angel. Will you let me take you somewhere safe?'

'Where's that?'

'I have some friends who are Quakers. They will find you somewhere safer and more comfortable to live. They might even find you a job.'

'I don't want no job.'

'At least let's go and talk to them.'

'Well, if you want. But I ain't agreein' anything.'

Richard had just enough time to take Nancy to Frenchay. He had already visited Charles and Hannah Penney, the Quaker family to whom Henry Scrope had written a letter of introduction. As promised, they had been very supportive and had promised Richard whatever assistance he needed. Now he wanted their help.

He marched Nancy to the White Hart where he was able to hire a horse. He pulled Nancy up to sit side-saddle in front of him and set off as quickly as he dared. Nancy, despite her fragile state, sat in wonderment at her first ride on a horse. They found Hannah at home, her husband out at a meeting.

'Come in Richard, and bring thy friend.'

'Thank you. Hannah, this is Nancy. She has been very helpful to me in our cause but is now in some danger because of it. She has already been beaten for helping me and I feel responsible for protecting her while I am away. I need to find somewhere for her to stay out of harm's way.'

'I'm all right I keep tellin' 'im.' Nancy addressed Hannah, who took no notice of her.

'Of course we'll look after her. She may be just what we are looking for. Our neighbours, who are also Friends, have need of a scullery maid. Nancy may be suited for that. Would thee like that Nancy?'

'I dunno. What is it?'

'Living in their house and helping their cook in the kitchen. Washing up and preparing vegetables mostly. They would give thee new clothes and a uniform and a bed of thine own.'

Nancy said nothing. It was clear she was torn. The idea of a real bed and new clothes appealed to her; but she had grown up wild and was clearly reluctant to give up her free life. Richard watched her with some anxiety for he didn't know what else he could do with her. At last she seemed to come to a decision.

'I'll see what it's like. I aint makin' no promises mind.'

Richard and Hannah smiled at one another at Nancy's way of suggesting she was doing them a favour.

'Stay here tonight Nancy and I'll take thee to my neighbours in the morning. Now, some treatment is needed for thy face.'

Richard realised he was no longer wanted and left. He felt pleased for having settled the problem of Nancy but as he rode back into the city he reflected that it was not just his own life that Ben Jackson's death had changed.

'Do come in Richard.' Frank Jackson smiled as he shook hands then ushered Richard through to the drawing room. Sarah was sitting by the fire and she, too, smiled at him with a warmth he found gratifying.

Frank Jackson continued: 'I'm sure you will excuse me for a few minutes while I finish off some important business. Dinner will be in half an hour and Sarah will entertain you until the other guests arrive.'

He left abruptly and Richard could not help but wonder whether his few minutes alone with Sarah had been contrived by one or the other, or perhaps both. Sarah stood up.

'Sherry, Richard?'

'Thank you, yes.'

Now that he had Sarah to himself he felt tongue-tied. They sat opposite each other, neither knowing how to broach the different subjects each had in mind. Richard felt a need to express his feelings at leaving her, but did not wish to sound presumptuous and risk a rebuff.

He began cautiously. 'I would like you to know how much I have appreciated your friendship over the last few weeks, Sarah.'

He thought he detected a little colour coming to her cheeks as she averted her eyes from his gaze. She did not respond, but changed the subject, a little abruptly Richard thought.

'Richard we do not have much time and I have a favour to ask you.'

Richard sat back as Sarah told him of her political involvement with Robert Harford, and her wish that he should contact some of their supporters in Virginia. He was surprised at her understanding of the complex political issues involved and of her failure to confide in her own father.

'So you see Richard it is vital to our efforts to have support and money from the Colonies. Robert has given me a list of some businessmen in Virginia who may be willing to help. We would like you to call on them.'

He was pleased that Sarah wanted him to help her although he felt some disappointment at her formal approach. He had hoped for an expression of personal sorrow at his going but he saw that this was to be denied him.

'I will do this very willingly,' he said, 'though you will realise that it will be many months before I reach Virginia and nearly a year before I am back in Bristol.'

'Yes we do understand that but we don't expect a General Election for two years or more.'

Richard started to tell her of his ship and its crew but to his deep disappointment he was almost immediately interrupted by the return of Frank Jackson bringing with him other guests. Richard felt a tightening in his stomach when he saw Laurence Willoughby, Joseph Terrill, and James Walter follow their host into the room.

Frank Jackson smiled at Richard's obvious surprise.

'I thought a little celebration dinner would be in order to wish you a safe and interesting journey, Richard.'

Richard felt embarrassment and concern at this unexpected farewell. He couldn't believe the evening would pass without an enquiry about his ship. And why had Sarah allowed Terrill to be invited when she knew of his intense dislike of the man? Was she trying to tell him something? Yes, that was it. A message to Richard that his friendship with her must remain strictly formal, whereas Terrill was to be seen as having a more intimate relationship with her. What a fool he had been! To allow himself even a thought of a deeper friendship with her, someone above his social position and whose future was surely mapped out. All these thoughts raced through his mind as the guests stood waiting for his response.

'I'm very grateful to you and your daughter sir. This is a complete surprise. Even Mr Willoughby didn't mention it.'

'If a lawyer can't keep a little secret, who can, eh?' Willoughby smiled at him, a twinkle in his eye.

As he looked round the dining table he wondered who would be the first to ask about his voyage. Sarah, who knew the truth, would say nothing and perhaps she had warned her father to avoid the subject. Lawrence Willoughby had never asked so would probably not do so now. The Mayor? Perhaps a misplaced but innocent question. Joseph Terrill would only speak to him directly if there was a chance to humiliate him.

He was deeply suspicious of Terrill and closely watched for signs of intimacy with Sarah, and even worse, her positive response. But after a while the conversation began to flow more easily with Willoughby prompting the politicians to debate the crisis over the American Colonies. The Mayor was conciliatory, Terrill strident in his support of the Government, and Sarah, to Richard's surprise, silent.

But he need not have worried. Lawrence Willoughby was in good voice and anxious to test the politicians views when he had the chance.

'Mr Terrill, please share with us, if you would, the Government's thinking on the problems in America.'

'With pleasure. Lord North believes we should maintain our right to tax the colonists, but apart from the tax on tea, he feels it should be in principle only.'

'Do you agree with that?'

'Yes, I do. But if the rebellious elements in the north continue to defy, it becomes a question of law and order, and a principle that must be enforced.'

'Would not that be playing into their hands?' asked James Walter. 'As I understand it, the rebels have support from only a minority of the population. Strong measures may rally support to their cause.'

'Spoken like a true Whig,' said Terrill. 'Willing the result without supporting the means. The Government takes a contrary view. If we let a small minority dictate to us, the few will soon become the many when they see what they can get away with.'

And so the debate went on, the most notable feature in Richard's eyes being the total silence of Sarah. He wondered what was going on in her mind. She was not usually reticent about speaking her mind. He was tempted to ask her but felt restrained. Was she a supporter of Joseph Terrill? That seemed unlikely. Or did she want to avoid disagreeing with him? If so, why?

As the evening went by he began to relax. He was easily able to avoid giving an opinion over the political problems because the politicians were more interested in their own and to the occasional question that came his way he was able to plead his desire to visit the Colonies with an open mind and form a view afterwards. He talked, with growing confidence, of the places he hoped to visit and the people he wished to meet. By the end of the meal he was beginning to enjoy himself. When they had finished, but before Sarah withdrew to allow the men their cigars and port, Frank Jackson stood up.

'As host of this little gathering I would like to propose a toast to our young friend here. We have come to know Richard well since my brother's death and have a high regard for him. His journey will be a long and arduous one.' More than you think, thought Richard. ' But we wish him well and look forward to having him back with us.'

He sat down and on cue Terrill rose.

'I should like to endorse those remarks. Sarah and I will look forward to your return with interest....'

Richard heard no more. 'Sarah and I' Terrill had said. So there was an understanding between them? An engagement perhaps? Was that why Joseph Terrill had been invited? His earlier gloom returned. He hardly noticed Sarah withdraw and although he smoked with the men he took in little of what was said and when the party broke up was able to utter only perfunctory thanks to his host. He was unable to speak to Sarah alone again, her reappearance coming only as he was leaving, when she came to wish him a safe voyage.

Disconsolately he walked slowly back to his lodgings. He was depressed at the thought of leaving Sarah under such circumstances but deep down he knew it was all he could expect. It seemed clear that Frank Jackson thought Terrill an acceptable suitor and apparently Sarah did not object. By the time he returned they would doubtless be married.

The cold night air gradually revived his spirits and he began to think of the voyage ahead. He looked up at the stars twinkling brightly in the clear night sky. They at least will stay with me throughout the voyage, he thought. He knew he was not going just to please Sarah and he took pleasure at the thought of the momentous step he was taking. He felt sorry he had not been able to confide in Lawrence Willoughby but knew he would have put every possible obstacle in his way.

Because of the early morning sailing Richard had decided to spend his last night aboard ship, so after reaching his lodgings he changed out of his evening clothes and walked down to the quayside with those few belongings that were not already stowed aboard.

Although it was past midnight, the streets around the harbour were busy. A number of vessels were sailing on the early morning tide and dozens of seamen were heading back to their ships from the pubs and brothels around the dock area. Many of the men were drunk and were being carried back to ship by their companions. All over the quayside, groups of two or three, arms around each other, were following an unsteady course, singing, or shouting at other groups, and occasionally brawling. Richard wondered about his own crewmen, many of whom did not want to join the ship at all.

But aboard the Amelia everything seemed under control. Captain Pinney and Samuel Baillie had known where to find most of the crew and had coaxed them aboard by a mixture of promises, threats, and brute force. Richard went aboard conscious that there was now no turning back. Standing on the deck he took a final look at his city and wondered when he would see it again. On one side, the tranquillity of Queen Square with its expensive housing. Beyond the Square, Marsh Street with its crime and squalor; and beyond again, the commercial centre at the heart of which lay Willoughby's chambers. And on the far side of the river he could see, behind the cathedral, Brandon Hill, with the new housing, some of it built by Frank Jackson, slowly creeping up towards the summit and Clifton beyond. In one of those houses Sarah would be asleep. Did it matter to her that when she woke he would be a good way through the Avon Gorge heading for the open sea? With mixed emotions Richard went below to his cabin to sleep for a few hours before the bustle of dawn should herald the beginning of his new life.

~ CHAPTER 6 ~

Distant voices, shouting, reached into Richard's consciousness. He thought at first he was dreaming, but the gentle rocking of his cot soon told him otherwise. He lay still, listening to the commotion outside until curiosity overcame him. He sat up and looked round the cabin but saw nothing save the black outline of his waistcoat hanging from a nail in a ceiling timber. He reached for his fob watch but it was too dark to read the time.

He swung his legs off the bed and onto the cold wooden floor. Shivering, he lit a candle. It was five o'clock. He stripped off his nightshirt, pulled on his breeches and poured cold water into an enamel bowl. After a moment's hesitation he doused his head in it. He shivered again, but now awake and invigorated he finished dressing and went up on deck. Ahead he could see the outline of the cliffs of the Avon Gorge approaching, the entrance to a long and tortuous passage from Hotwells down river to the mouth of the Avon and out into the Bristol Channel. Seagulls in their hordes swooped round the ship looking for and expecting scraps to be thrown overboard. But it was neither the view nor the birdlife that arrested Richard's attention. Towards the stern of the ship most of the crew were gathered, now silent and sullen. Tied to the mizzenmast was one of the seamen, stripped to the waist. A lamp stood on the deck nearby, illuminating the features of the mate Samuel Baillie, standing next to the tied man. He was holding a knotted rope in his right hand, curling it round with the other. Richard moved closer to the men to hear what was going on.

'So this is what all of 'ee'll get if you're not sharp about your duties.' The mate looked menacingly around at the crew, all silent and still.

'D'ye understand?'

There was but a low murmur. Richard could tell from the pale faces that most of the crew were too terrified to speak.

'D'ye understand?' bawled the mate.

'Aye,' came a resigned but more audible reply.

Baillie turned and launched himself at the hapless prisoner, the whip flying backwards and forwards onto the man's back, knots digging deep into his skin. After the first blow had found its mark the man moaned, but then remained silent. Richard counted ten lashes before the man passed out and buckled at the knees, his body propped against the mast, blood flowing from several flesh wounds.

'Let that be a lesson to you all,' Baillie growled. He then strode away, disappearing below. The crew moved off in small groups, silent still, and took up their allotted tasks. Only Richard and the surgeon William Daniel remained with the unfortunate crewman. The surgeon untied the man's bonds and taking his weight as he fell, laid him face downwards on the deck. Using strips of cloth he staunched the flow of blood and bound up the wounds. Then holding him in an upright position, held a mug of water to his lips.

'What was all that for?' asked Richard.

'This man wasn't too keen to start work this morning.'

'Is that all?'

'Oh yes. They always pick on one to start with. Usually a potential ringleader. To knock any rebelliousness out of him and serve as a warning to the others.'

The injured man, now fully conscious, pushed Daniel away and without a word struggled to his feet. Richard watched him as he stumbled off to join the rest of the crew.

'The mate will have to watch out for him,' said Richard.

Daniel chuckled. 'No. He'll be no trouble. It will be the slaves who will suffer for his resentment not the mate. The captain mistreats the crew, the crew abuse the slaves. That's how it is.'

'Was the flogging the captain's idea?'

'Yes probably.' Daniel stooped to wash his hands in a pitcher of water, then looked up at Richard. 'At least, in a manner of speaking. You won't be seeing much of Captain Pinney. He keeps to his cabin mostly. He controls the ship through Baillie. He probably ordered him to knock the crew into shape before we reach the Channel. Baillie is free to interpret these instructions as he will. This little exhibition was part of the process.'

'Why do the crew let him get away with it?'

Daniel shrugged his shoulders and smiled. 'They have no choice. There are six or seven trusted crew who collaborate with Baillie. They will have sailed with him for years. The more reluctant recruits will be picked off one by one like this man this morning. And they can't jump ship. They're watched too closely whilst we're in the Gorge. And once out to sea it's too late.'

He touched Richard lightly on the shoulder. 'Come on, let's have some breakfast.'

The two men walked to the galley and helped themselves to bread and beer. Richard's uneasiness was relieved by the companionship of the surgeon, from whom he was learning to survive. Do your job unobtrusively and keep out of the way. That was Daniel's unspoken message and one he resolved to copy.

'How long have you been a seaman, William?' asked Richard.

'About seven years.'

'How did you come to sign up?'

'The usual reasons that drive young men to sea. No other regular employment and a wish to see the world. My family comes from Gloucester. As a young boy I had occasional work in the docks there. Nothing regular. I used to envy those aboard the ships I watched setting off down the Severn. My family was not starving but there was little enough. One day I thought I could do better for myself so I came down to Bristol. It wasn't difficult at that time to find a berth.'

'Have you always worked on slave ships?'

'No. I started on the Portuguese run. Got my sea legs crossing Biscay. Then the opportunity came to do the Atlantic crossing. By then I had learned some skills at mending bodies, so here I am. This is my third voyage to Africa and the Colonies.'

'Doesn't it worry you, transporting human life to another continent?'

'Not really. I don't think about it like that. Such small skill as I have helps keep many of them alive. It would go on without me. Owning slaves is lawful, I just look after them as best I can.'

Another essentially kind man caught up in an evil trade, Richard thought. Are we all children, taught to accept a world we cannot control?

Richard's first day afloat was a busy one. It was his responsibility to check the cargo was properly fastened down for the heavy seas ahead, and to familiarise himself with where it was all stowed. The hold was crammed full of a multitude of different items that he knew was the price that would be paid for human cargo. Now packed full of crates and boxes, he could not imagine the hold full of human beings, particularly the number being spoken about. The ship seemed to him to be too small for its purpose, yet he knew it had made several such runs in the past.

By early evening he was beginning to feel sick. The ship had met a heavy swell north of Lundy Island and he was unable to walk the deck unaided. The rolling and pitching forced him to lie down, though this gave little relief. Throughout the night and the following day he was sick at regular intervals and by the second evening was regretting his decision to sign on. He kept to his bunk as the ship crossed the Bay of Biscay, undisturbed save for William Daniel who brought him water and bread from time to time and emptied his bucket, an act of kindness he would not forget.

But his sickness proved to be short lived and by the time they were opposite the Spanish coast he was able to stand up, tired and emaciated, but no longer feeling ill. Daniel insisted there would be no recurrence, for which reassurance Richard was grateful.

While Richard was sailing down the Avon, Sarah was breakfasting with her father. She felt listless and could find little to say to him nor do more than pick at her food.

'Are you going to miss that young man?' her father enquired gently. She did not answer the question directly.

'I am concerned for his safety. There are many dangers ahead for him.'

Her father leaned across the table and touched her arm reassuringly. 'Young men must travel my dear. But the act of living is dangerous. I'm not sure that sailing to the Colonies is very much more hazardous than walking the streets of Bristol at night.'

Sarah looked sharply at her father and waited for him to continue.

'He's been seen, you know. In Marsh Street, late at night. I can only guess what he goes there for.'

'How do you know this?'

'Willoughby told me. He takes no notice of course. But I think you ought to know.'

'Thank you father, but you need not concern yourself. I know why he has been going to Marsh Street. I knew before he ever went. He was seeking information.'

Her father smiled indulgently.

'And what information does a young professional man need that is to be found amidst the brothels and drinking dens?'

She fell silent and blushed, losing a little of her self-confidence.

'He was looking for a berth. He is not a wealthy man. He had to find a working passage, as you know. The shipping agents and captains are to be found in Marsh Street, so there he went.'

The conversation hung in mid air. Sarah could see doubt and suspicion in his eyes and dreaded his next question. Why should Richard visit shipping agents in brothels at night instead of their business offices during the day if he were seeking a position on a cargo ship? She could see from his eyes that the question was forming in his mind. She wished neither to tell him the truth, nor lie. But Frank Jackson decided not to ask the question. He had warned his daughter and that was enough. The silence allowed her to change the subject.

'Father, have you thought over the proposal to nominate you in Uncle Ben's place on the Common Council?'

'Indeed I have Sarah, but without coming to any definite conclusion. As a matter of fact I was wondering what your opinion is.'

'It is really for you to decide father. I will support whatever decision you make. My only anxiety is that you would lose your independence.'

'Do you think I would? It has not been suggested I should join the Tory cause.'

Sarah could not prevent a smile at her father's naivety. She leaned over and took his hand.

'You are a fine builder. But I fear you would not make a politician. They know how your conscience would make you feel indebted to those who had promoted you. They have no need to set out their price.'

Frank Jackson smiled at his daughter. 'Sometimes, my dear, I think you have a deal more political insight than many men. I don't know where your jaundiced view of men and affairs comes from. But I suppose you are right. Much as I like Mr Terrill, he is a politician to his fingertips and will expect my support. And that answers my own question.'

'As you have raised the name of Mr Terrill, father, there is something I should like to say relating to him.'

'Yes, my dear?'

'I realise that you have a present liking for him.'

'That is so. He is a clever and cultivated man.'

'You have had an opportunity to get to know him. And your opinion of him may be correct. But I know him less well so have formed no judgement. Yet he seems to be a little presumptuous about his relationship with our family. In particular with me. I hope you won't encourage him to be too familiar.'

She watched her father's face to judge the effect her remarks made and thought she could see a hint of disappointment in his eyes. But he said nothing.

'I'm not setting my face against Mr Terrill, father. I just wish for things to take their natural course.'

His eyes relaxed.

'Get yer 'ands off me.'

Nancy struggled as one pair of firm hands held her while another tried to lift off her dress.

'Now now young lady, let's have some cooperation.' The strong voice of Mrs Carraby tried to quieten her down.

'I ain't 'avin no bath.'

'Well, miss, if that's the way you want it.' So saying, she and the cook gave up trying to undress the new maid and threw her fully clothed into the tub. Nancy fought against the arms holding her down but gradually gave up the unequal struggle. By the time her two superiors had finished, her spirit was broken.

It was the last agony of a painful morning for Nancy. After Richard had left her the evening before in the Penney's house, she had been given a mattress in the large kitchen and had curled up beside the kitchen range as happily as any household pet. In the morning she was given food then taken to the house of James and Rachel Naylor next door and given over into their custody. With scarcely a word she was taken downstairs to the scullery and handed into the care of the housekeeper Mrs Carraby, and the cook. It seemed to Nancy that these two took an instant dislike to her, though she cared not. It was clear that the domestic staff took a pride in their employer's establishment and did not take kindly to the arrival of a dirty, smelly urchin as one of their number.

For a while, Nancy sat on the floor and sulked, whilst her two superiors openly displayed their feelings.

'I'm surprised that madam should be taking on such a smelly creature as this,' said the cook.

'We must do what we can with her,' replied Mrs Carraby. 'Cleaning her up is the first thing. I'm not putting her into one of our uniforms like that.'

They spoke as if Nancy was an animal that had wandered into the house uninvited.

'What's your name child?' asked the cook.

'Nancy. Just Nancy.'

'Where are you from?'

'Bristol. I 'aint got no proper 'ome.'

'Well Nancy,' said the housekeeper, 'if you cooperate and work hard, you'll have a good home here.'

Not having had to cooperate with anyone, or work hard, at any time during her life these simple proposals were painful to her. She sat on the floor, head bowed, and said nothing. Then came the ordeal of the bath when her physical resistance to her new situation was finally broken.

Over the next few weeks Nancy was trained into her new duties but she never took to the life of a domestic. Yet she soon discovered that compliance and silence were the best ways of keeping out of trouble. She lived in a state of uneasy truce with the other girls. No one was antagonistic towards her but there was no real warmth either.

But silent acquiescence bred boredom that would eventually transform itself into rebelliousness. Once she had decided it was not the life for her, it could only be a matter of time before she parted company with her employer.

'Good morning, Julia'

'Oh Nicholas, you startled me.' Julia increased her concentration on her sewing.

'I am sorry to do so. Where is my sister?'

'I think she is with Lady Manners. I had some sewing to complete and find the light brighter here in the library. But if you wish to work I can go elsewhere.'

'No, please don't think of leaving.' Nicholas sat down opposite her. 'It is pleasing to have an opportunity to speak to you. Except at dinner I see so little of you despite we live in the same house.'

'You have so much business to attend to, and I am but a companion to your sister.'

'That is no reason why we should not be friends.'

'I am not sure that would be appropriate. Your father may not approve.'

'My father does not decide with whom I speak.'

'That is kindly said no doubt, but I fear I must leave to disagree with you.' She bent her head lower over her work.

'I have offended you. I am sorry, I did not mean to do so. I have wanted to speak to you for some time.'

Julia did not reply, nor did she have to do so for to her relief the door opened and Lady Manners came in.

'Julia here you are. And Nicholas too.'

Both looked at the other. Julia felt an embarrassment she knew she need not feel.

'I was just catching up on some sewing while the light remains good. Mr Nicholas had just come in.' She looked at Lady Manners but saw no suspicion in her face.

'Julia, Jane wishes to speak to you. I think she needs your advice on what to wear to the ball. She is in her bedroom.'

Julia gathered up her sewing and with considerable relief left the room.

'Now, Nicholas,' said Lady Manners, 'I hope you are not becoming too familiar with Julia. Your father and I would not approve of such a friendship. Please do not compromise Julia's position in this house.'

'Mother, I...'

She put up her hand to stop him saying anything, making it clear that she expected no further discussion on the subject, and immediately turned and left the room.

'Sarah, how charming.' Joseph Terrill took Sarah's hand, bowed, then smiled confidently at her.

'Good evening Mr Terrill. I trust you are well.'

They were standing in the hallway of the Mayor's mansion in Queen Square. A civic banquet was being given to celebrate the year of office of James Walter, soon to end. The guest list was usually limited to Members of Parliament, Aldermen, Councillors, the Sheriff, and their wives. But this year Sarah and her father had been invited as a mark of respect to their late colleague.

Terrill offered his arm to Sarah, who after an anxious look towards her father, took it out of politeness. She was led towards a large reception room where a number of guests were already drinking sherry and talking in a dozen or more groups.

'Councillor Joseph Terrill and Miss Sarah Jackson.'

The booming voice of the liveried footman announcing them caused Sarah to stop momentarily in her stride. She had not expected this. She told herself: 'I've been led into a trap. My name publicly linked with Mr Terrill. This was not what I intended. What can I do?' She felt the heat of her fury rise in her neck and up into her face and hoped she had not visibly reddened. She held her composure whilst removing her arm from his and waited for her father to catch her up.

But Joseph Terrill was not a man to feel a slight.

'Sarah, have you met our two Members of Parliament?'

'I have not had that pleasure.'

'Perhaps you would like to do so now?'

Without waiting for an answer he touched her arm and led her to a group surrounding the Mayor. Sarah was surprised and impressed how easily he broke into the conversation.

'Sir Ralph, Mr Croder, may I introduce Miss Sarah Jackson and her father Mr Frank Jackson. They are, in a sense, guests of honour tonight. Though of course I hope that Mr Jackson will be one of our number on the council before long.'

Both men bowed. 'I am pleased to make your acquaintance, Miss Jackson, Mr Jackson,' said Henry Croder.

Frank Jackson was used to his daughter being the centre of attention and looked on admiringly. He had taught her the social graces and knew she would be able to cope in any society. Sarah contented herself with an appreciative bow of the head and a smile, then drew back to the edge of the group, offering nothing further, but listening intently to what was being said.

Sir Ralph carried on the conversation where it had broken off. 'Terrill, we were discussing the American Colonies. Croder here has a cousin in Boston who says the feeling there is most rebellious. I can't understand it myself. We fought to keep the French away from them, and now they don't want to help pay for that war. Disloyal I call it.'

'Perhaps they are wanting the same rights as British taxpayers.' The voice came from the back of the group. Everyone turned, except Sarah, who knew who it would be. Instead she watched Joseph Terrill and saw a sneer of pleasure cross his face.

'Oh it's you Harford.' Sir Ralph was clearly going to take him on. 'I might have expected as much. Against the King again are you?'

'Not at all, Sir Ralph.' Robert Harford moved forward, the group dissolving itself into two lines to watch the protagonists squaring up. Harford continued. 'I am as loyal a subject as any. But I would not wish His Majesty to receive advice that would lead the colonists to secede. They will remain with us only if we recognise and correct their legitimate grievances.'

Blackman laughed. 'Legitimate grievances? That's what you call them is it? We sent an army over to save them from the French. Now we protect them from the natives and safe passage for their shipping. And they object to helping with the cost and object to billeting our troops. '

Henry Croder intervened to support his fellow MP. 'Sir Ralph and I don't see eye to eye on many things, but we do on this issue. My cousin tells me that the damn colonists are stockpiling weapons and ammunition and that many are preparing to declare independence whatever we do. They say they no longer need the mother country. What would become of our plantations and other investments then? We would have no means of protecting them.'

'Quite right.' Terrill urged them on, seeing this as an opportunity for one of his political rivals to be publicly humiliated. Yet Harford was not to be put down.

'Why should our investments be at risk, Mr Croder? Their legal system gives adequate protection to the rights of foreign owners. And the colonists want more investment, not less. Bristol merchants want to see a vibrant economy over there, not one faced with the threat of war.'

Joseph Terrill was willing to push his rival over the brink. 'So you countenance a breakaway do you Harford? I'd call that treason.'

At this, Harford stepped up to him, eyes blazing and fists clenched. 'I'll not take that from you, sir.'

He stopped short of issuing a challenge, but for a few seconds the two men squared up to each other, as two prize fighters ready to start a bout. Sarah saw that no one else was prepared to intervene, and that a challenge or even a fight would be the inevitable outcome unless she herself took a hand.

'Speaking as a woman, and knowing very little about it, I can see how important it is for these matters to be resolved peacefully,' she said.

The irony in her comment was not lost on the guests watching the confrontation, and quiet laughter from around the group defused the situation.

'Hear hear.' Sir Ralph Blackman backed her up, realising that local rivalry had overtaken the discussion. 'Mr Mayor, how is the memorial fund progressing?'

Harford and Terrill backed away from each other to the anonymity of their own group of allies. Terrill knew when to withdraw. His anger had been contrived, designed to influence an opponent into an ill-judged response. In this he had succeeded for Robert Harford was easy game. His enthusiasm and sincerity often led him onto unsustainable ground. He had not yet learned to weave and tack, an art required for political success. He felt embarrassment at his loss of temper and was in no small measure relieved when the gong sounded for dinner. The guests followed the Mayor into the banqueting chamber, Terrill at ease with himself, Harford full of remorse.

Julia was very fond of the Manners family and she usually had a healthy appetite. But she found formal dinners with the family difficult, particularly when there were guests, as this evening.

There were eight sitting round the oak table. Sir John, as always, headed the table with his wife at the opposite end. Nicholas and Jane were on Sir John's right and left respectively. Julia sat next to Jane. On her left was Samuel Oliphant, a middle-aged bachelor and leading member of the Merchant Venturers Society of Bristol, a group of businessmen who both supported the interests of business in the city and raised money for a number of charities. On the opposite side were Sir Ralph Blackman and his wife Lady Angela. Dinner was usually an hour-long affair when just the family were present but with guests they were into the second hour and only the fish and chicken courses had been completed. A joint of beef was now placed before Sir John for carving. Servants bustled about clearing plates. Conversation continued as if they weren't there.

'Well, Ralph,' said Sir John, 'what is our Prime Minister planning for the American Colonies now?'

'I am a mere backbencher, John, not privy to all cabinet secrets. But I suspect Lord North will do as little as possible.'

'Is that wise?' Sir John attacked the joint as if attacking rebels in Boston. 'The northern colonists are still not satisfied. Perhaps they need teaching a lesson.'

'Sometimes, John, inactivity is the best policy. All Townsend's duties have been repealed except on tea, which as you know was retained as a symbolic gesture of the Crown's rights. The hotheads over there scent victory, of course, but there are many patriots in New York and elsewhere who just want the whole thing to blow over.'

'Will it come to war?' asked Lady Manners.

'I doubt it,' replied Sir Ralph, sounding less confident than his words suggested. 'The shooting of a few rioters in Boston last year didn't help. But the funny thing is that the British troops on trial for the shooting were represented by that radical lawyer John Adams.'

'Pah, lawyers will take any case for a fee,' said Sir John. 'Money always talks louder than conscience.'

'You gentlemen should wait until we have retired before talking politics,' said Lady Blackman. 'Nicholas, tell us your plans.'

He fleetingly looked across at Julia. 'Well, Ma'am, I am expecting to go to our plantation in Virginia for a while, then back here to take over more of the running of the business.'

'And to find a suitable wife, I hope,' said Sir John, 'and have a few bouncing babies. We have to keep the family name going, eh, Nicholas?'

'There are a number of suitable young ladies in Bristol who would jump at the chance to form a connection with our family,' said Lady Manners.

'There is plenty of time for that' said Nicholas, clearly not enjoying the turn in the conversation.

'And what about you, young lady?' said Samuel Oliphant turning to Julia. 'Have you an admirer?'

Julia felt her neck redden with embarrassment. 'I, no, I am in no position to think of such things.'

'That's a pity,' said Samuel, 'a pretty girl like you. Why if I was a bit younger myself...'

He didn't have time to finish. Julia dropped her knife and fork with a clatter onto her plate. 'Please excuse me.'

'What is the matter, Julia?' said Lady Manners.

' I don't feel too well. I will retire if you don't mind.'

She stood up, as did Jane and Nicholas.

'Nicholas, don't concern yourself, Jane will look after her,' said Lady Manners.

'Please, I will be alright,' said Julia. 'I just need to lie down. I'll go to my room. Jane please don't trouble yourself.' With that she left the room.

'A touchy subject there, Samuel,' said Sir John. 'And her only close relative, her brother, has just set sail for Virginia. He'll be visiting our plantation I believe.'

'I am sorry if I am the source of her discomfort,' said Samuel.

The diners concentrated on their beef more than the dish warranted and as soon as the meal was finished the ladies were pleased to leave the men to their port and cigars.

Although it was a cold morning, it was crisp and dry and Julia was well wrapped up as she walked slowly round the grounds of her employer's estate.

The incident at dinner the previous evening had upset her but she realised it was only because it brought to the forefront of her mind the seemingly inevitable future for both her and the Manners' family. With her brother gone, and no close friends with whom to share her sorrow, she felt that her world had closed in on her. Only the gentle exercise and fresh air cheered her spirits, and that but a little.

She had been walking for over half an hour around the parkland and now made her way back towards the house through the hedges and walls of the formal garden. As she approached the small lake with its central ornamental fountain she was surprised to find Nicholas Manners apparently waiting for her.

' Nicholas, what are you doing here?'

'Julia I can't say our meeting is accidental. I saw you walking this way.'

She waited for him to continue but he seemed hesitant, as if just meeting her had exhausted his courage. Julia was unsure whether to keep walking or wait to see what, if anything, he had to say. This he eventually did.

'I wanted to say how sorry I am about the behaviour of Mr Oliphant last night.'

'Nicholas, please don't concern yourself, it was not of your making.'

'That may be, but you are under our roof and should not be treated to such discourtesy. But his remarks do perhaps bring to a head what I really want to say to you.'

Julia could see that he was acutely embarrassed yet felt able neither to encourage him nor turn away.

'Julia, I want you to know that from the first time I saw you I have had the greatest esteem for you which has now grown to affection.'

She felt her face and neck redden.

'Do you think you should be saying such a thing, Nicholas? What about your father and his wishes?'

'Please do not speak of my father. He does not control my feelings. Please hear me out. Julia I would like to think that the feelings I have for you are reciprocated.'

'Nicholas I don't know what to say. Of course, yes, I am very fond of you, as I am of all your family, but as things stand the situation is impossible. I am truly flattered by your sentiments which in other circumstances...'

'I don't feel that the circumstances come into it Julia. It is only your family misfortune that puts you in your current relationship with our family.'

He took her hand. 'Julia, if you could just give me some hope.'

'Please don't press me Nicholas. It is...it is too quick. I would like time to think. I don't wish to lose my position in your house. And with my brother away I need time.'

He squeezed her hand then let it go. 'Now you have expressed your feelings Julia, I am content to say nothing to my family for the time being. But be under no illusion. I have made up my mind and will speak to my father as soon as you allow me to do so. I can do no other.'

~ CHAPTER 7 ~

3rd February 1771 ~ Off the West Coast of Africa.

It is by no means certain that I will survive this voyage. My wish is that if I do not, this record shall be placed in the hands of Miss Sarah Jackson of Bristol for delivery to Henry Scrope, Secretary to the London Committee for the Abolition of the Trade in Slaves. I have confided the existence of this diary only to the surgeon, Mr William Daniel, who has undertaken to deliver it to Miss Jackson.

I have already witnessed much that has shocked me and would shock decent British people if they were aware of it. The wanton cruelty shown by captain and mate towards the crew is appalling. There have been almost daily whippings and beatings, poor and insufficient rations and serious overwork. Scurvy is appearing and diarrhoea is endemic.

Of the captain, little has been seen. He keeps to his cabin issuing orders of a general nature to the mate, Samuel Baillie, who runs the ship as he wishes. I am certain Baillie enjoys inflicting cruelty for he interprets an order to keep discipline as an instruction to use the cat at every opportunity. More than half the crew have been whipped, yet there has been no general revolt. Punishment is accepted with remarkable calm, I believe because of the inability of the victims to organise themselves against the mate and his trusted allies. I fear that if an organiser appeared he would be thrown overboard.

Today we arrived at our first destination. We are anchored off the Slave Coast at a settlement near the slave port Whydah. The sea is calm and the setting sun to the west a fiery ball of orange. On land I can see a collection of round huts surrounding two or three more substantial buildings in the centre of the village. There is no one to be seen. On the shore is a row of fishing boats with nets spread about them. The beach, too, is deserted. Around the village is undulating grassland as far as can be seen from our ship, with clumps of trees scattered at intervals, no doubt supporting the birds whose cries come across the water. We have been at anchor for nearly three hours and I have yet to see my first human being.

The crew is relaxed and strangely elated. I fear that this is not just because we have reached land and will tomorrow be going ashore. The surgeon tells me it is because of the slaves. The persecuted crew will soon become the persecutors. Perhaps this is why the crew acquiesce in their own punishment. And soon there will be a plentiful supply of women for them to enjoy.

6th February

We have had two days of high winds and rough seas, making landing by small boats impossible until today. The initial high spirits of the crew at arriving soon turned to frustration as they stared at the land they could not reach and several times quarrelling and fighting broke out. But this morning I set foot on foreign soil for the first time. The day broke calmer, no wind, and bright sunshine. The boats were lowered almost at first light and I went in the first with the mate, the surgeon and six of the crew.

We were met by a small delegation of three, the leader being a sick looking Portuguese agent whose name is Rodriguez. He was waiting on the beach flanked by two tall graceful looking Africans, the first I had seen. Later in the day I learned they were his personal bodyguards, who were happy to safeguard him in exchange for food and accommodation and a liberal supply of gin. The mate was acquainted with Rodriguez and the two men greeted each other warmly. This did not commend the agent to me. The mate handed him a case of gin, no doubt a down payment for his services.

I felt it prudent to stay in the background and say as little as possible but I did ask Daniel where all the villagers were. It was then I learned the truth. The natives knew what we had come for and were frightened. All the villages for miles around would be deserted. It seems that although most slaves are bought from African dealers, slave traders are not averse to topping up their complement, when necessary, from whoever else happens to be around. The senior crewmen are allowed two or three slaves of their own to barter for their own profit, so they are always on the look out for strong young slaves who will fetch a good price.

I had already begun to feel the intense heat while we were rowing ashore, but as we followed Rodriguez up the beach towards the building that served as his office and home, the heat seemed to increase. I began to sweat and my clothes oppressed me. We were soon out of the breeze that had swept off the sea and it was a relief to enter the trading post, out of the sunlight. We were led into the only room downstairs, large and square, with an earth floor and covered only in the centre by a rug that had served as many meals for insects. By this time the rest of the crew had rowed ashore and I could hear the relieved laughter as the men ran about on the beach to exercise their limbs.

At one end of the room were a small table and a scattering of wooden chairs. We sat down and Rodriguez opened one of the bottles he had been given and offered drinks all round. I was the only one who declined but immediately realised it was a mistake. My refusal seemed to set me apart in Rodriguez eyes and my lame excuse that I felt unwell did nothing to heal the breach. Truth to tell I did feel faint, for the smell of drink pervaded the house.

The conversation was between the mate and Rodriguez, the latter speaking slowly and in broken English. Slaves were not mentioned by name. The agent reported that such and such a chief had so many head of cargo and offered to lead us to the various collection points. A handling charge was agreed without difficulty and plans were made to set out the following day to collect the first batch. We were assured that among them would be a number of young women suitable for the crew's pleasure.

We returned to the beach to find the crew all actively engaged in various tasks. Some were back aboard ship erecting netting along the sides. In my naivety I asked if this was to catch flying fish. The mate laughed. 'Tis to stop the cargo falling overboard, not to catch things coming aboard' he told me. It seems some of the slaves try to jump overboard to escape. Some believe they can swim ashore. Others know they will drown but believe their souls will fly back to Africa. I knew there was no chance of swimming ashore even from where the ship was anchored. It had already attracted the attention of several sharks that circulated the ship incessantly waiting to be fed.

Other members of the crew were at the far end of the beach in a clearing in some trees. I walked over and found them to be repairing a large wooden cage, some of the bars of which were loose. This was the compound in which slaves would be held until ready to be loaded aboard. All this activity made me realise how near the taking of our first slaves we were.

We rowed ashore early this morning, shortly after dawn. This time all of us left the ship save for a small number to keep it safe. Rodriguez met us once more, sweating and breathing heavily despite the early hour. He led us inland along a track through the savannah, his trusty bodyguards leading the way, hacking bushes aside where the path was overgrown. The men seemed nervous and had their rifles at the ready, whether to deal with attacks by natives or wild animals I know not. But their nervousness was infectious and I too was soon listening for every sound.

We walked for about two hours without rest and saw no other human beings. Sometimes a startled antelope would jump up and speed off. I am not sure whether it was the antelope or us who was the more frightened. Throughout our journey there was a continuous cacophony by insects, birds, and sometimes the howl of animals I could not identify. Everyone walked in silence, as if to hide our presence. But of course we made enough noise anyway to alert anyone or anything within a mile of us.

By mid morning the sun was becoming unbearable and we sheltered awhile under a clump of trees and drank water we had brought with us. I noticed Rodriguez took a swig of gin as well. I cannot help feeling the combination of the climate, disease, and drink will overcome him before he is much older. Perhaps he knows this.

We set out again, each of us covering our heads with whatever we were able to find on the ship. The canvas sailcloth proved an efficient material for making caps. After another hour or so we approached some low hills and could see at the head of a pass between the hills a settlement of mud huts, which was our destination. At first these, too, seemed deserted, but as we approached I began to make out many pairs of eyes staring out at us from behind the huts or nearby trees. They were obviously terrified of us even though they knew we had come to trade with their chief.

In the centre of the village was a much larger hut outside of which sat a delegation ready to receive us. Rodriguez and Baillie moved towards an imposing figure in full tribal dress of animal skins sitting on a raised platform as a mark of his rank and status. Two tall warriors standing stiffly to attention, looking splendid in feathered headgear and holding long spears, flanked him on either side. The Portuguese was familiar with the local dialect and acted as interpreter for Baillie. I was standing too far back to hear what was being said but after several minutes conversation there were smiles all round and I guessed that negotiations had been successful. Crew members started unloading their merchandise in front of the chief while one of his warriors led the rest of us through the village to what I could see was a wooden stockade beyond.

The main gate in front of us was open and as we approached I could see natives sitting around on the floor in what appeared to be mainly family groups. There were men, women and children, most of them naked, and everyone shackled at the ankle and to each other. Half a dozen warriors stood outside the compound armed with spears or clubs. The prisoners sat sullen and silent. Not one moved, nor spoke.

At the sight of our party their expressionless faces began to register fear. Some tried to crawl away from us but their bonds allowed them only a yard or so. Daniel told me it was not fear of slavery. They had been told that white men ate black slaves, and many believed it.

As they began to realise that they were not to be instantly killed they became still again, no longer pulling at their ties. Baillie and Daniel inspected them in turn as if they were cattle. Their heads had been shaved and their bodies rubbed with palm oil to disguise their ages. Thirty-five was the maximum age for a first class slave. Those older, or who suffered from defective eyesight, teeth, or limbs, were second rate and worth less. Daniel rejected about twenty as being too poor quality and the rest were then set in line, each manacled to the one before and the one behind. A fire was kindled and the slaves branded on the chest with the captain's mark.

We had our first batch of slaves and the Chief had his supply of tobacco, gin, guns and ammunition. It had been easy. I knew not where the slaves had come from save that they were described as prisoners of war. This I doubted for only a few were men of fighting age. My belief is that a tribal dispute had been resolved by force and the men who had not died in the fighting, together with the women and children had been rounded up. Their village would now be deserted save for those too old to be of value.

When we were ready for the return journey the slaves were lined up, half the crew in front, half behind. As we set off the captives started wailing which set off a crying and screaming from the birds and monkeys in the trees around. It was a pitiful scene. The men cried out through fear, the women for their men, and the children for their mothers. No attempt had been made to keep families together in the line. The slaves were fettered together, some by the ankle, others by the neck. I felt sick at being part of this barbaric act but took comfort at remembering my mission.

The journey back to the coast was slow but uneventful and the slaves were herded into the wooden cage, now made good by the crew who had remained behind. The Africans were exhausted and were thankful to lay down, unmindful of their new prison, or the ocean to the side. They were given water, and yams and bananas to eat. An armed guard was posted as night fell. We had our first one hundred and fifteen slaves. The last act before the rest of us returned to the ship was for the mate to select six young slave women and take them, protesting, aboard for the pleasure of the crew.

12th February

How changeable the climate is here! Yesterday we were again confined to the ship because of heavy seas. It rained all night, soaking the unfortunate slaves and their guards for there was little shelter. By mid-morning today we were able to land and Rodriguez came down to the beach to meet us. He was unshaven and his eyes bloodshot. On days such as yesterday he stays inside and drinks. We were to start on a two-day march today, but before doing so went to inspect the slave compound. The Africans were laying or sitting in groups, children being comforted by their mothers. They were quiet but watched us suspiciously. A few children started to cry. I noticed one couple embracing and I felt ashamed. The agent had made sure they were fed regularly and the night rain had been their drinking water. The growing piles of faeces were beginning to give off a smell that the sea breeze did not entirely dispel.

We set off in an easterly direction keeping quite close to the coast. The sun was by now fairly high in the sky and the earlier haze had evaporated. The savannah was dry and appeared untouched by the overnight rain. Three quarters of the crew were with us, all fully armed with guns and ample ammunition, for there was no need to take goods for barter this time. We were to take our slaves by force. I was given a rifle and some elementary instructions as we went along, but I resolved to use it only in self-defence. Rodriguez did not come with us. We were led by some Africans from the agent's village who had been promised immunity for them and their families in return for their assistance. We were heading for a small village nearly two days march from our landing site. The village was on the edge of the jungle strip that stretched down to the coast. There was no suitable bay for landing any nearer. The natives apparently regarded themselves immune from attack for this reason, but its headman had offended the villagers from our village and was going to pay the price.

Apart from an occasional sighting of the sea to our right, our journey passed through similar terrain to our previous one and was equally uneventful. But it was very hot, and the ground was hard on the feet. The seamen, although used to the tough routine aboard ship, where muscle and shoulder power is required, were not equipped physically for a long hot march, and neither was I. Our stops became more frequent as the day wore on. We were glad enough to camp for the night as the sun began to set. Yet tired as I was, I found difficulty sleeping, and slept but fitfully. Now accustomed to sleeping to the rocking of the ship, I felt awkward lying on land, sleeping under the stars. And the night was as noisy as the day, but not the chatter and cries of the monkeys, but the roars and screams of night animals on the prowl. I was mighty relieved that we had posted guards and kept a fire burning.

As I lay awake I thought of my home city and friends. I felt a little ashamed not to have done so more since leaving the Bristol Channel. But truth to tell my new life at sea absorbed my thoughts. Perhaps it was coming back to sleep on land that sent my mind back to Bristol and the three months that had passed since the fateful murder. And most of all I thought of Sarah. Would she be thinking of me?

We rose well before dawn to walk before the sun became unbearable. By mid-morning we were leaving the savannah and entering the jungle. Here the paths were almost gone, but our guides seemed to know the way instinctively, beating down the undergrowth, their noise frightening off any unwary animals or reptiles. We soon acquired some new companions, a tribe of monkeys who followed us for several miles, swinging from tree to tree, chattering and screaming, until giving up hope of food, they abruptly left us.

Towards mid-day our guides stopped and waved us forward to join them. It was clear we were approaching a village. I could hear in the distance the sound of a river and assumed the village was close to the bank. The guides indicated we were to fan out in a semi-circle and approach in silence. At a signal from the mate, us attackers were to close in rapidly and surround the natives before they had a chance to fight back or run away. Any native showing serious resistance was to be shot, but the intention was to take as many natives alive and unhurt as possible. William and I were to stay behind the line of attack. We were not expected to take part, for which I was thankful.

Twenty minutes later the attack began. The villagers were taken completely by surprise and stood no chance of escaping. Four or five young men seized spears but were immediately shot dead. There was no other resistance. None of our men was killed or even injured. It was a totally one-sided encounter. The shouting of our men and the crying of the Africans at their confusion soon turned to wails of pity as they realised their plight.

Once subdued, they were placed together in the centre of the village under armed guard while some of our number carried out a search for any who had hidden. Their huts were set alight and out from the burning timber several women and children appeared. Soon there was no one left. The surgeon's job was easier this time for not having been in a trader's hands there was little difficulty in settling their approximate ages. Daniel rejected about fifteen as being too weak or old, leaving us with another seventy-five towards our complement.

On the return journey the children cried, their parents wailed but there was no attempt at rescue, nor did we expect any. No one would come near us for fear of joining the captives. We camped at the same spot as before and reached the coast the next evening. It was too rough to attempt to reach the ship so the slaves spent the night in the compound. A few young women were forced out and taken away by the guards. This afternoon the wind dropped and we returned to the ship.

28th February

We have been sailing east for several days, putting in at small settlements along the way and buying a few slaves each time, usually captives from tribal disputes. This morning we completed our complement of four hundred and twenty together with a few extra for the senior officers to sell who we acquired in a most unpleasant incident that upset me considerably.

We had completed our business and were officially at maximum number. Just before setting sail a number of canoes were paddled out to us, the natives offering to sell food, and trinkets as souvenirs. The mate signalled to them to pull alongside, making out that we were to trade. As the two leading canoes pulled alongside, they were grabbed, and the protesting Africans pulled aboard. One tried to escape by diving into the sea but was immediately attacked by sharks. Eight others were pulled aboard and bound. They were all healthy young men and would fetch a good price. They were to be the private booty of the captain and senior officers. My reason tells me that this was no worse than the other crimes committed, but it upset me a deal.

We are now ready to set sail across the Atlantic and this afternoon for the first time I went below to where the slaves are stowed. Although I knew what to expect I was nonetheless sickened by the sight and smell. The slaves were lying tight against each other all the way round the hold, chained and fastened to the sides. I was told that each adult male was given a space of six feet by sixteen inches; an adult female five feet by fourteen inches; and children five foot six by twelve inches. The tallest were stowed amidships, the smaller ones and the children in the stern. No account was taken of the different sex and there was no facility for personal hygiene. They had to lay and sleep on their sides. There was a raised platform some three feet above the floor, with rows of slaves on this too. Over four hundred and twenty slaves have started this voyage. I wonder how many will reach our destination alive?

1st March

We set sail this morning under a gentle breeze that increased as the day wore on. Soon the groaning started from the slaves below, which grew louder as seasickness took hold. The slaves were sick where they lay. The crew grew alert to possible trouble, weapons available if required. The crew manned the small cannon on the upper deck pointing towards the door of the hold in case of a mass breakout. Ships' crews have been known to be overpowered, and the ship then lost, as the Africans have no knowledge of sea sailing or navigation.

Late this afternoon the first batch of slaves was brought up on deck for exercise. Each day about fifty will be allowed out for half an hour. They were ordered to jump up and down at pain of a whipping if they refused. Their movements were clumsy and pitiful to watch. They were manacled together and some continued to be sick. While on deck their part of the hold was washed down to remove blood and faeces and the result of their sickness.

3rd *March*

We have been at sea for two days now and the ship has settled into a routine. The slaves are given yams and beans, and sometimes biscuits, morning and night, and a number brought up for exercise each afternoon. This means that each slave has half an hour on deck once a week, which Daniel has told the mate is insufficient. Even my inexperienced eye can tell that the slaves are becoming physically weaker, and with many, the will to live is fading. I fear many will die before we reach our destination. They do not seem to fear death, believing their souls return to Africa. It is the fear of the unknown while alive that terrifies them. On our second evening two slaves tried to jump overboard while exercising and were prevented from doing so only with difficulty. One of them attacked a seaman who was trying to restrain him. He was shot in the leg and is now chained securely in the hold.

As I write this an appalling scene is being played out on deck. Some of the women are given more freedom to move about unfettered than most, I believe those who have been used by the crew. One of them, a girl who could not be more than seventeen, was caught stealing food. She was stripped naked and hung upside down by the ankles, where she remains. She is subject to regular beatings and abuse from the crew. Whether she will hang there until she dies, I know not. Likely she will be cut down and sent back below as a warning to the others. Even our cruel first mate realises that a dead slave is of no value.

I am beginning to see the full horrors of the trade in slaves. Below deck, there is a constant crying and moaning. Most of the slaves are seasick. They foul themselves where they lay and a growing number are succumbing to the flux. The crew have become brutalised and are treating the slaves ever more badly than they themselves were treated on the voyage out. No compassion is shown, except by the surgeon, whose job it is to keep the slaves alive and healthy. And, remarkably, we are being escorted across the Atlantic by a school of sharks that circles the ship continuously. They know that soon we will be jettisoning bodies.

4th March

The young woman who was tied to the mast has been cut down. For an hour she lay on the deck where she fell, only William Daniel attending her. He gave her water and covered her from the sun. It is his job to prevent her from dying. He knew the futility of telling the mate not to punish her in the first place. He could only observe, then repair the damage.

The first slave died today, a young child who had looked frail from the start. She provided the sharks with a reward for their patience. I watched her being thrown overboard. As her body hit the water, several fins headed towards her; there was turmoil on the water's surface as the sharks fought over the spoils. Within seconds all was peaceful again.

8th March

We have been at sea a week now and conditions aboard are beginning to become less tolerable. I dread to think what the ship will be like after three months. The smell coming up from the hold is appalling. The slaves are lying in their own faeces and vomit. The rats, which have been with us throughout the voyage, are now more in evidence, and several of the slaves have been bitten. The crew are by turns sick themselves, cruel to the captives, and drunk.

This afternoon William persuaded the mate to bring all the slaves out on deck together. This was not so much an act of kindness by Baillie. He was persuaded that many more would die unless conditions improved. It was a dangerous time for all of us. Some of the slaves were not yet beyond hope, and we were heavily outnumbered. Even the captain came out of his cabin to play a part. The entire crew took up vantage points with rifles at the ready as the slaves slowly and painfully emerged from the hold. Most of them could scarcely walk at first. They helped each other out and it took some time for their eyes to become accustomed to the light. But none gave any trouble. Family members found each other and embraced. Others stood or sat silently until ordered to dance to help circulate the blood. Several were struck with rifle butts to make them do so.

The crew took it in turns to go below two at a time to wash down the hold. It was a filthy job. Several of them were overcome by the stench and were sick. I saw no sign that they were sorry for the slaves but instead they unfairly blamed them for fouling their quarters. At the same time the crew brought up on deck for repair the spare sail and rigging, badly chewed by the rats.

11th March

Two more slaves have died of the flux. We have lost six so far and we are not a quarter of the way to our destination. Scurvy is now rife amongst the crew because of the poor diet. I too feel ill and depressed but my deprivations are nothing compared to what others are suffering.

The captain appeared on deck this morning for only the second time throughout the voyage. He looked sick and was foul tempered, abusing everyone except, I noticed, the mate upon whom he relies to run the ship. Drink is taking its toll on him, I fear. If we are to arrive safely we must hope that the captain allows the mate to keep control.

This afternoon several more slaves tried to escape and throw themselves overboard. They must know they cannot survive in the sea yet prefer death to lifelong captivity, or as some of them believe, being the victims of ritual killing and being eaten. It is difficult to control people who wish to die, for the ultimate sanction of death is not available as a threat. Only physical restraint can hold them.

15th March

A heavy swell has brought more sickness. There have been three more deaths, making nine in all. One of them was the young woman who was tortured for thieving. She never recovered from the ordeal and lay below in pain until she expired yesterday afternoon.

17th March

A slave jumped overboard today. He was the husband of one of the women who died last week. Baillie was furious at the loss and had the guards whipped for slackness. But truth to tell, the crew are tired and dispirited and I fear more such incidents before journey's end.

21st March

Three more deaths of the flux. The mate is blaming William. But God knows the conditions are beyond anything a medical man can deal with. William has urged more frequent swabbing out and more time on deck for the slaves, but the mate believes this to be too dangerous. The stronger the slaves and the weaker the crew the more danger there is of open revolt.

31st March

Over a week has passed since my last diary entry. Incidents I recorded when they first occurred now happen regularly. Eight more slaves have died. Eight more needless deaths of blameless Africans, providing a meal for the ever-present sharks.

We had our first death among the crew this morning. Chandler, a young man from Plymouth, died after having been ill for several days. His death disturbed the crew. They treat the death of slaves with distain. A loss of cargo they call it. But one of their number is a different matter. It strikes them as being against the natural order. They know that crew die on every voyage, and Chandler's death has made them wonder who will be next.

My own health is reasonably good and for some reason I feel less depressed. Perhaps it is because we are approaching the half way stage. We have made good time and are several days ahead of schedule. My own situation is helped by the mate of all people. He has behaved well towards me and I have no complaints against him. I have not had to undertake any physical labour and as far as rations go he has done his best to look after me.

15th April

We have been at sea for six weeks now and I have found a way of overcoming the monotony of the journey. There is little for a tally clerk to do in mid-ocean so I have taken to helping William with his duties. Not being a true medical man his methods are rudimentary but I have been pleased to learn from him. As well as the general debilitation of all on board he has to deal with injuries picked up by the crew. I have learned to deal with crushed fingers, a broken wrist, weals from whippings, toothache, and rat bites.

We have seen no other ships, which is just as well with so many privateers on the seas, and apart from the ever-present sharks there has been little to watch. My only comforts have been my books and the companionship of William Daniel, who I like more as time goes by. The rest of the crew regard me as of officer standing and treat me accordingly, though no one has been unpleasant to me. William by contrast has gone out of his way to befriend me and has given me invaluable lessons on how to stay out of trouble. On several occasions I have had it within me to protest at the treatment meted out but he has always been on hand to restrain me. I have tried to ask him why he comes on these voyages; he seems too compassionate to be party to this barbaric trade. But so far he has been reluctant to talk about himself. I suspect he has some personal grief that keeps him away from England, for he shows no enthusiasm to return. Perhaps he will talk more freely as he becomes easier in my company.

As the days go by I am inclined to think more about Bristol. The starting point of my thoughts is always Ben Jackson's tin box and the letter I found in it. Before then, I, like most other Englishmen, was aware of this trade yet gave it no serious thought. But confronted with it I have had to face up to the reality. Have I been foolhardy in coming? Would I have taken this on if Ben Jackson had not had such a charming niece? I hope I would but I am not sure.

How quiet Bristol will seem when I return. There will be plenty for me to do but my legal work will seem a little dull by comparison. It is hard to imagine the routine of life in the city continuing in its quiet orderly fashion while I am not there.

~ CHAPTER 8 ~

'Gone? What do you mean gone?'

Lawrence Willoughby shouted across the room at his clerk, who was standing by the door uncertain whether to remain or retreat.

'Jacobs has jumped ship, sir. No one knows for certain where he is.'

Steggles shifted his weight from one foot to another. Xerxes had already taken refuge under the desk. Both waited for the storm to subside, knowing that Willoughby's occasional flashes of temper rarely lasted long. Steggles had been with Willoughby for many years and knew his employer's moods. The outbursts were not directed at him personally, just a sign of frustration. The last reply was designed to steer Willoughby in a different direction and the ploy did not fail.

'No one knows for certain, eh? That means you have heard a rumour or two. Come on, man, tell me what you know.'

'It is only gossip you understand, sir, but some of the crew of the Hope believe that Jacobs has found it more profitable to smuggle full time.'

Willoughby started stubbing his fingers together as his patience again began to wear thin.

'Will you please come in and be so good as to tell me the whole story.'

'Of course, sir.' Steggles cautiously took a stride towards his employer's desk. He felt more confident now it was clear he was no longer held personally responsible for Jacob's disappearance. He had been surprised at the old lawyer's behaviour since Richard had left. Usually a mild man, irritation and temper had become increasingly frequent. He never made mention of Richard but Steggles knew he was missing him. Perhaps he saw Richard as the son he never had.

'Well, sir, I went down to the docks early this morning, knowing the Hope was due in today, and there she was, unloading. I asked for Abel, and the crew just laughed at me. One of the seamen, a Bristol man named Dunning, came over to me. "Your wine waiter's gone," he said. They all laughed again. They must have known of our arrangement'

Willoughby waved at him impatiently. 'Yes yes, I dare say they do. Pray continue.'

'"Where has he gone to?" I asked, " and when will he be back?" Dunning laughed again and said, "he ain't a-coming back. He scarpered down river as soon as we closed with the Somerset shore. Methinks he's joined Whittle's gang. Finds it more profitable than honest trading I'd say."

'I asked him how he knew this. He told me that Jacobs had become restless sailing back and forth to France on low wages and reckoned that if he was going to smuggle at all, he might as well do it properly.'

Steggles stopped and waited while the lawyer considered what he had heard. Willoughby sat down.

'I see. He'll be caught and hanged before long. He is too greedy for his own good.'

'There is something else sir.'

'And what is that, pray?'

'It seems Jacobs felt he was being watched.'

'Watched?'

'Yes. He told Dunning that every time he docked in Bristol and went ashore he felt someone was following him.'

'Did he say why that might be?'

'No Sir. But I doubt it was the excise.'

The lawyer sat thinking, eyes closed, fingertips together. Eventually he opened one eye and stared at his clerk.

'Was there any cargo aboard for us?'

'Indeed there was, sir. I took the opportunity of enquiring whether there was any wine for sale. I had no difficulty in obtaining our quota at the usual price. It seems that most crewmen enjoy a little private dealing of their own. I think they were quite pleased that a buyer had met them off the boat. It saved them a lot of trouble and provided cash for an immediate visit to Marsh Street.'

Willoughby opened the other eye and smiled contentedly.

'That's all right then. Perhaps we no longer need to worry about our former client though for his own sake I hope he keeps out of harm's way. He knows too much about too many people for his own good. What do you know about his new companions?'

Steggles had been advancing closer to his employer's desk, as the latter's humour improved, and now stood directly before him.

'Whittle is an ex-slaver who gave up the sea following an accident. He now operates a gang down at Pill. They cover the north Somerset coastline as far as Burnham, collecting from vessels coming up the Bristol Channel. They operate at night mostly, store the merchandise in farmhouses around the countryside and dispose of it when the hue and cry has died down.'

'Jacobs knows this man Whittle then?'

'Yes, he served with him on a voyage or two before Whittle had his accident. Jacobs then joined the crew of the *Demera* and was one of the few to be rescued when she went down off the Slave Coast.'

Willoughby nodded, closed his eyes, and leaned back in his chair, fingertips pressed together. Steggles knew the conversation was at an end and that his employer wished to be alone. He quickly backed towards the door. Only Xerxes watched him go.

Nancy put her ear to the keyhole and listened. All was quiet. She opened her door quietly and looked up and down the passageway. She could see the moonlight illuminating a window at the far end and there was no shadow between her and it. There was no one about. Closing the door quietly behind her she walked slowly towards the square patch of light. She could feel, and thought she could hear, her heart pounding. Would the noise of it wake the household? The only other sound was the ticking of the grandfather clock solemnly keeping time in the hall two floors below. As she passed the stairs she looked over the balustrade, down the stairwell, to the ground floor below. The stairs tempted her. An easier way out, but far more risky. The stairs would creak and she might wake the dogs if she went that way. And she could not slide the bolts on the large wooden front door without making a noise.

She had left the catch off the window earlier that evening so that when she reached it she was able to slide it open noiselessly. She lifted one leg over the sill, then stopped and looked back along the corridor. There was no sound. Almost with one movement her body was through the opening and the window closed behind her.

Nancy had been planning her escape for several days. At first she had accepted her new position in the house and had even consented to being scrubbed clean and put in uniform with only a perfunctory protest. But she had never found the routine of work and discipline acceptable. The novelty of a warm bed and regular meals did not outweigh the discipline required and she had soon had enough. The other domestics had never really taken to her, although they had not been unkind, and she missed the freedom of her former life.

She had planned her escape carefully. During the daytime she was never alone long enough to disappear unnoticed and she could not just walk out. To her mind, if she just disappeared overnight, no one would try to find her. She had left the uniform behind so as not to take anything that did not belong to her. Fortunately her old clothes had been given back to her to keep, enabling her to leave as she had arrived, with nothing but what she stood up in.

The window led out onto a flat-roofed extension to the main building. It was on two levels, the nearest being window level and at the far side a flight of steps down to a single storey over what was an outbuilding for gardening implements. With nothing to guide her except the moonlight Nancy walked across the roof and down the steps to the flat surface below. The rest of the descent would be trickier. There was no easy way down from this first floor level to the ground, but she had previously seen a way of doing it. Heaped against the back of this block was a pile of manure some five feet or so at its highest point against the building. Nancy was about twelve feet off the ground. She sat on the edge of the roof above the pile, turned, and gently lowered herself down the side until she was fully suspended, hanging on by her fingertips. Then she let go. The manure broke her fall, but she was unable to keep her balance and toppled backwards down the pile, landing at the bottom covered in manure and straw. She lay still for a few seconds to make sure there was no one about. Unhurt by the fall, she stood up and keeping off the gravel driveway, walked towards the main gate. She was relieved to have escaped so easily and, dirty and smelling, set out on the walk back to Bristol.

Sarah glanced at the note and then at her father, but he was engrossed in his newspaper.

'Father, I have to go out.'

'Of course, my dear. Another of your waifs and strays?' He did not look up from the newspaper.

Her father was indulgent, if not supportive, about her charitable work. Like many of his class he was sympathetic towards the poor but disinclined to help alleviate their condition. Sarah often wondered whether he thought that letting her become involved was a sufficient contribution from himself.

She smiled to herself but said nothing. That way she would not be misleading him.

'I will be only an hour or so.'

She left the room, called her maid, and within half an hour was once again in her carriage heading for Kings Down. Robert Harford was at his door to greet her.

'Come in Sarah. Thank you for coming so promptly.'

He ushered her into the sitting room. Hugh and Frances Berry were already there. Sarah accepted the offered seat and sat waiting to hear why the sudden summons. Robert Harford seemed agitated and excited.

'Sarah, Hugh has brought us some important news. I will let him tell you himself.'

She looked across towards the French windows to where Hugh Berry was standing.

'Blackman is seriously ill. He is not likely to live long, perhaps six months if he is lucky. There will have to be a by-election soon, whether or no he decides to leave Parliament before death.'

Sarah was puzzled. 'Why should this affect Robert's campaign? I thought we were going to challenge the Whig nomination at the next general election. Blackman is a Tory. The vacancy will be for them to fill.'

Berry nodded. 'That's usually the case. But it seems that some of our leading supporters in the city think the times are too perilous to continue the cosy two party arrangement and want to challenge for the seat when the vacancy occurs. Events are moving too quickly for Robert to let this opportunity to pass him by. A by-election will attract national attention to the issue of the Colonies. And what better place to have it than Bristol?'

'But Hugh, this will cost a fortune,' said Sarah, 'and would the Whigs in Bristol agree to do that? Without their support we would be hard pressed to fight a campaign on our own.'

Harford intervened. 'John Powell has been sounding them out Sarah. He will be here soon. The plan is to announce my candidacy for the next general election so that momentum is already building up for when the by-election comes, as it undoubtedly will.'

'I suppose you all know what you are doing, but to me it is distasteful,' she replied.

Robert Harford looked shocked. 'But why should you think that, Sarah?'

'Because you are in effect campaigning for a seat currently held by a sick man. Everyone will see through what you are doing. You will arouse as much contempt as support if you openly canvass for the seat of a dying man.'

'I agree with Sarah.'

Everyone turned to Frances Berry. She was not known for expressing political views.

'That is how women will see it, even if you men are too insensitive to do so. I know it is the men who vote, but are you certain none will be influenced by their wives? Or be dissuaded from making a financial contribution?'

The two men looked embarrassed.

'What do you advise, Sarah?' asked Harford.

She smiled. 'Do what you are already doing, only more quickly. Assume there will be an election within six months. Prepare your arguments, your helpers and your finances. Do everything behind the scenes to be ready to meet a by-election or general election sooner rather than later. But do not declare your candidacy yet.'

Harford nodded. 'How would we manage without the good sense of you ladies? You are right, of course.'

He walked over to the window and stared out as if he could see the American Colonies in the distance.

'I am just anxious that no time be lost. The situation is worsening by the month. An election now fought on the issue of trade and the Colonies just might make a difference. This seems an opportunity too good to miss.'

'So it is. And you will not miss it. But the opportunity will be lost if you lose votes because of an insensitivity towards the sitting member. You cannot bring the date forward by announcing your candidacy, but you can make sure you are ready.'

Their conversation was interrupted by the arrival of John Powell.

'Robert.' He strode across the room, briefly stopping to acknowledge the presence of others. 'The news is good. Your main backers are ready with funds just as soon as you say and are keen to see your campaign launched. I estimate that there is more than enough to get your campaign under way. And once we have started, funds should continue to flow.' He stopped, momentarily, to allow the pleasure of his news to sink in. 'But there is one worry.'

Everyone looked at him intently.

'We must anticipate that our opponents will attack us with the weapon of lack of patriotism, and self-interest. We shall be accused of siding with the King's enemies and selling out the interests of Bristol and the nation at large. Well, we can answer that. But we will be vulnerable on the question of campaign funds. Our backers here are concerned about this. There are many in the Colonies prepared to donate funds to your campaign. You will be challenged on this point. We must accept no contributions from plantation owners except those who are still English residents and who have property or investments here. Otherwise I fear colonial money will be our downfall.'

'It is too late.' Everyone looked at Sarah.

'We already have a representative on his way over to raise funds in Virginia. It is Richard. The list of names we gave him contains several who no longer have any connection with the home country. And he is seeking a campaign organiser who will open a fund in our name.'

Harford left the window and walked to the centre of the room. 'John is right. We must not play into the hands of our enemies. We thought we were preparing for a distant general election, but a by-election soon changes everything. If Richard collects money from non-English sources, it must be returned with thanks and a suitable explanation. Much as we need the money, we must turn it away.'

Dawn was breaking as Nancy came within sight of Lawford's Gate. The black shades of the numerous church spires that marked the Bristol landscape were gradually turning grey. A mist was rising from the Avon and it was bitterly cold. Several times on her walk from Frenchay Nancy had been minded to stop, so tired was she. It was a cold morning even for early April and she knew that laying or even just sitting down could have led to death from exposure. She had to keep walking.

When leaving Frenchay her one objective had been to return to Marsh Street. Yet now she was close, her confidence faltered. She felt nervous and uncertain. Would she be allowed back at the Flying Angel? Without friends or family she was at the mercy of whoever took her in and at whatever price she was asked to pay. The only man who had ever shown real kindness to her was either dead or thousands of miles away at sea. And his, to her, misguided kindness had cut her off from her own kind and the one regular resting place she had ever known, the cellar at the Flying Angel.

Yet it was to the Flying Angel that she went, stumbling and shuffling through the city streets which were empty of people save for the early morning scavengers rooting through refuse looking for something to eat or sell. When she reached her destination the doors and windows were locked and barred and she was too scared to knock. But she had expected this. Next to the door was a barrel roll in the pavement with a grill over it. Nancy knew that one end of the grill was loose and she was able to lift and slide it across sufficiently for her thin body to slide through. She had entered this way before, several times, and was not yet too full grown not to be able to do it again. Her cold fingers struggled with the grill and eventually it moved. She slid into the gap which had appeared and down the chute into the blackness below. The grill she could replace later, the gap being too narrow for anyone to fall through in the meantime.

As she landed she heard the soft rustle of rats running for cover. No other sound disturbed the morning stillness. It was too dark to see her way but she knew it instinctively. She walked slowly across the cellar to where she knew her familiar pile of sacks was kept. They were still there. She slid under the pile and closed her eyes.

'So you're back then?'

Nancy woke and for a moment thought she was in her attic in Frenchay. But recognition of the voice and the smell of beer pervading the air reminded her where she was. She looked out and saw Alfred Regan, the landlord, standing looking at her.

'Yes, I'm back.' She could see he was in a poor temper.

'What do ye mean by disappearing for so long? I could've done with your help.'

Nancy struggled out of her makeshift bed. 'Well, I'm back now and ain't goin' off no more.'

The landlord looked at her quizzically.

'I dare say I can use you. But you'll 'ave to do a few new jobs now.'

Nancy had been expecting this. She knew how the men who patronised the Marsh Street pubs were entertained and what would be expected of her sooner or later. She was neither scared nor disgusted. It was just a fact of life, part of growing up, in her world.

'If you want me to look after them sailors I'll need some new clothes.'

'You? Entertaining my customers? I wouldn't put my reputation at risk. You're just a thin bundle of bones. My customers like a bit o' meat on their women. No one'd want you. No, I want you to be a messenger for me sometimes. You can come in and out of the city, no questions asked. I want someone to take messages for me to friends around the Somerset coast way from time to time. If you do that and help in the bar, you can stay. And you can have the scraps to eat.'

To Nancy this was a generous offer. It would give her the freedom to come and go, with a dry bed and food whenever she wanted it. She knew the friends Regan referred to were smugglers and that she could be hanged if she were caught. But the chances of detection were slim. She would never have smuggled goods with her. No one could pin anything on her unless she was caught with the gang and that wasn't very likely. Yes, a better life than in service at Frenchay, she thought. She felt much better.

'I'll do it. Now what about some breakfast?'

By the time Sarah had returned home from the meeting at Robert Harford's there was another message waiting for her, this time from the Penney's at Frenchay. She read that Nancy had disappeared, but no sign of a forced abduction. She knew a little about Nancy's background and had wondered about Richard's interest in her. He wouldn't be able to help for many months yet. What would he expect her to do to help the girl? She didn't know where to start looking for her and decided against doing anything, at least for the time being. Nancy was probably back with her own people, she thought. That was no doubt for the best. It would be dangerous to try and take her again and isolate her from those she knew. In this she disagreed with Richard. He would help whoever came across his path. Sarah's compassion extended to mankind as a group.

She put Nancy out of her mind. Joseph Terrill was coming to dinner that evening and she had to confer with cook to ensure the kitchen arrangements were in order. And to prepare herself, as much to be a credit to her father as for her own benefit. There was no time left that day to think of Richard's protégé or what had become of her. She was looking forward to Terrill's visit more than usual. He may have some information about Blackman's condition. She wished the poor man no harm, but if he were to die, perhaps sooner would be better than later. For Robert Harford's sake; and for the country.

'You are looking particularly charming this evening Sarah, if I may say so.'

Terrill smiled across the dinner table at her, but not until he had noted her father's approval.

'Thank you Mr Terrill. I try to be a credit to my father.' She lowered her eyes, a little demurely, in order to camouflage the feeling behind her next question.

'But what is happening out in the world Mr Terrill? Father and I seem to miss so much, and we do like to keep up to date, don't we father?'

'Of course, my dear.' The older man was content to enjoy his salmon and leave the two younger ones to provide conversation.

Terrill began tentatively. 'I know I can speak with a certain amount of confidentiality in this house. There are one or two developments of interest. I understand Sir Ralph Blackman will not be a candidate at the next general election. He is not too well and has decided to stand down at the dissolution of Parliament. He feels that fifteen years in the House is enough. There is a body of opinion within the Tory Party in Bristol that I should replace him.'

Sarah failed to control a gasp of astonishment.

'You seem surprised, Sarah.'

'Indeed I am Mr Terrill. Not that you are unworthy of such an honour. It was unexpected, that's all.'

'Not too much of a surprise I hope to prevent you giving me your support should it happen?'

Sarah felt the conversation was getting beyond her control. Whether intentionally or not her father came to the rescue.

'Will there be a contest, Mr Terrill?' I thought the seats were allotted to the two main parties.'

'There should not a contest to secure the Tory nomination. The seat itself ought to be allocated to my party in accordance with custom. It saves money that way. And a little violence, too, I don't doubt. But I have heard a rumour,' he leaned forward conspiratorially, although there was no one else in the room, 'that the Whigs are split. Someone wants to precipitate a contest.'

So much for secrecy, Sarah thought. How did he know this?

'Mr Terrill, you hear such shocking things. Who might the candidate be?' She was determined to find out the extent of his knowledge.

'I don't know at present. Some local radical I believe. There are plenty of them in the city. He even supports the treacherous colonists. But I am confident the Whig machine will put him in his place.'

Sarah fell silent and attacked her dinner with vigour. She wanted to think through the implications of what she had heard. Within the next six months or so, the man she had befriended socially, and who was clearly playing court to her, whose increasing intimacy she had not rebuffed, was likely to be a candidate for Parliament in direct opposition to a man on whose campaign committee she played a major role. How had she brought herself into this difficulty? Should she, like other women, have stayed in the background, acting the dutiful daughter, and taking no side? And there was worse. Had she encouraged Richard to engage on a dangerous mission to please her? It was with relief that she heard her father take up the conversation. Her part in the rest of the evening was perfunctory only, as she longed for their guest to go so she could retire to her room and consider how she might extricate herself from her encircling embarrassment.

'Do come with us, Julia. I would be upset if you refuse.'

'I have done so little dancing lately Jane. But I will do so if you wish.'

With these words Julia had agreed to go with the family to the civic ball at the Assembly Rooms and the date was fast approaching. Her reluctance had been both her natural diffidence and the probable presence of Nicholas. She recognised the strength of her feelings for him but his very presence had an upsetting effect too. The situation between them seemed hopeless.

But having agreed to go, she had set to with her preparations with enthusiasm. In the days leading up to the night the women of the house were consumed by preparation of clothes, much to Sir John's amusement.

The steady rain on the evening did nothing to dampen their spirits as the Manners' coach pulled up outside the Assembly Rooms and took its turn in a long line to set down its passengers. The long ballroom was brilliantly lit and a large number of people were sitting and standing around the walls watching the dancing. Through open doors Julia could see through to the dining room where many others were taking refreshment and talking in groups.

It seemed that all Bristol society was present. The Mayor and Mayoress and all civic dignitaries, representatives of all political parties and none, mixing happily together. Sarah Jackson would be somewhere with her father. How people liked to enjoy themselves, she thought, perhaps to shut out the uncertainties of life, for a while at least.

'Do you enjoy dancing, Julia?'

She turned, knowing it was Nicholas standing behind her.

'I do, but have little recent experience, Nicholas. I used to love it.'

'There is a new French dance that has become popular in England recently, the cotillion. Have you heard of it?'

'I am afraid not.'

'Would you mark your card for me to show you? It is easy to pick up. Although the French dance it in squares, we English stick to our traditional lines, so you can just follow your neighbours.'

They did not have long to wait. The announcement of the cotillion was greeted by excited applause and couples quickly lined up.

'Come, Julia. Just do what we all do. You will follow the steps with ease.'

She soon became lost in concentration and after a few faltering steps she felt herself relax and surrendered herself to her partner. What a graceful dancer he is, she thought. And so considerate. Could she really continue to hide her feelings? She was entitled to happiness. If it is to be with this man then they must face the consequences together. How she wished Richard were home. But it would be another six months at the earliest before she saw him.

The sudden conclusion of the dance brought her out of her reverie. She smiled at Nicholas as he came to her side.

'I so much enjoyed that,' she said.

'And me. I feel I have been dancing with the most beautiful woman in the room.'

Julia laughed. 'That is kind. But I don't believe it.'

'Would you care for some refreshment? A sorbet?'

'That would be lovely, Nicholas. But I must return to Jane.'

'My sister is with that awful Samuel Oliphant. He marked her for the gavotte, which is next. She is not looking forward to it but as you know he is a friend of father's, and very powerful in business circles. She regards being pleasant to Mr Oliphant her filial duty. Ah, they are up. We can have our sorbet now.'

Together they walked into the refreshment area and sat waiting their turn to be served.

'Julia, I may not have another opportunity to speak with you privately tonight. I want you to know that what I said to you before remains so, and increasingly so. May I dare hope that you might accept an offer from me?'

Julia felt as if an electric shock had passed through her. Suddenly nothing else mattered but this man sitting beside her. But she knew what was required of her.

'Nicholas I am touched by your affection which I think you know I return. But please, don't force me to a decision until Richard returns. I promise a reply as soon as I have spoken to him. He is unlikely to influence my decision but we only have each other, I would hate to go behind his back.'

'Julia, I have said before. I am content to wait. You have made me a most happy man.'

~ CHAPTER 9 ~

Richard put down his pen and stared at the cabin wall in front of him. Usually he took no notice of the rocking of the ship or the creaking of the beams or hull but tonight even the smallest sound distracted him. His diary entries had become shorter and now he could write nothing. Yet incidents were still occurring daily, and slaves were dying. With a shudder he realised his senses were becoming numbed to it all. It worried him that he had become used to brutality and death and took no notice of it except to record the number of meals for the sharks. He was becoming as insensitive as the crew.

He looked at his tally: thirty-seven slaves had died so far. Thirty-seven unnecessary lives lost. Four crewmen had died too, and two more were seriously ill. Most of the slaves were in a poor condition, some close to death. Only the ministrations of the surgeon kept the death toll down. At his insistence the slaves were now allowed out on deck daily, and all at once, so their quarters could be cleaned. For there was no fight left in them; they were resigned just to survive if they could.

His thoughts were interrupted by a call from outside his cabin.

It was William. 'Richard will you come up on deck please. The captain wishes to speak to us.'

Richard closed his notebook and hid it away, buttoned his waistcoat and followed his friend up the stairs to the deck above. There he found the captain and Baillie awaiting them. He stood by, saying nothing, waiting for an explanation, which he correctly guessed, would come from the mate, not Joel Pinney.

'I want you to know that I have reported to the captain that we are dangerously low on water. There's been ne'er a drop of rain for a week now. If this continues, we'll run out long afore we reach land.'

Even Richard knew what effect this would have. 'How long before we reach Virginia?' he asked.

''Bout three weeks. But we're not quite sure of our position. After reaching the coast it may take a day or two to find somewhere to land. It's a bleak coastline with only a few suitable landing places. We are planning to make our water last another four weeks. That's about half the present ration for each man. The crew won't like the short rations no more'n the slaves. We shall have to be on our guard.'

William spoke up. 'I understand the situation. But keeping crew and cargo alive needs more water not less. If we cut back, more will die. Surely we can rely on rain during the next few weeks?'

The captain, to whom water was a matter of indifference as long as there was a plentiful supply of whisky, spoke for the first time.

'The mate has been expressing my orders. If it rains, we can increase the rations. If not, it is the best chance of more of the slaves surviving. I have asked Mr Baillie to supervise distribution, and there will be a flogging for anyone stealing or taking more than his share.'

Pinney turned, and with a heavy tread, shuffled away towards his cabin. To Richard he looked a very sick man, with bloodshot eyes, loose jowls and staggering steps. There was no more to be said. The captain had made this clear by his abrupt departure. The matter was settled. Richard recognised the problem but saw its origins in the overcrowding, with lack of proper medical and hygiene facilities. Now even more slaves would die unnecessarily. The crew would grumble but put up with it.

And put up with it they did, for they had no real choice. A further two weeks passed with no rain and the water supplies were jealously guarded. Each crewman was given three cupfuls a day, the slaves only two. Richard's rations were the same as other members of the crew. Only the surgeon was allowed more although no one knew about Baillie or the captain.

The ship continued on its course north-west with one and sometimes two slaves dying each day. At last, during the third week of short rations, evidence began to appear of land not far off. Floating branches were seen from time to time, and the number and variety of birds increased, some known not to fly too far from the coast. This led to a visible improvement in morale amongst the crew, which increased still further when the first shower fell for nearly a month. It was brief, but everything that could hold water was put on deck to catch what there was. At the shout of rain the crew had rushed to catch what they could in their hands and eagerly swallowing what fell into their open mouths. Richard felt no shame in joining in, pleased to get as soaked as the rest. He was suffering too much to care what others thought. No attempt was made to bring out the slaves: the shower was all too brief and the crew thought only of relieving their own suffering.

Three days later the morning routine was disturbed by a shout from the crow's nest.

'Ship sou' west.'

This was the first vessel sighted since leaving Africa and the interest aroused was tempered by a fear of what it might be. Richard joined Baillie who was watching the ship through a spyglass.

'Can you see what she is?'

'Nay, not yet. But we must take care. There's many a privateer operating these waters hoping to overcome exhausted crews and relieving them of their cargo.'

'Can we deal with it?'

'Oh aye, I expect we can. They're not looking for a fight, just easy pickings.'

He ordered the crew to reduce sail to let the stranger catch up. If friendly they might have water to spare. For twenty minutes they watched the cutter come steadily closer. When within about four hundred yards the mate turned abruptly and ran towards the bridge.

'It's hostile,' he shouted. 'Prepare to send a broadside. And prepare full sail.'

The gunning team manned one of the cannons and prepared to fire a warning shot while the Amelia was manoeuvred into position with the port cannons aimed at the enemy. The mate waited until the enemy was within three hundred yards.

'Fire.'

There was an explosion Richard found deafening. Smoke poured from the mouth of one of the cannons. Immediately a howling and shrieking started below deck.

The shot was not intended to hit its target but was close enough to send a cascade of water up over the deck of the intruder.

'That'll do,' shouted Baillie. 'Now, full sail ahead.'

They all knew the cutter could catch them eventually if it wished, but the message was clear. The crew of the Amelia would run, but if caught, would fight. The pirate ship shadowed them for twenty minutes, then gave up and went in search of easier prey.

It was seven o'clock the next morning when land was first sighted. The excitement amongst the crew was immense. Richard felt both exhilarated and relieved that the most dangerous part of his journey was complete. He stood close to the bow of the ship, William next to him and neither said a word for several minutes as the coastline of the eastern seaboard came steadily closer. But William had made the journey before and knew what Richard was feeling.

'You are finding it hard to believe we have arrived?'

'Yes. The Colonies have always been 'over there'. I cannot take in that I am there too. There are times when I thought I would never see land again.'

They watched the bow break through the water as if it knew the way and realised it was almost at its destination. Soon they could see the land in sufficient detail to notice the absence of settlements. After some minutes the mate ordered a change of direction and the Amelia swung round to a southerly direction, the coast now being on the starboard side. They would hug the coast until they found a natural harbour and safe anchorage.

But they were fortunate. Only a further twelve hours sailing was required before they came to the small port of Seahaven, a noted slaving port close to the centre of the Virginia plantation. After fifteen weeks at sea, the Amelia anchored in the safety of the harbour on 15th June in the early evening. They were to have another night aboard before setting foot on American soil.

Richard and William stood on a small hillock which gave them an uninterrupted view of the square in front of them. There was a raised platform in the centre with a crowd thronging round on three sides. Behind the platform a long line of slaves was waiting, hands tied behind their backs. Richard marvelled at the apparent condition of the slaves and at what his friend had achieved in the two weeks since they had arrived. The thin, emaciated bodies had been transformed. Now, they looked stronger and fitter, their oiled skins glistening in the morning sunlight. There were few signs of disease.

He had watched and admired his friend's skill since landing. It would have been dangerous to have acted too quickly and more deaths would have occurred. But Daniel had known his job. He had been given a fortnight in which to make the slaves a saleable commodity and he had used the time carefully. At first contenting himself with increasing the water allowance, he gradually increased and varied the diet. After a few days they were taking regular exercise. By the end of the first week they were going ashore in small groups for more exercise and to acclimatise themselves to their new surroundings. This reassured them that they were not to be killed or eaten. They were to work for a living and had learned that to survive they had to be well.

Towards the middle of the second week the personal grooming began. Hair was cut, chins shaved, hands and toes manicured. Cuts and infections were treated. By the time of the auction they were as near back to their natural state as it was possible for them to be. And early on this morning of the auction their bodies had been rubbed with natural oils to give them a shining and healthy look.

At exactly ten o'clock the auction began. The crowd, good natured and chattering, became silent. The slaves knew by now what was in store for them. They had only one anxiety – to stay together in families if possible. They were brought up onto the platform in batches of twelve, naked, and standing apart from one another. Families kept as close as possible in the hope that a buyer would take a group. But often the auctioneer sold them individually, forcing each one in turn to turn round full circle, stretch, bend, and jump up and down. When the first batch had completed their exercises several men from the front of the crowd moved forward to the auction block.

'What are they doing?' asked Richard.

'They are the buyers. They always stand at the front so they can examine the slaves more closely. The rest of the crowd is just here to watch.'

The bidders started examining the slaves individually, looking in their ears, mouths, and pulling down their eyelids. Each made careful notes and when they had finished the bidding began. One by one they were sold, but occasionally two or three together. Most bid for the young strong males, but one man seemed intent on buying only young girls. This puzzled Richard.

'What does he want the girls for?'

' I expect he breeds slaves. A lot of slave owners in Virginia breed them to sell on.'

The slaves, so quiet before the selling started, were now wailing and pleading with their buyers whenever they were to be separated from their families. But no effort was made to keep them together. Children were taken away from their mothers;

husbands from wives. In the eyes of the dealers and their customers they were like cattle.

Once sold each slave was tied up again and bundled into the buyer's buggy or cart. The youngest and strongest were sold first at a good price, but some of the older women failed to sell and were held back for a future occasion. By the end of the morning Richard had counted eighty slaves sold, with fifteen returning to the ship to rejoin those not yet put up for sale. There were to be two more auctions on successive mornings then those unsold would be taken overland to Kingsburg, a market town fifty miles away, where further selling would take place.

Richard stayed on and around the ship for the next two days watching the remaining auctions and arranging to hire a horse for his intended journey to Williamsburg. The ship would remain in port for a further six weeks for refitting and re-provisioning. He had secured leave of absence for three weeks, giving him sufficient time to execute his various commissions for Lawrence Willoughby and for Sarah, as well as trying to contact Amos Kettle, the former agent of the *Demera*. If all went according to plan he would be back three weeks before the ship was due to sail, giving plenty of time to supervise the loading of cargo for the return crossing to Bristol.

On the morning of his departure on leave Richard bade farewell to William and walked to the far end of the town to where he had arranged to hire a horse for his visit to Williamsburg.

His journey lay northwest, just over a hundred miles to the town that had fast become the capital city of the district. Most of the road lay through tobacco plantations. For the first few miles Richard found plenty to interest him as he rode along. On each side of the road as far as the eye could see were the huge plantations, African workers toiling under a hot sun, often singing songs the like of which he had never before heard. But he kept reminding himself that none of these workers was there through choice and virtually none was free to leave and go elsewhere. Overseers with rifles and whips were strategically placed around each plantation. Despite their presence, escape would not have been impossible: but there was nowhere for the slaves to go. They would be outlaws, like in medieval England, Richard thought, with no protection from the law, and nowhere to hide except to live rough, constantly moving on from ditch to wood. A few tried it, most were captured, some died of hunger. The majority decided to stay and make the most of their lives as best they could. They could marry and have children who in turn would become the property of the master.

After the first few miles the novelty of the scenery around him began to pall and Richard longed for a break in the monotony. He was excited at the prospect of going to Williamsburg. But deep down he felt a strong desire to be back in Bristol now his main task had been accomplished.

'Welcome to Williamsburg Mr Stourton.'

Richard took and shook the hand offered to him and studied his host. A big, bluff man with rounded red cheeks, he would not have been out of place running a Devon farm, Richard thought.

'My name is Jake Worrall. I own the plantation you would have ridden through on the outskirts of town. I am also the Mayor. Please follow me.'

Richard was invited into the hallway of a white clapboard building which was the main meeting room in the town centre. He had arrived some three hours before, reporting his arrival to the Mayor's office before taking a room in the main street hotel, and after a meal and a bath returned at an agreed time to the clerk's office. He was then taken across to the meeting room where the Mayor and a large crowd of farmers and businessmen had gathered to hear what he had to say. Richard was disconcerted by the throng.

'I had expected to meet a few people informally, not in a public meeting like this,' he said.

'This is how we do things here Mr Stourton, in open hearing. That way everyone gets to hear what is going on.' He grinned. 'Mind you, that doesn't mean we always agree. Far from it.'

As they mounted the steps to the raised platform at the front of the hall Richard began to have misgivings about his mission. He was not an experienced public speaker and had been hoping to approach potential financial donors in a less formal way. Now he was expected to argue his case publicly and the success or failure of his mission would no doubt depend on how convincing he sounded. The Mayor, however, was quite at ease and knew his audience.

'I mustn't detain you long gentlemen, I know you have a thirst to slake. We have an Englishman with us from Bristol, just over on a slaver. He has asked to meet you to discuss something of a political nature.' He gestured to Richard. 'Mr Stourton, the floor is yours.'

Richard felt the eyes of the assembly looking at him with mild, rather unenthusiastic interest. The hall was so silent, the only sound he could hear was the scrape of his chair legs on the wooden floor as he pushed it back to give himself room.

'I thank you for your interest, gentlemen. I understand that Englishmen are none too popular at the present time. Perhaps it is as well that I am not here on King's business else my time with you might be even shorter.'

He paused. There were growls of agreement. Hostility by American colonists had so far been limited to British officials sent out to collect the King's taxes and to billet the army. Little animosity had been shown to private citizens.

Richard stared straight ahead, not seeing the sea of faces, but concentrating on the wall at the back of the room. 'As you know, King George and his ministers take a view about the colonists that your leaders by and large do not share. I have to say, I largely agree with you. I represent a body of men in Bristol who are anxious to persuade His Majesty to take action that would prevent an irreparable split between us. At the next general election in Britain one of our members will stand as a candidate to oppose the government on this issue.'

Feeling more confident now, Richard looked round the room and was gratified to see nods of approval. He continued. 'But he is likely to have to stand as an Independent without the backing of either main party and fighting against both. For that he will need funds. A number of Bristol merchants who have interests here are also willing to contribute, but more donors are needed. This is why I am appealing to you.'

'But why should we fund an election in which we have no vote?'

Everyone turned to the back of the hall where a tall well-dressed man was standing. Richard could see from the shrugs and whispers of the audience that they appeared not to know who he was.

Satisfied that he had gained the ear of the meeting, the stranger continued.

' We have no vote, no say in the campaign, and we know nothing about the candidate or what he stands for. And you are asking us to fund his election campaign. Over here Mr Stourton we don't buy goods until we have seen them.'

From the front of the audience a different view was expressed.

'Mr Stourton, you should know that not all of us oppose the King. I for one have no wish to oppose the British Government.'

This provoked a fury of shouts, and some booing from around the hall. Richard was content to let the debate proceed without him for the time being, the better to let him gauge feelings. A third speaker started up.

'What does it matter what else this candidate stands for? British domestic issues are no concern of ours. If this man Mr Stourton is commending can argue our case in London, he is worthy of our support. All I want to know is where does he stand on taxes and duties?'

There was a hush in the hall. Platform and audience alike recognised that the question had gone to the heart of the issue. Richard knew that his mission would succeed or fail by his response.

He replied slowly. 'Our candidate, Robert Harford, believes in the British Parliament having only a minimum role in your affairs. This could perhaps be described as having the right to legislate but not tax.'

'What is the difference?' shouted the tall man at the back of the room.

'The difference is that the British Parliament is recognised by the Colonies, but that in return Parliament agrees that it should not have powers to tax without your agreement. On specific issues we believe that duty on tea from India should be abolished as other duties have been recently. And the indiscriminate billeting of troops should stop. Press gangs here for the British navy should be illegal. All these matters will be argued out in the campaign. If Councillor Harford is elected it will be as if you have your own representative in the House of Commons.'

This last statement met a mixed reception. Those nodding in approval equalled the bitter and scornful laughter of others. But the man at the back had not finished.

'So your man doesn't accept full independence then?'

'No sir, he does not.' Richard's reply was strong and unequivocal. 'But as I understand it, few over here do either. The security of the British army protecting you from attack by both the French and the natives, and the protection offered on the high seas by the British navy is of great value, as many of you recognise. How would you manage your tobacco plantations and your farms if your able-bodied had to defend your lands from constant attack?

And how would you sell your produce abroad with no navy to protect you? No, Robert Harford wishes the link to remain, but with as much autonomy for the thirteen Colonies as possible.'

Richard sat down to indicate he had said as much as he intended, leaving Jake Worrall to bring the meeting to a conclusion.

'Thank you, Mr Stourton. Would all those interested in contributing to the election fund please stay in the hall. Mr Stourton will be pleased to talk to you individually to answer any further queries you may have and I will explain how the fund will be organised. But before I close, are there any further questions?'

The questioner from the back had one last throw. 'Where does your candidate stand on the issue of slaves?'

This was the issue Richard hoped to avoid. The Virginian economy was reliant on a regular supply of slaves and no one present would countenance the supply drying up. Richard knew he would have to tread carefully. He thought for a moment before offering a reply.

'The trade in slaves would not be an issue in Councillor Harford's campaign. He wishes to concentrate on one issue alone in order to make it the subject of national debate. His personal views on other matters will not be allowed to cloud the issue. If the link can be maintained and strengthened by some form of representation, even if unofficial, then issues such as guaranteeing the success of your businesses will be resolved through mutual understanding. Parliament has no desire to interfere with the trade in slaves.'

Richard hoped that no one would point out that he had failed to answer the question, for that was as far as he was prepared to go. He knew that Robert Harford was personally against slavery and recognised his dilemma. The purpose of Harford's candidature was to air the colonists' grievances and argue for understanding of their case. Yet one of their deepest anxieties was to preserve the slave trade. Harford had resolved the question by allowing what he saw as the major issue to exclude the minor one. The question of slavery would have to wait. The voters of Bristol would not vote for a platform that included the destruction of the city's prosperity. Richard had been disappointed when Sarah had explained this to him. He could not then see why Robert Harford could not have fought the two issues at once. But now he was in the Colonies he saw the wisdom of the strategy. The relationship between Britain and the Colonies needed to be resolved quickly before it was too late. Starting an anti-slavery debate would be fatal.

As soon as he had finished, many in the audience stood up and left the hall without saying a word.

'I see a good number are leaving,' said Richard, unable to hide the disappointment in his voice.

'You must understand,' the Mayor replied, 'that there are as many different opinions here as in Britain. You will not receive support from those who want independence, nor from those who support the King.'

'Who was the tall man at the back who had so much to say?'

'I don't know, Mr Stourton. He is a stranger in this town. My guess is that he wants independence from Britain so will not support a sympathetic voice in case a compromise is reached. He wants the British Government to be uncompromising. But there are enough here to give you handsome support. Those who have remained in the hall will give you financial backing. Some of those who have left will probably do so too, but anonymously. You will have pledges enough.'

And so it proved. After three days in Williamsburg and the surrounding area Richard received financial pledges exceeding five thousand pounds, drawn equally from those with interests in Britain and those who did not. He saw no more of his chief questioner at the meeting.

While in Williamsburg, Richard had made enquiries after Amos Kettle, the former shipping agent mentioned by Jasper Cox in the Flying Angel. Kettle was now a plantation manager and lived some forty miles west of the capital. Richard's journey back to his ship allowed sufficient time for a detour to Kettle's plantation and on arriving at the settlement late one afternoon he had no difficulty in locating his man in the town's main bar.

'Amos Kettle?'

The man who turned towards him was a middle-aged square jawed man. Richard could see a purple scar running down his left cheek stretching the skin around his mouth, giving an almost permanent malicious smile.

'That's my name. What would you be wanting of me?'

Richard pointed to the man's glass and on receiving a nodded assent, ordered a refill. Kettle sat smoking, saying nothing more. Richard sat down beside him.

'I am over in Virginia from Bristol on business. Jasper Cox said I might find you in these parts.'

Kettle laughed and spat on the floor. 'That old blackguard. What is he after, Mr...'

'Stourton.'

'Mr Stourton.'

'Nothing. You misunderstand my purpose. It is I who has been looking for you, not Cox. I think he gave me your name to stop me bothering him.'

'About what, Mr Stourton? If you have something to say, then say it.'

He resumed drinking as if to signal that it was all the same to him whether anyone was looking for him or not.

'Thank you. I am interested in the *Demera* that sank some years ago. I believe you were the agent who contracted the crew.'

Richard could see a tightening of the forehead of his companion, as if he were pulling up a drawbridge. His eyes moved away from Richard's gaze and he started rubbing his hands together restlessly. Richard could tell it was going to be difficult.

'I would like to find out who the owner was.'

'Is that all?' asked Kettle.

'Yes.'

'Do you speak for insurers?'

'No. I represent no one else. I am neither a law officer nor an excise man.'

Kettle seemed to relax a little. He picked up his pipe from the table and took two or three draws.

'It was owned by one o' them joint stock companies. Name of Africol.'

'Thank you Mr Amos. Do you know who the major shareholders were by any chance?'

'I don't know about that. A company manager called Abraham Freker dealt with its affairs. My job was to find the crew. More'n that I can't tell you.'

Or won't, thought Richard. 'One more question Mr Kettle. Where does Abraham Freker have his office?'

'Nowhere, Mr Stourton. He died two years ago.'

Richard's final visit before rejoining his ship was to the plantation owned by Sir John Manners, some twenty miles from where his ship was anchored. He called on his American manager Bill Kenyon out of courtesy, explaining how his sister came to be living with Sir John and Lady Manners and was rewarded with refreshment and a tour round the plantation.

'We grow tobacco over about one hundred acres here, Mr Stourton, with the help of one hundred and fifty slaves and twenty overseers.'

'Are the Africans good workers Mr Kenyon?'

'Most are. They soon settle down. Regular meals, shelter, and fear of the whip keeps them in line. Some we let breed so we grow our own replacements, so to speak.'

'What happens when they are too old to work?'

'We don't kill them if that's what you think. We let them live out their lives, though most don't live long after their working days come to an end. Some of the older women look after the babies while the mothers go back to the fields.'

'Do they try to escape?'

'Only occasionally. There's one boy missing right now. But generally they don't go for in truth there is nowhere to run to. Mostly they decide to stay with their own kind.'

Richard bade farewell and rode slowly away from the plantation in the direction of Seahaven. He had gone but little distance when he heard a low call from the bushes alongside the track.

'Masser, help me.'

Richard stopped his horse and looked round but could see no one. He was about to set off again when he heard a rustle from the bushes and a small black face appeared. He dismounted and walked over.

'Come out, I won't hurt you.'

The bushes parted and a black boy of about nine or ten came slowly out. He looked tearful and dirty.

'Do you speak English, child?'

'I speak a little. Help please.'

Richard sat down by the track and waved the boy to him.

'You come from the plantation?'

'Yessir. I been an runaway.'

'Why have you done that? Have you no family there?'

'No family. I am in much pain. They hit me.'

He lifted his shirt and showed wheals on his back, still red from a recent whipping.

'Why did they hit you?'

'They say I no work hard. But I too tired.'

'What do you want me to do?'

'Take me away. I no go back. They will hit me again.'

It was clear to Richard that the running away was a spur of the moment decision and that the boy had no plan as to what to do. He would either go back and face more punishment or most probably die of starvation.

'I can't take you. I go on a big ship across the sea.'

'I come with you please.'

Richard was nonplussed at this unexpected situation and for a brief moment did not know what to do. His first instinct was to ride away. But then he wondered what his opinion on slavery was worth if he turned his back on the first person he could really help. He then knew what he was going to do.

'Come up on my horse, boy. I will take you to Seahaven then we will decide what is best. What is your name?'

'I am called Sam. I have no other name.'

'Why have you come out of hiding? I might have taken you back.'

'I have not eaten since running away and have nowhere to go.'

They rode slowly back to the port, where his ship was waiting.

'What have you got here Richard?' William was with a crowd of sailors when he saw the boy.

Richard had no wish to deceive his friend but with a crowd around him listening he could take no chance. He would explain later.

'I have bought a slave to take home with me. He will sell for a good price in Bristol or Bath. Young black servants are quite the fashion just now.'

William looked suspiciously at Richard but said nothing. The child was of no interest to the crew. Several of the officers took black slaves home with them, usually young men or women, so no one queried it. What Richard intended to do with the boy when he arrived back in England he had no idea.

~ CHAPTER 10 ~

It was daybreak when Nancy left the comfort and security of the city, making her way over the new bridge and along the southern bank of the Avon. A few travellers were abroad but no one attempted to stop her or question where she was going. There was a towpath along the riverbank and she followed it for a mile or so, the city always opposite her on the farther bank. She could feel the warmth of the thin autumn sunshine on her back as she headed towards the hills of north Somerset that rose steeply before her. She knew these hills well for she had been carrying messages from Bristol to many addresses in the area over the previous three months but today she was heading for a destination she had not been to before.

At the entrance to the Avon Gorge the towpath ended, but a track led away from the river and up Rownham Hill to the higher ground opposite the Hotwells. Nancy was beginning to feel hungry and stopped at the top to eat a hunk of bread she had brought with her. Sitting overlooking the river she watched a small yacht sailing up from Avonmouth and, as she had often done over the previous seven months, wondered if her kind young gentleman who had gone on the slaver was still alive.

She walked on for another hour until she reached the outskirts of Pill, a small village nestling at the foot of the hills, around a creek which fed into the Avon. This was her destination but she knew she would have to be careful as her way passed a customs watch-house close by the river. If questioned as to her purpose she was ready to say she was visiting her uncle but no one disturbed her as she passed it and approached a whitewashed stone cottage at the opposite side of the creek.

'Come on in, Nancy.'

The voice growled to her from somewhere within. The front door was ajar. She cautiously pushed it and found it opened directly onto a large square room, bare except for a fireplace, three wooden chairs and a small table. An old rug lay covering the centre of the earth floor. There were two men in the room both sitting in front of an open log fire, both smoking clay pipes.

One, who she assumed was John Pitts, the owner of the cottage, she did not know. But the other she did.

'You didn't expect to see me, eh Nancy?'

Nancy felt her blood run cold as she stared at the unexpected figure of Abel Jacobs grinning at her. She had known him for several years. At first, while she was just a child, she had been subjected to occasional bullying and petty violence; but as she had grown up his behaviour had turned to a more familiar intimacy that she had done nothing to encourage. He was a bully who took advantage of her sex and some months past had tried to be intimate with her. Few opportunities had presented themselves as their meetings had mostly been in the more public rooms of the Flying Angel and she had kept out of his way away from the bars. Now here she was in a lonely cottage with the man she dreaded, with only one other person present, a man likely to be as bad as Jacobs. She silently cursed Regan for sending her on this errand without warning her that Jacobs was amongst the north Somerset smuggling fraternity.

Looking at Pitts she decided to ignore her tormentor.

'Regan says you may have a message for me.'

'Aye,' he replied, 'tell your friend there's a shipment arriving at Portbury on Friday night. We'll want some help taking it to the barn at Easton-in-Gordano. 'Bout midnight, usual place, twenty donkeys. He'll know.'

Nancy listened carefully to her instructions. She knew the smuggling ships had regular dropping off points along the coast and that Portbury, at the mouth of the Avon, was one of them. Donkeys would take the merchandise to a safe haven before it was despatched to various parts of the country.

'What will be comin' in?' Nancy asked.

'Brandy mostly, and some tobacco. Now d'ye want to eat afore you leave?'

Nancy's hunger momentarily overcame her fear of Jacobs and she sat down to a table of cold meat and potatoes and a jug of beer. By the time she had finished Pitts had disappeared upstairs and only Jacobs remained in the room. Panic gripped her. Jacobs stood between her and the only door out of the room. She watched him put his pipe down and take a step towards her. The malevolent grin on his face revealed his intention.

'Well Nancy, I think we need to have a little talk.'

She sat in silence, head down, looking at the table in front of her.

Jacobs continued. 'That young man of yours, Richard Stourton I believe his name is. What is he to you?'

'I dunno what you mean.'

'Oh come now, I'm sure you do.' Jacobs moved close to Nancy, putting his face in front of hers. She could smell his bad breath laced with whisky. 'We know you've been to his lodgings.'

She was paralysed with fear. 'Twice only,' she said, without really thinking. Jacobs might have been guessing. Now he knew.

'Twice, eh Nancy? That must 'ave been very worthwhile for you. How much did 'e pay you?' Jacobs pressed his face right up to hers. 'Or did you give it 'im free?'

Nancy drew back. She wanted to scratch his face but was too frightened. 'It ain't like that. He's just been kind to me, no more.'

'Say what you like Nancy but I know what you get paid for. That and information. What's 'ee been asking you about?'

'It's none o' your business, Abel Jacobs.'

'Oh it ain't, ain't it? We'll see about that. You've been too clever for too long Nancy.'

Nancy pulled herself backwards but there was nowhere to go and Jacobs grabbed her by the arm and dragged her to the middle of the room. She screamed.

'Let me go, you're hurtin' my arm.'

He squeezed her wrist tighter. Her face contorted with pain. Then his grip loosened.

'I'll let you keep your precious secrets with yer fancy boy. But you'll have to be nice to me before you go.'

Nancy looked round in desperation but there was no sign of John Pitts nor was she strong enough to escape Jacobs' grasp.

'Come on now Nancy. We've been friends for years and you're a big girl now.'

He released her wrist but before she could move away he grabbed her by the shoulders and squeezed until the pain made her sink to the floor.

' I ain't 'avin' nothing to do with you!' she screamed out at him, at the same time catching the side of his head with her fist.

'Why you little vixen!' roared Jacobs. 'I'll soon teach you a lesson.'

He forced her onto the floor and tore at the shoulder of her dress whilst she struggled and hit out at him.

'You leave me alone Abel Jacobs. If you don't leave off and let me go the message won't be delivered. An' don't forget I know all about your smugglin'.

As Jacobs loosened his grip Nancy realised she had said too much. A threat to expose the smugglers would likely lead to her death. But she had said enough to cause her attacker to pull back as he thought about her words. He did not resist as she pulled herself free of his grip, rolled away from him and on hands and knees crawled across the room to the door. She expected him to pounce on her again but he made no further attempt to restrain her. She stood up and opened the door, then looked back. Jacobs was kneeling on the floor staring at her.

'All right Nancy I'll let you go this time. But remember, if those donkeys are not there on Friday, don't expect to see daylight the next day. You'll be in the river like that interfering councillor.'

It was only while running along the footpath back towards Bristol that Nancy thought out the implications of Abel Jacobs' last remark.

The shattering of glass shook the night air. Two men ran down the street, their boots clattering on the cobbles. Dogs started barking and somewhere a horse whinnied and snorted. Seconds later the door of the damaged building opened and a number of people ran out onto the pavement. But they were too late to catch the attackers. One by one they disappeared back inside, making for the front office where the damage had been done.

Robert Harford, whose office it was, walked over to the broken window, through which cold air was blowing into the room. He looked at the damage. One pane had been broken by a stone that lay on the floor amid a mosaic of broken glass. He picked it up and removed a sheet of paper tied round it. Someone brought a lantern over to where he was standing. There was a crudely scrawled message on it which he read out to his companions.

'No radical traitor for Bristol. Signed, for the committee for the return of a loyal subject of His Majesty King George III.'

Robert shrugged his shoulders. 'It has started then. Just as we expected.'

No one spoke, as no one knew what to say. Robert moved towards the door. 'Shall we resume our meeting?' he said.

There was no bitterness in his voice, just resignation. Blackman had died three weeks before, releasing tensions that had been building up for several weeks. The agreement between the two political parties for the sharing of the Bristol seats in Parliament had worked well for a time, but with fundamental disagreements growing over the issue of the American Colonies, the concord acted to stifle debate. Elections were often violent and disorderly even when there was no contest, and it was becoming clearer by the day that the impending by-election would be an opportunity for people to show their feelings on the issue.

Robert had been forced to show his hand soon after Blackman's funeral. Had he not done so, a writ for the by-election would have been moved immediately and the Whig hierarchy would have declared their support for a Tory replacement. Pledges to the Tories would have been given by his potential supporters, which could not have been withdrawn. As a result of his declaration most of the Whig establishment had come out against him, the Tories watching from the sidelines, delighted at their rival's discomfiture. Happy to attack both wings of the Whig party, the Tories nevertheless directed most of their fire at him. Some of the Whig hierarchy joined in.

The electors of Bristol had soon found themselves divided into three different camps, a luxury not often afforded to them, and an opportunity for the citizens, whether or not on the electoral roll, to create more than the usual disorder. Two of the three groups attacked Robert and his supporters. A poster campaign had started accusing him of disloyalty to the Crown and constitution. With limited funds so far, he had no resources with which to fight back.

But his first target was to secure the Whig nomination. To achieve this he had to persuade a majority of the city Whig party to fight the seat at all, and if that were successfully achieved, to secure the nomination for himself, with the party behind him, and start campaigning against the Tory candidate.

Until the shattered window there had been no real violence. Abuse in the streets, the cold shoulder from former party colleagues, and some lively heckling at meetings of the Common Council were much as he had expected. Personal and political pamphlets and attacks in the press were also part of the electioneering process. Yet this time the process had started before even the vacancy had been declared and the writ issued for a by-election, and now the first act of violence had taken place.

Robert instructed his servant to clear up the debris of broken glass and board up the window and resumed the meeting in the library at the back of the building. Everyone waited for his lead.

'It is clear we are in for a rough campaign. The eyes of the country will be upon us. Bristol will be seen as a test of opinion on the Government's policy on the Colonies. I have a duty to go on with it but I would not wish to risk any of you coming to harm. Most of you have families and businesses to protect. If any of you wish to withdraw I will quite understand.'

No one moved. After a short interval John Powell spoke. 'Robert I think it is clear we are all behind you and will see it through with you. And, as you say, we have a duty. If we don't stand for what we believe to be right on this issue, that point of view will have no means of expression. We need to give the public an opportunity to express itself, and send a timely message to the Government.'

He paused, then looked across at Sarah. 'My only reservation is not for me, but for Sarah. There is resentment at women being involved in politics at all, let alone on your election committee. With respect to you, Sarah, I think you would be well advised to play a less prominent role.'

There was a sharp intake of breath around the table. Everyone knew where this was leading. Sarah, ever defiant, shook her head in a vigorous denial.

'I am sorry, John, but I don't agree. I know your remarks are intended kindly and I thank you for them. But I see no reason to do as you suggest. I never travel anywhere unaccompanied and I do not seek to speak at public meetings. Perhaps being a woman will give me a measure of protection.'

'What about your relationship with Joseph Terrill?'

This question was put by a newcomer to the committee, Thomas Butcher, one of the establishment Whigs won over to Harford's cause. He was a solid middle-aged trader, well versed in political intrigue and the sort of man Robert Harford was keen to attract to add weight to an otherwise young and inexperienced team. His question had been put sympathetically but Sarah felt vulnerable and replied in a tone she afterwards regretted.

'What business is that of yours or anyone else's?' She felt the colour flowing to her cheeks. 'I mean, it is nothing to do with this issue. Mr Terrill is a friend of my father. As my father's daughter I have a duty to entertain his guests. There is nothing more to it than that. His politics are anathema to me.'

'It is rumoured that Terrill will be the Tory candidate,' persisted Thomas Butcher.

'Then he will be too busy to visit my home and the problem will not arise.'

There were chuckles around the room.

'All the same..' began Butcher.

'All the same, what?' snapped Sarah. 'If you are suggesting I spy for Mr Terrill, then say so.'

Robert Harford and John Powell were content to let the matter be aired. It had worried them, not because they thought that Sarah had divided loyalties, but that her own position and that of her father would be compromised. They were happy to let her argue her case.

But Thomas Butcher was satisfied. 'No of course not Sarah. I just feel it would be intolerable for you to have a social relationship with one candidate when actively working for another.'

'Thank you for your concern,' she said with pursed lips which could not conceal her displeasure. 'I would imagine that the first time Mr Terrill asks me for my support and I tell him I have given it to Robert he will feel less inclined to visit our home.'

This seemed to bring an end to the debate and the tension eased.

'There is one other matter I want to bring to your attention,' said Robert. 'I don't think our campaign can expect to be successful without the help of an election agent. I have approached Jeremy Sly who has experience of contested campaigns in the West Country and he has agreed. I have asked him to tell me how much the campaign will cost and what actions he recommends we take.'

'I agree with this Robert,' said John Powell 'We all need to know what we have to do and the price we will have to pay. Has he started work yet?'

'He has done some preliminary planning. He tells me that a large number of the Bristol electorate live outside the city, some even in London. It seems eligible freemen retain their voting rights even after leaving the city. They will all need to be contacted and encouraged to return to vote. That will be expensive.'

'A fortune, money lost for the candidate who fails,' said Sarah, 'but I suppose we have to do it to give ourselves the best chance of winning.'

'I propose we appoint Jeremy Sly,' said John Powell, and there was general agreement.

As they left the building later that evening, Robert Harford held Sarah in conversation until the others had gone.

'I admire what you said to Thomas this evening Sarah.'

'Thank you Robert. John's advice was sound, of course. But I couldn't agree publicly to keep in the background. I will be careful though. It will not help women in society if I was seen to be an easy target.'

'I was thinking more of your friendship with Mr Terrill, Sarah. I rather fear that the political situation is leading you to a decision you had not yet determined to take.'

She smiled and put her hand on his arm. 'You need not concern yourself on that score. I am not making a personal sacrifice if that's what you think. My friendship with Mr Terrill was as much on my father's account as my own. I had not made a personal decision because there had been no need to. But once faced with it, as I am now, my position was clear. And there is a young man on the other side of the world who will be delighted.'

Her eyes sparkled as they smiled at one another. He helped her into her carriage. 'God bless you Sarah,' he said as he waved her carriage away.

Sarah heard the commotion long before the carriage carrying her and Mary Harford reached Prince Street. As they turned from Broad Quay towards the junction of Marsh Street and King Street the driver slowed down, then halted. The women looked out anxiously. They were some hundred yards short of their destination, the Assembly Rooms, and between them the way was blocked by an excited, jostling crowd. The driver climbed down and stood by the carriage window.

'Pardon ma'am but I can drive you no further.'

Mary nodded. 'That will not matter. We can walk from here.'

The two women got out. It was a damp November evening with no wind. Instinctively they pulled their cloaks around them more for protection than against the cold, and, picking up their skirts, they started walking towards the throng. Although noisy and restless, the milling crowd was good humoured and as they approached, a passageway between people opened before them. Some, supporters and opponents alike, recognised them and there was spasmodic cheering and booing alike from the respective sides.

Robert Harford was waiting at the door of the Assembly Rooms to welcome them and he escorted them upstairs to the musicians' gallery that overlooked the main ballroom. Several other ladies had already taken their seats. Sarah recognised a number of them as wives of leading Whig Councillors and officials in the city and was dismayed by the frosty acknowledgement she received from most in response to her greeting.

They took seats in the second row from where Sarah could see the main body of the ballroom below. At the far end a temporary platform had been erected which would enable her to see the faces of the platform party when it arrived. She looked round the room. Built some twenty years before in Palladian style with much rococo ornamentation, it was designed for genteel evenings of music and dance, and seemed unsuited for acrimonious political debate. The clerestory of windows on the south wall was too high for outsiders to look in. Deliberately built this way to protect dancers from prying eyes it effectively prevented the interested crowd out in the street from knowing what might be going on inside.

Although over eighty feet long, the room was soon full and Sarah watched minor skirmishes at the main door as the attendants tried to prevent more gaining entry. Eventually the door was closed and barred and she turned her attention to the empty platform at the far end. On the wall behind the platform was a large clock dial framed with rococo ornaments. The hands were approaching eight thirty.

At exactly that time a panelled door beneath the clock opened and the platform party entered. Sarah watched as three men filed in, the Mayor James Walter, Robert Harford, and Hugh Berry. The crowd became hushed. Sarah thought Robert looked pale and tense but he had good reason to be. The meeting had been called to decide whether he would be the official Whig candidate at the forthcoming by-election or whether he would have to fight alone.

The tension was broken by a moment of farce as the party mounted the steps to the platform. Clearly no thought had been given to the seating arrangements and there was a jockeying for position. Was this to be a meeting of the Whig Party, to be presided over by the Mayor or was it a private meeting called by Robert's supporters, under the chairmanship of Hugh Berry? After a minute's hurried whisperings between members of the platform party, encouraged by exhortations from the floor to 'get on with it,' the diplomacy was concluded by two chairs being placed side by side in the centre of the platform affording equal seniority to the bottoms that would occupy them, with Robert sitting between them but slightly behind. The audience quietened again after the unexpected entertainment and the Mayor rose to address them.

'In deference to the office I hold Mr Berry and Councillor Harford have invited me to open this meeting. I do so formally, without comment at this stage on the merits of the question at issue. This is not an adoption meeting called by the Whigs in Bristol. It has been called by Mr Berry to announce Councillor Harford's intentions, and, I understand, to seek the support of our party.'

He paused to allow a challenge to his interpretation, but there was none. The Mayor continued.

'It has been agreed that Mr Berry will speak first to be followed by Councillor Harford. As leader of the Whigs in Bristol I will then respond. After discussion from the floor, the matter will be put to a vote.'

Sarah looked round the hall. When the audience had filed in earlier she had seen some faces she recognised, but the majority were strangers to her. Most of the Whig city councillors and senior party officials were there. As she looked down at the sea of heads – only the backs of which she could see – she wondered about this arbitrary group of people who would be deciding Robert's future. She knew his friends had tried to dragoon potential supporters into attending, but no doubt so had his Whig opponents, and they had more influence. The outcome could depend on who had managed to push to the front of the crowd and secure a place in the hall. That Robert would stand as a candidate was now beyond doubt. The question was whether as official Whig candidate or as an independent. As the former, his chances of winning were infinitely greater.

The Mayor resumed his seat and Hugh Berry took centre stage. He was not a man to prevaricate.

'Citizens of Bristol, we have called this meeting to seek your support and the support of the Whig party for Robert Harford as a candidate in the forthcoming by-election.'

Sarah could not resist a smile. Politicians always addressed 'the citizens of Bristol' yet everyone knew the audience comprised only a small fraction of the total citizenry and most of those persons were already committed supporters of either the Whig Party or Robert Harford.

'Since 1756 there has been an agreement between the two main parties in this city for the Bristol seats in Parliament to be shared, one Whig, one Tory. This agreement has been based on expediency. The last contested election, in 1754, cost our party £20,000.

'But expediency leads to complacency and, I regret to say, in certain areas of policy, to the disadvantage of Bristol. Our two members elected in 1768, one now deceased, were both strong supporters of the King and his government over the issue of the American Colonies. If we allow the Tories to nominate a successor to Sir Ralph Blackman unopposed, that will continue. Councillor Harford and those who think like him believe this to be unacceptable and a situation that does not serve this city well. My colleague himself will tell you why.'

He sat down to a buzz of voices around the hall as each man present volunteered an opinion to his neighbour. Sarah, from her vantage point above the throng, tried to judge the mood from the cacophony that rose up to her. But she received confused signals, sharp disagreements, and a wave of restlessness and even discontent, sweeping the hall. Members of a crowd like to think that they are in sympathy with everyone around them, but this was clearly not the case here. Sarah feared that the Whig leaders had planted agitators amongst the audience to try to stir opinion their way.

Robert appeared to sense this too as he stood patiently waiting for the debate to subside. Sarah turned to Mary and took hold of her hand. She looked as pale and anxious as her husband did, waiting to address an unsympathetic audience. But Sarah knew that he was brave, if inexperienced, and would cope with his ordeal.

At last the hall was hushed.

'Gentlemen. I am grateful to you for allowing me to address you. What Hugh has said is correct. It is the issue of the American Colonies that has persuaded me to take this step. This great city of ours,' – a great sweep of his arm suggesting the city was laid out in the hall in front of him – 'second only to London in trade with the rest of the world, is dependent on good relations with our cousins in the thirteen Colonies. Bristol merchants own plantations and other businesses there. All of us in this city would suffer if those links were lost.'

He paused for a moment to allow time for the point to sink in. But this gave an opportunity for a heckler to intervene.

'Seeking to look after your own pocket and that of your friends, are you?' This led to laughter and a chorus of agreement from around the room.

Robert stood passively before responding, then spoke in a quiet voice to compel silence from his audience to enable then to hear him.

'Perhaps the gentleman at the back would consider this. How many families in this city are dependent on the port for their livelihood?'

He raised his voice a little.

'How many men and women supply services for seamen who come ashore? Clothing. Ship refurbishment and supplies. Food, drink and entertainment. How many people work in our china and glass industries, which export so much to our Colonies?' He was almost shouting now.

'I do not seek to safeguard businesses just for the sake of the merchants. I seek to preserve the jobs and livelihood of all our citizens.' This time it was his supporters who could cheer and point at their opponents as if to say 'you must do better than that.'

Robert's successful rejoinder to the heckler discouraged others and he was able to complete his speech with few outright interruptions but to a background of murmurings from those who did not want his words to be heard. When he sat down it was to sporadic cheering and clapping although a substantial part of the audience remained silent. Sarah judged that he had enthused his own supporters, but not won many converts. The few who were open-minded were awaiting the Mayor's reply.

Quiet and undemonstrative by nature, James Walter's political success had been steady rather than spectacular. His advance had been by offending no one and with the passing years he had acquired the aura of an elder statesman. Local Whigs would often wait to see which side of a question he would take before expressing their own opinion. He was the centre of gravity in Whig politics. Yet when he did take a position on a particular issue he was resolute and would not be easily dissuaded. He accepted his status in the party with pride. It was a matter of honour to behave with dignity and receive respect in return. It mattered not to him whether the issue fell to him as Mayor or as leader locally of his party.

He stood with dignity waiting for the hubbub that had followed Robert Harford's speech to subside. It was not for a Mayor of Bristol to raise his voice to be heard.

'Gentlemen, I wish to say a few words on this matter. I have known Robert Harford for several years as a colleague on our

Council and value his work for Bristol and the party. It therefore saddens me to have to say publicly that in this matter I believe him to be in error.'

Sarah felt her body tense as she realised what was going to happen. This kind and gentle man, a close companion of her father and a frequent guest at her table, was going to destroy the campaign before it had barely begun.

James Walter continued. 'The agreement with the Tories has been to the immense benefit of this city. It has led to a united approach to Bristol's affairs by both political parties and by the corporation. Our Members of Parliament have been able to represent this great city's interests shoulder to shoulder, without rancour or bitterness.'

Did he realise what he was doing, Sarah wondered? She tried to read the answer from the expression on his face but she was too far away. She knew that unwittingly or not, the Mayor was providing an argument against Robert around which every petty place seeker and jealous Whig could unite whatever their political motives.

There was complete silence in the hall now as the Mayor developed his argument.

'The 1756 agreement was made to last three Parliaments. It was understood that the party whose member had died or retired would fill the vacancy. It has held through the 1761 Parliament and so far in this one that started in 1768 and has one more to go after this one. The Tories have so far honoured the agreement and so have we. I am not prepared to see our party break faith. I have spoken with our Member, Mr Croder, and he agrees with me. I say quite openly that whatever happens in this hall tonight I will support the Tory nominee, whoever he may be.'

He stood, defiantly, looking round the room, daring anyone to gainsay him. No one spoke. The effect of his words was to stun Harford's supporters into silence, and offer a clear lead to the doubters. Sarah leaned over to whisper to her companion.

'I had expected the Mayor to be unhappy, but not this.'

'Why is he going against his own party?' Mary looked straight at Sarah, her eyes glistening with tears for her husband.

'He will not have to. He knows perfectly well that such a strong denunciation will be sufficient to swing the vote his way. If Robert loses tonight he will have to stand as a Radical so there would be no Whig candidate, leaving the Mayor free to vote Tory without opposing his party.'

The Mayor had said all he intended to say and started to take points from the floor. Robert's supporters attempted to rally by asking him whether he supported their candidate's policy over the Colonies, but the Mayor would not be drawn, pointing out that that was just one issue amongst many and he was arguing on a point of principle. But the tension had gone, and no one had the stomach to argue further. The power of the party was too great to oppose its will. Yet Sarah knew there was more to it. Robert was a young man. If elected now he would be in Parliament for twenty or more years. There were several ambitious Whigs who had no wish to see such a young man installed. Far better to let the Tories keep the seat until the agreement expires and a new candidate is sought. No, a few local dignitaries harboured their own Parliamentary ambitions, and would not block their own chance for the future.

The vote produced no surprise. The Mayor's resolution 'That this meeting resolves that the Whig Party of Bristol shall not contest the forthcoming Parliamentary by-election and will process with the Tory candidate to the official handing in of his nomination paper' was carried on a show of hands, no count being necessary. Robert had a respectable body of support but failed by a substantial margin to carry the day.

In the same hall exactly one week later the Bristol Tory party enthusiastically and unanimously adopted Joseph Terrill as its candidate.

~ CHAPTER 11 ~

'You have returned then?'

Lawrence Willoughby's voice boomed down the stairs at Richard.

'I have indeed sir.'

Richard wondered how much of his time his principal spent looking out of his window, for his return to Bristol and this first visit to the office were both unannounced. The reception committee at the top of the stairs comprised the old lawyer, Xerxes peering through his legs, and Steggles the clerk, standing behind Willoughby, just tall enough for his eyes to peer down from over his employer's shoulder.

'Welcome back, sir,' said the clerk, sensing that Willoughby would not bring himself to express pleasure at his pupil's return. In this assumption he was right for the lawyer merely ushered Richard into his room without a further word and closed the door, Steggles excluded. Xerxes squeezed through before the door closed but sensing trouble took refuge under his master's desk.

'Sit down my boy, and tell me about it.'

Knowing that his principal was a man of few words when it came to social conversation, Richard spent little time on preliminaries and confined himself to his report on the various commissions he had undertaken for the firm. Of his other activities he said nothing. But Willoughby had other ideas and waited until Richard had finished before speaking.

'You have been on a slaver I hear.'

Richard was momentarily silenced. 'I have sir.'

'You did not tell me that was your intention.'

'I thought you would not approve.'

Willoughby scowled. 'In that assumption you were right. I would have forbidden it. I expect you know now what a risk you took.'

'I do, sir. But how did you find out?'

'Let us just say one of my former clients heard about your escapade. He felt it right to tell me, but by then it was too late. You had already set sail.'

'I am sorry if I have distressed you. I felt it was something I had to do. And as you see, I have come to no harm.'

'No doubt, no doubt.' Willoughby pressed his fingertips together several times, expressing his irritation. For a moment it seemed to Richard almost as if his principal wanted him to come to harm just to prove he was right, but he dismissed the thought as unworthy. 'And what do you intend to do with the knowledge you have gained about the trade? I presume you had a purpose?'

The old lawyer sat back in his chair, eyes averted but almost closed, touching fingertips now still. All this indicated to Richard that Willoughby felt he was entitled to an explanation and was going to have one. Richard, too, sat in silence, listening to the hooves of horses stamping impatiently outside the Bush Hotel next door. The clock of St James Church opposite struck the half hour. He had often thought of these sounds while away, these and many like it. He knew he would now have to give an explanation. His chosen course would be unpopular, but how far would it alienate those whose respect he most sought?

Willoughby, sitting opposite him now, would be the first test. Was he feeling let down, betrayed even, or just disapproving? It was hard to tell. Richard had not been intending to talk about his experience so soon and wanted to hear about Sarah and Nancy first, and to think over all he had seen. But he was being forced to declare his position now. Perhaps that was Willoughby's intention. On the return voyage Richard had taken William into his confidence a little, but had implied that his investigations into Ben Jackson's death was in the nature of a murder enquiry not a political campaign and his friend had not suspected the truth. Now he felt he should emphasise his loathing of the slave trade and leave alone the question of Ben Jackson's death.

He began tentatively. ' You should know, sir, that before I sailed I was in contact with the London Anti-Slave Trade Committee and met one of their supporters in the House of Commons.'

Willoughby opened one eye and stared at his pupil. 'They put you up to it, did they?'

'No, they did not. Quite the reverse. They tried to dissuade me. They were honest enough to point out the dangers and that I would be on my own and beyond help. Only when they realised I was set upon my course did they give me their support.' Richard felt Willoughby's full concentration on him. At least he takes me seriously, he thought.

'I expect, Richard, they want to take advantage of your evidence nonetheless.'

'Of course. I offered it to them.'

'I see. And why do you think there are people in London who are against the slave trade?'

Richard was given no time to answer what he quickly saw was a rhetorical question. Willoughby stood up, and, leaning across the desk on his knuckles, answered his own question.

'I will tell you why.' His voice had a sharp, almost triumphant edge to it. 'Because London has lost its share in the trade to Bristol and Liverpool. Does it not strike you as odd that for fifty years while London was the dominant slave port there was scarcely a voice raised against it? Now their trade has all but gone, committees are set up expressing revulsion at the whole idea. I tell you this. Liverpool has now overtaken our city as the major slave port. If it ever obtains a virtual monopoly, I predict voices will be heard in Bristol condemning the trade as barbaric. People have consciences only when it does not affect their pockets.'

He sat back, and in a voice less strained, more sympathetic, resumed his role as counsellor.

'If you will take my advice Richard, you will be very careful. This city is not yet ready to turn virtuous. To do so its merchants must find other, more profitable, activities. And the church must recognise slavery as an evil, which it is not yet ready to do.'

Willoughby stood up and turned towards the window and nodded towards the Exchange opposite. 'Those people deal in slaves as they deal in tobacco, cotton, pots and pans. It has been so throughout their lifetime and I doubt one in a hundred considers the morality of it. And the few that do? Why, they just think that if the trade did not come to Bristol it would go somewhere else.'

He stood silently, now leaning against the sill as if the articulation of his thoughts had tired him. Richard had already noticed how much older and more weary he looked than before he had gone away and wondered whether his long absence had contributed to it. Willoughby's speech had taken him by surprise, and not just because it was the longest exposition of his views on any subject at all that the old man had ever given him. Richard found his cynicism of men and events almost too much to grasp. And yet he was surprised at Willoughby's hint that he himself had misgivings. He had not said as much, and yet admitting there was a moral argument at all indicated an open mind. But he knew where Willoughby's argument was leading.

'I am grateful to you for your advice,' he said. 'I can see that a radical campaigning lawyer would not enhance your business. It is not my intention to cause you embarrassment or distress. Quite the opposite. I had hoped to offer you more support in the practice. Perhaps you would advise me what I should do.'

Willoughby turned towards him. Richard saw the hint of a smile flicker across his face and the eyes betray the satisfaction of success. So that was it! He feared he would lose his influence once his pupil had struck out independently. By asking for his advice, Richard thought, I appear to be back under his control. So be it. I have no wish to hurt him and will accommodate his wishes as far as possible. He waited for Willoughby to set his terms.

'Deal with it as a lawyer, my boy, not as a politician. Prepare your evidence, obtain sworn affidavits from those who are willing to testify and send it all to the London Committee. Then forget the whole business. You will have achieved your purpose at minimum risk to yourself. Above all, do not make any public statement here in Bristol unless you have to, and even then only if you have sworn testimony to support it.'

Richard sat silent, head bowed. This was not what he had wanted to hear. Yet deep down he knew he could expect nothing else.

'Thank you, sir. I will reflect on what you have said.'

Both men knew that Richard was not promising to follow Willoughby's advice and both knew the discussion had ended, their thoughts hanging in mid-air. Richard made no move to leave the room and remained seated in front of the desk. He had another matter on his mind. 'I was wondering whether you have had any dealings with Frank Jackson while I was away. And whether the mystery surrounding Ben Jackson's death had been solved.' His question was intended to lead to information about Sarah and he felt himself tense up in anticipation eyes half closed, fingers clenched.

'I have seen little of the Jacksons, Richard. Winding up Ben Jackson's estate is more or less complete, but I have met the family socially from time to time. As for his murder, nothing new has come to light. It is assumed he was set on by footpads.'

'Is Sarah Jackson still living with her father?'

'As far as I am aware. She is not yet married, if that is what you are asking. Taken to politics I understand. Can't think why. It is no sort of pursuit for a woman. I think her father is over indulgent.'

Richard could not help himself. 'And Councillor Terrill?'

'He is making quite a name for himself. Regarded by most as an up and coming young man. Terrill and Miss Jackson are frequently together at civic functions. They make quite a striking partnership. There will be a formal announcement soon I shouldn't wonder.'

Richard felt a sense of desolation and loss and wished to hear no more. He rose to leave. He paused but could think of nothing more to say. 'I will start work tomorrow morning if that is convenient to you.'

The older man smiled. 'That will suit very well. I am pleased to have you back.'

As Richard was going down the stairs to the street the sound of footsteps behind him made him stop. He turned to see Steggles following him. 'Mr Stourton, sir.'

Richard waited for him to catch up.

'I have this letter for you. It has been here for eight months.'

He took it and went out into the street before opening it. It was dated April 1771 and was from the Penneys at Frenchay telling him that Nancy had run away.

Richard felt bitter as he walked slowly down Corn Street towards the river, and his lodgings beyond. Everything he was trying to achieve was falling apart in his hands. His future with Lawrence Willoughby was in doubt unless he abandoned his anti-slave trade activities. Sarah seemed committed to life as a society hostess married to Joseph Terrill. Nancy had run away, no doubt back to a life of poverty and prostitution. The chain of events that had started with the murder of Ben Jackson had now run its course. There was no way forward except the quiet humdrum life he had known before. At the time, he had been content. To qualify as an attorney and become Willoughby's partner had seemed a goal worth attaining. But he had since glimpsed other possibilities. Now those possibilities were vanishing. Yet, nagging in the back of his mind was something that told him he had not come to a dead end and: that there was a loose strand not followed. What was it?

As he reached the river he stood and looked at the tall sailing ships moored along the quayside, some recently arrived, others soon to depart for destinations all over the world. One or two would be going back to the American Colonies, perhaps even on the slave run. His thoughts turned to Williamsburg and the lives the colonists were living.

Then it came to him. The loose thread. It was Amos Kettle. Or rather, Kettle's disclosure that a consortium from Bristol under the name of the Africol Trading Company had owned the *Demera*.

That was the unanswered question. He must find out who was in the consortium, if only to satisfy his own curiosity. His low spirits began to revive as this task presented itself to him and it was with a more purposeful step that he crossed the river and returned to his lodgings.

As he retraced his footsteps to Frogmore Street his thoughts turned to the African boy waiting at his lodgings. His ship had returned to Bristol with him still not knowing what to do with Sam but he was clear that he could not just disown him. He was responsible for bringing him to England and had to look after him at least in the short term.

For the first few days back in England Richard had kept the boy in his room but his presence could not be kept from his landlady for long and she soon discovered him. At first shocked and angry, she had come to pity the child and even befriend him. Now he found her feeding him. She had also dressed him in some old clothes of her husband's to keep him warm.

'What are you going to do with the boy Mr Stourton?' she asked. 'He can't stay here all day and every day, what with you working such long hours. He needs to be placed with rich folk who have need of servants.'

'Yes, I know, Mrs Browning. I have one or two people I can speak to about him.'

Richard watched the boy finish his meal then they sat together by the fireside.

'Do you miss home?'

'No it was like a prison.'

'There are servants like you with families in Bristol and Bath. I will try and find you somewhere to live and work. You will not be beaten. Would you like that?'

'I want that sir.'

Richard's next call was to his sister in Henbury. He had sent her a note telling of his return and that he would call to see her at the coming weekend, so when he knocked on the door the following Saturday morning he knew he was expected. The footman let him in but on entering the library he found Julia with Sir John. Julia looked frightened and his welcome from Sir John was cold and formal.

'Good day Sir John. Julia how are you?' He walked over and embraced her but although she smiled he could see she was tense.

'Good day to you, Mr Stourton. I trust you have recovered from your journey?'

'Yes thank you sir. And how is Lady Manners?'

'My wife is well, thank you. But I'll come straight to the point. We understand you have some property of mine.'

Richard looked from one to the other, Sir John angry, and Julia tearful.

'I do not understand your meaning Sir John. I know of no such property. Perhaps you would explain?'

'You have a runaway slave at your lodgings belonging to my estate in Virginia. Sam I believe to be his name. Is that correct sir?'

Richard began to feel uncomfortable. 'You are misinformed, Sir John. The boy left Virginia of his own free will. I did not steal him.'

'Slaves do not have free will as you put it. I am sure you know that. But perhaps we need not argue the point. He is here now and I would be grateful if you would return him to me and I will call that an end to the matter.'

'I am afraid I cannot do that. With all respect to you, Sam is in England now where slavery is not acceptable. If I hand him over you will no doubt send him back to your plantation.'

'I most certainly will,' said Sir John. 'The boy belongs to me and I will have him.'

'Sir John it deeply saddens me to disagree with you so soon after my return and I hope it will not reflect ill on my sister, who knows nothing of this matter. But I do not intend to hand him over.'

'You must accept the consequences of that, Mr Stourton. I will have him even if I have to go to law to do so. Now, I will leave you with your sister for a while, but in future you will not be welcome in this house. Unless of course you think better of the situation. Good day to you sir.'

He strode out of the room, slamming the door behind him.

Julia was sobbing quietly. 'Oh Richard, what have you done?'

'I am so sorry Julia. Circumstances have made things this way; it was never my intention to create problems for you. If you could have seen Sam when I found him at the roadside, terrified and bruised from ill treatment, with no family to protect him, I am sure you would have made the same choice. You are a dear kind sister who I know would not have left him to his miserable future.'

'How did they find out so quickly?'

'I expect I was seen with the boy in Seahaven and a letter was sent, probably on the same ship that I sailed on, advising Sir John of what I had done. Anyway it doesn't matter how they found out. The fact is they have and I will have to face up to whatever they do. I will have to confer with Mr Willoughby about the legality of the situation. I am not so confident as I may have sounded.'

Julia put her handkerchief to her eyes but could not stop sobbing. Richard walked over to her and sitting down next to her put his arm round her shoulders.

'Come, Julia, please do not cry. It is a silly quarrel which will not affect your position here, I am sure.'

She leaned against him and he felt her sobs gradually subside.

'I am sorry, Richard. I am sure you are right about the boy. When will it be resolved?'

'That depends on Sir John. If he goes to court as he threatens, it will take some months. Perhaps though he will calm down and gradually accept the situation.'

'I don't think he will. He chairs the Bristol League of Support for the African Trade and cannot be seen to be recognising legal rights for slaves. I have heard him say so. He will have to attempt to recover Sam through the courts.'

'Well that we shall see.' He gently detached himself from his sister's embrace and walked over to the window.

'Have you seen Sarah while I have been away?'

'Yes. I have visited her on several occasions. I like her very much.'

'Was anyone else there?'

'Not usually. I met her father, of course, and on one occasion Councillor Terrill called. But they just talked of her uncle's memorial for a few minutes, then he left.'

'Did you like him?'

'I was not in his company for sufficient time to form a judgement. He did seem a little too sure of himself. But that may be the confidence he has gained through being successful'

Their conversation lapsed. Julia sat quietly, Richard returned to the window and stared out. It was raining and the wind was blowing in squalls. Watching the clouds blow across the sky he was reminded of the changes in the weather that so affected all aboard the Amelia. There had been moments when he thought the ship would not survive a storm, the elements seemed too powerful to resist. He thought of his father's investment in a ship that could not withstand nature at its worst.

'Do you think of father often, Julia?' he asked at last.

'Oh yes,' she replied, 'I think of him frequently when I am alone. I like to think of the happy times we had with him and what our lives would have been like had he lived.'

Richard said: 'Truth to tell I suspect my life would not have been too dissimilar to what I now enjoy. I would have taken over his business, or gone into my profession, as I have done. But your life would have been so different.'

He turned to look at his sister and saw a flicker of sadness across her face. He continued. 'I am still intent on trying to find out what happened to father's fortune. Not with much success so far I fear. But I have not yet given up.'

'I know you are doing your best, Richard, and I continue to support you, but so far there has just been sadness.' Julia played with the thought of telling Richard about Nicholas. She desperately wanted to, but feared he would feel torn between his love for her and his sense of duty over Sam. That was not a dilemma she wished him to struggle with.

'Julia, don't despair. I have some enquiries still to make. All is not at an end. And perhaps next time you are invited to the Jackson's home I could visit you there. I might even have good news for you.'

To the Gentlemen, Clergy, Freeholders and Freemen of the City of Bristol
GENTLEMEN AND FELLOW CITIZENS
This by-election is now upon us. I am conscious that I have served in this City for several years as a councillor and have never deviated from my duty and attachment to you the electorate and the public. I deem it a great honour to be chosen to lay myself before you to be a Member of Parliament for this great City. I ask for your favour and votes by supporting the King and his Government to protect the commercial interests

of the City and the wellbeing of the people. I will continue in Parliament to show the same honesty, diligence and independence as I have hitherto shown in my civic duties. I intend to conduct myself throughout this campaign with dignity and without challenging the personal integrity of any other Candidate.

However, I regret that there is one who believes he should represent the City by pandering to those who would by our weakness take from us that which has made this City and nation great and prosperous. I trust that such a voice will be ignored.

I am, with esteem and respect,
Gentlemen,
Your most faithful and devoted, humble servant,
JOSEPH TERRILL
Clifton, November 1771

◆ ◆ ◆

To the Gentlemen, Clergy, Freeholders and Freemen of the City of Bristol
GENTLEMEN AND FELLOW CITIZENS
I am aware that several unfavourable reports have been circulated respecting my intention to stand as a Candidate for the honour of representing this City in Parliament. I think it is right that I should assure you that I have received many promises of support and it is these numerous applications that have determined me to offer you my service.

I am conscious of my inadequacies but I venture to hope that by spirit, good faith, and honesty I shall render myself worthy of your confidence. I would add that my intention if elected is to seek a peaceful resolution of our current disagreement with the American Colonies so that trade between the Colonies and this great City will suffer no further disruption, for the benefit of all who live here.

Gentlemen,
Your faithful and obedient servant,
ROBERT HARFORD
November 1771

◆ ◆ ◆

To the Gentlemen, Clergy, Freeholders and Freemen of the City of Bristol

GENTLEMEN AND FELLOW CITIZENS

I feel bound to draw to the attention of all loyal citizens the contents of a scurrilous leaflet from one who purports to seek your support in a most duplicitous way. Whilst claiming to seek your support by promising to protect our trade he is in fact in league with those in the American Colonies who seek to sever the link that is the true cause of our wealth and fortune. Such is the danger that he presents to us that neither Whig nor Tory is willing to allow him a platform.

I am with esteem and respect,
Gentlemen
Your most esteemed and humble servant,
JOSEPH TERRILL
Clifton November 1771

♦ ♦ ♦

To the Gentlemen, Clergy, Freeholders and Freemen of the City of Bristol
GENTLEMEN AND FELLOW CITIZENS
I wish to advise my friends and fellow supporters that I am strongly attached to the principles of our glorious constitution and if elected to Parliament I will study and support and defend our civil and religious rights, and promote your particular interests, to extend the commerce of this great City, with which I am so essentially connected. It is because I am so attached to ancient rights and liberties that I seek to maintain those same rights and liberties for those of our fellow citizens and their descendents who have settled in the Colonies. Those who suggest I am giving comfort to any who conspire against our King and constitution are in grievous error,

Gentlemen,
Your faithful and obedient servant,
ROBERT HARFORD
November 1771

'What do you think so far, Sarah?' said Robert Harford. Sarah put the leaflets back on the table.

'Well you seem to be matching the opposition, but can you keep it up?'

'We must thank Mr Sly for writing them for me, but the cost of paying for them to be distributed around the streets on top of the usual cost of supporting the voters is a heavy one. And voting has not yet started. What do you think, Mr Sly?'

The three of them were standing in Robert's office, temporarily turned into his campaign headquarters, with the usual election chaos around. Piles of literature, posters, and bunting lay around the floor, chairs and desktops. Of medium height and build, his spiky black hair and black suit gave Jeremy Sly an appearance of imperturbability and authority.

'Well Mr Harford, sir, if you can find the money, I can spend it. But there is a cheaper way if needs be. The local press are ever interested in elections, particularly if contested. Once voting starts, some of your supporters may take to their pens.'

'We must be careful what they say. A word in the wrong place could cause untold damage.'

'Oh no sir, you misunderstand me. They will use their pens just to sign the letters. I will write them.'

Robert and Sarah smiled to one another as if to confirm their election agent was worth his fee.

'I am in your hands as ever, Mr Sly,' said Robert.

There was plenty of work awaiting Richard when he returned to the office the following morning and for several days he had no opportunity to pursue his investigations. Nor did he attempt to see Sarah. He brooded over his situation, sometimes thinking of her, sometimes immersing himself in work in a vain attempt to put her from his mind. He was desperately keen to visit her yet could not face what he expected to be her rejection of him as anything more than a casual friend.

A week after his return his mind was made up for him. A note arrived, the messenger instructed to await a reply. He opened it and read.

> *I hear you are back and yet you have not paid us a visit. Father and I would be pleased for you to dine with us tomorrow at six.*
> *Sarah Jackson.*

Richard scribbled an acceptance and sent the messenger on his way before he could change his mind. The invitation spurred him into activity. He decided that before he saw Sarah he would follow up the Africol lead, and also start to look for Nancy.

Darkness was beginning to fall when Richard entered Castle House in St Nicholas Street later that same day. Sitting behind a desk with a single candle beside him was an elderly clerk apparently intent on copying the details of a letter into a ledger. Richard waited patiently in front of him. Eventually the clerk looked up over his glasses, laid his quill on the desk and without a word sat back waiting for Richard to speak.

'Good day sir. I would like to examine, if I may, the records of the various shipping companies operating out of this port ten years ago.'

The clerk sighed. It was clearly a chore he would have rather done without.

'Any one in particular, sir?'

'The Africol Trading Company. I wish to see whether the company operated a ship called the *Demera*.'

The clerk screwed up his face and peered at Richard. 'A popular ship, sir.'

'What do you mean?'

The clerk pushed his glasses further up his nose. 'You are the third person to ask after her, the first about a year back. The second one was about six months ago. What is so special about her?'

'She foundered in a storm nine years ago and is at the bottom of the Atlantic. Your records are all that remains of her.'

The clerk, shrugging his shoulders in an indication it was of little consequence to him, slid off his stool and picking up his candle bade Richard follow him. They walked down a long corridor and into a room on the left at the end. The clerk lit another lamp which he held up at the back of the room alongside tall shelving stretching almost to the ceiling.

'The records are kept chronologically. You will have to start some time before the sinking to find reference to your company, and the ship.'

'Will it contain the names of the crew?'

'Not necessarily. Sometimes the officers. But the shareholders in the company should be there.'

'Thank you.'

Richard lit another candle from that carried by the clerk, took down the volumes for the years 1760-1770 and sat at a desk to begin work. There was complete silence throughout the building and he had the impression he and the clerk were the only people in it. He took his time studying each entry. On every page under the name of a shipping or trading company, apparently in random order was a synopsis of its main trading activities, details of the share capital, and a list of directors and shareholders. Shipping companies had the names of their ships listed and various details of their voyages. This latter information was rather haphazard. Some entries contained full descriptions of their ships voyages and cargoes. Others, just ships' names. Richard supposed it depended on what information the shipping agents passed on.

After about twenty minutes Richard was disturbed by what he thought were footsteps in the corridor outside the room. He was not normally a nervous man but alone in this dark room he felt distinctly uneasy. He called out, supposing it to be the clerk returning to enquire after his progress, but there was no reply. He picked up his candle and walked cautiously over to the door. Opening it he looked in both directions along the corridor but saw no one. He tried to tell himself he had heard a rat scuttling about, and returning to the room continued his search through the records. It took him a further fifteen minutes to find what he was looking for. He felt a thrill of excitement as he read the entry.

Africol Trading Company. Ship: *Demera..* Cargo: weapons, clothes, kitchen utensils. Owners: page 347.

There was no mention of slaves. Eagerly he turned the pages. Then stopped and stared. Page 347, or most of it, had been torn out. He scanned what was left, turned it over, read the next page, and then read the preceding page. There was no doubt about it. The entry for the Africol Trading Company was missing. He sighed, closed his eyes, and leaned forward, chest resting against the desk. Who were the two previous enquirers? Had one of them been Ben Jackson? Had the first enquirer or the second torn the page out? Perhaps Ben Jackson had been the first visitor, found out who the owner was, confronted him with the killing of the Negroes and the insurance swindle, and been murdered to keep him quiet. Then the owner had come here to destroy the evidence. If that is what happened, what could he do now?

After some moments of anguish he opened his eyes and found himself staring closely at the page, just below the tear. There was some writing remaining, just a line and a few words. He looked closely to see what it said. The writing was none to clear but he could just make it out.

'...the crew, only J Cox, S Baillie, and A Jacobs are known to have survived.'

So he was not quite at the end of the trail. Cox and Baillie would tell him nothing, but if he could find the man Jacobs, he might be willing to testify. Nancy may know of him and where to find him. But where was Nancy? The only place to look would be back in Marsh Street. He resolved to go there that evening.

He returned to his lodgings and spent the next two hours writing up his detailed account of his voyage. Despite Lawrence Willoughby's advice he had decided to prepare an affidavit of his own evidence, even if he could not substantiate it. Perhaps William could be persuaded to join him in exposing the cruelties.

It was still early, about nine o'clock, when he reached the Flying Angel, yet the house was already full and as noisy as ever. He bought a mug of beer and sat in an unobtrusive corner and waited for Nancy to appear. By ten o'clock he had tired of waiting and decided to risk asking the barman about her. He had put off doing this for as long as possible as he was aware that his interest in her could put her in personal danger again. He pushed his way through the throng and attracted the barman's attention by waving his empty tankard.

'Is Nancy here?'

The barman grinned. 'What would you be wanting her for? I have some fine ladies upstairs any one of whom would be pleased to talk with you.'

'No thank you. It is Nancy I am looking for.'

'Then you've come to the wrong place. She's not so often here now. Sleeps here occasionally, that's all.'

Do you know where I might find her?'

The barman shrugged his shoulders. 'She spends most of her time down at Pill helping a man called Jacobs. More'n that I can't say.'

Or perhaps won't, thought Richard. But he persisted. 'The man Jacobs. Would that be Abel Jacobs?'

'The same.'

The barman looked across the room then turned away abruptly. Half turning, Richard could see one of Cox's men watching him. It was time to leave.

Despite it being a cold night there were a number of people about, mostly in groups of twos and threes, often women escorting sailors from the docks into the drinking dens to help them enjoy spending their wages.

Crossing the river, Richard turned into Denmark Street. At the far end he saw two men leaning against the corner wall of the end house. Richard walked towards them trying to look unconcerned but watching them carefully, if surreptitiously. As he reached them, one of them called out.

'Mr Stourton?'

Richard slowed down. 'Yes.'

'We would like a word with you.'

He looked at them both, one now on either side of him, but he recognised neither. From their rugged appearance he took them as sailors. He could just make out their swarthy, dark features and strong, square shoulders, the tell tale sign of men used to the rigours of sailing. He noticed that each of them now held a knotted club, which must have been concealed under their coats. Images of Ben Jackson flashed into his mind. Is this how he met his end? He wondered whether to make a run for it. His lodgings were only fifty yards away, yet he would never have time to unlock his door and escape before they would be on him. And if they got him inside he would be even more at their mercy. Shouting for help would bring no relief either. Honest folk kept inside locked doors at night and those out for pleasure would keep away. His only hope was to keep calm and keep the men talking until someone came along. He was no match for the men on his own. He had his cane but that would not withstand the force of the weapons the strangers had.

He tried to hide the fear that he felt. 'How can I help you gentlemen?'

'You have been asking too many questions, Mr Stourton. It makes folk feel uncomfortable.'

'Who sent you?'

'There you are,' said the same man, 'another question.' He grinned, showing even in the darkness a mouth almost devoid of teeth, save three or four, yellow and black.

'We are here to persuade you to give up looking for whatever it is you hope to discover.'

The two men closed in on him. There was still no sign of anyone else about. Richard tried to keep them talking.

'What is it I might find that frightens your masters?'

As he made this remark he realised how many different interests may have put these men on to him. Ben Jackson's murder? The *Demera*? His anti-slave trade activities? His political fund raising? Even his search for Nancy. Or was he in danger of stumbling into something else, something of what he was not yet aware? Perhaps even that which caused his own father's ruin.

There was no reply to his question. He knew now they were going to attack him. He could not retreat down Denmark Street. His best hope was to run past his lodgings towards the new housing in Orchard Street and cry out for assistance.

But he was too late. In a sudden movement the first man lifted his cudgel and brought it down on Richard's left shoulder. He cried out with pain and shock. His legs buckled momentarily but he kept to his feet and tried to run. The second blow pushed him forward onto his knees, his own cane falling from his grasp. He rolled over onto his back, hands over his face to protect his head, and kicked out with his feet. He caught the first assailant on the knee causing him to curse, and stop. The second man was not deterred and stood over Richard ready to strike him again.

'Stop or I will shoot.'

A man's voice came from the shadows outside Richard's lodgings. The attackers stood motionless. The owner of the voice moved forward a step, revealing the outline of his head and shoulders, the rest of him remaining in shadow.

'Now go or I will hand you over to the magistrates.'

Richard's assailants needed no further encouragement. Without a further look at their victim or his rescuer they turned and disappeared back down Denmark Street. Richard felt himself losing consciousness. He felt sick and dizzy and was unable to move. He was dimly aware of a man kneeling over him and gently lifting his head off the ground. It took several seconds for his eyes to focus.

'William?'

'Aye, it is. But say no more now. Do you think you can stand, with my help?' William put his arm under his friend's shoulders and lifted him onto his feet, leading him the few yards to his home.

Sam was there and showed much concern at Richard's condition. On William's prompting he warmed some water on the stove and offered such further help that the surgeon might require.

'I thought you were going to sell that boy when we got back home.' William grinned.

'You didn't believe me when I said that, did you?'

'Not really, no.'

It took the surgeon but a few minutes to tend Richard's injuries during which time neither man spoke. Richard was sufficiently conscious to appreciate the skill of his friend in making him comfortable and tending a deep cut on his shoulder. Soon all he felt was an aching back whenever he tried to move.

'I owe you my life William, what were you doing here?'

The surgeon smiled. 'I had called at your lodgings a few minutes earlier and was standing at the door wondering whether to wait for you when I heard those two men approach. My instinct was to walk the other way but I heard one of them say 'he's coming.' I realised they were probably up to no good and wondered if it was you they were waiting for. They were obviously unaware of my presence so I stood still to see what would happen.'

'Which was fortunate for me,' said Richard. 'But how did you come to have a pistol with you?'

Daniel laughed. 'I had no weapon. It was bluff. I realised they were unable to see me so I gambled on them believing me. If they had known the truth I would have been as helpless as you, but they were disinclined to take the risk.'

'But what are you doing back in Bristol?'

'A man must work. I have come to look for my next berth. Not to sail quite yet I hope, but to arrange something for the future.'

'Where are you staying? Surely you are not going back to Gloucester tonight?'

'No. I was hoping to presume upon your hospitality for a night or two.'

'By all means, my friend, I would be delighted. It would be comforting for the next few days in case my assailants decide to come back. I don't know whether they were intending to kill me or just give a warning. It depends on who sent them and how much he thinks I know.'

'I will sleep in the kitchen,' said Sam. Without further word he stripped the bedclothes from his bed and made to carry them out.

'Sam before you go there is something I want to tell you. Come and sit down.' The boy did as he was requested.

'You are not safe in Bristol. Your former master knows you are in the city and may guess you are lodging here. Please do not go out alone nor open the door to any strangers.'

' What would happen to me if I was took?'

'You would be taken in chains to a ship and returned to Virginia. If that doesn't happen, it is likely that a law court will decide your future.'

'How long will that take?'

'I am afraid it could take some months.'

Sam nodded and left the room.

'That's a problem you could have done without, Richard,' said William.

'Yes, I know, but what could I have done? But there is so much to talk about William. Now we are back in England I can be more open with you. I had no wish to compromise your position while we were at sea, but I would value your help now.'

CHAPTER 12

By the following evening Richard had little but bruising and an aching shoulder to remind him of his attack. He had spent the day at home resting while William had been out looking for work. His incapacity showed Richard the growing affection of Sam. The boy willingly bustled around, making up the fire, fetching blankets, and even bringing him his food. While Richard appreciated this valuable help, he realised that Sam was becoming attached to him and it would be more of a wrench for both of them when he had to leave to take up a servant's job elsewhere.

Richard had sent a note via William to Steggles explaining his absence from the office due to indisposition. He felt unable to tell him the whole truth yet it played on his conscience to be less than frank and it concerned him that his activities were becoming more secretive. He knew that Willoughby would stop him if he could and wished neither to give up nor go against his wishes.

William returned about an hour before Richard was due to go to Sarah's for dinner. Richard was pleased to have his company and while dressing he related the whole story. Just confiding in someone revived his spirits. He had not at first intended to tell him everything but the various elements were so intertwined that each was incomplete without the others. Although only a young man, William seemed experienced beyond his years and Richard had no difficulty in telling him not only the true reason for his voyage but also of his investigation into Ben Jackson's death, his feelings for Sarah, the election fundraising, and even of his disagreement with Lawrence Willoughby. It was not until he had finished that he realised how much of a burden he had been carrying and felt quite light headed at having shared it with a trusted friend who showed such interest and concern.

'Well Richard,' said William when he had finished, 'you have certainly been caught up in a complicated situation. There must be any number of people wanting to silence you, and for a variety of different reasons. You must be careful from now on. Whoever put those two men up to attack you may well do so again.'

It was agreed that William would stay at Richard's lodgings a few days longer than originally intended, and it was with some reluctance that William agreed to Richard walking alone up Brandon Hill to Sarah's home in Clifton. But Richard insisted on being on his own for a few minutes, to clear his mind of the events of the last twenty-four hours and to think about what he should say to Sarah. He would not tell her of the attack for fear of frightening her. He knew she thought she was partly responsible for him having gone on the voyage, and he had no wish to add to her burden of guilt.

The night was clear and crisp, with none of the fog that had covered the city since his return. As he walked up the hill towards Clifton he looked up at the stars and thought of the many nights at sea when he had watched the same night sky. What could he tell Sarah of the agony aboard ship for so many? The poverty experienced by many in Bristol did not seem to affect those more fortunate who lived close by. What hope did he have of persuading those same people of the immorality of a trade thousands of miles away?

On approaching the Jackson's home he began to lose his nerve. He walked past the house, trying to calm himself. Then, pulling his cloak tight about him as if to give himself moral strength, he walked briskly to the front door and rang without hesitation lest he should change his mind and walk away altogether. The door opened almost immediately and there, in the hall waiting to greet him, was Sarah.

'Richard. How wonderful to see you. Please come in.'

She held out her hands to him, and almost overcome with emotion, he took them. For a brief moment they stood looking at each other, arms outstretched, hands clasped. Then the formality of the hostess took over and withdrawing her hands she bade him give his cloak to the maid and ushered him into the drawing room. Richard felt his chest tightening when he saw several people already gathered in a group talking. But his eyes told him Joseph Terrill was not among them and he relaxed. Frank Jackson walked over to him.

'Richard, welcome. You are well I trust?'

'I am thank you sir. And yourself?'

'Well enough thank you. Allow me to introduce my other guests. I believe you already know Robert and Mary Harford? Richard bowed and in turn was introduced to Hugh and Elizabeth Berry and John and Joan Powell. Clearly a political gathering.

'I am much relieved to see you again, Richard,' said Robert Harford. 'We were fearful for your safety when Sarah told us of the nature of your voyage. There will be much more you can tell us.'

'Thank you. Yes it was a perilous trip. But one can come to as much harm here in Bristol.' The irony of this remark was lost on his audience. Richard was pleased by their interest and pleased, too, that Sarah had thought sufficiently of him to tell her friends the purpose of his voyage.

Yet despite his warm reception Richard could not relax. He found himself listening for other guests to arrive until he could contain himself no more. 'Are there any other guests coming this evening Mr Jackson?'

Sarah laughed and answered for him. 'No, Richard, your old sparring partner is not coming tonight.' She turned to the other guest. 'Richard used to enjoy arguing with Mr Terrill. But he wouldn't want to be among our number tonight.'

They all laughed, leaving Richard perplexed. Mary Harford saw his embarrassment and chided her husband. 'Robert, you forget that Richard has only recently returned. Richard, please forgive us for laughing at your expense. While you were away Sir Ralph Blackman died. A by-election is to take place in the New Year. Mr Terrill is the Tory candidate to succeed him. Robert is his only opponent that we know of and is standing as an independent Radical. We are virtually all there is of his election committee. We are the last people Mr Terrill would dine with at present.'

Richard looked at Sarah and tried to read her thoughts but without success. What did she think of the situation? Was her friendship with Terrill over, damaged beyond repair because of political differences? Or would she divorce politics from her personal life, wait until the election was over, and then resume her relationship with him? Richard could not decide in his own mind whether the news was pleasing to him or not. Terrill in London would be Terrill out of the way. Yet his elevated position if he were to win might make him an even more attractive suitor. Sarah's eyes gave him no clue. Perhaps she wanted to keep him guessing. Or perhaps she didn't know herself.

'Come now,' said Frank Jackson, 'no more election talk tonight. We are here for a quite different purpose. You should understand, Richard, that I am not on this election committee. Truth to tell, I'm not sure I sympathise with it. I cannot really understand why my daughter wants to be involved in politics at all. But her friends are most welcome to our house and she has invited them tonight to hear of your experiences. Perhaps over dinner you will enlighten us.'

And tell them he did. Not of his suspicions about Ben Jackson's death, but of the taking of slaves, their treatment aboard ship and the treatment of the crew, and of the slave auctions. They listened in respectful silence, interrupting occasionally to ask a question. Robert sat pensively, concentrating as if taking in every fact on offer. When Richard finished his account with the slave auctions, he asked for more.

'Richard, tell us if you will of your trip to Williamsburg. Of the mood of the colonists.'

'It is very clear that the feeling is mixed. No one point of view predominates. There are a number of local leaders advocating independence. But there are many wishing to maintain the link whatever the cost. They are mainly those with strong business connections with this country. Yet the majority is undecided and are waiting to see how things fall. They would like to maintain the link but wish our Parliament would behave better towards them and understand their point of view. In their minds, the question is wholly undecided. I believe our Parliament has it within it to settle the matter either way.'

'Excellent' said Hugh Berry. 'Just as we had hoped. Our campaign has a live issue on which to fight.'

'But it still needs funds,' cut in John Powell. 'Did you have any success raising money Richard?'

Richard felt some unease that the slavery issue seemed to have slid from view so quickly. He was determined to revive it if a suitable opportunity arose.

'I have a list of subscribers and the banks through which their pledges are to be honoured. Over £5,000 is being made available to you.'

There were audible gasps around the room.

'You have done extremely well Richard,' said Robert, 'I congratulate you. But unfortunately a problem has since arisen. It would be politically unwise to accept pledges from those who have no link with this country. I am sorry but some of the pledges must be declined. Can we do that?'

'Yes we can Robert. On that basis I would reckon that just less than one half would have to be refused.'

'Good,' said Robert. 'The amount left, added to our own funds, should still be just about enough. Now, I have one further favour to ask of you. It would help me immeasurably if you would be willing to campaign on my behalf. Speaking at meetings, helping write the literature, that kind of thing. A first hand eye witness account would be of great benefit.'

This was what Richard had wanted to hear. An active political role working alongside Sarah to oppose Joseph Terrill.

'I will gladly help you. I have kept a detailed account of life on a slave ship...'

Berry interrupted. 'No, not the slavery issue.'

'But I thought you were all against the trade in slaves?' Richard was perplexed and looked to Robert Harford for an explanation.

'That is true. But it is neither an election winner, nor even an issue at present. Quite the reverse. The public is not yet ready I fear. Only among the Quakers and Evangelicals is there much support. And I do not want to dilute my message. This by-election, if it is to have any national significance must be on the single issue of the link with the colonists. Introducing other issues, however worthy, will give the voters an excuse to support Terrill. And it will divert the publicity. We have a unique opportunity to bring the issue of the American Colonies to national prominence, unclouded by factional fighting on other issues.'

Richard had anticipated this reply but could not hide his disappointment.

When dinner was over and the ladies had withdrawn, Richard's sole preoccupation was how to speak to Sarah alone before the evening was over. But it was not to be. The ladies returned only when it was time for the guests to take their leave, and apart from a farewell as warm as the welcome had been, Sarah gave no clue as to her feelings. But at least the first meeting had taken place.

'Nicholas my boy, come in.'

Sir John Manners waved his son to a seat beside his desk and poured him a glass of sherry. Nicholas rarely entered his father's study. As a boy he had learned that this was where his father did his thinking and work and was not to be disturbed. Despite coming to manhood and sharing the burdens of the business he still regarded the study to be his father's domain, to be entered by invitation only. Such invitations were rare and a prelude to a business discussion. Today he was surprised to find his mother present also and tried without success to recall a previous occasion when she had been there with him.

'Good morning father. Mother.'

'Nicholas, your mother and I would like to discuss your future with you.'

This was it, thought Nicholas, now is the time I am to be sent to the plantation.

'You wish me to go to Virginia, father?'

'No. At least, not yet. We think you ought to be married first. It would be good for you to have a companion over there with you.'

'I see. At least I think I see.' He paused. 'No actually, I don't see at all. I am not about to be married, so, with respect, isn't it a little premature to talk about married life in Virginia?'

'That is exactly the point. An opportunity has arisen for you to make a splendid match.'

Nicholas struggled in his mind to know how to respond to this and eventually decided to remain silent. He looked at his mother but she sat still and expressionless. He could not gauge her thoughts. His father continued.

'You will know, Nicholas, that Samuel Oliphant also owns a plantation in Virginia and has sizeable investments in merchant shipping. Or rather, he and his sister do. Margaret Oliphant is twenty-three and owns half the business. Mr Oliphant has approached me about a union between our two families. I have been briefly introduced to Miss Oliphant and she seems a decent enough young woman, quite pretty in her own way.'

He stopped. Nicholas could see he was trying to judge his reaction before going any further.

'Father, I have not had the pleasure of meeting her but even if I had, I fear it unlikely I would be attracted to her....'

'Oh, come, come Nicholas don't let us have any of these new ideas. Families in our situation are best placed to arrange these things. Coming from a similar background I am sure you will find the union a comfortable one and I daresay affection and even love will grow. That is what usually happens. Look at your mother and I....'

'Forgive me for interrupting father, I have no wish to disappoint you or mother, but I am afraid I see things differently. Perhaps if I had been in the young lady's company for some time things may have been different. Anyway, what does Miss Oliphant think of the proposal?'

Nicholas watched as his father started drumming his fingers on the desk, a sign of rising impatience and anger.

'She has the good sense to be open about the suggestion. She relies on her brother's judgement in business matters, as you should rely on mine. Just think, there would be two plantations you could supervise while over there. I hope you are not going to disappoint your mother and I.'

Lady Manners remained silent and still Nicholas could read nothing in her expression. But he feared that if pressed she would side with his father. He decided not to offer her the opportunity.

'Father I am sorry I am going to disappoint you but I regard my choice of wife to be in no way connected to the business. I would naturally expect a wife to support me and be a credit to the family. My choice is likely to fall on someone who has those qualities. But I regret it is not possible for me to agree to your proposal.'

Sir John stood up, pushing his chair back with a violence that sent it crashing to the floor.

'I am afraid, Nicholas, I am not prepared to take that as your final answer. I suggest you give the matter further thought. Your mother and I are most disappointed at your reaction. We were expecting you to entertain the idea; we would then arrange a meeting, a dinner party perhaps, so that you could meet informally. I expect you to reconsider the matter. Good day to you sir.'

With a despairing glance towards his still inscrutable mother, Nicholas stood up and with a respectful nod towards his father, left the room.

Early on the first Saturday in the New Year, Richard and William left Bristol following the same path that Nancy had taken some months before. They were heading for the same cottage. Richard was determined to follow the lead given him by the barman at the Flying Angel, believing that if he could find Nancy he would find Abel Jacobs as well. It was a bitterly cold January morning; a light powdering of snow on the surrounding hills, and the track they were following heavily rutted yet rock hard, making walking dangerous. Both men wore heavy overcoats, and scarves muffled round their throats and mouths. Neither attempted to speak during the two hours it took to reach Pill.

They had no difficulty recognising the cottage Regan had described to them. William favoured keeping it under surveillance for a while but Richard saw no point in delay and finding the door unlocked pushed it half open.

'Is anyone there?' he called.

There was no reply. It was dark inside, save for the low glow of burning coals in a grate in a fireplace along one wall, and it took Richard some seconds to adjust. Gradually shapes began to appear, a table and some chairs underneath the window, some stairs leading to an upstairs room, and in the corner a pile of sacks. He called out again, this time a little louder.

'Hello. Is there anyone here?'

A small voice came from the pile of sacks. 'Who is it?'

'Is that you Nancy? It's me, Richard. Richard Stourton.'

A figure rose from the sacking. He recognised her at once, but she seemed puzzled and confused.

'Don't be frightened Nancy. I haven't come to take you away.'

'I thought you was dead.'

Richard smiled. 'No. I am very much alive. I returned to Bristol before Christmas.'

He turned to William. 'This is my friend William. He was with me on the ship and has come to help me.'

' 'Elp you do what?' Nancy sounded suspicious as well as uncomprehending.

Richard did not answer but looked towards the staircase. 'Is there anyone else here?'

'No, they are both out until tonight.'

'Is there a lamp we can light Nancy?' said Richard.

She walked over to the fireplace and taking a piece of burning wood lit a lamp hanging from a bracket on the wall. To Richard she seemed thinner than when he had last seen her and was very pale. Undernourished, he thought. She was still wearing only a thin shift, despite the cold, though the sacking that served as her bed no doubt kept her warm enough. She had probably been laying there for warmth rather than sleep.

'Do you live here now, Nancy?'

'Most times. 'Ee makes me.'

'Who? Abel Jacobs?'

Richard saw the look of fear in the girl's eyes. What sort of a hold did this man have over her? For all that she was little more than a child she had always struck Richard as being able to look after herself. Yet now she seemed too frightened to talk to him even though they were alone.

Richard crossed the room and sat at the table and motioned to Nancy to join him. 'Come and sit down and tell me all about it, Nancy,' he said.

William walked over to Nancy's bed and picked up two of the thick sacks and draped them round her shoulders. She smiled nervously at this small act of kindness. The three of them sat at the table, William and Richard at opposite ends, Nancy between. She started talking, hesitatingly and quiet at first.

'I couldn't get on at your friends 'ouse. I weren't used to that sort o' life. I ran away. I didn't take nothin' though. I ain't a thief. Least, not from friends o' yours.'

She looked anxiously at each of them in turn, but neither showed any sign of displeasure.

'I walked back to the Angel. Regan were cross I'd left 'im. 'Ee said I could only stay if I took messages to the smugglers, Jacobs mostly.'

She paused, as if surprised at how much she could say in one speech. The two men sat waiting patiently, recognising her self-consciousness. 'Go on, Nancy,' said Richard eventually, but gently.

'When I first came here, 'bout six months since, 'ee, that's Jacobs, well, 'ee wanted me. You know. I said I'd tell 'bout 'im smuggling. That stopped 'im. But next time I came here 'ee said I were to live 'ere, where 'ee could keep an eye on me. If I was to tell anyone what I know, he'd kill me.'

'Has he tried to force himself on you since?' asked William.

'No. 'Ee ain't interested no more. Gets 'is pleasure in Bristol now. I just look after this place and take messages.'

'Why don't you just run away?' said William.

''Ee'd come after me. I ain't got nowhere to go 'cept Bristol and he'd soon find me there.'

Richard felt sorry for the girl and angry that she had to put up with whatever life threw at her. He could see her condition was little better than slavery, that she would most likely spend her life at the bidding of men and end up drinking herself to death. That was the lot of so many young girls – early prostitution, solace in gin, then a premature end. He was tempted to take her away, but what effect would that have? And he already had Sam under his protection. He could not support her forever, and taking her away from her own class for a while would make her less able to manage, like a wild animal taken into captivity later to be released back into its natural surroundings. He could see from the expression on William's face that he, too, was moved by her plight. As he listened to her story, Richard wondered how much his interference had worsened her position. If he had not befriended her, would she be here in this cottage now? Probably not, but what would her life have been? No better, surely. Prostitution or starvation, the only alternatives for girls with no family to support them. Yet he had altered her life, whether for better or worse he was not sure. And so he felt involved.

'Nancy,' said Richard when she had finished, 'we would like to help you when we can. But we can't yet as there are other things we have to do first. We are looking for Jacobs. Can you tell me where we can find him?'

Nancy's eyes betrayed her alarm. 'You won't talk to 'im 'bout me?'

'No. I promise you we won't. I need to speak to him about something quite different.'

Nancy sat quiet for a moment, then seemed to reach a decision. 'There were a landing last night. Down at Portbury. Brandy and tobacco I think. 'Ee was there to take the stuff into 'iding. He'll be at the 'iding place now.

'Where is that Nancy?'

'Down Easton in Gordano way. There is a barn there on a farm where they 'ide it 'till its wanted.'

'Can you direct us there?'

'I ain't goin' there. I've been once an' I ain't goin' again. I don't want 'im to know we've been talkin'. I can tell you how to get there though.'

'That will do Nancy. We will find it ourselves.'

'That must be the place.' Richard caught hold of William's sleeve and pointed to a low-roofed barn at the edge of, and at right angles to, a farm courtyard. It was early afternoon and a fine rain was falling, warming the air but gradually seeping through the men's clothes. They had followed the route to Easton in Gordano as described by Nancy and had stopped at the only inn in the village for refreshment before the final part of the journey to the barn where Jacobs might be found. The farm lay about a mile west of the village on the Portishead road. The farmhouse itself was about a hundred yards from the road, along a rough track that led up to, then behind the house to a courtyard of low buildings.

No one disturbed them as they walked up the track and round the house but as they approached the courtyard a black and white sheepdog, which walked towards them, at first growling, then barking, revealed their presence. The noise brought two men out of the barn who stood at the door and stared at them.

'What do you think you're doing here?' one of the men shouted.

'I'm looking for Abel Jacobs,' shouted back Richard. 'Are you he?'

'No. Who wants him?'

'Stourton. Richard Stourton.'

By now Richard and William were almost at the barn door, sufficiently close for someone inside to hear and reply.

'All right, Pitts, I know who this is.'

A man strode out of the barn. 'I've been expecting you sooner or later Mr Stourton, but not here. How did you find me?'

Richard was not prepared to betray Nancy. 'I know my way round Marsh Street Mr Jacobs, and who to talk to. But we are not here to cause you trouble or expose your activities.'

Jacobs ignored this and looked towards William. 'And who is this?'

'My name is William Daniel, a ship's surgeon and a friend of Mr Stourton. We were recently at sea together.'

'Oh aye. I have heard about your voyage. A slaver weren't she?'

Richard nodded.

'Well,' said Jacobs,' best not stand out here. Too risky. Come inside.'

They followed him into the barn. Just inside the entrance was a large number of panniers and the two men who had first confronted Richard started shifting them to the back of the barn, behind some large hay bales and under a tarpaulin. Richard judged there to be about fifty panniers altogether, not counting any already hidden from view. Most of them were closed, concealing their contents, but the few that were open revealed smaller boxes and packets.

It was widely known how smugglers operated and apart from the excise men most turned a blind eye. Ships would unload their cargo at night, twenty or so donkeys would carry the goods to a safe haven – in this case the barn – and the smuggled goods would then be redistributed in smaller batches and sold to purchasers mainly in the Bristol area. Everyone involved in the landing would be paid, yet the goods would still be substantially cheaper than the lawfully imported produce upon which import duties were levied.

'What would you be wanting me for then Mr Stourton?' asked Jacobs. Richard's thoughts were jolted back to the task in hand.

'You are a client of Lawrence Willoughby's I believe?'

Jacobs spat, then smirked. 'I have given him a little business, yes.'

'As a result of his help you avoided the gallows and went to sea.'

Jacobs stood waiting, showing no inclination to answer further. Richard continued.

'According to the records one of the ships you sailed on was the *Demera*.'

'Aye,' said Jacobs. 'But she foundered and is now at the bottom of the sea.'

Jacob's companions took no interest in the exchanges and were out of sight now behind the hay bales.

'Mr Jacobs I am interested in finding out who owned her.'

'Are you now. And why might that be?' Jacobs spoke mockingly, as if he realised he had information that was valuable to someone. He sneered. 'Didn't the records office tell you that?'

But the conversation got no further. The dogs started barking again, then six men burst into the barn brandishing pistols pointed at Richard and his two companions. There was no response from Jacobs and no sound from the two men behind the hay bales. One of the armed men stepped forward.

'We are excise officers and in the name of His Majesty I am arresting all three of you on a charge of smuggling.'

Jacobs glowered at Richard. 'You young fool, you were followed.'

He spat on the ground again but made no move to escape. Richard knew there was nothing he could say that would help the situation. He was implicated in a serious crime and what was worse, had involved William. He realised immediately how foolish he had been to come here.

The two men at the back of the barn remained undetected and it was with deep embarrassment and humility that Richard, together with William Daniel and Abel Jacobs, was taken back to Bristol to be locked up in Newgate gaol. After they had gone, Pitts and his companion walked back to Pill and told Nancy what had happened.

Richard woke early. It was the rats rustling in the straw that woke him. He turned his head to look round but it was too dark to make out anything but two shapes, William and Jacobs, who, like Richard, were curled up on straw bedding, sacks over them to keep warm. The cell was but a few square feet. It was damp and smelled of stale urine and rats. He shivered and drew the sacking up around his shoulders. He felt depressed. Not because of the physical deprivations, he could cope with that. Nearly a year at sea had hardened him. No, as he lay there he felt that everything he had touched had broken in his hands. Now to add to his growing list of misfortunes he was in gaol, a humiliation in front of his friends. The reaction of Lawrence Willoughby didn't bear thinking about. And he had dragged William into the same plight. Was there no end to his misery? Yet it had all been for the best possible motives. Or had it? Was that why it had all gone wrong? Was he genuinely concerned for the slaves, or the future of the colonists, or even for finding out who murdered Ben Jackson? Or was he deluding himself, merely seeking to increase his esteem in Sarah's eyes?

As the grey of dawn began to penetrate the cell, so his mind cleared and his depression lifted a little. It was no use bemoaning their situation; he must do something about it. He was innocent of smuggling and must fight the false charges.

He stood up and walked the few steps to the cell door to bring life back into his cold limbs. His two companions stirred. Jacobs looked round, realised where he was, and turned over to resume his sleep. William got up and walked over to Richard.

'How are you feeling, Richard?'

'Wretched. Not in body. Wretched for involving you in this.'

'Nonsense. It is not your fault. I didn't have to go with you. Anyway, we are here now and must make the best of it. And the first problem is breakfast.'

He took hold of the bars of the cell door and shook them. 'Anyone there?' he shouted.

A voice sounded, some distance away, followed by footsteps on the stone stairs that led down to their cell. The gaoler, a thickset man with the jaundiced look of someone who sees insufficient daylight, stood before them holding an oil lamp.

'What're ye hollerin' about?'

'I have some money here,' said William, 'it's yours if you can find us some breakfast.'

The gaoler nodded and turned back up the stairs.

'You seem to know what to do William,' said Richard, 'have you been in gaol before?'

William laughed. 'No, but money will buy a crust of bread anywhere. Gaol is no exception. In places like this if you've no money you don't eat.'

Within minutes the gaoler returned with enough bread and beer to satisfy three hungry men, and William paid the expected price. From his mattress Jacobs had watched the negotiations in silence but willingly joined in for his share. The meal revived their spirits.

'How do we get out of this situation, Richard?' asked William.

'We must find a way to send a message to Mr Willoughby. Much as I dread him knowing what has happened, he will be the person to know what to do.'

Jacobs snorted. 'Ye'll be lucky to get out of this. We will all hang more'n likely. I've a good mind to do for ye myself, leading the excise on like that.'

'You don't know that we did,' said Richard, with little conviction.

' Course you did. I 'xpect they had informers in Marsh Street and you talked too much 'bout what you was doin' and led them straight to us. Caught red handed we were. There be no way out for us now.'

He sat down on his mattress and put his head in his hands. Richard was disturbed by the finality of Jacob's opinion. He knew that smuggling carried severe penalties and was sorry he had interfered. Jacobs might not deserve better he thought, but he regretted he was the instrument of the man's arrest nonetheless.

Jacobs looked up again. 'Anyway, you never finished tellin' me what you wanted to know about the *Demera*.'

'I wanted to ask you if you knew who owned the ship.'

'Well I reckon it don't matter much tellin' you now. It were owned by a company run by a couple of local councillors.'

'Who were they?'

'Joseph Terrill and James Walter.'

'Are you sure?'

'As sure as I'm a dead man.'

Richard looked across at William. Neither spoke, each nursing his own thoughts. Richard lay down on his mattress and stared at the ceiling, all thoughts of his present situation temporarily banished. How did this piece of information fit into the collection of facts that he now had? A Whig Mayor and a soon to be Tory MP in the slave trade together. Their ship sinking but before it does so slaves are thrown overboard to drown. Another prominent Whig Councillor finds this out and is murdered. Why? Surely they were not worried about their business activities becoming public knowledge? It was not illegal to deal in slaves, nor even reprehensible in most people's eyes. There must be some other reason. But what was it? He looked across at William, but he had curled up again and seemed to be in a deep sleep. Jacobs sat motionless on his bed of straw, head once again in his hands. I must watch out for him, Richard thought. If his mood changes from despair to anger, it will be directed against me.

But Richard did not have long to worry or to wonder. Shortly before ten o'clock he heard a familiar heavy tread coming down the steps and soon the robust figure of Lawrence Willoughby came into view followed by the gaoler. The lawyer walked straight up to the cell and without looking towards Richard, grasped the bars and called out.

'Jacobs.'

Jacobs looked up and stared sullenly at the visitor.

'Abel, come over here.'

Jacobs slowly rose and ambled over, saying nothing.

Willoughby pressed his face close to the bars. 'I want a word with you. The gaoler has agreed we can talk alone for a few minutes. He has locked the upper door, so don't try to escape.'

The gaoler unlocked the door letting Jacobs out and locking it again behind him. Jacobs and Willoughby disappeared into an empty cell nearby. A quarter of an hour later the process was repeated, but in reverse. When Jacobs was secure back in his cell, Willoughby turned away and dragged himself back up the stairs. Not a word, or even a glance had passed from the lawyer to Richard. It was as if Jacobs had been the cell's only occupant. Richard felt too humiliated to call after his employer, and clearly Jacobs was not going to offer an explanation. He just lay on his back and turned his face to the wall.

'Who was that?' enquired William.

'My employer, Lawrence Willoughby.'

'Methinks your former employer,' replied William.

'I fear so.'

❖ ❖ ❖

'Wake up and come with us.'

Richard was not aware of having fallen asleep, but his fob watch showed it was noon, some two hours since Willoughby had come and gone. Outside the cell the gaoler and three constables waited. The prisoners filed out and under escort followed the gaoler down a long corridor that led away from the steps down which they had originally come. The stone floor echoed to their footsteps and the occasional candles affixed to the wall threw large flickering shadows down its length. After following the passage for twenty yards or so they came to another set of stone steps, which this time they ascended. This led them out into the street from where it was but a short walk to the magistrates' court.

Richard had been in the court before in a professional capacity but this was the first time he had seen it from the vantage point of an accused. How different it seemed, and how noisy. In front of the dock sat two rows of lawyers talking with an exaggerated boisterousness. To his left he could see the press bench, occupied by two red-faced scribes taking it in turns to drink from a bottle of whisky only half concealed. And to his right, and behind, the public benches crammed full as usual with relatives of those charged, with vagrants looking for warmth and shelter, but mostly with the curious and interested bystanders for whom a visit to the courts is an opportunity for entertainment in otherwise grey and hard lives. He had heard many times before the shouting and ribaldry from the public benches and had taken no notice. Now they seemed there just to mock him and he found their presence intrusive and offensive.

The raised dais at the front of the court was presently empty. The magistrate had retired, for his glass of whisky Richard guessed, but within a minute or so an usher appeared through a door behind the magistrate's chair and called for silence and for the court to rise. In these requests he was only partially successful. The legal benches heeded the injunction and the journalists concealed their bottle. The public benches gave only partial support. The babble, cross-chat and laughter continued, but quieter. On the whole, Richard thought, the usher's words had been worthwhile.

Richard had now acclimatised and the figures around him began to take on shapes he recognised. Most of the lawyers he knew, and he recognised the back and head of Lawrence Willoughby sitting motionless on the front bench.

The magistrate came in and after exchanging bows of respectful greetings with the lawyers as if acknowledging mutual membership of a secret club, sat down. Richard knew the magistrate to be Samuel Hopkins, a local vintner, and a man not known to be sympathetic to smugglers.

When all had settled down the usher formally identified the three prisoners, who acknowledged their names and addresses, and put the charges to them. Before they had an opportunity to respond, Willoughby was on his feet.

'May it please you sir, I represent all three accused.'

Richard could not help smiling to himself. Trust Willoughby to assume his instructions without a word to himself or William. He listened with interest to what his lawyer was going to say.

'When this matter comes to trial my client Jacobs will plead guilty. Stourton and Daniel will not. Their defence will be that they were innocent bystanders arrested by mistake. I am content for Jacobs to remain in custody but seek bail for the other two.'

The magistrate looked surprised. 'It is unusual, Mr Willoughby, to seek bail on a charge as serious as this. You must convince me there are extenuating circumstances and that there are sureties available.'

'Of course.' Willoughby bowed. Deference never harmed an application Richard remembered his principal had once told him.

'Your worship,' Willoughby continued, 'the defendant Stourton is a trainee attorney, Daniel a ship's surgeon. Both respectable young men with no previous convictions.' He paused whilst the magistrate stared at the dock trying to make up his own mind about their respectability. Willoughby knew the secret of securing the magistrate's undivided attention and waited until his gaze turned back towards him.

'They were looking for the defendant Jacobs to seek information on a quite different matter. I have a witness, a serving girl, who can testify if required that she directed Stourton and Daniel to the third, Jacobs.'

'It won't be necessary to call her, Mr Willoughby.'

Willoughby bowed again. 'I am obliged. Jacobs can also testify to the truth of this.'

The magistrate looked across at the dock. 'Abel Jacobs. Are you able to confirm this?'

Jacobs spoke in a quiet and resigned way. 'Aye, your worship. They were nothing to do with it.'

'Thank you. Mr Willoughby, do you have sureties?'

Willoughby turned round and gestured to the back of the courtroom. Richard followed his gaze. Working their way through the concourse of people were Frank Jackson and Robert Harford. Then he saw Sarah, sitting in the corner of the back row. Their eyes met and she bowed slightly in recognition.

Sureties sworn, Richard and William were soon released but Jacobs was remanded in custody until his trial at the next assize. Richard watched him disappear through the trapdoor from the dock and wondered whether he would ever have the chance of thanking him for helping secure his freedom.

Once outside the courthouse Richard gave William the key to his lodgings and bade him return there for food and a bath while he went for the inevitable confrontation with Willoughby. There were others he would have to thank, but Frank Jackson and Robert Harford had disappeared. Richard appreciated their tact in not adding to his embarrassment at the present time.

Steggles was waiting for him in Willoughby's room. 'I am very pleased to see you sir. Mr Willoughby was most concerned about you.'

'Concerned?' repeated Richard 'Very angry I dare say.'

On this point he was correct. Willoughby arrived a few minutes later, threw his cloak at Steggles and told him to go away and close the door behind him. The clerk was only too willing to oblige. Without a word Willoughby pointed Richard to a chair and started pacing up and down the room muttering to himself and clearly trying to retain his self-control. Richard had thought through this scene many times whilst languishing in gaol, but still did not know how to handle it. All he could grasp was that if he could engage his principal in prolonged conversation, the anger would begin to abate.

'I am truly sorry for...' But he got no further.

'I don't want an apology,' bellowed the lawyer, 'I want an explanation!' He stopped pacing about and walking up to Richard's chair held the back of it with fists tight, knuckled white. 'You have made this firm a laughing stock, humiliated me and embarrassed your friends, our former clients. I doubt you will be a welcome guest at their houses any longer. They stood surety only as a personal favour to me.'

Richard doubted the truth of this last remark, but recognised the lawyer's wish to be seen as the one who sorted out the mess. But Willoughby was not finished.

'I took you in when your father died, and set you on the path to a worthwhile career. I had hoped to see you take over my practice when I retire. And how do you repay me?' His voice rose as his anger grew. 'By going off in a slaver in order to threaten the livelihood of hundreds of people in this city. Now you are arrested on a smuggling charge alongside Abel Jacobs.'

He stopped, a thick silence between them as Richard struggled frantically to think how to divert Willoughby's train of thought.

'How did you find out so quickly where I was?' he asked.

Willoughby tutted his impatience. 'It is not important, but it was the child, the girl Nancy who came to find me. She must have run all the way from Pill. I found her exhausted on the doorstep. Why she should have troubled on your account I do not know. She didn't know where you had been taken of course but it was not difficult for me to find you. I then sent Steggles to seek assistance from Frank Jackson. I am led to believe that Sarah Jackson involved Robert Harford. Apparently he knows you. So I suppose you have been involved in politics as well without telling me.'

Richard said a silent prayer for Nancy. 'And Jacobs? How did you persuade him to cooperate?'

Willoughby perhaps realised that Richard was flattering him, talking of his efforts on his behalf and Richard could tell from the tenor of his voice that his anger was abating.

'That was not difficult. He is facing the death penalty. I told him so. That if he did not help you I would let him hang. With my assistance he may be transported to the American Colonies instead. His admission of guilt and speaking the truth about you will be mitigating factors.'

'What are his chances?'

'Less than even. He has a bad record. That haul in the barn was substantial, suggesting a highly organised gang at work. Apparently there were others who escaped detection. Presumably it was they who alerted Nancy.'

Willoughby was calming down now, like a flood river that reaches its peak then silently subsides.

'What should I do now?' Richard asked.

'Nothing. You have done enough already. I blame you for the plight of your friend Daniel. The charges have not been dropped yet but I am hopeful that they will be. The prosecution must realise that no jury would convict you. Just keep out of the way for a few days. I would like some peace and quiet to sort this out and no doubt you could do with some rest.'

But Willoughby did not see his wish fulfilled nor did Richard gain more than a few hours rest. Within twenty-four hours of Richard's release on bail, the by-election was called and campaigning began in earnest. On the following day news came that Abel Jacobs had escaped from custody.

~ CHAPTER 13 ~

The news that the by-election had been called came in a note from Sarah. It was brief and formal. It told him that polling would take place between 1st and 14th March and that so far only two candidates, Joseph Terrill and Robert Harford, had declared themselves. There was no warmth in her message, no invitation to call or take part in the campaign. Richard longed to see her but felt constrained from doing so. Instead he sent a formal response thanking her for the message and making himself available to help if required.

The two weeks following his arrest was a bleak period for him. His relationship with Willoughby was brittle, formal to the point of coldness. Neither man had been willing to take the first step towards reconciliation, Willoughby through pride, Richard through shame. They worked closely together as always, but the old intimacy had gone. Richard understood the older man's disappointment in him but felt unable to console him. He decided that time must be the healer.

Of Nancy there was no word. Richard did not return to the cottage at Pill or to Marsh Street. He would have liked to have thanked her for her part in securing his early release from gaol but felt that his intervention in her life had on the whole been to her detriment. Jacobs, too, had disappeared. The authorities had assumed he had fled the country and appeared to have no desire to bring him back.

The only comfort for him at this time was the continued presence of William. He showed no inclination to return to Gloucester, or to leave Richard's lodgings. His departure was never discussed. While Richard was at work, William himself was out, looking for his next ship, Richard assumed, although he would not be able to sail until his bail terms had been lifted.

But as the New Year brings new hopes, so those hopes are sometimes fulfilled. One morning in late January Willoughby appeared at the door of Richard's room, an event unusual in itself, for it was Richard who was normally expected to make the short journey along the corridor between their offices. Richard stood up and waited.

'You are a fortunate young man, Richard.' Richard remained silent, knowing he was expected neither to confirm nor deny the statement. Willoughby continued.

'The proceedings against you and your friend are to be dropped. You will both be required to attend the assizes in February when the Judge will direct the Grand Jury to dismiss the charges.'

Although this news was expected, Richard was nevertheless reassured. 'I am very pleased, of course,' he said. 'And most grateful to you for the part you have played in this. Perhaps when you have some time to spare I could tell you the whole story.'

Willoughby crossed the room and sat down close to Richard's desk. 'I think now would be as good a time as any, Richard.'

So that was it, Richard thought. The reason for Willoughby's coldness was not just the impending court case but also the feeling he was keeping something from him. And so, over a year after Ben Jackson's death, Richard told him the whole story, starting with the letter amongst the dead man's papers, through to his recent arrest. He told of his ineffective attempt to help Nancy: of his relationship with Sarah; and of his meeting with Amos Kettle in Virginia. And of Abel Jacobs, and the allegation that Joseph Terrill and James Walter owned the *Demera* and were possibly involved in fraud. Finally he told him of Sam and the unpleasant conversation with Sir John Manners. Willoughby listened in silence, his solemn countenance showing his concentration. When he had finished, Richard sat back watching the lawyer's expression, waiting for a reaction that took some minutes to come, slowly and cautiously. But when it came, it surprised him.

'Your case is by no means complete, Richard. You have no convincing evidence of the ownership of the *Demera*. And what if you did? You can prove nothing. A page torn out of an official record. A beating by footpads. A verbal statement from a wanted criminal who is most probably abroad. None of this offers a shred of evidence that Ben Jackson was murdered other than by common thieves.'

Richard leaned across the desk, relieved that Willoughby had decided to think about the problem rather than his own behaviour. 'Do you think I should forget all about it? If only I could find a motive.'

'A motive? That will not be difficult to provide.'

Richard looked at him with surprise. 'You know then?'

'No I don't. But I can make a very good guess. Insurance. That is the key. It is likely that the slaves were insured against natural calamities but not against their wilful destruction, which is what was committed when they were thrown overboard. You told me you were the third person in the last few months to search the records of the ship owners. I think you were right to believe that Ben Jackson was probably the first. Whoever tore the page out was the second visitor, and you were the third.'

Richard sat back, breathing excitedly. That must be it, he thought. A false insurance claim which Ben Jackson found out about, probably in Marsh Street, and for which he paid the ultimate price. Now he had another line of investigation to follow.

'Do you think the details of the insurance claim are recorded somewhere?'

'I expect so,' answered Willoughby, 'but do you think it wise to continue? I think your conclusion that Joseph Terrill and James Walter killed Ben to silence him is preposterous. But suppose it was true. You would yourself be in a perilous position. You have been attacked once and were saved by a lucky intervention. Next time may be different.' He paused for a moment. 'Having a theory is of no benefit without facts to support it. Amos Kettle is abroad, so too is Abel Jacobs if he knows what is good for him. Mere ownership of the *Demera* proves nothing. Your voyage, the dangers you faced at sea and now back home, have all been for nothing.'

Richard shook his head in disappointment. 'With respect, I see things differently. From a legal point of view your analysis is correct. But I am trying to solve a murder. That requires a different approach. I must search out the facts, and to know where to look I need to start from a motive. You have provided me with one.'

Richard surprised himself with the strength of his response, arguing with the one person to whom he usually deferred. He understood Willoughby's view of events. Lawyers tended to take a detached view of the world. They watched events, saw the traps people fell into, and tried to avoid them themselves. They worked on the margin of society, arguing whatever case their clients required. They did not need to take a consistent or even moral stand on anything.

But he knew that Willoughby was right about one thing. His mission to bring Ben Jackson's murderer to justice would fail without evidence. He had none on which he could rely. Yet having established a plausible motive, perhaps he could look in the right direction for supporting facts. He knew he had made up his mind. He would go on.

'Thank you for your opinion, which is very helpful. What you say about lack of evidence is of course right, and is my central problem. But I am not prepared to give up yet. I would appreciate your help in tracing the insurance records. If no fraud can be proved I promise to give up. You have my word on that.'

Richard saw the beginning of a smile at the corners of Willoughby's mouth, though it was soon smothered.

'I accept that, my boy, and I will help you. Give me a day or so to make some enquiries. As for that Negro boy you have befriended, let's see what Sir John does about it. There could be some awkward legal issues here.'

Without waiting for a response, and breathing heavily, he pulled himself out of his chair and walked slowly from the room.

Later that day a letter was delivered to Richard by hand. It was from Robert Harford. He eagerly tore it open.

> *Congratulations.*
>
> *I am delighted the charges against you and your friend have proved unfounded and are to be dropped. I would be most grateful if you would join my election committee. Perhaps you would speak of your American experiences at one or two meetings.*
>
> *S. sends her regards.*
>
> *Robert*

Richard's capacity for despair when things went wrong was matched by his ability to build success on the slimmest evidence and the inclusion of a message from Sarah doubled his pleasure at his reconciliation with Robert Harford. The renewal of a degree of intimacy with Willoughby, Harford, and Sarah all on one bleak January day put him in an exuberant mood. He scribbled a hasty acknowledgement and resolved to call on the candidate the following evening.

His good humour had not abated by the evening and William added his congratulations at the turn of events.

'I am delighted for you Richard. Truth will out.'

Richard was not so sure. 'Truth about our wrongful arrest yes. But I am no nearer solving the murder.'

William smiled, his eyes twinkling. 'Can you take more good news in one day?'

Richard looked at his friend whose face betrayed he had a secret to tell. 'What is it William? Have you found work?'

'Gracious, no. In truth I have not much been looking for work these few days since. But I have found what I was looking for. I have found Nancy.'

William calmly leaned forward and lit a pipe, eyeing Richard as he did so to enjoy the reaction. Richard, struck dumb, stared in disbelief for a few seconds. Then both men started laughing.

'Is that true William?' Richard asked. 'You have really found her? For goodness sake, tell me all about it.'

William sat back, smoking contentedly. Richard could see he was going to make the most of his story but he didn't mind that. It was a day that had changed the course of events and he was in no hurry to end it. If his friend wanted to tell his story at length then he was prepared to listen. He too lit a pipe... and waited.

'When I first came here, Richard, I was keen to secure another berth. My reason for lodging with you was quite genuine on that count. Having no close family I can move when and where I want. But after a week or so it became clear there was little work around. I visited all the shipping agents, to no avail. The problems with the American Colonies are having an effect on trade and the French, of course, are happy to make mischief and take our markets.

'I soon realised the agents had nothing for me so I decided to make a direct approach. I knew where the captains and mates spent their time, and there I went. I must have frequented upwards of a dozen pubs. Just being there, listening to the conversation, joining in occasionally. Nothing to frighten them off, you understand. Many's the fortune I have been offered at cards and many's the time I was almost tricked into signing up for a slaver. But deckhand is not for me, nor do I want another slave ship. Surgeon or tally clerk on a regular merchant vessel, why that would be fine, but I was not offered that chance.'

He stopped to refill his pipe. Richard silently applauded the dramatic effect of the pause before he reached the critical point of his story. To spur him on Richard poured him a sherry. William held his glass up to Richard and they offered each other a silent toast. The surgeon continued his story.

'One afternoon I fell into conversation with some seamen in a tavern in Victoria Street, the Shakespeare I believe it is called. I had met these men before. They had no suspicion of me and talked amongst themselves most freely. The subject turned to smuggling. Imagine my surprise when one of them mentioned he knew a man named Pitts who he believed had been in the barn when "Abel and that lawyer were took." Those were his words.

'As you would expect I listened carefully to the conversation as it developed. It seems that the man Pitts lives in the cottage at Pill where we found Nancy. There is a customs house near the cottage, supposedly to keep an eye open for smugglers in the Gorge. Well, the joke is that Pitts keeps an eye on them, the excise men. All part of the dangerous game.

'" Is that where the girl Nancy lives?" says I, trying to sound calm. They were a little suspicious, but I had to risk that before the conversation turned away from the subject. They looked at me a bit canny like. "How do you know that?" one of them asked. "Oh" I replied, "it is common knowledge that the girl ran half the night from Pill to Bristol to tell the young man's lawyer about the arrest."

This satisfied them but I had to be careful.

"Aye," one of them said, "she used to live in Pitts cottage. Kept Abel's bed warm so I'm told." They all laughed. I was not best pleased to hear these words but managed to control my feelings.

"And where is she now?" I asked.

"Want to take her now Abel's gone?" the sailor said, and they all laughed again. I joined in the joke, much against my true feelings. "No," I said, "just curious."

"She's been seen down St Phillips," the sailor went on, " a bit of skivvying in a pub down there for a crust of bread and a bed. Does a bit of washing up, that sort of thing." He didn't seem too clear about it so I didn't press him and resolved to go to St Phillips myself.'

He stopped for a few draws on his pipe. Richard was so engrossed in the story that the events of the day were temporarily blotted out from his mind. He was surprised how talkative William had become. He remembered him aboard ship as a man of few words, knowing how to keep out of trouble, to look after himself. Now, away from the sea, he was acting quite out of character, putting himself in the way of danger and judging by the length of his narrative, quite enjoying the experience. And he seemed to Richard to have become more personally involved than would be expected.

The ritual delay over, William resumed. 'There are a great many drinking houses in St Phillip's I can tell you and I visited most of them. I didn't go in asking for Nancy for I neither wanted to frighten her away nor put her into any danger. I used my job-hunting as a reason to be seen in unfamiliar haunts.

'There were a lot of young girls working in a large number of public houses and after a while I began to doubt whether I would recognise her. You will recall I met her only the once. But then, one lunchtime, I saw her, in the Albatross in Albion Street. I had been there nigh on two hours and was all for giving up when she came out through a door behind the serving bar and started clearing away empty tankards. It happened I was sitting alone with a few empty glasses in front of me and eventually she reached my table and started clearing up without so much as a glance in my direction.

"Nancy," I whispered. Richard, you should have seen the look on that girl's face. She jumped, startled, then looked down at me. I could tell immediately she knew who I was. "What do you want?" she half whispered.

"Can we talk?" I said. She started wiping the table.

"Not here. They are watching me the whole time," she said.

"When and where then?" I asked her.

"I don't know," she replied. "I'm here most nights. Come again and I will think of something. Don't bring him though," -that's you, Richard, - "they'd know who he was." They were her exact words.

'With that she moved away, giving equal attention to the other tables. I tell you, Richard, she was mighty frightened. I don't know whether anyone was watching her then, but I am sure no one suspected anything.'

'You have done well, William,' said Richard, 'I thought we had lost her for good. The poor girl must be half scared to death. We must take her away from all this.'

William smiled. 'Your first attempt wasn't very successful, was it? You can't just uproot the girl and set her down somewhere else and expect her to fend alone in new surroundings. This is her world. She has come back to it despite all its horrors. She knows no other life.'

The two men smoked in silence for a while both lost in their own thoughts. Richard still felt a responsibility towards Nancy, and now gratitude too, but saw no immediate means of improving her lot. He noticed William smiling to himself from time to time, but his friend said nothing.

'Perhaps Sarah will have some idea of what to do for her,' said Richard at last.

'Perhaps,' replied William.

'Your thoughts seem to be elsewhere, William.'

'Not really. Still with Nancy. I was wondering how we could arrange a meeting with her that would not endanger her. I presume you would like to?'

'Yes, I must continue what I have started. Nancy may know where Jacobs can be found. I need to have sworn testimony from him. I will probably see Sarah tomorrow when I meet Robert.'

'Mother, you said nothing.'

Nicholas knew from her silence that his mother understood that he was referring to his father's attempt to choose him a wife.

He and Lady Manners were riding to Bristol together, he with the reins, his mother sitting silently staring at the countryside as if she had not seen it before. It was the first time they had been alone together since the meeting. Sir John had not spoken to him since and his mother said little. Whether she too was angry with him or out of deference to her husband he could not tell. She did not respond to his prompting.

'Are we going to live in silence, mother?'

She turned to look at him, a weak smile barely illuminating her face.

At last she spoke: 'There is more to it than you told your father, isn't there?'

'He didn't ask, Mother, and I had no wish to add to his disappointment. But how did you know?'

'Mothers know these things. A change in the way you and Julia talk to each other. Secret smiles. A mother notices. A father rarely does.'

'Would you be opposed to such a match?'

'Please don't ask, Nicholas. Of course I want to see my children happy but I have a duty to your father and to the family. Does Jane know?'

'I think not. I have said nothing and Julia would not commit herself until her brother returned. But now we have this wretched business with the slave boy.'

'Has she told Richard?'

'No. She was going to but the row that blew up over Sam made it impossible for her to do so. She had no wish to put the dilemma on Richard's shoulders. He would either have to give the boy back to appease father, or hold on to him knowing he was damaging his sister's prospects.'

'You know she is penniless?'

'I do. And that matters not at all. It is not her fault. She is refined, well educated, and has seen at close hand what will be expected of me in the business. I believe she would make me happy.'

'I will not be disloyal to your father, but let things be for a while. Perhaps the situation with the slave boy will be resolved. Let Julia tell Jane though. She is entitled to know. But not a word to your father.'

Nicholas realised that was as close to support he could expect from his mother and was content to let the subject drop.

Bristol Daily 15th February 1772

We who are hundreds in number wish it to be known on the eve of this by-election to return a new Member of Parliament, that it is the wish of many in this City to bring change in our representation.

We sincerely wish that the gentlemen who are privileged to vote will pay the more serious attention to the peace and welfare of the City of Bristol than is offered by the Tory candidate. Such a conduct is more than especially necessary at this time. Our trade is greatly suffering, and causing much distress among the citizens, which makes every lover of this country and City fear the return of the disturbances and commotions which we experienced on a former occasion.

We must look to the wellbeing of our City that is so dependent upon trade and commerce. We must however, express our warmest wishes that such a member may be returned as shall contribute to the commercial interests and ably support the wellbeing of this great City.

Upon this occasion we cannot but congratulate our fellow citizens for declaring the candidacy of a gentleman whose extensive connection in trade, and knowledge of the commercial interests of this city, exceed our highest expectations.

We are delighted to hear it is intended to nominate Councillor Robert Harford as our candidate.

That he may be well supported is the united wish of
HUNDREDS OF CITIZENS

◆ ◆ ◆

Bristol Daily, 16th February 1772

Very many of the Bristol traders of the City present their compliments to the friends of Councillor Robert Harford and wish to assure them that it is not the general wish that he be our representative in Parliament. Having felt the ill effects of contested elections, we believe it is right that the agreement of the two great parties of state reached many years ago to share representation is in the best interests of the citizens of Bristol. We urge our citizens to return a Tory to replace our late beloved member in accordance with the current agreement.

◆ ◆ ◆

Bristol Daily, 17th February 1772

What kind of traders those are, who have the assurance to declare that we would wish to return a Tory to parliament whose policies would be a continuation of the late member's and whose party would alienate still further those in the American Colonies with whom the merchants of Bristol would wish to trade?

'A good blow to us, Richard, don't you think?' As he put the papers down, Jeremy Sly had a twinkle in his eye and a broad smile that Richard found hard to understand.

'I confess I am not a politician, Mr Sly. It seems that Terrill's men have framed an adequate reply.' Richard looked again at the newspapers as if expecting an explanation to jump off the pages.

Sly laughed. 'That is the point. The electors do not perceive what is happening, yet we will have gained their interest. First of all we have dealt with the need to have a contest at all. That was always going to be a problem for us. By tackling it now the question should be forgotten in a few days. The Tories can't run it for three weeks or more. Second, we have put the issue of the American Colonies at the forefront of our campaign. It is our strongest issue and Terrill's weakest. And with all due modesty, you will have noticed our candidate's name mentioned twice, Terrill's not at all.'

'I see I have a lot to learn, Mr Sly. In what way can I be of assistance?'

Richard's visit to Robert Harford had found the candidate and his supporters deep in election strategy under the skilled tuition of the election agent. Sarah was of their number, and apart from Mary Harford, was the only woman present. The desk in Harford's study, and the floor for several feet around it, was strewn with newspapers, pamphlets and assorted papers. Evidence, Richard thought, of an election being fought without the backing of the Whig Party. He had been greeted warmly enough by all present including Sarah, who made no mention of his embarrassment of being arrested. Richard understood that there was only one subject of importance now, to secure votes for their champion. There would be no opportunity to discuss his own affairs or Nancy.

'There are many things you can do to help, Richard,' said Sly. 'Visiting a number of public houses is the most important.'

Richard felt his neck and cheeks tense and redden, as he believed Sly to be joking at his expense, but his discomfiture was soon relieved.

'At election time,' the agent explained, 'there are Whig houses and there are Tory houses. The publicans fly the appropriate party flag and the party's candidate is expected to pay for drinks and provide polling money to the customers to make sure they vote. That's what makes elections so expensive, even if uncontested, for the publicans will not deliver their customers unless these expenses are paid.'

'You want me to deliver the payments?'

'Not at this stage. We know the Whig landlords, but do not know which of them will support Robert rather than follow the party lead and support Terrill. That is what I would like you to find out. John Powell has the list.'

'How many voters are there?'

'As far as we can tell about two thousand five hundred, but I hope to double that by the close of poll.'

'How can you do that?'

'Well, there are many potential freemen who have not registered. Some live away from Bristol, or are sons of freemen provided they were born in the city. And there will be many widows or daughters of freemen who have remarried or are about to. Their husbands are entitled to vote by virtue of their marriage. Your job, Richard, is to help me find them.'

'Can these new freemen vote if the ballot has started before they are registered?'

'Most certainly they can. There was an argument about this in the 1734 election but it came to nothing. To make sure we will persuade the first new freeman to vote for Mr Terrill. He won't then be able to object.'

'What about existing freemen?'

'Many have no party loyalties and can be persuaded.'

'How do we do that? By presenting our case to each of them in turn?'

'Not exactly. By paying their expenses. The current rate is 7s 6d plus refreshments which I will provide.'

'Isn't that illegal?'

'Both parties do it. And the electorate won't complain as they are the beneficiaries.'

Robert Harford was listening to this lesson on modern politics with mild amusement. Richard now turned to him

'And, Robert, the public meetings? You mentioned me speaking at one or two which I am willing to do.'

'Yes, public meetings too. I have some planned already. It would be good if you were to speak before I do. About your American experiences.'

'Yes of course. I should be delighted to.'

'And nothing about slavery?

'Nothing,' Richard promised, with a note of disappointment.

'Richard, some bad news I am afraid.' Lawrence Willoughby was standing at his desk as Richard went in for his morning meeting. 'Sir John Manners has issued a writ against you for the return of the slave boy. I fear you have a nasty High Court action on your hands. It could be ruinously expensive for you if you lose.'

'I'll not give him back,' said Richard sharply.

'Calm down, my boy, I am not going to suggest that you do. I am just suggesting we must be sure of what is at stake here. I cannot advise you of your chances of successfully defending this claim. I suspect we are in new legal territory. There is no doubt that in the Colonies the boy is a slave and is owned by Sir John and like any other property should be returned. I just don't know whether such a ruling would be enforced in England. I would suggest we take the advice of Sir Arthur Jenkinson before deciding what to do.'

Richard was a little chagrined at Willoughby's assumption that he would not only run the case, but also decide what he should do. But after his previous activities that required his principal's assistance, he could not complain. And deep down he felt relieved that he was taking some of the worry off his shoulders.

'What you suggest seems the best course. I do not wish to give the boy up only for him to be returned to the plantation. This is an issue of conscience for me. But in truth I cannot keep him. I was hoping to place him with a good family as a servant.'

'I am afraid that won't be possible for the time being. Until Sir John's claim is decided by a court of law, no one would take the boy on, and if they did he would face the constant fear of being forcibly removed.'

'I must speak to Julia. It must be very difficult for her.'

'Sir John is a fair man, I believe,' said Willoughby, 'I don't believe he will act unkindly towards your sister at the present time. But I must confess I have always felt uncomfortable with him. He is a man with ambition and the ruthlessness to go with it. I am sure he would not wish to be worsted about the slave boy and will do whatever is necessary to recover him. If the dispute is protracted it might affect his attitude towards your sister.'

When Richard returned to his lodgings that afternoon he found an agitated landlady awaiting him.

'Oh Mr Richard, I am so pleased to see you.'

'What is the matter Mrs Browning?'

'It's Sam. He's been taken.'

'What do you mean taken? Who by?'

'I don't know, sir. I was outside scrubbing the front step and these two men came up the street and stopped near me. They asked if you lived here. Well, I said you did but you weren't home. Then they just pushed past me into the house and grabbed Sam and dragged him out.'

She became very distressed so Richard helped her inside and sat her down.

'What happened next Mrs Browning?'

'Well sir they dragged him away 'gainst his wishes. He was hollerin' but no one was about and neighbours won't get involved. That's the last I saw of them.'

'How long ago was this?'

'About an hour. Mr William came back shortly after and went straight out looking for them.'

'Which direction did they go?'

'Down towards the docks. That poor boy, I don't know what will become of him.'

'Well I do Mrs Browning. He will be aboard a slave ship by now. I'll go and see if I can find him or William.'

As he made his way towards the quayside he saw William among the crowd of dockers standing close to a schooner, the Juliana.

'Richard, I am pleased to see you. He's on that ship. Several people saw him dragged up the gangplank. He made quite a struggle against it apparently.'

'I'm not surprised. It's likely to be a slaver and Sam is to be one of a batch for sale. You must wait here and watch what goes on. I will try and obtain a writ I can serve on the captain.'

'Can you do that?'

'I don't know, but it is our only chance.'

Richard hurried away, across the bridge and along by the river towards the city centre and the courts to persuade the court clerk to find a magistrate to hear an application. This he was able to do and within a few minutes was on his feet asking for a writ.

'The position sir, is this. I have living at my home a black boy of ten who in my opinion is a free man. He was a slave in the Colonies under Virginian law and his former master, a Bristol citizen, is claiming him back. The matter is before the High Court for a decision. The boy has been seized and forcefully taken aboard a slave ship. Whether by his former master or another, I know not. Either way, a forced removal is unacceptable under English law and I seek a writ of habeas corpus to have him released. Nothing short of that will prevent him being taken out of English jurisdiction.'

'Mr Stourton,' said the magistrate, 'if it is the boy's master who has taken him, isn't it right that he should be able to take back his own property?'

Richard could feel himself getting angry. 'Sir, that may be the outcome in due course. But with respect, it is for the High Court to decide. And at present we do not know who has taken him. All I ask is that the English court be not deprived of its jurisdiction to decide what is right in these circumstances.'

The magistrate sat quietly considering the situation whilst Richard stood patiently waiting.

'Mr Stourton, I have decided that I will grant the writ you ask for. But it must be clear that I am not suggesting that the court agrees the boy is a free man. I am accepting your argument that if the boy is forcibly removed the court will lose the right to say. I have to say that if it were for me to pronounce I would refer the boy to his rightful owner.'

'I am grateful to you sir. I am just glad that when the matter is finally decided it will not be before you.'

'Be careful Mr Stourton, you might persuade me to revoke the decision I have just made.'

Richard bowed and left the court, cross with himself for having lost control of his temper. The writ was drawn up and after taking it to the Mayor's office for endorsement, he returned to the Juliana where William was still keeping watch.

'I'm glad to see you Richard. I was just trying to work out how to stop the ship sailing. They appear to be nearly ready and the tide is right.'

Together they went aboard and were immediately approached by the mate.

'What can I do for you gentlemen?'

'My name is Stourton, I am a lawyer, and I have a writ for the captain.'

'He don't want no warrant and you can't make him accept it.'

'It's not a warrant it's a writ of habeas corpus and it will prevent your ship leaving if he doesn't comply with it.'

The man spat on the deck. 'Wait here then.'

He turned and went down the stairs to find the captain who heralded his arrival by steady footsteps on the wooden stair rungs.

'What do you want Mr Stourton?'

'You have kidnapped a free black boy and the court has ordered his immediate release. I would like to go down into the hold and release him.'

The captain looked at the writ. 'Wait here, you've no right to walk about my ship.'

He disappeared, shortly reappearing with a tearful Sam in tow. 'Here he is, Mr Stourton, now get off my ship.'

Together the three of them walked back down the gangplank and away.

On the way home Sam said: 'They were going to take me back to the Colonies and sell me again.'

'I guessed as much,' said Richard. 'I don't think this was Sir John Manners' doing. There are slave catchers at work in all ports where foreigners live. They seize them whether they be slaves or free men. I suspect they saw you with me. A chance kidnap.'

'How do you know it wasn't Sir John?' said William.

'Sir John wouldn't want to re-sell him. And I was suspicious when they wouldn't let me go below. I expect they have others there. Is that right, Sam?'

'Yes there are two others, both chained up.'

'By the way, Richard, how were you going to hold the ship up?' said William.

'I have no idea. But as you were able to pretend you had a pistol when I was in trouble, I thought I could try a bluff too. They both laughed, releasing the tension they both felt. Sam continued crying at his lucky escape not understanding his rescuers good humour.

The list of potential supporters among Bristol publicans proved to be a long one. He soon discovered it was slow work and after four evenings had visited fifteen. Each landlord needed to be listened to, flattered, and wooed. The purchase of at least one glass of ale was obligatory just to persuade a landlord to listen. Most would listen, then argue, and then give the opinion they first held. It was a ritual that had to be played at every election, contested or not. By the end of the fourth evening, a Friday, twelve had turned him down, two had accepted, and one remained undecided. Only two to exhibit Robert Harford's favours did not auger well especially as public houses all over Bristol began to fly the Tory favours. Of the twelve who were not willing to support an independent candidate, six switched to supporting Terrill, largely to attract Tory largesse, and six agreed to take Robert's money to stay away from the Tory camp and remain neutral.

The following day Richard's route took him into St Phillips. He had discovered early on that Nancy's new employer was on the list and he wrestled with his conscience for some time before deciding he would call. He was willing to deceive himself into believing that if he called for a reason other than to see Nancy, she would be in no danger.

As it was a Saturday he decided to call at mid-day in the hope that there would be fewer customers than of an evening, and he would not ask for Nancy for fear of arousing suspicion. If he saw her, all well and good; if not, he would leave it to William to make contact.

The bar was more crowded than he had expected. Most of the tables were occupied, other customers standing in groups of twos and threes between the tables and the bar. Here and there Richard noticed single, silent drinkers, and felt uneasy. At the bar a middle-aged woman, dark haired and fat, stood serving ale to those who came up to her for their orders. Two younger women were carrying drinks to the tables and returning empty tankards through a scullery door. Richard approached the bar and waited until the older woman came over to him.

'Is the landlord here?' he asked.

'Who wants him?' she replied in a tone a shade too aggressive for Richard's liking.

'I am here about the parliamentary by-election.'

'What election?' The woman sounded interested. Richard explained and saw that the woman did not know who Bristol's MPs were, nor that one had died and was to be replaced. It was clear to him that her interest was limited to the business potential of such an event.

'My husband's the landlord here. He's in the cellar. I'll fetch him.'

She turned to the scullery door behind her. 'Nancy!' she shouted, 'come and look after things here will you? There's a gent wants a drink.'

The frail form of Nancy emerged from the back kitchen, wiping her hands on a dirty cloth. It was only when she reached the bar and looked up that she saw who stood before her. She looked startled.

'You! What do you want?' She became agitated and looked about her anxiously.

'Don't worry Nancy, I have come on election business, not to disturb you.'

She drew some beer and pushed a brimming glass towards him. Richard watched her closely but she kept her eyes averted and said nothing. The bar area was beginning to fill up. Two men next to Richard started to enjoy a joke. On his other side a man with a lonely face stood staring into his glass. Richard leaned across the bar and whispered to Nancy.

'Do you know where Abel Jacobs is? Has he gone to France?'

She shook her head. 'No. He is still in Bristol hiding from the constables.'

Richard was surprised but suppressed his elation. 'Do you know where he is?'

She nodded. Other customers began to demand attention. Richard knew his time was limited and that the landlord would soon reappear.

'Can you lead me there Nancy?'

He could see concern in her eyes. He knew he was asking a lot of her, but he was desperate to speak to Jacobs before he disappeared and had to take a chance.

'Please Nancy. I won't ask any more of you.'

'Be outside 'ere at eleven tonight then,' she said quietly. 'Wait outside an' keep well hidden. I'll come out. Just follow. Don't catch me. 'eell let me in if I'm alone. I'll tell 'im your there. Then its up to 'im.'

She moved away to serve other customers before he had a chance to reply. The solitary drinker next to Richard drained his glass and left. Before Richard could say any more, the landlord and his wife arrived and Nancy returned to the kitchen without a backward glance.

Richard pulled his cloak tighter round his neck and turned to William. 'She's not coming.'

'Be patient my friend,' said William. 'It is but eleven now, give her time.'

They stood in the darkened doorway of a shop on the opposite side of the road from the Albatross from where they could see the main entrance and the coming and going of customers. Lights were ablaze inside, and the shadows of people moving backwards and forwards were thrown onto the window blinds. The house seemed to be packed. Richard assumed that Nancy had chosen this time so that her absence would not be missed in the throng.

It was a cold, clear night, crisp and dry. There was already a frost underfoot and late night revellers were struggling to keep their balance, shouting and laughing at every slip and slide. Despite the cold, prostitutes stood in many of the doorways, especially outside the taverns and alehouses. This was the world in which Nancy had grown up and would probably never leave.

It was ten minutes after eleven when they saw her. She emerged from an alleyway at the side of the building, looked up and down the street, across to where they were concealed, then turned to her left and walked briskly away. They followed at a discreet distance. Groups of revellers repeatedly blocked their view of her and they had to approach closer than they would have wished, but after a few minutes they crossed the Bath Road into a quiet quarter where only the darkness caused problems. Eventually she headed up hill towards the Redcliffe district and turned into another maze of alleys, streets and congested houses. Only the moonlight guided them in their way, her thin figure silhouetted against the background. She looked around her once or twice, not so much to see if they were following but to alert her to any thieves or vagrants into whose path she may have strayed.

At last she turned into an even narrower street where the houses were so close together, leaning drunkenly over the road that little moonlight penetrated. By the time Richard and William had turned into this street, Nancy had stopped outside a house, half way along on the left hand side. They waited, pressed up against a wall about thirty yards away as Nancy knocked, quietly at first, then more loudly. Soon she had disappeared through the door and all was quiet again. They could not see who had let her in.

They waited a minute or two but Nancy did not reappear.

'I don't like this, I'm going in,' said William.

Richard, too, felt uneasy. It was too quiet. No lights, no sound. Had Nancy led them into a trap, or had she herself been betrayed? He could not decide what to do for the best. 'Let's wait a few moments longer,' he replied.

They did so, but with no result. William was clearly getting more agitated and Richard sought to restrain him no more. They stepped out of the protective shadow of the wall and walked briskly towards the house into which Nancy had disappeared.

They did not reach the house. When several yards short, a whistle blew and running feet brought men from both directions. Two men ran past them shouting, and two appeared from the shadows further up the street. The four men reached the front door first, shouldered it open and rushed in. Richard and William followed them in to find the four men running from room to room.

'Upstairs' one of them shouted. The four ran upstairs followed by a bewildered Richard, William close behind. All six burst into an upstairs room, then stopped and stared in horror. Lying on the floor on the opposite side of the room was a man, blood flowing from his stomach. He lay still, apparently dead. Kneeling beside the body, holding a knife, itself bloody, was Nancy. Her clothes were splattered with blood from the dead man. Richard recognised him immediately as Abel Jacobs. He would have to flee from justice no more.

'We're too late,' one of the men said, and it was only then that Richard recognised the voice and features of Constable Skinner. 'Put the knife down, young lady.'

Nancy looked at the knife as if unable to believe it was in her hand, and with a shiver of revulsion threw it onto the floor. She wiped her hands down her dress then stood up, head bowed.

'What's your name?' asked Skinner.

Richard stepped forward. 'I know this girl. Her name is Nancy.'

'Nancy,' repeated the constable, 'I am arresting you for the murder of Abel Jacobs.'

Nancy made no reply. She stood up and walked past the group of men still standing shocked and motionless. Constable Skinner followed her out of the room. Richard and William watched, unable to articulate a word, as Nancy, Constable Skinner, and the other three men disappeared down the stairs.

~ CHAPTER 14 ~

'I cannot believe she killed him. I will not believe it.'

Richard shouted at Willoughby who sat patiently waiting for his pupil's frustration to subside.

'My dear boy, just calm yourself. I did not say she did, nor even that I believe she did. I said it looks as if she did. Do you see what I am suggesting?'

Richard stared at Willoughby's face, calm and analytical, and waited for what came next. Willoughby continued.

'If it looks as if she did, then either she did plunge the knife in – and heaven knows she had good reason to – or someone wanted to make it seem as if she did. Now why would they want to do that?'

Richard was beginning to see where Willoughby's thoughts were leading and was content to let the lawyer develop his argument.

Willoughby answered his own question. 'To deflect the suspicion away from themselves and onto someone who probably could not prove her innocence. To test the theory we need to find a motive, and perhaps a reason to put Nancy out of the way too. The girl must have some information – she may not even know she has it – that would help convict someone else of a crime. What better way of disposing of one adversary than arranging his murder to look as if it was committed by someone else who is a danger to him.'

'So we must start with Nancy?' enquired Richard.

'Exactly. That is why we are going to see her this morning. We have no time to lose.'

'How many weeks do we have?'

'Four at the most. In a few days time the magistrates will commit her for trial at the assize. Unless we can find a defence she will be convicted and hanged soon after.' With that Willoughby was down the stairs and into the street before Richard had retrieved his cloak.

Richard took comfort in Willoughby's undoubted interest in the case, more than just professional. Willoughby was not by nature a crusading lawyer, but would take facts as presented to him and make what he could of them. This was the first time Richard had known him take an investigative attitude to a criminal case, and without payment either.

Richard had not only not slept the night before; he had not even gone to bed. He had sat up with William, in turns brooding and talking, going over all the events that had led to this tragedy time and time again, trying to make some sense of it all. Neither for one minute believed Nancy to be guilty of this terrible crime. They were ready to believe her capable of thieving, of lying, even of prostitution to prevent starvation in a world where she had learned that keeping alive was the only code to follow. But murder? That was a different matter altogether. There was no economic necessity to kill Abel Jacobs, even if he had abused her. And why should she kill him knowing that Richard was about to enter the house? He did not believe she had the wit to double bluff – commit the murder at the worst possible moment in order to make people believe she would not have done it then. The only possible scenario either could think of in the long night hours was self-defence. Had Jacobs taken the knife to her and somehow had been stabbed himself? If so, why had she not said so?

The streets were crowded as they walked through the city to Narrow Wine Street to Newgate Gaol. Shopkeepers stood in their doorways beckoning them in; barrow boys called out to sample their wares; and by the city wall a small crowd was listening to a speaker urging them to repent of their sins. Richard felt affronted that life carried on as normal while only yards away an innocent young girl was in custody for a crime she probably did not commit. His heart felt that there should be a public outcry at the injustice but his head told him otherwise. The weak, the poor, and the unprotected had little defence against the legal system, which favoured those who could afford lawyers.

At Newgate they went down the familiar steps to the cells below. Richard's nose wrinkled with disgust as the stench rose to meet him and reminded him of his own imprisonment not long before. Nancy was in a cell further along the corridor, a large square room, overcrowded, mostly drunks, pickpockets and whores, men women and children locked in together with no privacy. Richard's arrival caused more interest amongst the other women than to Nancy, who sat in a corner motionless.

'Here's a nice one!' shouted one of the women prisoners, flattening herself against the bars of the door. 'Come to take me 'ome 'ave you my lovely?' The other women started laughing and crowding round the door.

'Perhaps 'is favourite girl is 'ere,' said another 'and 'ee can't do without 'er.' Several arms reached through the bars as Richard approached and he recoiled out of reach.

'Get back, all of you,' shouted the gaoler, and to Richard's surprise they did. 'I'm the one who feeds 'em,' the gaoler explained, 'they do as I tell them else I forget meal times. Nancy come out, will you?'

There were shrieks of laughter from the other women as Nancy came forward, head bowed.

'Likes 'em young don't 'ee?' one shouted. 'She won't teach you much,' called out another. The gaoler took no notice and led the party to a small room at the end of the corridor, the same room where Willoughby had interviewed Jacobs not so long before, though Richard did not know that. The gaoler locked them in.

'I'll leave you alone,' he said, 'shout when you want to come out.'

Richard sat opposite Nancy, a table between them. Willoughby sat in a corner from where he could watch Nancy's face. The girl sat, head bowed, hands in her lap, saying nothing. It seemed to Richard she was completely bewildered by what had happened. She had walked from cell to interview room as if in a trance and now sat, expressionless eyes staring down in front of her. Richard was not even sure she knew he was there.

'Nancy, it's me, Richard. Richard Stourton. And Mr Willoughby is with me. You remember him, don't you? You came to him when I was in trouble. Now we have come to help you.'

She half looked up, caught Willoughby's eye, then lowered her head again. Richard tried once more.

'If we are to help, you must talk to us about what happened.'

The girl stirred and looked at Richard for the first time.

'I dunno what 'appened,' she said softly. 'I didn't kill 'im.'

'What did you see Nancy?' asked Willoughby. His authoritative voice seemed to jolt her out of her trance-like state and she began, haltingly at first, to tell her story.

'I knocked on the door. There was no reply. It weren't locked so I went in. It were dark downstairs but I could see the glow of a lamp upstairs, so up I went. As I were going up I thought I heard a voice downstairs at the back, but it were dark there so I kept going up towards the light.' Her voice began to tail off. The two men said nothing but waited patiently for her to continue.

'As I got to the top I heard a moan from the room where the light was. I found 'im lying there, on the floor just as 'ee were when you came. 'ee were alive when I found 'im. The knife were sticking in 'im. I pulled it out.' She started sobbing. ''ee just lay still. The moaning stopped and I knew 'ee were dead. Then you came in.'

'Did you see anyone else?' asked Richard.

She shook her head.

'It sounds as if he was stabbed just before Nancy came in,' surmised Willoughby, 'his assailant must have escaped out of the back. Nancy probably heard him. It looks too much of a coincidence not to have been deliberate. Whoever it was must have been waiting for her, to put the blame on her. The murderer must have known she was coming. And there is another thing. Unless the murderer had hidden himself in the house, which is unlikely, he must have been with Jacobs, someone the dead man knew and trusted.'

They talked to Nancy for another half hour or so but learned nothing new. She denied telling anyone about her arrangement with Richard. Mostly they talked about her life and people she knew. Richard was certain she knew something that put her at risk, but whenever the discussion approached the subject of Jacobs she froze and the conversation dried up. Even though he was dead she was still clearly frightened of him and what he represented. When they left her they were very little further forward.

It was arranged that Richard and William would visit Nancy alternately, and as often as possible, just to see if in talking she let slip any clue that might help her. But a week passed, then ten days, then her committal to the assize and still they learned nothing that would help build a defence. The prosecution case looked formidable. A girl, subjected to humiliating treatment from the dead man, found kneeling over her victim, holding the murder weapon. For the defence, no alternative theories, just an appeal to the jury that it was impossible that she would choose that moment to gain her revenge. Yet supposing Jacobs, not suspecting that Richard was outside, had attempted another assault? She could have stabbed him for self-protection. A plea of self-defence might prevent her going to the gallows, but would still end in transportation for life for manslaughter, and Nancy denied stabbing him anyway. And if that is what happened, where did the knife come from. If she took it with her, the murder was premeditated.

The only other possible enquiry they could make was how Constable Skinner came to be following Richard and William, but this too, led to a dead end. Willoughby reported that Skinner had told him an informer had said Jacobs was probably still in the city and that Nancy knew where he was. She was watched in the hope she might lead them there, which she had done, but with fatal consequences.

Carberry's coffee shop in London's Strand, opposite the Law Courts, was a favourite haunt of the Bar. It was darkly lit, furnished in dark mahogany and had an acrid smell of coffee beans and tobacco. In it, cases were argued over, compromised, and settled with all the ardour shown in the courts themselves. The proprietor, James Carberry, knew his trade. Divided into semi private booths and open from early morning to late at night, it was an ideal place for opposing barristers to meet, and having already agreed their brief fees with their instructing solicitors, settle their cases without a foot being set inside the Royal Courts.

In one such booth in early February, two men sat drinking coffee. One was Lawrence Willoughby. The other was a tall slim man of about forty, languid in manner and speech. He wore pin stripe trousers and a winged collar that established him, like most of the patrons of the establishment, as a barrister. He was Sir Arthur Jenkinson, who although qualified as a barrister only fifteen years earlier, had established his reputation as an authority on the laws of trade on both land and the high seas.

'What chance do you think we have of preventing the shipping of the Negro boy back to Virginia?' asked Willoughby.

'The whole subject is determined by case law, which in the circumstances of this case is inconclusive but not encouraging. Sir John will argue that slavery is in fact in existence in England, being fairly common here in London, and in Bath. It is considered an example of the status of the slave owner and is the height of fashion. You will see slaves advertised. Ladies tend to prefer small, plump faced boys who they dress in exotic eastern clothes and tease as pets. Padlocks for them can be bought from reputable locksmiths who trade quite openly and who advertise them as suitable for Blacks or Dogs. Gentlemen like black servants too. They dress them in sober livery often with a silver collar engraved with the name of the master and sometimes with a coat of arms. Sir John's argument will be that as slaves exist in England and are owned by their masters, taking a slave away is theft.'

Willoughby stayed silent for a minute or two. 'The circumstances you describe are different in this case. Usually slaves are brought to England by their masters. In our case the slave was no longer under the control of his owner when he arrived here. He had escaped from slavery in Virginia.'

'Unfortunately that argument does not take us far. There is no doubt that by the law of Virginia the boy belonged to Sir John. There is no example in English law of a slave being forcibly freed, that is to say freed against the wishes of the owner.'

'What about the cases of English sailors being taken into slavery by Musselmen on the Barbary Coast? When we rescue them they are then freed.'

'Unfortunately the two cases are not the same. We do not recognise the laws of the Barbary Coast. We do recognise the laws of Virginia. Therein lies the difference.'

Both men lapsed into silence. Around them the buzz of conversation continued.

'But the picture is not altogether hopeless,' said Sir Arthur at last. 'There was a case five or six years ago when a slave owner in England lost his temper with a slave, beat him almost to death, then threw him out into the street. The slave wandered the London streets for some weeks until the master saw him recovered and tried to take him back again. The slave, whose name was Jonathan Strong, had been befriended by a clerk who sympathised with him and supported him at the trial. The court allowed the slave to go free, but the reason given was lack of evidence. I do not know what was in the Judge's mind.'

'So how clear is the law?' asked Willoughby.

'Not at all I am afraid. There has been no court decision that states in terms that as soon as a slave sets foot in England he shall be free. But there are other cases we can call in support. Granville Sharpe, the civil servant who was involved in the Strong case, has taken up the cause of slaves who have secured some freedom in England but are faced with arrest or kidnap and return to their former masters.

'Sharpe brought another case before Lord Mansfield last year, a black slave called Thomas Lewis. The jury let Lewis go free but again the judge made no declaratory statement against slavery in England, merely observing there was no bill of sale to prove ownership of the slave. It seems the courts don't want to permit slavery to continue on English soil but are wary of interfering with property rights.'

'We may need to break new legal ground to win then?'

'I fear so. But the law adapts to change and public opinion might favour such an advance.'

'Have you seen much of Richard, Julia?' asked Jane one morning.

'I see him from time to time, but he is extremely busy.'

'He has been in a few scrapes, I hear.'

Julia smiled. 'Nothing too serious. He was mistaken for a smuggler and taken by the excise men, but it has been sorted out.'

'Your brother seems to be able to find trouble,' said Jane. 'What will he be involved in next?'

Jane laughed at her joke but Julia merely smiled.

'My father is still extremely angry with him,' Jane continued. 'I fear their dispute will not be resolved easily.'

'What does Nicholas think about it, Jane?'

'I am not sure. He doesn't seem to want to talk about it. He and father discuss business all the time, of course, but I have never heard him talk of Richard. I expect he just wants it settled.'

Julia felt that the time had come to confide in her charge. 'Jane there is something I have been wanting to tell you. It has weighed heavily on my mind for some time.'

Jane looked attentively at her companion. 'Is it something important, Julia? I can keep a secret.'

'It is important. Your brother...Nicholas, well, we have an understanding.'

Jane's eyes widened and her lips quivered. 'You? And Nicholas?'

'Yes. It has worried me that I have been deceiving you. It is something that has developed slowly, but at the ball...'

'I could see you were enjoying each other's company, but I had no idea...'

'It is not something I intended to happen. These things are rarely planned. And I intended to tell you as soon as Richard returned, but then there was all this bother about the slave boy.'

'Julia please do not apologise. There is nothing to apologise for. I am delighted. And thrilled. You will be my sister. How wonderful.'

Julia smiled at the innocence of an eighteen year old. 'I doubt it will be possible Jane. Even without this wretched dispute, I doubt your father would sanction such a union.'

'Then we shall have to persuade him how splendid the match would be,' said Jane.

'And how do you propose we do that?' said Julia, her voice laced with scepticism.

'By working on my mother. If she can be persuaded of Nicholas' happiness then she will accept you. She would be a valuable ally.'

'Jane, please speak to Nicholas first.' Julia was becoming alarmed that the situation would spin beyond her control. 'He needs to approve and be ready for whatever may happen. I will tell Richard when we next meet. It is hanging heavily on his mind that he has been the cause of such unhappiness to me.'

Jane took hold of Julia's hand and gently squeezed it. 'We will make it all right, Julia. That I promise you.'

The by-election campaign was gathering pace, supporters of the two candidates trading insults by pamphlets, letters in the press, and at public meetings. It became clear to Richard that the more the insults flew, the more Jeremy Sly appeared to be enjoying the contest. He had a knack of judging what Joseph Terrill was going to say next and as soon as he said it there was a pamphlet setting out Robert's views on the subject on the streets. When he agreed with Terrill, he took the credit; if he disagreed, the case against was put first.

One evening in late February Robert Harford asked Richard to speak at a meeting at the Merchants Venturers Hall in King Street to outline his impressions of the state of feeling in Virginia. His heart was no longer in it, his thoughts being dominated by Nancy's plight, but having already promised to do so he agreed to honour that commitment.

It was a wet night, a squally February evening with a swirling wind whipping rain into the faces of all who ventured out. Yet the hall was packed. The campaign had attracted national interest, questions in Parliament, even a hint from King George himself that Terrill's candidature was approved in royal circles. As a result, Robert Harford had attracted something of a hero's status amongst the underprivileged and less wealthy shopkeepers, most of whom had no vote. In vain had Harford tried to explain to the wealthy burghers of the city how their prospects would improve if only the King's Government would cease its pernicious interference with the proud colonists. But most of the merchants were not ready to see this. Many of them had interests overseas, and owned shares in the plantations. It was not uncommon for Bristol businesses to send partners to live and work in the new world; yet most had not been there for many years and were not aware of how quickly sentiment was changing. They feared the colonists would break away altogether if concessions were made, confiscating their lands and businesses, bankrupting their companies.

This was the first election meeting Richard had attended and as he took his seat on the platform alongside Robert Harford and John Powell he surveyed the sea of faces in front of him. It was a cheerful, boisterous crowd, come for entertainment; some were laughing and pointing, others in small groups, heads bowed, were debating earnestly. Here and there, on either side, and in the galleries, good-natured banter was shouted across the hall from one group of supporters to another. It seemed that the audience had decided that having braved the weather, it would enjoy itself.

At eight o'clock precisely John Powell called the meeting to order, or at least to as much order as was likely to prevail. The hubbub abated somewhat, not to complete silence, that could not be expected, but enough to enable the chairman to introduce himself and the two speakers. A volley of catcalls and booing at the mention of his name made Richard uneasy, and contrasted with the reception of the candidate who was booed and cheered in equal measure.

Richard spoke first, hesitantly to start with, feeling his way, trying to judge the mood of his audience. There was, for a few minutes, an interested silence. It was a novelty for a young man, unheard of by most present, to address an election meeting in this way. He told of his journey from the coast to Williamsburg, talked of the plantations and those working them, and of the need for the tobacco growers to find markets for their produce. He described Williamsburg, its buildings and people. Yet as he spoke he sensed he was losing his audience, that it was becoming restless. From the corner of his eye he could see even Robert shifting uneasily in his chair.

But it was when he came to speak of the Williamsburg meeting that he ran into trouble.

'Mr Chairman,' a voice from the back shouted. Richard stopped speaking, looked at John Powell, then sat down.

'What do you want to say?' Powell called to the interrupter.

'There's some of us here want some questions answered before we hear any more,' the voice continued. Richard tried to make out who was speaking but his view was obstructed by rows of men standing about ten deep forming a barrier between the last row of chairs and the back of the hall. He realised that this man, whoever he was, could not be ignored otherwise the rest of his speech would be punctuated with interruptions. He turned and spoke quietly to John Powell.

'I will deal with this John.'

He faced his audience again.

'I will be perfectly happy to answer the gentleman's question if he would be so kind as to make himself visible.'

There was movement and jostling at the back of the room and eventually a man emerged from the crowd and stood between the seated audience in front and the standing ranks behind. Richard recognised him at once. He was the questioner who had so much interrupted his meeting in Williamsburg several months before. What was he doing in Bristol he wondered? Was it a coincidence or was he following him, either to disrupt or simply see what he was doing? For the time being he decided not to reveal that he recognised him.

The audience went silent.

'I should like to know, Mr Stourton, how many of the farmers of Virginia have the vote in this by-election?'

'The answer to that, sir, is not many. There are a number of Bristol merchants who own shares in farms in Virginia and who have the vote as burgesses of this city, but otherwise, none.'

There was a hush around the hall as the audience waited to see where the questioning would lead.

'Then how many of these non-voting colonist farmers have contributed to your candidate's election fund?'

Murmuring rose from around the hall, but before Richard could reply to that question, another was put.

'And is it true Mr Stourton that you raised money at your meeting in Williamsburg?'

Richard's heart began to beat fiercely and his face and throat flushed. He knew this was his first big test on a public platform. Giving a talk on events as he remembered them in front of several hundred people, many openly hostile, was difficult enough, but to cope with malicious questions and produce the right answer immediately required other skills.

'You know full well that I did, as you were present at the meeting. There is nothing unusual in that.'

The audience was transfixed by the exchange. This was more interesting than a speech. A gladiatorial contest was more to their liking. They turned to the questioner, eager for more, and he did not disappoint them.

'Is it true that you collected donations from any who would give? Irrespective of whether they had connections with Bristol?'

Richard thought fast. Be careful, he told himself, a hastily considered answer will cause much damage.

'It is true,' he spoke slowly, choosing his words with care, ' that at the end of that meeting a number of people came forward to pledge funds for Councillor Harford's campaign. In each case I enquired whether they had connections with Bristol, and what those connections were. It was subsequently decided that those with no connection should be thanked but their offer declined. I am satisfied that that is what happened. We took the view that colonists with no roots in our city should not be involved in our election.'

This time it was the turn of Harford's supporters to cheer and mock the questioner who they felt had been adequately rebuffed. But there was more to come. It soon became clear that there was a concerted attempt to discredit Richard as a way of getting at the candidate, for almost immediately another voice arose, this time from one side of the hall where a group of young men lounged against the wall. One of then took up the questioning.

'Mr Stourton, is it true you are currently on bail facing a charge of smuggling?'

This brought a mixed, but noisy reaction from the crowd, some merely gasping in shock, others clearly anticipating this question and cheering the questioner. Richard exploded in anger at this attempt to sabotage the meeting.

'My private life is none of your business,' he shouted, 'but as you have raised the matter, yes, a charge of smuggling was recently, and wrongly, brought against me. The prosecution has admitted the error and it will be formally dismissed at the next assize.'

'So you say,' persisted the questioner, 'but isn't it also true that your fellow smuggler has been murdered by a young lady of your acquaintance, who you visit regularly in gaol?'

At this remark the meeting boiled over. People stood shouting, some to remonstrate, others to support the speaker. Arguments broke out all over the hall, and here and there fists flew. Richard tried to shout above the tumult.

'I am a lawyer. She is a client of my firm and I visit her...' But he could say no more. No one was listening. He sat down, beaten and dejected. It took some minutes for John Powell to restore order by which time a number of people had left the hall. Robert Harford was left to speak to those who remained, largely his own supporters. After the meeting had ended, he tried to console Richard.

'Don't worry about this. It was not your fault.'

'It was. I should never have taken part.'

'I knew all the risks,' said Robert, 'it was I who took the chance. Besides, it may rebound to our advantage. There were many here who disliked what happened. That may turn into sympathy votes. But I think we should use your help in less prominent ways for the rest of the campaign.'

William looked at Nancy across the desk that separated them. His frequent visits had at last broken down the barriers between them and she appeared to look forward to seeing him. She offered little by way of conversation, but answered his questions quite readily and occasionally offered a smile. Yet so far he had failed to find anything that would help her. The days were passing and the assize was shortly to start. He looked at the thin emaciated girl in front of him with growing feeling and even affection and felt ashamed that she had endured the life she had, only to end up in a situation which she barely understood, and could not explain.

'Are you feeling well today, Nancy?'

'Enough. I ain't eating much though.'

'Are they treating you properly?'

'No one speaks much. Not to me any rate. They don't care for murderers in 'ere. But they do me no 'arm.'

William had put off discussing Nancy's relationship with Jacobs, but felt it could be avoided no longer. To his surprise he found it was a subject that pained him personally. He had not appreciated he had growing feelings for Nancy until he thought of her treatment by Jacobs, which made him angry and upset. Yet he knew it had to be tackled and that he would have to lead her into it gently.

'What made you leave Marsh Street and go to live in the cottage?'

He watched her thinking about it, twisting a rag nervously between her fingers. She replied softly; he had to strain to catch her words.

'I were only allowed back to Marsh Street if I took messages to them at Pill.'

'And one of them was Jacobs?'

'Yes.'

'Did he harm you?'

''ee knocked me about. And once, like I told you at the cottage, he tried to – well, you know.'

'Did he threaten you?'

'Once he said 'e'ed kill me. That I'd end up like that man.'

William was all attention now. 'What man Nancy?'

'That council man, you know, what was found in the river.'

'Ben Jackson.'

'Yes, that were 'is name. I said if he tried it on again I'd tell 'bout his smuggling. 'ee said if I weren't careful I'd end up in the river.'

'Did he indeed.' William thought for a few moments, wondering if a breakthrough had come at last.

'Why do you think he mentioned him? Many bodies are found, murdered, both in the river and out. Why mention that one?'

She did not reply, but twisted the rag more tightly between her fingers.

'Are you frightened to talk Nancy?'

She nodded. He understood how her fear of the man continued beyond his death. The world of smuggling, slave ships, and drinking dens held its own terror and anyone caught up in it found it difficult to break free. Jacobs had not worked alone. He had had many contacts who were still at large and no doubt knew of Nancy and her friendship with Richard and himself.

'There is no need to fear him now,' he said, stretching across the table and gently squeezing her hand. 'You must help yourself as much as possible. Soon you will have to go to court. The jury must be convinced there was a reason for someone else killing him and blaming you.'

Nancy seemed to accept this. 'That other man, the council man, 'ee was askin' 'bout the slaver what sunk. They didn't like that in Marsh Street. Jacobs was told to warn 'im off.'

William could barely contain his excitement. She had never spoken of this before. Take it easy, he told himself, don't frighten her.

'How do you know that, Nancy?'

'I 'eard 'im say so. In the 'Angel. I served drinks there most nights. I 'eard 'im talkin' to Jasper Cox 'bout it. Jacobs said your council man weren't easily put off. 'ee said 'e'ed 'ave to be, I forget his words, 'ee meant break a few bones.'

'Do you know who paid Jacobs to do this?'

'No. I never 'eard 'im talked of.'

'Who else was present when Jacobs said this?'

'There were a few seamen there. I don't know their names. 'xcept one. Samuel Baillie.'

William could not resist a smile. 'I know him. Richard and I served on the same ship as him. A nasty piece of work he is. Nancy, you have given us something to work on at last.'

Voting started on 1st March. A week before, Robert Harford had processed through the city streets to hand in his declaration of candidacy, escorted by two dozen supporters and a band. They had met with generally good-natured abuse from citizens watching from the windows of houses along the route. No more vegetables or slops had been thrown at them than was customary and Robert was optimistic that he had won the argument even if he were to lose the vote. Terrill had processed later that same day, almost turning it into a civic occasion. Leading councillors from both parties processed with him, together with the Mayor, several hundred supporters, and two bands. Robert had walked, but Terrill was chaired through the streets, hoisted aloft and carried by four burly supporters.

During the days leading up to the opening of the poll, each side had sought to enrol more freemen onto the voters list. An expensive business, Terrill had seemingly inexhaustible funds whereas Robert was running low and would be hard pressed to keep going until close of poll in two weeks time.

On the eve of poll all Bristol was celebrating and few went to bed until the early hours, if at all. Supporters of both candidates were out in force, calling on electors, encouraging those believed to be sympathetic, intimidating those who were not. As much pressure was put on opposition supporters not to vote as in pressing supporters to declare. Debtors were politely reminded that continual credit required the goodwill of their creditors, employees of where their employers' interests lay. Shopkeepers were promised undreamt of custom, or threatened that business would go elsewhere.

As dawn broke on the cold, dry morning when the polls were to open, large mobs began to gather round the voting booth. Everyone, whether eligible to vote or not, was a supporter of one or other of the candidates and was determined to cheer every vote for their champion and abuse those who took a contrary decision. Throughout the day, electors arrived, sometimes alone, often under escort, to announce their vote loudly enough for those at the front of the crowd to hear, and each declaration was greeted accordingly.

In the Jackson household there was turmoil and tension. Sarah had worked feverishly for several days past visiting wives of voters, seeking influence here, exerting pressure there. Now she could but wait. All day she fretted, seeking information from whoever chanced to pass by, but accounts were contradictory and unreliable, reflecting the views of those presenting them. At last, an hour after the poll closed on the first day, Robert sent a note.

> Sarah,
> An exhausting first day. Much work still to be done. Terrill decided on a show of strength to begin with to dishearten us and persuade us to withdraw. As a consequence, many of his closest supporters have voted on this first day. I have every confidence we can hold him and catch up over the next few. The official count at close of poll is:
> Terrill 135 votes, Harford 75.
> Robert

~ CHAPTER 15 ~

'Mr Baillie!' Richard stepped out of the shadow of the doorway and put his hand on Baillie's shoulder. 'A pleasure to see you again.'

Samuel Baillie pulled back in surprise but Richard did not lose his grip. Realising he was not being attacked, Baillie peered at his unexpected companion.

'Oh it's you, Stourton, what d'you want?'

'I should like to talk to you, somewhere private.'

'Well I ain't wantin' to talk to you.' He tried to wrench himself free. Another figure emerged from the darkness and seized the other arm. A third figure stood behind him. Baillie looked round at the features of William Daniel and Constable Skinner, struggled briefly, then realised he was held fast.

'Damn you Stourton, what do you think you're doin'?'

'You are going to talk to us whether you want to or not, Mr Baillie. I suggest you make no trouble or the Constable here might decide you are causing a breach of the peace.'

Constable Skinner had taken some persuading that Baillie should be forcibly abducted for questioning but gave in after Willoughby's impassioned plea on behalf of the helpless Nancy. William had recounted Nancy's story to the lawyer and together they had gone to see Skinner to seek his help. Out of respect for Lawrence Willoughby, Skinner had, with misgivings, agreed and now they escorted Baillie away from Marsh Street and up Corn Street to Willoughby's chambers where they sat him down with a glass of whisky. Willoughby waited for Baillie to take a drink and relax a little before he started his questioning.

'Mr Baillie, evidence has come to light that you mistreated your crew on a recent voyage.'

Baillie looked up at Richard and the trace of a smile crossed his face. 'What's that got to do wi' you? How the ship is run is up to the captain. Is that all you've brought me here for?'

'No it is not. But I want you to be aware of the consequences of not co-operating. It matters not that you were at sea; offences against British subjects are punishable by British courts wherever committed. Mr Stourton and Mr Daniel will be happy not to press the point if you give satisfactory answers to other questions.'

Baillie reached for the bottle to pour another glass. His interrogators could see he was uncertain whether they spoke the truth.

'What do you want to know?' He spoke uncertainly and with hesitation.

'That's better,' said Willoughby. 'We want to ask you about Abel Jacobs.'

"Ee's dead ain't 'ee.'

'Yes he is. But it is what happened back in 1770 that we are interested in. Do you remember Councillor Ben Jackson?'

"Ee were murdered too, weren't 'ee.'

'Yes. Did Jacobs tell you anything about him?'

Baillie sat silent, fingering his tumbler, clearly weighing up his options.

'Come on, Mr Baillie,' said Skinner, 'I am sure you remember. We have one witness already. It will be better for you to help us now.'

'Damn you all!' he shouted, standing up as if to leave. Two pairs of hands restrained him.

'No you don't,' said Skinner. 'If you leave here without telling us, it will be to Newgate.'

Baillie looked at each of the determined faces in turn and knew he was no match for them. He turned to Willoughby. 'All I know is that Jacobs told us one night how 'ee was paid to keep Jackson quiet and how 'ee was finding it difficult. 'Ee said 'ee'd been offered a purse to do it, no questions asked. It were a handsome sum, 'ee said, and 'ee weren't going to lose it.'

'And who was paying him?'

"Ee didn't say. But it were something to do with the *Demera*. There was a secret about 'er. I dunno what it was. That's all I can tell you.'

'That will be sufficient Mr Baillie,' said Willoughby. 'Now all we want is for you to sign a statement about what you have just told us. Please help yourself to more whisky while I write it out.'

'Secret? There's no secret,' said Lawrence Willoughby after Baillie had left them. Richard, William, and Constable Skinner all looked at him expectantly. There was a twinkle in the old lawyer's eye as there often was when he had an advantage over his audience.

'You will remember, Richard, that after you were released on bail I promised I would investigate the insurance claim made after the *Demera* went down. That I have done. It seems the insurers paid out on the basis of the ship foundering with a full cargo. The owners did not disclose that part of the cargo had been jettisoned overboard. Those slaves would not have been covered by the insurance had the company known. Ben Jackson undoubtedly found this out and decided to use it in his investigation, with the unfortunate result that we all know.'

Richard leapt to his feet. 'So Joseph Terrill is our man. And probably James Walter too. They owned the *Demera*, defrauded the insurers, had Ben Jackson murdered, then arranged the murder of Abel Jacobs – who was probably Ben Jackson's assassin – and have neatly cast the blame on Nancy, who is the only person who could possibly incriminate them.'

'Hold fast, Richard,' said Willoughby. 'We have a theory, little more. Certainly not enough either to acquit Nancy or condemn Joseph Terrill and James Walter. But I agree, we have a motive.'

'Not enough for criminal proceedings,' said Skinner. 'Your problem is where to go from here. You have insufficient evidence with which to incriminate Councillor Terrill and even less for James Walter. And Joseph Terrill will be a Member of Parliament soon, and a very influential figure. A case based on the flimsiest of evidence, supported only by a serving girl on a murder charge, and a disreputable seaman, will stand no chance of success and would be thrown out by the magistrate at the first hearing. A challenge to Terrill now will put him on his guard making your task more difficult. Jasper Cox is at sea, not expected to be back for months, and Nancy is likely to be hanged within the month.'

'Could you tell me the name of the insurers?' asked Richard. 'I would like to talk to them myself.'

'Of course. It is the Western Fire & Commerce Insurance company.'

'Sam, come and sit down. I want to talk to you,' said Richard.

'Yes sir.' He sat down but Richard could see from his fidgeting that he was nervous.

'I am afraid it is too risky for you to live here any longer. William and I have too much to do to be with you very often and after the last incident many bad people will know you are here.'

Richard saw the immediate pain in the boy's face.

'Don't turn me out, sir please. I can't go back.' Tears began to well up in his eyes.

'Have no fear Sam, I am not going to turn you out into the street or give you back to Sir John Manners. I am going to take you somewhere where you will be safe. Would you like to ride on a horse?'

He could see that this prospect of a ride had stopped the tears.

'I would like that. Where are we going?'

'I have some friends who live on the outskirts of Bristol who don't believe in slavery and will look after you until the court decides what is to happen to you. They will find you jobs to do about the house. But I want you to promise not to run away. I took someone else there once and she ran away and is now in serious trouble. Will you promise me?'

'Yes sir, I won't run away.'

'Then pack your things together and we will be off. William is coming with us.'

Together the two men walked to Lawford's Gate with Sam between them to hire two horses to take them to Frenchay.

'Who are we going to Richard?' asked William.

'My friends are the Penneys. They are part of the Quaker community. They, and the Evangelicals in Bristol are about the only people who oppose not only the trade but slavery itself.'

But William's thoughts were elsewhere. 'Do you think there will be enough evidence to save Nancy, Richard?'

'I fear not, Baillie's statement is not enough. That just tells us that Jacobs was a criminal, but that is known already. But it does raise the possibility that someone murdered him because of his involvement in Ben Jackson's death. If that is what happened, of course. But even that is supposition. The murder of Jacobs could be unrelated and for reasons we will never find out about.'

'And there is not much time left either,' said William.

'No. The assize starts soon and Nancy's trial is likely to be in the first week.'

They rode into the driveway of the Penney's home, an early century three storey stone building, square and imposing. Hannah and Charles Penney were on the doorstep as they pulled up.

'Richard, welcome. It is so long since we last saw thee.'

'Good morning, Hannah. May I introduce my friend William Daniel? And this is Sam'

'Won't you all come in?'

Sam needed some encouragement and Richard could see he was overwhelmed by the size of the hallway though he soon made his way to the huge stone fireplace with blazing log fire.

'Hannah I feel embarrassed about Nancy and have Sam's word that he will not run away.'

'There is no need to feel awkward about the girl. Nancy was obviously an independent spirit who found the discipline of service too much. She worked well when she was with the Naylors and stole nothing. We will keep Sam with us. Charles can find work to keep him occupied.'

'I certainly can. Sam would thee like to see the stables?'

Sam needed no second bidding and together he and Charles left them Richard stood up. 'I think this is a good time to go,' he said.

The Manners' estate occupied high ground to the north of Bristol and extended over several hundred acres of farmsteads, formal gardens and parkland. The house itself was at the lower end of the park from whence a line of trees led to a wooded hill through which a path wound its way up the hill to an open grassy knoll at the top. Immediately beyond that the estate ended at the edge of a cliff overlooking the Avon gorge through which the river flowed towards the sea. This was a favourite walk for Julia; she could usually count on being alone except for a few rabbits nibbling grass contentedly on the edge of the field closest to the sanctuary of the wood, and occasionally the white flash of a startled deer running through the undergrowth on sensing her approach. Despite the biting February cold, Julia stood on the cliff edge and looked across the gorge below. In the distance she could see a sailing ship being towed along the river by men and horses, Pill men she thought, from the village further upstream from where pilots and tug men had plied their trade for many generations.

Recently, at these quiet moments, her thoughts were always the same. Perhaps it was the sight of the river, she thought. It reminded her of Richard's voyage and the consequences for both of them that had resulted. The impossibility of her situation with

Nicholas; the embarrassment with the Manners family over Sam; and the effect all this was having on her brother.

Yet she could not condemn him nor did she even feel anger that it had happened. Just a melancholic understanding that sadness could follow even the best of intentions. She thought back to the poem that Jane had read to her. Were they all children caught up in a system to which few had given much thought and fewer could control?

The snapping of a twig caused her to jump and she turned round.

'Nicholas.'

'I am sorry to startle you.'

'I was day dreaming.'

'I could see that. I didn't know how to approach without frightening you. Snapping a twig seemed the best way.'

He paused. ' I know you come here often. I have never sought to intrude on your place of refuge but today I so much wanted to speak with you alone.'

Julia watched him walk towards her. She felt a pride and a longing for this tall smiling figure who came to her side. It was as much as she could do not to touch his cheek as he came to stand in front of her.

'I love this spot, Nicholas, there is something about looking down over the river. It helps lift my spirits above the daily world. Perhaps it is because the river flows into the Severn, and from the estuary into the ocean beyond.'

Nicholas moved a little closer to her. 'I think I understand. Perhaps it helps you rise above the cares of the day. But what about us, Julia?'

She stood looking at him. She saw a longing in his eyes and a questioning shape to his lips. She waited, not sure if he expected an answer.

'Have you spoken to your brother?'

'Not yet, Nicholas.'

'Don't you think the time has come?'

'It is difficult for him, you must understand. He will want me to be happy, naturally but....'

'But what? Will he think me unworthy of you?'

She smiled. 'No, of course not. It is just that the argument between him and your father over Sam will make it difficult for him to think of a union between our families.'

She looked anxiously at him trying to gauge his reaction. At last he took her hand and caressed it gently.

'Dear Julia, how you are caught between three men. My love for you, your affection and loyalty to your brother, and his quarrel with my father.'

'Which was not of Richard's making, Nicholas.'

'That is true. But it exists nonetheless.'

He tightened his grip on her hand then with his free hand gently brushed a stray strand of hair from her brow.

'What are we to do, Julia?'

'Nicholas you must know that my heart is yours. But please let's wait a little longer. Until the argument over Sam is resolved. I know Richard will put that behind him, whatever the outcome.'

'But how long will that be? I find it so hard to keep my feelings secret. I know you have told Jane. She keeps giving me knowing smiles.'

They both laughed, pleased to break the tension.

'My brother thinks the court will determine Sam's future in a few weeks time. Please let's wait until then.'

Together they walked back through the wood towards the house. How strongly she felt for this man. The urge to take his arm almost overcame her discretion but the sight of Lady Manners standing on the terrace watching their approach suppressed the thought within her.

The second day of polling saw the same excited crowds gather at the voting booth although the number of electors voting was fewer than on the first day. Robert Harford instructed half his committee to vote to prevent Terrill building up an unassailable lead and by 1 p.m. the voting figures were:

Terrill 170 – Harford 130.

After a hearty lunch Joseph Terrill led his supporters on a noisy procession through the city ending at the White Lion in Broad Street, the Tories usual meeting place, where he had planned to give a speech from the first floor balcony. Richard mingled amongst the excited crowd, most of whom sported the Tory favours. At four o'clock a huge cheer went up as their champion appeared on the balcony smiling broadly and bowing in acknowledgement. Richard felt sick at heart. Convinced of this man's guilt, yet unable to do anything about it, he waited to hear what his detested rival for Sarah's affections had to say.

'Good citizens of Bristol,' Terrill began, 'first I must thank you for your show of support today.' Cheers echoed around the square. 'You will know that we already have a substantial lead in the poll' – more cheering- 'and I expect the lead to grow as the days pass. I would go so far as to predict that our victory will be so crushing that those who are opposed to us now will wish they had never done so.' This produced a prolonged bout of cheering and cries of 'hear hear' from around the concourse.

Terrill spoke for an hour. Despite himself Richard could not but be impressed with his oratory, but his admiration at the man's skill with words turned to anger as the Tory candidate neared the end.

'My final comment today,' said Terrill, raising his voice, 'concerns the subject of law enforcement. As your Member of Parliament I will not see the honest endeavours of the citizens of Bristol be thwarted by thieves and criminals. I believe in tougher penalties for lawbreakers whether they be footpads on the Bath road, or treasonous colonists in America. In that pledge you have my word.'

He finished to a tumultuous cheering and shouting that went on for some minutes before the crowd was united by a call for three cheers. Richard could see that Terrill revelled in the adulation, bowing and waving to the crowd, before retiring back through the casement window from which he had emerged more than an hour before. After a final stare at the now empty balcony Richard turned away and walked disconsolately up Broad Street and along Welsh Back before turning into King Street on his way back to his lodgings.

His way took him past the Mayor's mansion house and on impulse – forethought would have stopped him doing so – he stepped up to the front door and rang the bell. A footman ushered him in and bade him wait in an anteroom whilst James Walter was advised of his call.

'Richard, a pleasure.' The Mayor stood up as Richard was ushered into his presence. 'Have you just come from the election rally? Your man is not doing too well I gather.'

'Well enough, I think,' replied Richard. 'Yes, I have just come from listening to Mr Terrill. A formidable speaker, I grant you.'

The social formalities over, both men fell silent. The spontaneity of his action now dawned on Richard. Here he was in the presence of the Mayor of Bristol, serving a second year, a former business partner of the man who would probably be the next M.P.

for the city, about to interrogate him about his possible involvement in an insurance fraud. There was every chance he would be thrown out and reported to Willoughby, with Terrill warned of what was afoot, just what Constable Skinner had advised him against. Yet it was too late to withdraw now.

'It is kind of you to see me without an appointment. Councillor Harford is making something of a show but we always knew it would be a struggle against the combined strength of the two parties.'

James Walter smiled. 'I do not mind the contest. Young men must make their way. Both are highly capable and both would make excellent representatives of our city in Parliament.' He walked across to a side table. 'You will take a sherry? Good. I am just sorry that Robert rejected the advice of older heads and perhaps blighted his future in Bristol for good.'

Richard took the proffered glass. 'Thank you. I think he feels the issue of the Colonies too pressing to wait.'

'Ah yes,' said Walter benevolently, 'young men are always in a hurry. It should be us older heads hurrying, we have less time at our disposal. But I am sure you did not come here to discuss the election. How can I be of service to you?'

He ushered Richard to a chair and resumed his own seat behind his desk.

'I am on something of a delicate mission and hope you won't take offence at what I am going to ask.'

'I will answer as best I can,' the Mayor replied tactfully.

Richard hesitated but for a second. 'I understand that some years ago you were in partnership with Mr Terrill in the shipping business.'

The Mayor looked puzzled. 'That is true. But how can that possibly be of interest to you? It is nearly ten years since our relationship finally ended.'

'Were you in business with him for long?'

'To tell the truth, no. It was too risky a business for me. Mr Terrill was anxious to invest in overseas trade and sought capital from a few businessmen in Bristol of whom I was one. Your father was another I believe. Mr Terrill had other business interests at the time that required considerable capital but as they prospered and made profits, so he bought out, one by one, those of us who had invested in his shipping line. I was relieved to go. I fear I did not have the nerve for long term risk.'

Richard began to relax a little. The Mayor did not seem to resent the questioning so far and had not even sought an explanation.

'It is the *Demera* in which I am particularly interested.'

A hint of impatience flitted across the Mayor's face. 'I am a little surprised, Richard, that you persist in your questions without any explanation or reason, on business matters which if I may say so, are no concern of yours.' He hesitated. 'But if it will satisfy you, yes, I did have an interest in the vessel for a while, but sold out to Mr Terrill before she foundered.'

'So you had nothing to do with the insurance settlement?'

The Mayor laughed, his moment of annoyance passed. 'No, my timidity counted against me there. I had sold out a few months before. Had I held on, no doubt I would have received a handsome insurance settlement. But tell me, pray, why all these questions?'

Richard thought fast. Could he trust this man? He felt he had to. He was not prepared to lie to him.

'I am not sure of your present relationship with Mr Terrill but the question of the insurance settlement has recently been raised and I have been asked to investigate the circumstances under which it was made. I can tell you I am relieved to hear you were not involved.'

The Mayor looked serious. 'I don't know what is behind what you are doing, nor do I want to, but do be careful. I may be a temporary political supporter of Councillor Terrill's campaign for Parliament, but that is a question of principle, honouring an agreement. He is not a personal friend. But he is powerful and dangerous. If he hears of your enquiries he will bring all his considerable influence to bear against you, including, no doubt, a writ for slander.' He relaxed again. 'And isn't there something of a personal animosity between you over the affections of Miss Jackson?' His eyes twinkled as he spoke. Richard realised he should take matters no further. He made light of the Mayor's ribbing and politely took his leave, shaking visibly at the audacity of his action and his escape from possible disaster.

Richard had no difficulty finding the Western Fire and Commerce Insurance Company, not because it advertised its services widely, but because Small Street lived up to its name and counted but a few businesses. The company advertised itself by a small plate adjacent to a front door that was unlocked and led directly up some stairs to an office that could have been mistaken for lawyers premises had Richard not known better. At the top of the stairs Richard found an open door that led into a large room with an imposing desk in the middle, surrounded by piles of files on the floor around, like an island in a sea of parchment. Behind the desk, marooned with it unless he were to escape by treading across the parchment clad floor, sat an elderly man, portly and bald, with a pair of glasses fixed more adjacent to the point of his nose than across his eyes.

'Maurice Woolston at your service, what can I do for you young man?'

'I am an attorney, investigating an insurance matter on behalf of the relatives of a deceased client. I believe you were the insurer of a ship named the *Demera* that sank off the Slave Coast in 1764. Am I correct?'

'The man screwed his face up in a quizzical way. 'Let me see now. Yes I believe that is the case. But what is your interest in the ship exactly?'

'I am looking after the interests of the family of a deceased shareholder in the owning company.'

Woolston got up and walked over a few parchments to a large set of wooden racks affixed along the wall. After some study and some false alarms he eventually alighted on a large volume forming part of a set. Without a word he carried it back to his desk and started to leaf through its pages. 'Yes I have the details here. What is it you want to know?'

'Could you tell me the type of insurance cover that was taken out, the amount paid in settlement, and to whom it was paid?'

Richard was not certain he would be given all the information he sought but saw no guile in the man's eyes.

'I have most of that information here. As you may know, a merchant ship can be insured in a number of ways. It is all a matter of risk, you see. Sometimes we insure cargo that subsequently has to be thrown overboard for the safety of the vessel. Legal jettison we call it. Sometimes we insure cargo that founders with the ship. In this case the insurance cover was the latter. Cargo, that is to say, livestock, went down with the ship. I am not able to tell you the settlement figure, but it was very substantial.'

Richard studied the insurance agent's expression to try and gauge whether he could press him further. 'Are you able to tell me to whom the settlement sum was paid?'

'Indeed I cannot, sir. That is er... confidential. The ship and cargo was owned by a Bristol company that I recall had some problems with its registration. In the event I paid the company secretary. And no, I cannot reveal his name.'

It was a particularly cold March and Bristol was experiencing sharp frosts at night and bitter days. The city was full of people, for as always, the assize opened in a carnival atmosphere. The first to arrive, during the week before, were the traders and street vendors from all over north Somerset and south Gloucestershire, who came to take advantage of the extra concentration of people. Across the entrance of the alleyways and side streets off Corn Street, Broad Street and around the harbour, temporary stalls were erected to exhibit a variety of goods from traditional local produce to foreign luxuries imported through the docks. Shopkeepers spent the weekend cleaning their shops and the cobbled roadway in front, putting up bunting and redesigning their window displays.

Throughout the Monday of the opening week of the assize carriages arrived from all over the hinterland bringing county squires, the gentry, and their families. Every London coach brought its complement of clerks, attorneys, and barristers. The most expensive hotels were booked, each with its crowd of onlookers around the main entrance to gape at the wealthy and well-dressed arrivals.

By late Tuesday afternoon the Bull Hotel was the centre of attention, for it was there that the grand jury dinner followed by assize ball would take place. From early evening carriages arrived one after another in quick succession, dropping off their passengers under the watchful eye of a large and critical audience. Anyone who was, or aspired to be, anyone in Bristol came to the assize ball. Daughters of wealthy merchants hoping to catch the eye of up and coming politicians, and impecunious barristers seeking a wealthy marriage.

On the Wednesday morning the crowds were out and about early, lining the route from Corn Street to the Cathedral on the Green. It was another sharp day, bright but cold. Children, trying to keep warm, congregated around the braziers of the hot chestnut sellers, and an array of street cleaners moved steadily along with shovels, buckets, and dung carts, clearing the streets of horse dung, the water cart following behind to wash the cobbles.

For this was the route of the assize procession, a walk of a quarter of a mile or so by all connected with it to the cathedral for the traditional assize service. The unwholesome smell of the streets gradually lifted, to be replaced by the sweet aroma of coffee beans as the coffee houses along the route opened their doors to the cold and muffled customers waiting outside. The streets were full of noise. The chestnut sellers and other vendors shouted their wares, children squealed with excitement, carriages rattled their way across Bristol Bridge and up High Street.

Eventually the procession was assembled and set off along Corn Street. At the head, the Judges, dressed in ankle length red tunics pulled in at the waist by a wide black belt. They were full-wigged and each carried the traditional lace handkerchief and posy of flowers, a hangover from the days when the first duty of the visiting assize was to inspect the prisons to ensure no one was held except by due process of law. The gaols being pestilential and diseased, the perfume from the posy was believed to keep the Judges safe from infection.

Behind the Judges processed the clerks, attorneys and barristers, followed by the city dignitaries, the Mayor, aldermen and councillors, and the Member of Parliament, Henry Croder. The Mayor, James Walter, was resplendent in black suit and knickerbockers, crimson gown and two-cornered hat. The councillors wore mauve coats trimmed with fur at collar and hem. Among the councillors walked the two parliamentary candidates, civic pride and duty for this morning at least pushing the election into the background.

By ten o'clock everyone who was attending had arrived and settled themselves in the Cathedral awaiting their Bishop who was to conduct the traditional service of prayer for wise counsel, fair trials and just judgements. Harford and Terrill sat a few feet away from each other, each studiously avoiding catching the other's eye, giving the appearance of close attention to the service but in reality thinking and planning the rest of their campaigns. Voting was now half over and Terrill was maintaining a comfortable lead over his opponent, but for today the drama of the campaign was set aside for the tradition and ritual of one of the city's great civic occasions.

But not everyone connected with the assize was able to enjoy the surrounding pomp and ceremony. At the same time as the choir and congregation were lifting their voices to God, others were immersed in quite different thoughts. Richard and William, waiting for the charges against themselves to be dropped, were thinking of Nancy and her coming trial. Willoughby was in his office making final preparations for her defence, Nancy herself sat in her cell, thinking of nothing very much, waiting without hope for whatever fate held for her.

Shortly before midday, Willoughby and Richard went to Newgate to visit her. 'What's goin' on?' she asked.

'The assize service has ended,' replied Willoughby. 'The hearings will start this afternoon.'

'How much longer will Nancy have to wait?' asked Richard.

'First will be the swearing in of the Grand Jury. The prosecution will then run through each case one after the other, with the Judge advising on each. The Grand Jury will then retire to decide whether there is sufficient evidence to allow trials to proceed. That's when yours will be dismissed, Richard. Assuming Nancy's goes ahead, as I expect it will, it will be second, after another murder trial. It is likely to start on Friday morning.'

'Is there any chance of the Grand Jury throwing the case out?' asked Richard.

'Virtually none I am afraid. Magistrates' committals are rarely challenged and I understand the Judge will give a strong lead. We can only pray the trial jury will eventually give Nancy the benefit of the doubt.'

'Richard, come with me, if you would be so kind, I have a job for you.'

Richard looked up from the pile of papers he was working on in Robert Harford's office and saw Jeremy Sly smiling at him from the doorway.

'What are we doing this morning, Mr Sly?'

'We are going to a wedding. In fact five weddings to be precise.'

Sly grinned at Richard's bemused face and total lack of comprehension.

'I am not sure I have time to attend one wedding let alone five. I have committed myself to helping Robert today.'

'Don't worry, nothing could be more important to the campaign than this.'

Richard grabbed his coat and ran after the agent who was already on his way down the street. Turning into Lewins Mead they walked the few yards to St James church.

Outside the church stood a group of men and women standing silently and seemingly embarrassed at being there.

'Come on,' waved Sly, 'the vicar will be waiting. Please choose a partner.'

Awkwardly they began to line up in pairs, each one of a pair approximately the same age as each other. They filed into the church, the first couple to the altar, the others sitting down to wait their turn. Richard and Jeremy Sly stood at the alter rail as witnesses. The marriage ceremony was brief but not without humour as the respective brides and grooms did not know each other's names. The five ceremonies were over in twenty minutes, at the end of which Sly hustled them out of the door.

'Now Richard we are taking them to the town clerk's office to have the claims of the new husbands investigated for them to be enrolled as freemen.'

' I am sure you know what you are doing Mr Sly, but I don't, so please enlighten me.'

Sly laughed. He was clearly enjoying himself. 'It is quite simple really. The five brides are widows or daughters of freemen. Two of them come from the workhouse, two from almshouses, and the fifth from her own home. Their new husbands are entitled to be on the register as freemen. Within the hour we shall have five new voters.'

'But the couples appear not to know each other, how did you persuade them to marry?'

'Oh, they were paid their expenses, and each marriage will be of short duration. In fact once the husbands receive their certificates we will be returning to the church to witness the unfortunate end of the marriages.'

Sly chuckled to himself. Richard did not know whether to admire the man or show his disquiet at such practice.

Armed with new marriage certificates, there was little the Town Clerk could do but issue each man with a certificate. The Mayor, James Walter, had been warned to attend for it was the custom in the city for the Mayor to sign the certificates as well. In fact there was no dispute, for the Town Clerk was paid a fee for his work. Following receipt of the certificates the party trooped off to the office of the Chamberlain, who for another fee enrolled the names in the book of burgesses.

'Now, Richard, the next stop is for our new freemen to vote. We will lead our tally of voters together. This may be a little dangerous. I will lead and you will bring up the rear, if you would be so good.'

But there was no trouble. Sly had thoughtfully arranged for two burly bludgeon men armed with staves to accompany the small party to the polling station where the first man was directed to vote for Joseph Terrill, the rest for Robert Harford.

'Now for the final part of the proceedings, Richard. Back to St James.'

On returning to the church, so recently the scene of wedded bliss, instead of entering the church itself, the entire party was taken to meet the vicar, now waiting in the graveyard. Couple by couple, the newlyweds were invited to stand on the opposite sides of a grave. The vicar muttered a few words, some of which Richard recognised as having a passing resemblance to a funeral service, then each couple in turn were encouraged to shout 'death do us part' to each other across the grave.

Their duty over, the five brides of such short duration were dismissed by Sly, with their expenses, and returned from whence he had found them. The five freemen also left, fees in their pockets, their civic duty done.

But Richard's morning of excitement was not yet done. Back in the election office, the agent outlined a new duty for him.

'Richard, there is a solicitor called Jeremiah Clarke who is entitled to be enrolled as a freeman. Unfortunately there is a dispute as to whether he was born in Bristol. I want you to find out, if you would be so good.'

'Do we have any clues, Mr Sly?'

'I can tell you the exact house. It is in Limekiln Lane. Unfortunately the Bristol and Gloucestershire boundary goes right through the middle of the house. If you go to Mr Clarke's office he will take you to the place of his birth and identify the very room, which I trust you will find to be the correct side of the border.'

Richard raised his eyes heavenwards. 'I am beginning to see why you enjoy elections so much Mr Sly.'

'I have a surprise for you all.' Robert Harford looked at the expectant faces of his closest supporters sitting round the table in the conference room in his election headquarters. It was clear to his audience that he had decided to tease them a little. 'Before telling you, I would like us to take stock of our position. John perhaps you would be so kind.'

John Powell shuffled nervously the few sheets of paper in front of him betraying that he was a not a man about to deliver good news.

'Thank you Robert. The count, as you all know, currently stands at Terrill 1,028 votes, Robert 936. There are five days to go before polls close. We have polled well against the combined forces of our opposition. I fear, though, that the final few days will see us slipping further behind.' He paused, to make sure he had the attention of everyone present. Robert nodded in agreement, everyone else sat motionless. 'All our pledges have now voted, and the uncommitted we have visited twice. There are no new sympathetic freemen to be made up and our funds are almost exhausted. The Tories have enough money to keep their supporters happy and many of Terrill's election committee have yet to vote. Unless we can find a new appeal, the cause is lost.'

Sarah looked round at the other committee members, the shock and disappointment clearly registering on their faces. They were perplexed and confused. Against the two major parties acting together they had kept within range of Terrill's vote; and had won the arguments with the non-voting population at large who cheered their candidate at every opportunity. Yet now they were being told that they would lose. They needed a lift, she could see that. Was Robert about to give them one?

'Thank you, John,' said Robert, 'you are correct in your analysis. I came to much the same conclusion two days ago. I have decided that win or lose, we must finish with a stir. I should like you all to know that I have sent a message to London and that the day after tomorrow Sir Edwin Bulwer arrives in Bristol to champion our cause.'

There was a sharp intake of breath from some of the faces around him.

'The Irishman?' asked Hugh Berry.

'The same. He is the greatest platform and House of Commons orator of our time and a staunch advocate of the colonists' cause. He also has strong doubts about the slave trade. If anyone can rouse the electorate to our support it is he.'

'Aren't you taking something of a risk, Robert?' asked Hugh Berry. 'Bristolians do not take too kindly to outsiders, and an Irishman at that.'

Sarah felt herself flush with anger. 'What have we got to lose, Hugh? We have just been told we cannot catch the Tories as we are. I applaud Robert's initiative. It may or may not be successful.

If it fails we will be in no worse a position than we are now. And Mr Bulwer's intervention will allow Robert's case to be given national prominence.'

Hugh Berry smiled benignly, acknowledging the strength of her argument, and no one else sought to disagree.

After the meeting was over and everyone was leaving, Robert asked Sarah to stay and talk further.

'Thank you for your support, Sarah. But I want to ask you what has become of Richard? We have not seen him recently. Has his experience at the hustings deterred him from politics?'

Sarah looked solemn. 'No, it is not that, Robert. He has a more serious problem to deal with.' She told him of Nancy's plight. Neither the public nor the press had made any connection between the trial and the by-election even though both were being widely discussed. Sarah realised that Richard knew he was the connecting link and following the intervention at the one public meeting at which he had attempted to speak, had decided to keep away for fear of further damaging their cause.

Robert listened impassively to Sarah's story.

'I wish I could help him,' he said at last. 'There is a lot of good in that young man as I think you have discovered, Sarah. But tell me, when does the trial start?'

'Friday morning I believe.'

'The morning Bulwer and I process through the city to a rally at the Bush Hotel. Poor Nancy. While we will be campaigning she will be fighting for her life only a few yards away.'

~ CHAPTER 16 ~

Richard hardly slept on Thursday night and the following morning he and William went early to court to secure William a seat in the public gallery. Richard was likely to give evidence so had to remain outside the courtroom. Normally a trial would attract only friends or relatives of those charged, with a sprinkling of vagrants on a cold day seeking shelter, warmth and entertainment. Today the court was full, for a murder trial provided great interest and all around them sat an excited crowd attracted to what they believed would be a grand public spectacle. Two special constables were stationed in the vestibule to control the jostling spectators and long before the start time of 11.00 o'clock the public gallery was full and even overflowing both into the well of the court and out of the court door.

The court itself was a square room with dark panelled windows which let in little light, and a dais at one end on which stood the judges' chairs. On one side were two raised benches for journalists and on the opposite side the jury benches. The dock was in the centre of the court, behind the lawyers' benches and in front of the seats set aside for the public.

On the advocates' benches sat two barristers with two attorneys behind them. The lawyers were engaged in active, if quiet, conversation. There were smiles and nods between them, which William found disconcerting. The camaraderie of the bar, an accepted part of a lawyer's professional life, now seemed inappropriate when two of them were seeking a death sentence and the other two trying to prevent it.

At the stroke of 11.00 an usher appeared.

'The court will rise.'

There was immediate silence and with something less than military precision everyone stood up. The lawyers were the first to rise, being familiar with, and expecting the call. The public lagged behind, being a little slow to realise the invocation applied to them. The Judge, Mr Justice Jeffard, followed by two magistrates and the High Sheriff shuffled in, bows were exchanged with the bar in a conspiratorial fashion, and the court was ready.

The jury was sworn in, twelve local men of trade and commerce, and then Nancy appeared in the dock. She was deathly pale, her hair ragged and unkempt, and she kept her head down taking in nothing of her surroundings.

For the next two hours William sat transfixed by the struggle that was unfolding before him. Feeling so personally involved he heard the arguments as if he was in the dock himself as a helpless victim and wondered what Nancy thought of it all, if she understood any of it, or even thought about it.

When counsel for the Crown, Sir Spenser Cartwright, had finished his opening speech, the prosecution evidence began to unfold. It soon became clear that far from abandoning hope of recapturing Abel Jacobs the authorities had decided that his associates might well lead them to him. The first witness told of his instructions to follow Richard in the belief that he would lead him to Nancy, who in turn would sooner or later lead him to Jacobs. This strategy had worked more easily than expected. Standing next to Richard in the bar of the Albatross he had overheard the arrangements for the late night rendezvous.

The second witness, a special constable, gave evidence of the entry into the house and subsequent discovery of Nancy bending over the body, knife in hand. William watched the faces of the jurors as a detailed description was given. It appeared to be a case of a loose-living woman gaining revenge on a former client. How many of the jurors had themselves visited the women of Marsh Street? Would their sympathy lie with the victim?

At about the time that Nancy's trial was opening, a quite different scene was being enacted not a hundred yards away at Bristol Bridge. A huge crowd had gathered, noisy and boisterous. From its size it seemed that everyone in Bristol who had not found a seat in the courthouse had come here instead. Robert Harford's supporters had been abroad early with leaflets and loud hailers advising of a grand procession to the Bush Hotel at which Edwin Bulwer would address a rally. Bulwer's reputation as an orator was spread throughout the land and he was one of few politicians who inspired enthusiasm rather than contempt.

Sarah, her cape pulled tightly round her shoulders, and hood up, mingled with the excited crowd eager for a glimpse of the great man. Her father had declined to join her but had insisted on her maid accompanying her for protection. A crowd was an incitement to rowdy behaviour and petty thieving.

She knew that Sir Edwin and Robert were to be chaired at the head of the procession, escorted by two bands and a parade of supporters wearing favours in their candidate's colours. The colour had been selected with care. Sufficiently to be associated with the Whigs, but sufficiently dissimilar to show Harford's independence.

It was clear to Sarah that the arrival of the famous orator had caught the imagination of the people, at least of the ordinary citizens, who loved a spectacle. Whether the voting freemen were similarly impressed had yet to be made clear. As she waited in the throng she was encouraged by the remarks of those around her.

'He speaks his mind, this Bulwer.'

'Aye,' said another. 'I don't agree with all he says, but he's an honest man.'

Soon there was a loud hurrah and cheering from the back of the crowd. Turning, Sarah could see the two men had arrived, chaired precariously aloft by their supporters.

They were set down by the bridge from where Bulwer addressed them. 'Citizens of Bristol. I come here today to commend Robert Harford as the candidate you should support. Join with us in a procession of strength to where I will tell you why I think Robert Harford should be your next Member of Parliament.'

A loud cheer greeted these words and the excited throng began to form a semi orderly line behind the two leaders. Up went the chairs again, a small band fell into formation immediately behind them, then the populace, and behind them another, larger, band.

Sarah made to join the procession, but as she did so, a roughly dressed elderly man sidled up to her. She recoiled from being accosted by such a man.

'Miss Jackson?'

She stopped and looked more closely at him. She did not recognise him, but judged from his weather beaten features that he had spent some years at sea.

'Yes, that is my name.' Sarah looked round to make sure her maid was at hand.

'Can I have a word, miss?'

'What about? The procession is about to begin.'

'I want to tell you about the girl Nancy.'

He had her full attention now. 'You have some information about her?'

'I have. I know she didn't kill Abel Jacobs.'

Sarah touched the man's arm. 'Come with me.'

All thought of the procession and Bulwer's speech went out of her mind, as did her care for her own personal safety.

She led him up the High Street to an alleyway leading off from the street, just below the Corn Market. Robert Harford's office was open for election helpers who were still actively coming and going. There was work to be done and not everyone could go to the rally. She led the stranger into the boardroom and asked her maid to wait outside the door.

'Now, Mr ....'

'Pitts.'

'Mr Pitts, what do you want to tell me?'

Pitts looked round the room. Sarah thought the formal surroundings had made him agitated and nervous and began to think she had made a mistake bringing him there. His resolve seemed to be weakening. Clearly it had taken some effort for him to come to her.

'Anything you tell me, Mr Pitts, will be treated with discretion. You have my word on that.'

She watched him look round the room. Then his whole body seemed to relax.

'Well, miss, I live in a cottage in Pill. Jacobs lived there too, for a while. So did Nancy. Jacobs and I did a little trade, you might say, and Nancy ran messenger. But Jacobs weren't never satisfied with just a bit o' liquor. He were into other things. I didn't hold with what he were up to, but it weren't for me to say.'

Sarah took a step towards him. In the distance she could hear one of the bands playing, interspersed with good-natured shouting. The procession was on its way, but no longer seemed important to her.

'What sort of things, Mr Pitt?'

He shrugged his shoulders. 'I don't rightly know. All I can say is he were paid by someone in Bristol to do his bidding.'

'What did he have to do?'

'He once told me he was paid to stop people asking questions.'

'What has all this got to do with Nancy, Mr Pitts?'

'Like I said, he were never content. After his escape from gaol, two men came looking for him. He weren't with me at the time.

They told me to tell him that their employer weren't going to be blackmailed no more and was going to settle with him.'

'Do you know what they meant?'

'Knowing Abel, I reasoned he had come to know so much that he asked to be paid to keep quiet. He didn't seem to understand that if he could be paid to kill, then someone could be paid to kill him too.'

'Kill? Who was killed?'

Pitts began to fidget in his seat and look round. Sarah could tell he had said more than he intended and had frightened himself.

'I... I don't know ma'am.' He fell silent for a while. Sarah wondered how to encourage him to tell the full story. She spoke quietly, gently encouraging him.

'I think you do, Mr Pitts. If you want to protect yourself, I am the person who can best help you.'

Sarah wasn't sure whether she was right to say that, but told herself that at least she would be able to find Pitts a good lawyer. She watched his face, which revealed he was turning the matter over in his mind, His eyes dulled and his lips quivered.

'Miss Jackson, I believe he murdered your uncle.'

Sarah froze. Outside the band grew louder as the procession made its way down Corn Street. She felt dizzy and gripped the table. So Richard had been right all along. Uncle Ben's death had not been a casual robbery, Jacobs had been paid to kill him, then tried to blackmail his hirer and had himself been killed for his pains. The band was now outside the office drowning her thoughts. She wanted to scream. Would the noise never stop?

'Mr Pitts,' she croaked, 'you must come to the law courts and tell your story to Nancy's lawyer. That is the only way Nancy can be saved.'

This was too much for the frightened man.

'I ain't goin' to no courts. You promised you wouldn't tell. Now you know what happened, you must save her yourself. I've done all I'm goin' to do.'

Sarah was unable to restrain him. He strode over to the door and before she could think what to do, he was gone.

Richard was pacing up and down the waiting room fretfully when Sarah burst in unexpectedly. In his career as a trainee attorney he had spent many tedious hours in court, sitting behind counsel, representing clients, and had found time passed slowly enough. But being a witness and kept out of the court-room itself, not knowing what was going on, was even worse. When he saw Sarah come in looking so agitated he felt a mixture of both alarm and relief. He ushered her to a bench away from other witnesses waiting their turn in the other courts and Sarah told her of Pitt's revelations.

'We must let Arthur Collins know of this as soon as possible' he said excitedly when she had finished. 'Even if we cannot prove what Pitts says is true, it might sow sufficient doubt in the minds of the jury to enable them to acquit Nancy. It always weakens a prosecution case when there is another possible explanation and motive.'

He looked at his pocket watch. 'Unfortunately we will be un-able to speak to him until the court rises, which won't be for another hour or so.'

'Will it be too late then?' Sarah showed from her voice how anxious she was.

'No. The prosecution case will last most of today and the de-fence will go on into Monday. If we can find Pitts and bring him back here, we must do so by then.'

'Should we let Robert know?'

'I have been wondering that. Yes I think we should. Whether he takes it up is for his judgement.'

Together they left the court and hastened to the Bush Hotel. They found that the procession had arrived and a large crowd was listening attentively to Edwin Bulwer who was speaking to them from the balcony above. On any other occasion Richard would have been pleased to be there, but now it represented a diversion and delay from the more serious business. Yet he resigned himself to listening, for there was nothing he could do until it was finished. As they edged further into the crowd they began to pick up Bulwer's words. His powerful and melodic voice penetrated even to the edge of the assembled crowd. The onlookers stood in the main in respectful silence save for a small group of agitators clustered together near the back.

'The Government must revert to old principles.' Richard picked up Bulwer's words and despite himself, the mellifluence of the famous orator arrested his attention.

'We are as a nation coming to a crisis in our affairs. It calls for wise counsels. I speak of the unhappy dispute with America. There are many opinions on how to deal with the situation. I do not seek to imply lack of integrity of any opinion even if I do not agree with it. But the solution is not obvious. There are many questions: of constitution and of trade. We must send to Parliament a man who is prepared to tackle these issues sympathetically and with understanding of the points of view of all who are in contention. This great commercial city will find its livelihood endangered if there be the slightest mistake. Do not misunderstand. I support the constitutional position of Great Britain. But this superiority must maintain the liberties of sober spirited Americans. No colonist should be put in a position of not being a freeman. I believe the superiority of Great Britain and the liberty of the colonists can both be maintained. So seek peace, not conflict, with our cousins in the Colonies.'

Even the agitators had fallen silent. Richard could see that Bulwer had the entire crowd eating out of his hand. The Terrill supporters would one minute nod in agreement, and then next realise they didn't agree with him at all.

Then he stopped. People leaned forward, eager to hear more. Now in a whisper, he brought his speech to a close.

'And the only way to stop this happening is to vote for Robert Harford, and by so doing you will be sending a signal to Westminster that cannot be ignored. That is why I am in Bristol today. In your hands perhaps lies the fate of the American colonists. Do not let them down.'

For just a few minutes Richard had forgotten Nancy and been swept up in the tidal wave of enthusiasm. He found himself clapping and cheering with the crowd and was gratified to find Sarah was responding to the orator in the same way. But there were almost as many boos and jeers as cheers, as supporters and opponents alike tried to out voice each other.

Robert stepped forward, holding his hands up in a vain attempt to quieten the crowd.

'With your support,' he began, but his words were drowned out by the noise. He tried again. 'With your support we can put up such a show that the Tories will regret ever having contested the seat. By close of poll we shall be so far ahead that Bristol will have sent such a message to Government that they will be unable to ignore it.' Richard could see that the audience had been lost and that only the first two or three rows of listeners would have heard what Robert had said. But he pressed on.

'Go out and bring in those who have the vote, help the sick and the old. Do not be put off from voting by the bullies supporting the Tory candidate. Victory will be ours.'

He could say no more. All around the street there was cheering and jeering from different factions intent on out shouting each other.

Robert and Sir Edwin bowed, waved, then bowed again, then repeated the exercise. It was some ten minutes before the crowd began to disperse, in good spirits and without incident. The two speakers then disappeared into the hotel and Richard and Sarah found them in a first floor sitting room, sprawled in armchairs, resting and reflecting on the success of the rally. Robert was not too carried away by the occasion to not be surprised by the appearance of Richard, away from the law courts.

'A spirited reply to the Tories, eh Richard? That will frighten Mr Terrill don't you think?' He did not wait for a reply. 'But what brings you here? I thought you were to remain at Nancy's trial.'

'I am here because of Nancy, Robert. Sarah has some important information which may have some relevance to your campaign.'

Robert looked across at Bulwer. 'I am not sure this business will interest you, Edwin.'

'On the contrary, anything that might affect the election is of interest to me. Mr Stourton and I met over a year ago before he went on the slaver. Is your voyage part of the story Mr Stourton? If so, I would like to hear it. It will relax and divert us after our exertions.' He slumped back into his armchair to listen what Richard had to say.

Recounting the events took some time, for Bulwer was unaware of much of the background, although he had read Richard's report on his voyage on the Amelia and the disposal of the slaves. To Richard's surprise Bulwer showed great interest in the suspected insurance swindle and questioned him closely about it. When Richard had brought the story up to that very morning, Sarah recounted her meeting with Pitts. The two men sat silent for a while after she had finished.

'I see the connection between Nancy's trial and this by-election,' said Robert. 'Your appearance in the witness box and the evidence you and Sarah would give could have serious repercussions. Nancy's attorney must decide how best to handle the evidence to her best advantage, but any suggestion that Mr Terrill is involved without substantial evidence to back it up will be construed as a smear and a tactic that could rebound against our campaign.'

Richard could see the dilemma. 'Would you mind, Robert?'

'No,' Robert replied without hesitation. 'A human life is at stake here. That is far more important than a few votes. You must do what you are advised is best for that poor girl. Don't you agree Edwin?'

They all looked at the MP for confirmation. He was lying back in his armchair, eyes closed, breathing peacefully.

Punctually at 10 o'clock on the following morning, a Saturday, Richard stood on the doorstep of the Jackson house for a meeting with Julia. He was feeling depressed over the trial; and the steady downpour of rain did nothing to lift his spirits as he shook and stamped his feet to rid himself of dripping water.

Sarah opened the door herself. 'Richard, come in. We are so pleased to see you.'

The sight of Sarah and his sister together began to restore his humour and a glass of sherry combined with a blazing log fire in the morning room completed the process.

'It is not an easy time, Richard,' said Sarah, 'how is the trial going?'

'Not well I fear. The prosecution case finished yesterday. They rely on the evidence we all saw and will admit of no other suggestions without supporting evidence. Which of course we have not got. I give evidence on Monday morning. I can only talk of circumstantial matters such as you have told me and the judge will not like that. In all probability he will rule it inadmissible. But that is for another day. How are you, Julia?'

'I am well enough, Richard.' She fell silent.

Sarah said: 'Julia and I have had quite a talk this morning and there is something she wishes to tell you.'

Richard looked at his sister who seemed reluctant to tell him anything. 'Julia, what is it?'

'Richard, you remember that before you went away I told you of Nicholas and his attentions. Well, we have since come to an understanding. We would like your blessing and that of his parents to a union between us.'

Richard's features froze, but his mind started racing. Should he feel pleased for his sister? Or angry that she wanted to join herself to a slave owning family?

'I have not agreed to marry Nicholas,' she said. 'He has made me an offer but has agreed to wait for my answer until you returned and I had been able to talk to you about it. I intended to do so sooner, but the question of Sam prevented it. I have told Jane and she approves. I hope you will too.'

'Julia there is nothing I would wish more than your happiness,' he said. 'And I have nothing personally against Nicholas. I am just concerned about you living in a household dependent upon the income earned on a slave plantation.'

'Forgive me from speaking on a family matter, Richard,' said Sarah, ' but I believe Nicholas has quite different ideas to those of his father.'

'That is so,' said Julia. 'We have talked about this. He believes slaves should be treated more humanely than is usually the case, taught to read, and encouraged to convert to Christianity. He also believes that in time they should be able to gain their freedom.'

'That is certainly far-sighted,' said Richard, 'but while his father is alive...'

'He has talked to his father about it and has made it clear that if he goes to Virginia as overseer it will be on his own terms for running the plantation.'

Richard thought for some moments then realised that his feelings for his sister had overcome any doubts he had.

'Julia, that is wonderful news, of course you have my blessing,' he said. Nicholas is a fine man, and if you are sure it is what you want, then I will not stand in the way of your happiness.'

~ CHAPTER 17 ~

Richard slowly climbed into the witness box and gripping the front rail to steady his nerves, looked round. In the dock sat Nancy, head bowed, taking nothing in. Willoughby and Arthur Collins sat on the benches in front of her, William sat behind.

The prosecution case had concluded the previous Friday evening. The only witnesses called were those who had seen Nancy in the house at the time Jacob's body was discovered. It was not the function of the prosecution to open up the case for speculation; that might sow doubt in the minds of the jurors. Four witnesses had given virtually identical evidence, defiantly challenging the defence to gainsay the facts. Arthur Collins had made no impression on them in cross-examination and knew he would incur the wrath of the judge if he subjected the witnesses to speculative questions.

Richard was the first defence witness. It had always struck him as odd that the accused in a criminal trial was not allowed to give evidence on oath on his or her own behalf. Yet now he saw some merit in the rule. Nancy would be wholly unable to cope giving evidence and might easily succumb to suggestion on cross-examination. Or she might simply say nothing at all, condemning herself by her silence.

How different was the perspective of the court from the witness box. Richard had often sat behind counsel, listening to evidence being given, usually haltingly, often contradictorily, or even untruthfully. His indoctrination into the attitudes and traditions of his profession, learned over several years with Willoughby, deserted him and he began to think as a layman. He could see why most Englishmen were of the opinion that the best way to view the legal system was from as far away as possible. It struck him forcibly that for the Nancys of the world, the law was a foreign country with its own language and customs, and that lawyers operated in their own timescales, almost timeless. Now he realised how difficult it was to give evidence. Perhaps Nancy's life depended on how he dealt with the questions. Desperate as he was to save her, he knew that any embroidering of what he wanted to say would soon be found out, making her position worse. It was a relief to be questioned first by the sympathetic Arthur Collins, who led him gently through the events of that night. How he had sought out Nancy as a means of speaking to Abel Jacobs: the late night meeting; following her through the dark streets; and his surprise when officers rushed past him into the house.

His evidence about what he saw differed little from that of the prosecution witnesses. Yes, he agreed that Nancy was bending over the body, knife in hand. Yes, she was alone. No he neither saw nor heard anyone else. And yes, she would have just about had time to commit the offence. But he was able to score two minor victories.

'Mr Stourton, did you hear anyone else in the house when you went in?' asked Arthur Collins.

'I did not, but then I wouldn't have.'

'Why would that be?'

'Because the officers entered the house before me, making so much noise that I wouldn't have heard anything else.'

'Mr Stourton, I want to ask you about the knife. Would you look at it please? Is that the one that killed Abel Jacobs?'

'As far as I can tell, yes it is.'

'It is fairly large isn't it?'

'It is.'

'Would you have noticed if the accused had carried it from the public house to the scene of the killing?'

'Almost certainly. She wore no coat and would have had great difficulty concealing it.'

'Did you see her carrying it?'

'No, I did not.'

'So we can assume that it was at the house when she arrived.'

'I think that is a fair assumption.'

All this gave the jury the impression he was not trying to hide anything. Richard began to feel a little more composed as Arthur Collins came to the more difficult part of his testimony.

'Mr Stourton, perhaps you would tell the jury why you wanted to speak to Abel Jacobs.'

The whole court became hushed. This was something new. Jury and public alike had grown bored with the same facts being reiterated over and again and had grown impatient to hear Nancy's defence. Now, at last, a new line of questioning was opening up.

'I had been investigating the circumstances surrounding the loss of a merchant ship that sunk in 1764. Abel Jacobs was one of the crew. I knew he was wanted on smuggling charges and it was important to talk to him before he was rearrested or fled the country. I thought that Nancy might know where he was. As you have heard, she did.'

'What did you hope to hear from him?'

'I had reason to believe there might have been some fraudulent conduct concerning the insurance claim. I believed he had information about the loss of the ship that might have confirmed my suspicions. I also feared he was at risk because of this knowledge.'

'What do you mean, at risk?'

For the first time since the trial started the courtroom was absolutely silent. Richard felt his heart beating and felt everyone else heard it too. The only person who seemed less than enthralled was the judge, who squirmed uncomfortably in his chair, clearly wanting to intervene yet unwilling to do so because of the interest aroused, not least among the jurors. Richard knew the judge would intervene as soon as he felt able to do so without the jury sympathising with Nancy, and was determined to say what he wanted to before that happened.

Richard replied. 'I have been told that Abel Jacobs was blackmailing an important person in this city and was silenced because of it, not by an innocent young girl.'

There was uproar in the court. On the public benches talking and shouting broke out. The jurors looked baffled and started talking amongst themselves. Prosecuting counsel stood up and tried to make an objection but was drowned out by the noise. Yet he had no need to do so for the judge could restrain himself no longer.

'Mr Stourton, do you have any evidence to support this astounding accusation? If not, it should be withdrawn.'

'I have no direct evidence, my lord, but....'

'Then your evidence is not to be regarded.' The judge turned towards the jury.

'This witness is not reliable on the matter just raised. He has no evidence to support his testimony which will be struck from the record.'

'My lord, I will be calling another witness on this point and together...' began Arthur Collins.

But he could say no more. Judge Jeffard had taken a view and was not to be moved.

'Don't try my patience any more Mr Collins. I will not have witnesses coming into my court throwing out wild unsubstantiated rumours simply in an attempt to confuse the jury.'

He calmed a little. 'Is there anything else you want to ask this witness?'

'No, my lord.' Arthur Collins was not too dissatisfied. He had expected that reaction yet had made his point. It was easier to expunge a statement from the written record than from a juror's mind. A seed of doubt had been sown and he would nurture it carefully.

He sat down. All he could do now was hope that the cross- examination would not destroy the small gain he had made.

Sir Spenser Cartwright, prosecuting counsel, was a short weaselly figure with a voice that was thin and whiney, insinuous in tone and insinuating in manner. His technique was neither domineering nor forensic. His skill lay in simply pursuing a point until he had broken down the witness, much like scratching at a sore. Sometimes his victims were not aware of what he was doing, so subtle was his approach. But Richard knew of his reputation and methods having watched him in action on several occasions. This was the first time he had to face him personally.

'Mr Stourton, how long have you known the accused?'

'About fifteen months.'

'Where did you meet her?'

'In a public house in Marsh Street.'

'Which one?'

'The Flying Angel.'

Sir Spenser looked across at the jury to see if they showed sign of recognition. The jurors sat motionless. If they did know it, they were not going to let it be known.

'One of those public houses that carry a reputation for prostitution?' he continued.

'A number of public houses have that reputation, whether deserved or not I do not know.'

'The Flying Angel is one of them is it not?'

'So I believe.'

'How did you come to meet her there?'

'I didn't go there to meet her. When I went, I did not know her. She came up and spoke to me.'

'What about?'

'She asked if she could help me.'

'So she was offering you...what shall we say? Some business?'

'I don't believe she was offering herself if that is what you mean, Sir Spenser.'

'What was she offering then?' Sir Spenser's voice was loud and quizzical, the tone intended to show the jury he did not believe a word of it.

'She works for the landlord serving and cleaning up. I assumed at the time she was just acting as a good hostess when a stranger walks in.'

'And what did you ask for?'

'I had gone to try and find a Captain Cox and told her so. When she showed me where he was I gave her a penny. She seemed very pleased with that. Had she been offering herself, a penny would have been a disappointment.'

There was laughter in the public gallery, brought to an abrupt end by a stern look from the judge. Sir Spenser continued.

'Where was your second meeting with her?'

'At my lodgings. Or I should say, near my lodgings.'

'Why was that?'

'She followed me home.'

Richard looked across at Nancy but she remained motionless with head bowed. It was not clear whether she was following or even listening to the exchange.

'She followed you home did she? Why would she do that? To earn two pence this time perhaps?'

This brought another bout of laughter from the public gallery and several of the jurors smiled. But Judge Jeffard was not amused.

'I insist on silence in the public gallery. Anyone making a further disturbance will be evicted from the court. Carry on Sir Spenser.'

'Did you meet her frequently after that?'

'No. It was shortly after that when I went abroad. I was away for almost a year. I saw her once more before I left, and again on my return.'

'Ah yes, on your return from the Colonies. Was she still at the Flying Angel?'

'No. She was by then living at a cottage in Pill.'

'With the deceased?'

'With him and a other man.'

'What did you discover?'

'She told me that Jacobs had forced her to live there.'

'Did you believe that?'

'I did. She seemed frightened of him. I think she knew too much about him.'

'That is speculation, Mr Stourton,' said Judge Jeffard. Your opinion does not count as evidence. Please stick to the facts. Proceed Sir Spenser.'

'Thank my lord. So let us be clear, Mr Stourton. In the time you knew her she was living at either the Flying Angel or the cottage in Pill with two men one of whom, the deceased, was subsequently arrested for smuggling.'

'That is correct.'

'If what you say is true, that the accused was frightened of Jacobs, that would be an ample motive for killing him, would it not?'

'I don't believe the accused is capable of killing anyone.'

Sir Spenser looked towards the jury. 'Answer my question please, Mr Stourton'

'There are many people similarly circumstanced as Nancy. Very few resort to murder. It takes something more than that to turn someone to be a killer.'

'A way out, perhaps?' said Sir Spenser.

Richard treated the question as rhetorical and did not attempt to reply. Sir Spenser spent some seconds staring at the jury to make sure they had absorbed the point, then shuffled his papers and continued.

'Mr Stourton this trial is in its second day and no other plausible explanation has come forward, has it? We have a body. The accused bending over the body. And holding a knife. The best you can do is say you don't think she did it and you have no other explanation. That is the position, isn't it?'

'Sir Spenser, rules of evidence have prevented me from giving an alternative explanation,' replied Richard.

Richard's tormentor raised his voice. He wanted the close attention of the jury.

'The rules of evidence are correct, are they not? You were going to offer an explanation unsupported by any evidence weren't you, Mr Stourton?'

'Direct evidence, yes, Sir Spenser, but circumstantial....'

Richard's intended explanation was too much for the judge.

'Mr Stourton, be careful what you say. I have already ruled such statements inadmissible.'

Richard realised the judge saw things the same way as the prosecution. 'My lord, I was seeking to answer the question.'

For a further thirty minutes Richard had to endure the seemingly endless probing into his private life and motivation yet whenever he tried to explain the real reason for his visits to Marsh Street and to Pill the judge blocked him. It seemed there was a conspiracy against him and against Nancy. He hoped the jury would realise what was happening and be swayed by sympathy, but he could not be sure.

'That was well done, my boy.' Richard did not find Willoughby's tone convincing, nor was he convinced.

'Do you think so?'

'The problems you had were apparent before we called you. We had to take the risk. You were not to blame. Besides, we have started so sow a doubt in the minds of the jurors.'

They were standing outside the court, William Daniel between them. The public gallery was emptying, a feeling of intoxication sweeping through the crowd of onlookers as they pushed their way out of the court building. Some noticed Richard and grinned and pointed. He had livened things up for them and was therefore something of a celebrity. Richard was anxious to put the morning behind him and find a task more suited to his energy and enthusiasm.

Richard turned to Willoughby. 'What can we do now?'

'We have until tomorrow morning to find Samuel Baillie or John Pitts, or preferably both. Collins will keep the trial going until then. We have a few character witnesses lined up including the landlord of the Flying Angel. The witnesses will have limited impact, coming from Nancy's station in life, but will keep the court busy and Sir Spenser will take his time with them. He is not to know what we are doing. But tomorrow is our last chance.'

But their efforts came to nought. Baillie had disappeared, likely to have gone back to sea, his signed statement useless without him. Pitts had just vanished. Bulwer was back in London and Robert Harford was engrossed in his election campaign. By the following morning Richard and William were dispirited and depressed. After visiting Pill the afternoon before they had toured the drinking dens in Marsh Street and St Phillips at night, to no avail. No one who knew the truth about the murder of Abel Jacobs could be found. Despite the strictures of the judge the previous day, Arthur Collins felt he had no alternative but to call Sarah to recount her meeting with Pitts. She spoke in careful, measured tones. She could offer no certainty that Pitts was telling the truth. The judge was circumspect in his interventions. No one doubted that she had met the man Pitts and that her account of what he said was accurate, he told the jury, but no one knew whether what he said was true and therefore could not be accepted as evidence. The judge asked the jury to be careful when considering the hearsay evidence of a smuggler who could not be found.

And so the evidence came to an end in some sort of stalemate. The prosecution case was as strong at the conclusion as it had been at the beginning. The defence relied on a possible alternative which they could not prove. All turned on the final speech of Arthur Collins and the partiality of the judge in his summing up.

Arthur Collins faced a dilemma. It had been in the back of his mind throughout the trial but nothing had happened to lead to its resolution. As he prepared to address the jury he knew he had to make a decision that could, quite literally, mean life or death. If he posed to the jury a straight question of guilt or innocence, conviction or acquittal, what chance was there of the latter? The jury might feel sufficiently uneasy to acquit. But if not, the result would be fatal. Would he not do better to offer a half way house – argue that if she is guilty of killing Jacobs, then it was manslaughter on the grounds of extreme provocation, but not murder. This would enable the jury to convict her, as they were likely to do, but of the lesser crime, which would mean transportation for Nancy, not the gallows. But if offered that choice, might the jury not take it instead of an outright acquittal? No one could help him in this dilemma. Nancy herself neither understood the situation nor expressed a view. He could not transfer the responsibility to Willoughby or Richard.

Strangely enough he had found he could talk to William Daniel. Not being a lawyer, William had not felt the burden of responsibility transferred to him and was sufficiently detached from that responsibility to see the matter objectively. As he stood up to address the jury, William's words were in his ears. 'Keep her alive, Mr Collins. Don't let her die. Anything but the gallows.'

Anything but the gallows. That was his view too. A mistake cannot be rectified after an execution. Better transportation or prison than death. He knew the rigours of a convict's life in the Colonies but many made good. Nancy had grown up looking after herself and was the sort to adapt and even thrive in that type of environment. And there was always the possibility of a return if it could subsequently be proved that she was innocent. As he stood silent, facing the jury, waiting with a theatrical pause for their attention, he knew the right path to take.

The early part of his speech was devoted to outlining the facts and he lost no opportunity to repeat that no one had actually seen Nancy plunge the knife in. He then moved on to his submission.

'Gentlemen of the jury, put yourselves in the position of this young girl. Suppose you had been the first one into the house. Had gone upstairs, found Jacobs, and pulled the knife from his body. Could it not have happened to any one of you? Is the first one on the scene after the death necessarily the guilty party? How outraged would you be to be arrested and charged? If you could imagine it happening to you, can you imagine it happening to this girl too?

'And if you were planning a murder, would you do so when others were right behind you? What folly it would be! Not even the most foolish murderer would act in this way. And Nancy? She knew where Jacobs was living. She could have gone there at any time, unseen, alone, committed the crime then disappeared into the night.'

He stopped, taking a sip of water to give time for his words to sink in.

'I turn now to the question of motive. It is said that to find a murderer you need but find the opportunity and a motive. I have, I think, demonstrated that the opportunity was poorly chosen if this girl did the deed. So inopportune as to almost discount it. But what of her motive? If she had a motive does that preclude anyone else having a motive too? Need someone have only one enemy? Of course not. It was suggested by the prosecution that Nancy's motive was revenge for the abuse she had suffered. But abuse and molestation are rife amongst Nancy's class. It seldom leads to murder. Yet you have heard from Mr Stourton and Miss Jackson of deeper stirrings. Of possible fraud, even blackmail. I do not intend to pursue that theme. My lord the judge has rightly pointed out there is no evidence of such.' He glanced at the judge to see if he was going to be interrupted, but the judge did not stir. 'I cannot prove that someone else murdered Abel Jacobs, or that there was any blackmail going on. But in my submission I do not have to. It is enough to demonstrate to you that there could be other motives for this murder. I say to you, members of the jury, that there is no clear first hand evidence that the accused wielded the knife, nor that any alleged motive she may have is the only possible motive for murder.'

He looked at the jurors. Everyone sat motionless and without expression. What were they thinking? Would they acquit? Even if they were minded to do so now, would they hold to that intention after hearing the judge's summing up? No, Daniel was right. He could not gamble on one throw of the dice. He must play the safer card.

'Gentlemen of the jury, it is my belief that this girl is innocent and that the evidence is sufficient to secure her acquittal. But if – and I must emphasise I do not subscribe to this view – if you think she killed him, then surely it must have been an unpre-meditated attack. With Mr Stourton and others just outside she would never have planned to kill Jacobs when better opportuni-ties were available. And you have heard from Mr Stourton that there was no sign of the Defendant having carried the knife with her. In fact that was ruled out.

'If she did plunge in the knife – and I don't believe it – but if she did, then there must have been extreme provocation. Perhaps he threatened to abuse her again, or even threatened her life. Perhaps he tried to assault her. If so, I would suggest a verdict of guilty of murder followed by the gallows would be inappropriate. The right verdict would be manslaughter.'

Collins knew there was not the slightest evidence of provoca-tion and that the judge would tell them so. But the escape route had been opened up. If they felt pressured by the judge to con-vict, yet felt she did not deserve to hang, this was the way out. Not necessarily logical, but who knew whether logic or emotion carried most weight in the jury room?

As he sat down, Collins felt he had said all he could. He looked round at Lawrence Willoughby who nodded discretely, the signal between lawyers that nothing had been omitted that should have been said. Both waited anxiously for the judge to begin his sum-ming up. From his first words, their worst fears were realised. There was little attempt at impartiality. Whilst he did summarise the evidence on both sides, he referred to the prosecution evi-dence as facts, but the defence as supposition. For almost an hour the jury was treated to the judge's view of the trial. The only glimmer of light in an otherwise gloomy picture presented was the admission that manslaughter was possible on the facts, but extremely remote because of lack of credible evidence to support it. He, too, appeared to be a little unsure of how a jury would view the matter and felt the accused should not be allowed to get away scot-free. When the jury retired, Nancy's lawyers and friends made a sombre party outside the courtroom.

As Richard sat waiting in silence he was once again struck by the disinterested, almost careless, routine followed by the courts. Within perhaps a matter of minutes a decision would be made whether a young girl would live or die; yet while the jury was deliberating the judge was hearing other applications, apparently without a thought for what was going on in the jury room. Bail applications and sentencing went on for one, then two, hours before there was any sign that the jury had reached a verdict. Then, suddenly, everyone sprung to life. The usher appeared and nodded to Arthur Collins and the court rapidly filled up again. The jurors were already filing back. William secured his usual seat beside the dock and when all were settled and quiet Nancy appeared up the steps from the cells below. She looked pale and frightened. She stood up, swaying a little, her weak legs betraying her emotions.

Finally the Judge entered, bowed, sat down and turned to the jury.

'Gentlemen, have you reached a verdict?'

'We have, my lord,' said their spokesman.

'Is it a verdict you all agree?'

'It is, my lord.'

Richard found he could barely breath and his heart pounded.

'How find you the accused, guilty or not guilty?'

'Guilty my lord.' There was a sharp intake of breath around the court. 'But guilty of manslaughter not murder, on the grounds of provocation.'

The judge turned to Nancy. 'Prisoner at the bar, you have been found guilty of unlawful killing. The jury has decided that your actions fall short of murder but it is my duty to punish this offence as severely as the law allows. You will be transported to the Colonies for life. Take her away.'

But before she could be led down the steps to the cells below her legs gave way under her. William stretched across the dock and caught her, gripping her tight. As the warders came to take her away he had time to whisper in her ear. 'Don't worry Nancy, I won't desert you.' He had no idea whether she heard him, as she gave no sign of life when dragged downstairs, the trapdoor from the court banging noisily behind her.

✣ ✣ ✣

To the citizens of Bristol
Gentlemen,
Friends of Councillor Joseph Terrill were saddened to see
that the eminent Irish orator Sir Edwin Bulwer has recently
visited this City to speak on behalf of the radical traitor
Robert Harford. Are you acquainted with the views of this
Irishman? That he was once the driving force behind the late
government is not to be gainsaid. We grant that they re-
pealed the American stamp duty. But at the same time they
are responsible for all the disturbances that have happened
since and may continue to happen. If the Act had merely been
amended, and then have been enforced, we would not have
our present troubles. They then enacted a law for securing
the Dependence of the Colonies upon the Mother Country but
declared themselves sovereign having first refused to exercise
that power.
A WARNING
March 1772

Jeremy Sly rubbed his hands together with glee.

'That's just what we wanted, Robert. Those who were unaware
of Sir Edwin's visit will now know of it. What excellent publicity.
And how it will attract Whig voters unsure whether to support
you or abstain.'

'Do you think I should reply,' asked Robert Harford.

'You have already done so. At least, here is the draft of your
reply. If you are happy with it we can print it immediately.'

Robert smiled to himself and took the proffered document.

To the citizens of Bristol, greetings,
Gentlemen,
I have been handed a leaflet attacking the recent visit to
Bristol of the eminent parliamentarian Sir Edwin Bulwer who
was kind enough to support my candidature. Those who were
fortunate to hear Sir Edwin speak will have been impressed
by several points. He made it clear to all who cared to listen
that his first consideration was the welfare of commerce,
which is of great importance to this City and the realm in
general. The second point was to stress the serious situation
in which the country finds itself at the present time. Much will
depend on the calibre of men representing us in Parliament. I

have been honoured with the judgement of Sir Edwin that I
am that man who is best suited to represent this constituency
in place of our late member. I feel humble that such an emi-
nent man has given me this sacred duty and I trust the voters
of Bristol will follow his recommendation.
   Gentlemen,
   Your ever faithful and obedient servant,
   ROBERT HARFORD
   March 1772

'What can I say, Mr Sly? It captures the mood exactly. Please distribute it.'

Nicholas had waited patiently for an opportunity to speak to his parents about Julia. Yet his father seemed to be in a constant bad mood. He knew the cause. It was Julia's brother. The issue with the slave boy was insult enough to his father. But in his father's eyes there was a catalogue of other misdemeanours. The story of Richard's arrest with the smugglers was known abroad. He was involved in the election campaign of the young radical who dared challenge the traditional Tory view. And, worst of all, there were rumours that Richard was not supportive of the slave trade, as his attitude over the slave boy demonstrated. Any one of these would have been enough to condemn Richard in his father's eyes. Nicholas could see that. Yet he could not himself condemn Richard. Whilst brought up a Tory, he did not feel instinctively against any of the views that Richard supported. It was comforting to be in a Tory household, where stability and respect for the existing order bred security and comfort. Yet he knew that times were changing, and that Tories usually found themselves on the wrong side of an argument when that happened.

Despite the difficulties he felt the time had come to speak out. Jane already knew and approved of the attachment. She was now away visiting a cousin so as dinner for Nicholas and his parents came to an end and the servants dismissed, Nicholas felt the moment had come.

'Father there is something I wish to talk to you about.'

His mother stood up to leave. 'No, please stay mother, it concerns you too.'

She sat down again and waited for what she guessed was coming.

'There is no way of breaking this gently. I have formed an attachment for Julia.'

His father stared at him for several seconds then threw his serviette down on the table.

'The devil you have,' he said.

'And she has returned my affection.'

'I don't want to hear any more about it, Nicholas, it is out of the question, so let that be the end of the matter.'

Lady Manners stared at her son, expressionless and silent. At first Nicholas daren't look at his father but after this first inevitable outburst he slowly turned his head. Instead of an angry man he saw an unhappy one.

'Father, this will make no difference to the business. Julia and I wish to be married and she accepts I want to continue the business at your side...'

'She's got no money to bring to the marriage.'

'I know that, father, but money is not the issue. She is a charming, educated woman and she makes me happy. I love her. She has seen what commitment the business will require and what my responsibilities will be. She completely supports me.'

'I tried to discourage this, John,' said Lady Manners. 'But a son in a contented marriage will be of great benefit to you. More so than if he is unhappy. A dowry would mean nothing then.'

Sir John looked at his wife reproachfully. 'So you knew of this, Elizabeth? Has my whole family been conspiring against me?'

'Father, no,' said Nicholas. 'Mother tried to discourage me, as she has said. Julia told Jane and she is pleased. We want but your approval and blessing.'

'Her brother will have to give up my slave first.'

'Father I have thought of that. Julia and I will need to set up our own household. Young Sam would make a fine servant, provided of course he chooses voluntarily to do so.'

Sir John looked squarely at his son for the first time, a smile beginning to form in the corners of his mouth.

'You have inherited some craftiness from your old father after all.'

He offered him his hand. 'Go and call my prospective daughter in law down. She must be at her wits end.'

~ CHAPTER 18 ~

It took less than twenty-four hours for the shock of the conviction and sentence to wear off. By the following afternoon Lawrence Willoughby was at work drafting an appeal and an application for a stay of execution of the sentence. A mid-day conference with Arthur Collins had resulted in the decision to appeal although both knew it had little chance of success without fresh evidence. Richard was given a week's leave of absence from the office to work on Nancy's behalf. Robert Harford had sent a note to Edwin Bulwer telling him of the outcome and that Richard was travelling to London to confer with him. Sarah agreed to visit Nancy daily to comfort her while William continued the search for the missing witnesses.

As the London coach rattled along the road towards Bath Richard reflected on his previous visit to the capital when he had first met Edwin Bulwer and the representatives of the anti-slave trade committee. So much had happened since then, so many lives changed. Abel Jacobs dead; Nancy in prison convicted of his killing; and either Robert Harford or Joseph Terrill on the verge of a Parliamentary career. Sarah, at first so close to Terrill, now estranged through political differences and deep suspicion of Terrill's involvement in crime. And William, who he had not then met, now so involved with all of them. As for himself? What had happened to him? Then, an unknown would-be attorney with ambitions that did not extend beyond the walls of Willoughby's office. A seemingly routine probate, a chance letter, had led to a voyage across the Atlantic, an attempt on his life, arrested, and humiliated at a public meeting. He was the link between a number of dramas being played out across the city, some of national, even international importance. Had all this happened because he had found Ben Jackson's letter? Or would it have happened anyway, but without him? He looked at the faces of the other passengers, all sitting in silence and wrapped against the cold, and he wondered about their lives. Were they involved in mysteries and intrigues as had befallen him? Their expressions revealed nothing, but then perhaps neither did his.

Doubts about his visit to London began to surface in his mind as the coach left Bath on the next stage of its journey, to Chippenham. Perhaps it was the extreme cold felt crossing the Wiltshire Downs, so black and empty this time of the year. Had his need for action clouded his judgement? How would Bulwer help? Even if he wanted to do, there was only so much he could achieve. The influence of a member of parliament extended only so far, and interfering with the judicial system was beyond that limit. What could Bulwer do?

'What can I do?' boomed the triumphant voice of Edwin Bulwer as he ushered Richard into his study. 'What you should be asking, my friend, is what have I done?' He chuckled and smiled at Richard, his engaging eyes twinkling at the possession of a secret. 'I have some guests coming shortly who you will find most interesting. But before they arrive, pray bring me up to date with the news from Bristol, though I was there but three days since.'

Richard had arrived in London the evening before and found at his hotel a note from Bulwer inviting him to call at six o'clock the following evening. A good dinner and a comfortable bed had revived his spirits, as had the note from Bulwer. Now, he recounted the details of the trial and up-to-date news of the by-election with less pessimism than he had felt on the journey,

Bulwer seemed genuinely interested. 'So Harford's making a run of it, is he? How stood the poll when you left?'

'Terrill is still ahead but the gap is closing. The count stood at Terrill 2140 to Harford's 2079. Robert has performed respectably whatever the eventual result. The Government will have to take notice.'

Bulwer shook his head. 'I am afraid not Richard. Only a victory for Robert will shake the Government. They will regard a victory by Terrill by one vote as being as good as a hundred. Any victory will be a vindication of their position.'

Richard's pleasure at having a political discussion with so eminent a figure could not altogether subdue his anxiety to know who the visitors would be but he did not have long to wait. At half past six he heard the bell followed by footsteps in the hallway outside. A knock, and two men were ushered in. One, Richard did not recognise. The other he did. It was the stranger who had heckled him in both Virginia and Bristol.

Bulwer smiled at Richard's obvious discomfiture 'Richard, allow me to introduce Sir Charles Godolphin, permanent under secretary at the trade department, and Thomas Deakin whose position will become clear to you in due course. Mr Deakin I believe you have already met.'

Bulwer poured sherry while introductions were completed. The MP was in charge and was clearly going to enjoy himself. 'Pray sit down gentlemen. Now Richard, let me enlighten you about this little gathering. Sir Charles is the head of the overseas division of the trade department. His responsibilities include trade regulation, customs duties and so on. Within his department are the fraud investigators. They have the power to look at the papers of any insurance settlement arising from loss or damage to merchant shipping. Any criminal activity detected is passed on for possible prosecution. I referred the case of the *Demera* to the department. Perhaps, Sir Charles, you would tell us what you have found.'

'Thank you Sir Edwin. Mr Stourton, my department has looked at the file of the insurance company that dealt with the *Demera* settlement. The papers contain signed statements that the entire cargo was lost at sea during a storm. Mr Terrill was one of the signatories. There were also statements from the captain and mate, both signed their mark.'

'Was there no way of checking those statements?' asked Richard.

'The fact is the insurance companies have insufficient resources to check this type of claim. Remember, the disaster occurred a long way from England and there were few survivors. Those who did survive remained in Mr Terrill's pay for some time and would have admitted nothing anyway. As you see, the two senior officers on the ship supported the claim anyway. It is extremely unusual for a claim of this nature to be re-opened so long after the event.

'What we now believe happened is that the insurance company was not told slaves had been thrown overboard so paid out in full. But the minority shareholders were probably told there had been no insurance settlement because of the jettisoning of the slaves.

'And there is one other aspect of this that you should know about. The settlement sum was paid to Mr Terrill as the largest investor and shareholder in the enterprise. He was the company secretary at the time. There is no evidence as to whether or not he passed on the appropriate portion to other investors. Records show that one of these was your father. I am not saying Mr Terrill didn't account to them, I simply don't know. But if he told them there was no insurance settlement, well, need I say more? '

Richard sat in silence for a while to consider this. At last some evidence as to how his father lost so much money. But could it be proved?

'What will happen now?' he asked.

'I will be handing the file over to the department's prosecution department but I fear the evidence may still be insufficient. We need to be sure of our witnesses before any official prosecution can take place. I understand that most of the survivors have since died or disappeared.'

'Nancy knows what was said about the wreck,' said Richard, 'but she is facing transportation and will shortly be out of reach.'

'I can help you there, Mr Stourton,' said Sir Charles. 'If we can mount a prosecution at all, and this Nancy is a necessary witness, we can secure a delay in her departure.'

'That is wonderful news,' said Richard, 'I feel we are making some progress at last. And I can now look further into my late father's affairs to see if he was defrauded at the time. Perhaps there is some way of checking the bank records for payments.'

His gaze shifted from the permanent under secretary to the other man who had so far sat in silence.

'Mr Thomas Deakin here,' began Edwin Bulwer, 'is one of a number of persons employed by His Majesty's Government on what we call security work.'

Richard studied the man carefully. So he is a Government spy, he thought. Their two previous meetings had been at the public meetings when this stranger had stood at the back of crowded halls making it difficult from the platform to take him in. He was a tall man of irregular features but with shrewd piercing eyes. He wore a dark frock coat with dark breeches and waistcoat. There was nothing about his manner or dress which made him stand out. Ideal as a spy, Richard thought.

'So you are a Government informer? ' began Richard with a touch of bitterness. Edwin Bulwer held his hand up to Deakin to remain silent.

'Perhaps I should explain, Richard. It is a legitimate function of all governments to keep themselves informed by less public methods. In the field of international trade and foreign relations it is essential. Successive Governments employ such agents, often the same ones. Governments may fall and change but the need for such information goes on. Thomas has served Whig and Tory administrations alike. In that respect he is like a civil servant. In fact, he is one, in a manner of speaking. But perhaps, Thomas, you will tell Richard your story. I am afraid some of it involves policy that I do not agree with, though I accept the Government has acted lawfully and in accordance with its policy beliefs.'

Thomas Deakin smiled, bowing obsequiously to Edwin Bulwer. Richard thought how difficult it would be to like this man.

'What Sir Edwin says is true. My work for the Government is in defence of the country's interests. In recent years I have been largely involved in the Government's difficulties with the American Colonies. You will understand that I take no political position over this. My job is to gather facts and opinions and report back. I have been to the Colonies on several occasions.' He stopped, and smiled again. 'I like to think I have built up some experience in the importation of tobacco. That is my cover.

'In the winter of 1770 the Government was advised of an interest developing in Bristol in the anti-slave trade movement. The Government believes that such a movement could damage our trade, though I appreciate Sir Edwin takes a different view. I was instructed to investigate and on hearing of your intended voyage and its destination I went across to await your arrival. By the time we had both returned the by-election was imminent.'

Richard was following the man's story intently. 'Why did you come to Bristol for the meetings?'

'For one simple reason, Mr Stourton. The Government supporter who warned of the anti-slave trade movement in the city had become the Tory candidate.'

'Joseph Terrill.'

'Exactly.'

Richard paused and sat back in his chair. 'One thing puzzles me Mr Deakin. Why have you come forward now? Do your paymasters know you have spoken to Sir Edwin?'

'They do, Richard,' said Bulwer. 'Once I realised that their candidate might have been involved in an insurance fraud I felt it right to let the Government know. A great deal of embarrassment it has caused them as you may imagine. They soon realised that the warnings from Terrill might have been motivated by his desire to cover up his criminal activity so they have dropped Mr Deakin's investigations without hesitation. One advantage of having a semi-secret agent is that you can drop him at a moment's notice.'

Richard turned back to Deakin. 'Was your harassment of me in Richmond and Bristol part of Government strategy too?' He spoke with feeling, his humiliation still playing on his mind.

'I am sorry about that,' Deakin said without sounding it. 'It was nothing personal. My intention in Williamsburg was to find out what you were planning and how far you were willing to disclose your views and those of your candidate on slavery. As for the Bristol meeting, let's say it was a little thank you to Joseph Terrill for his help to the Government. We did not then know the background to his dealings, of course. The position now is quite different. The Government is acutely embarrassed about the whole thing and is continuing its own investigations, as you now know.'

'What is the next move, Sir Edwin?' asked Richard. Can we really prevent Nancy being transported soon?'

'Yes, without doubt. Even if the judicial process fails and her appeal is turned down, she can be held here by administrative action if wanted as a Crown witness. But we cannot cancel the conviction or sentence. Only new evidence can do that. Let us hope our missing witnesses can be found.'

'Your man is not doing too well, is he?' Sir John Manners beamed at Richard across the dinner table.

Richard looked at Sir John and saw a benevolent gleam in his eye, the magnanimity that a winning party usually shows to the losing side.

'He has polled well considering he has been independent of party and little support save that of volunteers.' He felt relaxed and confident in a verbal joust with his host.

This was the first time he had been invited to dine with the Manners family though previous visits had reconciled the family to him and he to them. Sam had jumped at the chance of freedom as a servant to Nicholas and Julia and the court action for his recovery had been withdrawn. The dinner was clearly arranged to put a seal on the reconciliation. He had been urged to persuade Sarah to accept an invitation, too, as a favour to Julia and he and Sarah had travelled to the Manners' home together.

Julia herself had said little so far. She had seen her position in the family change perceptibly from companion to future daughter in law, and like all converts Sir John had shown the most kindness and consideration.

'Nicholas and Julia think a spring wedding would be suitable, Richard,' said Lady Manners. 'They see no reason to delay. Would you agree?'

'I do indeed,' said Richard. 'When will you be going to Virginia, Nicholas?'

'Not for some months, perhaps in the autumn. You will come and visit us, I hope. But by a more comfortable berth than your last voyage.'

They all laughed.

'Of course I will come. I have to make sure you are not mistreating Sam.'

They laughed again, a confident laugh of a family comfortable with itself.

Nicholas continued. 'I will be looking for someone to act as overseer and help with the health and wellbeing of the slaves. I suppose your friend William couldn't be persuade to join us, could he?'

'Am I to be deprived of all my family and friends?' said Richard. 'Yes of course I will ask him. It is time he found some work to do.'

'What about me?' said Jane. 'I thought I was gaining a sister but now I am to be losing a brother. Can I go with them father?'

Lady Manners replied. 'No you may not, young lady. We need you here. Nicholas and Julia will be away for two years at the most and will then be back to settle in Bristol. You will see plenty of them then.'

'And perhaps a nephew or niece to spoil,' said Sir John.

'Jane you must come and see me frequently,' said Sarah. 'We may even be able to arrange a few visits to the theatre and perhaps a ball or two.'

Jane beamed. 'That would be wonderful Sarah. You see, Julia, you are deserting me but I have a new companion already.'

'What news of the servant girl, Richard?' asked Sir John.

'We are still hopeful of a successful appeal, Sir John. I think it is becoming clearer to everyone that Nancy did not kill Jacobs. There is a good chance the transportation will be postponed. Nancy is a key witness in a matter involving the Government. I cannot say more at present, but we are hopeful.'

Jane turned to Sarah. 'I am to be bridesmaid. Will you help me with a dress?'

Richard sat back and relaxed as the women discussed the wedding arrangements. So much had happened in the last fifteen months; he could hardly take it in. A murder, a chance letter, a voyage, another murder. Was the saga now moving towards a close? Some hope for Nancy; some possibility that Ben Jackson's murderer would be arrested; even some possibility of recovering his family's lost fortune. His sister settled and his friendship with Sarah deepened. Sam's future resolved. Yet there were still issues unresolved. Nancy had not yet been cleared of involvement in Abel Jacobs death and Joseph Terrill was seemingly heading to victory in the election. On a wider front, the trouble with the American Colonies was worsening; and no one believed the trade in slaves would be halted. The one certainty, Julia's future, had nothing to do with him, In fact he had almost wrecked it, albeit unknowingly.

'What do you think, Richard?'

He realised everyone was looking at him. 'I am sorry, Lady Manners, I did not catch what you said.'

'Sir John and I have suggested that after their wedding, Nicholas and Julia should spend a month travelling in Europe, to Italy perhaps. What do you think?'

'That would be most appropriate,' said Richard.

'Have you been listening, Richard?' teased Sarah. 'Or are you thinking of other things?'

'Thinking of the by-election, I'll be bound,' said Sir John. 'Your man cannot win now, you know. Good thing too if you ask me. Anyway we shall know in a couple of days. Well ladies, it is time you left us to our port.'

The men stood up and Richard watched Jane leave, arm in arm with Sarah, as if she were one of the family. Is it possible, he thought to himself as he settled down again to the good -hearted banter of his host?

The evening before the close of poll is always a night of excitement, especially so at a by-election. Usually the result is known by then, the last few votes on the last day making little difference. Supporters of the winning candidate are out celebrating without waiting for the official declaration. Celebrations include drinking the victorious pubs almost dry, tearing down opposition posters, and breaking the windows of leading opposition supporters, this last activity being a means of solace for supporters of the losing candidate also. But eve of poll in the Bristol by-election was different because the result was still in doubt. The momentum given to Robert Harford's campaign following the intervention of Edwin Bulwer had carried his campaign along until Terrill was almost caught. The poll that night recorded Terrill 2342 votes, Harford 2329. Rival gangs roamed the streets looking for unwary opponents to beat up and for stray voters to be coerced into supporting their man. The sick and the lame had already been carried to the vote, one dying on the way back because of the effort involved and the treatment meted out to him, which was somewhat rougher on the return journey. Every stretcher carrying a freeman to vote had had to fight its way through the opposition throng, the stretcher-bearers carrying their burden with one hand, throwing punches with the other. Lists of electors had been read and re-read. Everyone who could have been made a freeman was so honoured. Now only the obstinate or the dithering had still to vote, together with a few expected to arrive in Bristol the next morning.

The mood at the headquarters of both candidates was remarkably similar. Terrill and his supporters had remained confident throughout, although a degree of nervousness had crept in. Robert Harford had polled better than expected and it was unsettling to find him steadily closing the gap between the two. Terrill had held back a few supporters until the last day to counter any last minute surge by his opponent. Yet there remained some anxiety in the Tory camp.

Among Robert's supporters there was a mood of quiet excitement. The voting was relentlessly moving their way, but not by a sufficient margin to guarantee victory.

Robert had called together a number of his leading supporters, including Sarah, for an eve of final poll discussion. Ten men and two women sat around the boardroom table in Robert's office; twelve people, exhausted, exhilarated but united in a determination to keep going for one more day.

'By this time tomorrow,' Robert began, 'the result will be well known. I want you all to know that win or lose, you have my undying gratitude for your support and effort over this long campaign. Let no one tell you the Government has not been worried, nay, frightened. I know that ministers have been running scared at the possibility of our success. And if we fail? We now know that any failure will be by only a handful of votes. That is very significant. It means that almost one half of the electorate is concerned about the British Government's policies on the American Colonies. Without the backing of either major party we have demonstrated the strength of feeling on this issue. Whatever happens tomorrow, that alone should give us deep satisfaction.'

The mood was one of sober satisfaction rather than jubilation as the committee left Robert's office. As had often happened before, Sarah and John Powell stayed behind to keep company with their candidate. Robert had time for thoughts other than just the election campaign.

'Sarah,' he said, ' I am much concerned about the peril Richard's young friend is in. Richard has been very supportive of me despite his own personal problems. I hope that with the campaign over tomorrow we shall be able to repay his kindness. Are you in touch with him?'

'I have heard nothing of him for several days. He has been to London. I have seen him but once since his return.'

'Will you be seeing him soon?'

'I believe so. But he will not rest until he has saved Nancy. He holds himself responsible for what has happened to her.'

They walked towards the door.

'Perhaps tomorrow we shall find someway to help him. Goodnight Sarah.'

'Goodnight.'

Sarah's carriage was waiting outside and she climbed in and settled back for the drive down over the river and up Brandon Hill. She thought of Richard and regretted she had seen so little of him recently. She wondered if she had been a little cold, perhaps even unkind, towards him. He had many fine qualities, which she admired and she wondered...

The carriage jolting to a sudden halt interrupted her thoughts, throwing her across to the seat opposite. A little shaken, she looked out of the window.

'What is the matter, Spinks?'

'Nothing to fear Ma'am. A young idiot jumped out in front of the horse.'

She peered out into the darkness and saw a young boy of about ten standing near the horse's head. He saw Sarah and walked along by the carriage towards her.

'Miss Jackson, Ma'am.'

'Yes. What do you want?'

'I have been asked to lead you to Marsh Street. There is some-one who wants to meet yer.'

Who is that?'

'I don't know 'is name Ma'am. 'ee ain't no gentleman. Says 'ees seen you afore.'

'Perhaps you will wait here while I fetch a male companion.'

'No Ma'am. 'ee said unless you was to come alone I weren't to bring you.'

Her mind started racing. Think of all the danger she told her-self. A lady never goes into Marsh Street alone during the day, let alone at night. But how great was the risk against the possible prize? There was no doubt in her mind. She opened the carriage door and stepped down into the muddy street.

'Spinks, follow me in the carriage at a discreet distance please. If I turn and wave you away, drive back to this spot and wait until I return.'

'Yes Ma'am, but do you not think...'

'Do as I bid please. I can take care of myself.'

She drew her cape close round her shoulders and followed the boy. After a few yards she turned and looked back but the car-riage was barely distinguishable in the gloom. The doorways on either side were full of women who silently watched her as she passed. One or two men walked up to her but turned away when she stepped purposefully on, ignoring them. Somewhere a baby cried. A woman shouted and a door slammed. Behind her the steady slow clop of the horses feet. She sensed she was being led to the Flying Angel and she was right. She had not been in one of these drinking houses before and although she knew what to expect the noise and smell coming through the doorway made her catch her breath and almost retch. But she would not give up now and turned to Spinks and waved him away. Her hopes were sufficiently raised to keep her following the boy, even through the main bar into a passageway behind and up an ill-lit stairway at the end. Half way up she encountered a sailor going the other way, drunk and barely able to walk down. Had there not been a banister rail to hold on to he would most certainly have fallen. Sarah shuddered, not out of fear, but loathing, mixed with some sorrow as to the human condition. Her liberal upbringing had made her aware how some people lived, but she had little direct experience.

At the end of the upstairs corridor the boy stopped and opened a door. 'She's 'ere,' he called out.

'Is she alone?' The voice struck her as one of an old seafaring man, throaty, perhaps once loud and rich, now losing its strength.

'Yes, like yer said.'

Sarah pushed the door wide open and saw, not John Pitts as she had expected, but a stranger, sitting on a wooden stool, back against the far wall. She was unable to contain her surprise.

'Oh! You are not who I expected.'

'No, I ain't,' the stranger replied. "Xpectin' to see Pitts was yer?'

'Yes I was.' She began to regain her composure despite the disappearance of her young guide. 'Do you know where he is?'

'Aye, I might that.'

'And who are you, Mr...?

'Baillie is my name, Samuel Baillie. Ye've heard of me perhaps?'

'I have Mr Baillie. A number of people are looking for you.'

'Aye, I don't doubt that. They won't find me though unless I want to be found.'

Sarah looked round for somewhere to sit but the room was bare apart from a rough bed and she wasn't going to sit on that. She preferred to stand near the door, with Baillie sitting at the far end of the room. She had some hope of escape if need be, though she did not feel in any danger from this man.

'You have a purpose in bringing me here, Mr Baillie?'

'Aye. I want to offer your friends some help.'

'What kind of help?'

'Nancy didn't do for Abel Jacobs. She were trapped. I reckon Pitts and I know enough to free her.'

'Why have you chosen to speak to me, Mr Baillie?'

'Cause we be wantin' something in return.'

Sarah had feared the possibility of violence or kidnap. Being asked for a bribe was not what she had expected and was something of a relief.

'I really don't think, Mr Baillie, we can offer you any money to...'

'Nay, I ain't talking about money. I want assurances.'

'What assurances?'

'That I won't be charged with no offence. Pitts neither.'

He's frightened she thought to herself. He's really frightened. As Pitts was. Go easy. Don't provoke him, he feels cornered. 'I cannot promise you. The law...'

'Don't give me no law. You have influence 'mongst them who can change things.'

'I am not sure about that but I can talk to my friends. Something may be possible if neither of you are too much involved. Where can I contact you again? Here?'

'Nay, I ain't fallin' into that trap. The lad will find you. Say the day after tomorrow?'

'I agree. What about John Pitts?'

'I know where 'ee be. An' what 'eell agree. No charges agin us mind. You understand?'

'Perfectly Mr Baillie. Goodnight to you.'

Shortly before four o'clock on the following afternoon a large crowd began to gather round the hustings. The mood was sombre. The steady downpour of rain had had its effect in dampening spirits and foreknowledge of the result took away any sense of excitement. No one had cast a vote during the final two hours and at four o'clock precisely the Mayor appeared to declare the poll closed and announce the result. One section of the crowd made a half-hearted attempt at enthusiasm but cheers soon died out. The rain had done its job. Everyone was soaked and wanted the official result to be declared so they could disperse to warmth and shelter to celebrate and commiserate.

Processing behind the Mayor were two officials, Constable Skinner, and the two candidates. Terrill had made a show of gaiety, being dressed in but the effect was neutralised by heavy cloak worn against the weather. Robert, as always, was dressed soberly. Watching from the back of the crowd were Sarah and Richard. Neither spoke, each watching the proceedings to their formal conclusion

James Walter stepped forward to the edge of the platform and held up his hand for silence. As if by cause and effect the rain began to ease and the squally wind dropped. The crowd stood in silence.

'As Mayor of this city I am called upon to announce the result of this election. The votes cast for the candidates were – Joseph Terrill 2,415, Robert Harford 2,389. I declare that Joseph Terrill is elected Member of Parliament for Bristol.'

CHAPTER 19

'Look at me Nancy.'

Nancy sat silent, head bowed. William sat opposite her, quiet, patient. He stretched across and held her hand. 'I have some news for you Nancy. Do you want to hear it?'

Somewhere in the background he heard screaming. He supposed two of the women prisoners were fighting. Locked in overcrowded cells for hours on end was too much for most and tempers flared easily. William had visited regularly since Nancy had been convicted but had never grown accustomed to the inhuman conditions or the smell. He had known worse, of course, on the slave ships but somehow on board ship hardships were the natural order of things. Here, in the centre of Bristol, it seemed so wrong, so cruel.

Nancy lifted her head and stared across at him. At least she is listening William thought.

'Your departure to the Colonies has been delayed, Nancy.' He watched her face. Her expressionless features gave way to the hint of pleasure, but no more.

'Why?' Her voice sounded functional rather than interested.

'Some evidence has come to light about crimes committed by others who were involved with Abel. There may be another trial and you might be wanted as a witness for the Crown.'

'They ain't goin' to let me stay then? Just long enough to 'elp 'em, then I go.' Her flash of anger pleased William. A sign of re-engaging her emotions then, and a sharp perception of the situation, he thought.

'Not necessarily, Nancy. A new trial might have a bearing on your situation. It might even prove that you are innocent. If evidence comes forward that someone else probably killed Abel, they will have to pardon you.'

He gave her hand a squeeze. 'Don't you see, Nancy, this nightmare could be over for you?'

'I can't believe nothin' till it 'appens. And I don't want to stay in Bristol neither. I wouldn't feel safe no more.'

'Where would you want to go Nancy?'

'Perhaps them Colonies ain't so bad. Better'n a cellar in Marsh Street.'

They talked some more, William pleased to have found something that interested Nancy. Gradually life seemed to return to her. The spark of hope had turned into a small flame. They talked of the future. William was able to tell her of the life of colonists. He told her of the farms and plantations, the towns and villages that he had seen, and the vastness of the country. It was as if the shock of the sentence had opened up the closed mind of the girl whose horizons had before been limited to Bristol and its environs. William felt an empathy with her, for travel was in his blood.

'Perhaps we could travel to the Colonies together,' he said shortly before visiting time ended.

Nancy smiled weakly. 'Thank you for comin'.' she said. It was the first time since her arrest that she had any appreciation or even understanding of the companionship he had given her. William left the cells with a spring in his step and an idea forming in his mind.

'Richard my boy, how delightful to see you. Sarah will be pleased to know you have arrived.'

Frank Jackson shook Richard's hand warmly and led him into the drawing room. Sarah was sitting by an open fireplace. Her smile seemed to Richard as warm as the glow from the logs burning beside her.

'Good evening, Richard. Do sit down.' She indicated a chair close by her. He took her hand, thrilled at the warmth of her welcome. Her father sat on the other side of the fireplace.

'Robert and Mary, and Lawrence Willoughby will be joining us shortly for dinner,' she continued. 'Father thinks we will talk about the election all evening, so invited Mr Willoughby to provide him with different conversation.' She paused. 'I- that is we- have seen so little of you lately we thought we would like a few minutes with you on your own, didn't we, father?'

Frank Jackson smiled and bowed to her. 'If you say so, my dear.'

Richard replied: 'I was pleased to be invited. I had heard from Mr Willoughby of your visit to Marsh Street. I am glad I did not know of it before your safe return.'

'Hear, hear,' said her father. 'I cannot think what possessed you to go in alone. I shudder at what might have happened.'

Sarah laughed. 'You men want all the adventure for yourselves. Just think about what did happen. The case against Joseph Terrill is almost complete.' She shivered. 'I shudder to think how intimate we had become with that man.'

'Will he be arrested soon?' Richard asked.

'We don't know,' said Frank Jackson. 'Lawrence should know more. But tell us about you, Richard, what lies ahead for you?'

Richard glanced at Sarah. He felt uneasy about this question, which was the one he hoped to avoid. What did the future hold for him? For over fifteen months he had been swept along by events, which demanded attention leaving no time to look ahead. Now that was coming to an end. What was left for him? For the time being he could continue his career with Willoughby, to whom he was grateful. But he had some prospects of recovering from Terrill the money stolen from his father, and he had become involved in business and politics, and a wider horizon than a Bristol legal practice could offer.

'I really don't know yet. Practising law I suppose.'

'You don't sound too excited at the prospect,' said Sarah.

'I must not sound ungrateful. I am not. It is just that I have seen a wider world and so much injustice in it.'

Sarah smiled. 'I like you as you are. You will always be welcome at our house, won't he father?'

'Of course. But would you excuse me? I have to welcome the other guests who I believe have just arrived.'

Richard saw Sarah's eyes watching her father leave the room. Now he and Sarah were alone he did not know what to say, but he did not have to say anything.

'Richard we will not be alone for long so forgive me for saying this. Is your discontent in any way caused by a feeling of – how shall I put this – unworthiness? Is that the right word? If that is so, you need not concern yourself. I like and admire you for what and who you are. Both father and I regard you as a worthy friend who is always welcome here. That is quite apart from the gratitude we owe you for finding out what happened to Uncle Ben.'

There was no time for Richard to reply. Robert and Mary Harford and Lawrence Willoughby were announced together and soon after, they were called to dinner.

It was a restrained, almost sombre dinner party. Robert Harford was suffering the low moments known by all failed candidates, and all knew the drama involving Joseph Terrill was reaching its climax. And Nancy was still in gaol facing eventual transportation.

Sarah voiced all their feelings. 'We are anxious to know what might be happening, Mr Willoughby.'

'My dear girl I know very little. I am not involved directly. Sir Edwin has passed all the evidence to the authorities, and thanks to your visit to Samuel Baillie we now have him and John Pitts available. They wanted immunity from any prosecution in respect of their smuggling activities, and that was easily given. Though they have been warned they do not have immunity for future behaviour. It is likely there will be an arrest soon, but when I don't know.'

'I presume Mr Terrill will not be able to continue as a Member of Parliament,' said Frank Jackson. 'Will that mean another by-election?'

'I am afraid it will,' said Robert.

'You will win next time, Robert,' said Sarah.

'No. It is unlikely I will stand again. I have made my point. I have some fences to repair with my party, I don't wish to antagonise them further. They must seek their own candidate next time, if they contest it at all.'

As he walked down Park Street back to his lodgings that night Richard had much to think about. His relationship with Sarah had strengthened immeasurably. She had made it very clear how she felt about him, but how could he aspire to her? His means were still limited. He had no social position to speak of. Would Sarah ever contemplate anything other than friendship? He thought it would be unfair on her for him to even try.

Edwin Bulwer looked round the chamber. Members of Parliament were in a boisterous mood, shouting and gesticulating to one another. It was always thus when a new member was to be introduced following a by-election. The successful party endeavoured to make the most of their victory and made extravagant claims. Every policy had been endorsed by the electors when their own man was successful. The unsuccessful party attributed its lack of success to local circumstances. On this occasion the Whigs had much to say. They had not fielded an official candidate, indeed had campaigned against the independent, yet the Tory victory was by the slimmest of margins. Not what a Government should expect. But to the Tories, every victory, however slim, was welcome.

Bulwer did not join in the high spirits. He sat on the backbenches, fingers pushed firmly into his waistcoat pocket, face grave and sombre. As he watched the scenes around him he contemplated the changes in fortune which could occur so quickly and which were about to do so now. The Tories were jubilant in their man's victory. He had enjoyed a smooth path to a successful business, local politics, and now Parliament. Yet Bulwer knew it would shortly be torn away from him. Terrill's tenure in the House would be brief, and if the evidence against him stood up to cross examination, so would his life. Jubilant Tory backbenchers were unaware of the drama that was about to unfold. Ministers did, and were conspicuously absent from the Front Bench.

After prayers, two supporters led Terrill in to a tumultuous cheering and waving of order papers. He was their hero. He had taken the Government's case on the American Colonies to the people and won. Bulwer watched him take the oath of allegiance and settle himself down on the green benches behind the empty Government Front Bench. The debate that followed was on the American Colonies, chosen by Government backbenchers to take full advantage of their man's victory. The Minister for Trade, who had come in after the swearing in process was complete, rehearsed all the old arguments for a tough stance by the Crown, but added a claim to a popular mandate. Bulwer noticed that he did not mention or refer to the new member, but simply to the success of the cause. Few members left the chamber for word had passed round that Bulwer was to lead for the Opposition and he was a popular speaker. Both sides soon became bored and restless with the Government speaker and the cheer that arose when he sat down was more of relief that he had finished than in support of his message.

Bulwer rose and stood, silent and still, the House hushed, anxious not to miss a word.

'Mr Speaker,' he began, 'we have witnessed today something that I hoped would not happen. We have in our midst a Parliamentary leper. A fraud, a cheat, a man riddled with deceit and double-dealing. I refer to the new member so recently introduced.'

There was a gasp of horror around the chamber, and angry shouts of 'no' from the Tory benches. This was the most astonishing attack on a new member that the House could remember, and coming from a source hitherto so respected for his oratory, conviction, and support of Parliamentary procedures. Members from all sides stood to intervene, but Bulwer refused to give way. A backbencher called point of order and the Speaker called on Bulwer to sit.

'Is it in order Mr Speaker, for an experienced member to attack a new member with language which if uttered outside of this House would lead to a writ for defamation of character?'

The Speaker hesitated, giving the appearance of confusion and uncertainty, and an unwillingness to criticise so senior a figure.

He said: 'the procedures and rules of this house apply equally to new and old members alike. It is not a point of order that has been raised. Members must defend themselves. The honourable member under attack will have ample opportunity to reply if he wishes.

Bulwer rose to continue his speech. 'Members will I think have judged me on my record to be a fair man. I will only say that events will vindicate what I am saying. I notice that Government Ministers are largely absent. My expectation is that within a few hours we will see the truth of my words.'

He was content to say no more on that subject and turned to the colonial issue itself. The House soon put his opening salvo to one side and for three quarters of an hour sat transfixed as Bulwer once again attacked the government for its handling of the American issue. When he eventually sat down, members turned to see if Terrill was ready to answer the attack. But his place in the chamber was empty. Bulwer smiled as whispered conversations started around him.

'Where is your champion now?' shouted one Whig. No one knew, except Bulwer and the Prime Minister's Whipper-in. They knew that Terrill had fled. Bulwer's words were plain for anyone who could read them. The game was up. Terrill was to be arrested.

He did not get far. Once outside the Palace of Westminster he was arrested and later escorted back to Bristol. His interrogation lasted several days but at last he gave in and admitted what was now proven against him. Once Pitts, Baillie, and Nancy had signed statements there was no way out. Joseph Terrill was charged with procuring the murders of Ben Jackson and Abel Jacobs. Knowing nothing could now save him from the gallows, he admitted that Jacobs had killed Ben Jackson and named the person he had paid to silence Jacobs. The paid assassin was arrested shortly afterwards, admitted the crime and Nancy was exonerated.

Other admissions followed. The insurance fraud, and the swindling of various people including Richard's father, were fully recounted. The procedure was started to have Terrill's assets sequestered and handed back to the families of those from whom they had been taken, including Richard on behalf of his father. One month after his arrest, Terrill was tried, convicted, and sentenced to death.

Throughout the month from Terrill's arrest to the conviction, Richard was a frequent visitor to the Jackson home. His emotions were mixed. There was a sense of relief; occasionally elation, and a growing feeling of confidence when it became clear his father's wealth would be restored to Julia and himself. At the same time the delayed shock of what so nearly resulted for Sarah and Nancy prevented him from expressing unbounded joy. Sarah may have married a murderer; Nancy transported for a crime she did not commit; and he could have been killed in the attack near his home. Only the chance presence of William had saved him. And on the issue of the slave trade, he had made no impact save present a full dossier of information to the London Committee. Neither Parliament nor public were ready it seemed to turn against the practice.

With his father's money he would be able to afford to buy himself a family home and invest profitably in business. Yet he had no great desire to do so. He felt he would continue in Willoughby's legal practice but that there was something else for him to do in the world, as yet undefined. But he knew he would be able to make a fine settlement on Julia's marriage.

One evening, after Terrill had been convicted but before the sentence was due to be carried out, the Mayor, James Walter, hosted an informal reception at the mansion house for all who had been involved in the drama. Richard noticed on arrival how animated the Mayor seemed, as if he had news to impart. Richard had been the first to arrive, with Julia and Nicholas, and had been met with an excessive show of friendliness that was repeated with Robert Harford, whose actions had originally split the Whig Party in Bristol. With the Harfords were Hugh and Elizabeth Berry, and John Powell and his wife Frances. Next to arrive were

Lawrence Willoughby, with William Daniel, both of them dragging a terrified Nancy in with them. Finally to make up the party were Frank and Sarah Jackson. The impending hanging of Joseph Terrill still cast a pall over the participants in the drama, but conversation soon flowed, though not for long as the Mayor was clearly anxious to make a speech.

'Thank you for coming this evening,' he began. 'I have invited you because you have all to a greater or lesser extent been involved in the events with which Bristol has been engulfed following the murder of our dear friend Ben Jackson.

'There will as you know, have to be another by-election soon to fill the vacancy that will arise with the death of Joseph Terrill. In that connection I have some news for you all. My Whig colleagues have been discussing the situation with me. We take the view that the agreement to share seats for three elections has been fulfilled with the recent by-election being the third election in Bristol. We are therefore free to contest the next by-election that will be called shortly. Now issues of honour are out of the way, I can tell you that the Party has decided to invite Robert to be our official candidate next time. I have it on good authority that the Tories will probably not field a candidate, so great is their embarrassment over recent events.'

There was universal delight at this announcement. Robert beamed, doubts about standing again resolved by the support of his local Party. 'James I thank you from the bottom of my heart,' he said. He then turned to his wife.

'What do you think, Mary?'

'Do you still want to go into Parliament Robert?'

'Yes I do.'

'Then that is your answer and I will support you.'

'If the Party is willing to support me, then I gratefully accept,' he said.

The Mayor turned to Richard. 'I have some news for you, too, Richard. When Robert takes his place in Parliament there will be a vacancy on the Common Council. The Whigs on the Council have asked me to ask if you would allow them to nominate you to fill that place.'

'Congratulations, Richard. You will accept, of course?' asked Robert.

'Yes, I will,' said Richard, smiling broadly. 'But I have to be elected first. There must be the opportunity for a contest. The Council must feel free to nominate more than one candidate if it so wishes. Remember what you said Robert in council after Ben's death. Richard looked at Lawrence Willoughby, who spoke next.

'Richard, the Mayor had mentioned this to me and I have assured him I have no objection, and indeed welcome it. The business will not suffer having one of its partners a city councillor. And yes, as soon as you qualify, I want you to take a share of the business as my junior partner and eventual successor.'

There was a silence as if the news was too much to take in on one evening, but William Daniel was waiting his turn. ' I have come late on the scene but shared many difficult moments on board ship with Richard and endorse the view that he will make a good, and if I may say so, compassionate, local politician. But I too have had some good fortune. My frequent visits to Nancy in gaol have led us into an understanding that we should spend our lives together. She wishes to start a new life in the American Colonies and I will be going with her just as soon as we can arrange marriage and book our passage. And Nicholas has offered me the post of overseer on his plantation. He has explained his plans to improve the lot of the slaves working there, and I fully approve.'

Richard walked over to his friend. 'William I am delighted. May I be the first to congratulate you both? We shall miss you, but wish you well in your chosen life together.'

'And Sam?' said Sarah.

'That is settled,' replied Nicholas. 'We have offered him his freedom and he has accepted a job with Julia and I as a servant in our household. Even my father thinks honour is satisfied.'

They all laughed.

James Walter's surprises at an end the little party gathered together to congratulation each other and talk of the future. Richard saw Sarah sitting alone by the fire and went over to her.

'You seem to do your thinking by the firelight,' he said, sitting down close by, but saying nothing further for a minute or two. Then he recovered his courage.

'Sarah when all this is over, would I dare to hope that you might allow me to make you an offer? I am now in a position to keep you in a manner to which you are accustomed.'

Sarah blushed, then laughed. 'That's very formal Richard. Is that all that has been holding you back?'

'Yes, it is.'

'You wouldn't insist I kept out of politics?' she teased.

It was his turn to laugh. 'Of course not. You and I would be Robert's staunchest allies. And I have another idea too. I would like to see if we could found a home and education for the Nancys of Bristol, young girls with no parents who would otherwise drift into crime. I thought that might interest you.'

'Wonderfully so,' she said.

'I ought to speak to your father.'

'Yes, but you don't really need to. Fathers know.'

They stood up together and Sarah put her arm through Richard's as they crossed the room back to their friends.

Two nights later a runner from Constable Skinner's office summoned Richard from his lodgings.

'Sir, would you come at once. Mr Terrill has escaped from gaol and no one knows where he is.'

'How could this have happened?' asked Richard.

'I believe he bribed the gaoler. He has gone too.'

Richard and William set out at once, fearing that Terrill might get clean away from Bristol, or worse, seek revenge against one of his accusers, possibly even Nancy. They ran to Marsh Street to the Flying Angel and found her unharmed. William told her what had happened and warned her to keep in a safe place and with other people who would protect her. They then went down to Welsh Back where Constable Skinner and his men had gone in search of the fugitive who might be seeking a boat to make his escape. They found Skinner, two special constables, Willoughby and Xerxes moving along the riverside with lanterns held high to see the gangplanks to the various craft moored alongside.

'Perhaps we should spread out,' said Skinner, 'but keep in sight of Xerxes, I think he has picked up the scent. This they did, with Richard moving towards Bristol Bridge. It was a foggy night with the lanterns making little impact except to show up the holder rather than illuminate much of the surrounding area. Suddenly Richard heard a noise and before he could look around, his arm was being held. 'Just who I wanted, Stourton.' Richard recognised Terrill's voice. He wrenched himself away and turned to see his opponent facing him with a knife in his hand. Richard was pinned against the stone stanchion of the bridge, unable to escape. 'You have been the cause of all my problems, Stourton, and you are not going to get away with it. If I have to suffer, then you will too.'

He lifted his knife to strike. But at that moment a scuffling noise followed by a growl came from behind him as Xerxes leapt at Terrill and his jaws locked onto Terrill's knife arm. Terrill dropped the knife but kicked out at Xerxes, who momentarily eased his grip allowing Terrill to pull free and turn and run. But he was too late. Voices and running feet came from all directions, cutting off Terrill's means of escape. As a desperate last attempt to escape he clambered up onto the side of the bridge to attempt to climb down. Xerxes jumped up at him. Terrill lost his footing, slipped over the side, hitting his head on the stone parapet before falling into the icy waters below.

The boys came out at first light, as they always did, looking for discarded scraps and other debris floating in the river. Today they were lucky. A body floated gently on the morning tide.

~ End ~